Praise for *Murphy's Gambit*

"Mitchell combines first-rate hard-SF storytelling with a strong female protagonist in a fast-paced space adventure."
—*Library Journal*

"An enjoyable high-tech space opera . . . a well-designed tale. . . . Readers will line up for book two."
—*Midwest Book Review*

"The fast pace and high adventure make for good fun."
—*Locus*

"You forget you're reading an author's first book. The future society explored here is fascinating, complex, and fully realized. I was reminded . . . of Robert Heinlein's *The Moon Is a Harsh Mistress*."
—Duane Wilkins, *Talebones*

"Pure, unadulterated pleasure. Syne is a born teacher and storyteller. Murphy is as realistic and appealing as any character in science fiction. Talent like Syne Mitchell's is the kind you can't afford to let slip by."
—Lisa DuMond, SF Site and MEviews.com

"A fun tale."   —*University City Review* (Philadelphia)

"*Murphy's G[...] [...]thing: adamantine-hard science fiction v[...]*
—E[...] *[...]l Shattered*

Don't miss Syne Mitchell's first vision
of the future. . . .

MURPHY'S GAMBIT

TECHNOGENESIS

Syne Mitchell

A ROC BOOK

ROC
Published by New American Library, a division of
Penguin Putnam Inc., 375 Hudson Street,
New York, New York 10014, U.S.A.
Penguin Books Ltd, 80 Strand,
London WC2R 0RL, England
Penguin Books Australia Ltd, Ringwood,
Victoria, Australia
Penguin Books Canada Ltd, 10 Alcorn Avenue,
Toronto, Ontario, Canada M4V 3B2
Penguin Books (N.Z.) Ltd, 182–190 Wairau Road,
Auckland 10, New Zealand

Penguin Books Ltd, Registered Offices:
Harmondsworth, Middlesex, England

First published by Roc, an imprint of New American Library,
a division of Penguin Putnam Inc.

First Printing, January 2002
10 9 8 7 6 5 4 3 2 1

Copyright © Syne Mitchell, 2002
All rights reserved

Cover design by Ray Lundgren

 REGISTERED TRADEMARK—MARCA REGISTRADA

Printed in the United States of America

For Eric,
my partner in love, life, and writing.

ACKNOWLEDGMENTS

Many people graciously donated their time and knowledge to help me research and edit this book—some of them on very short notice. Any mistakes remaining are entirely my own invention.

Dr. Howard Davidson, for reviewing the computer science details and for telephone conferences in which he tempered my wilder flights of fancy with fact.

Joe Decker for details about the California Institute of Technology.

Dr. Öjvind Bernander for further Caltech details and information about neural nets and brain science.

Leah Cutter for a speedy critique.

Dr. Richard Kline for checking the physics and general science.

Dr. Jennifer DeCamp for pointing me to publicly available information about the government.

Philip Chang for a last-minute muscial education.

Eric Nylund, for endless encouragement and insightful critiques.

Bob and Sara Schwager for catching my bloopers during copyediting.

Editor Jennifer Heddle, for her enthusiasm for the project and suggestions that improved the story.

Agents Jennifer Jackson and Donald Maass, for handling the business details so I can spend more time writing.

And most of all, the readers, who make all this effort worthwhile.

PART ONE

"If you gaze long into an abyss, the abyss will gaze back into you."
—Friedrich Nietzsche (1844–1900)

CHAPTER 1

Jasmine Reese was a god. Standing on an endless sea of data, she cast her net into the waters and drew out strands of conversation, lumps of encrypted transactions like clams waiting to be cracked, and writhing, flopping calculations. She walked on pulses of transmissions, riding the waves of networked information exchanged by the ten billion people who lived on the planet—then she was nothing.

The data mask flickered—a strobe of her desk and office walls, then the Net—office—Net—office—Net. She pulled the mask off in frustration. The delicate filigree of wires that crossed her face horizontally appeared intact. Jaz couldn't see anything wrong with the processor gems that dotted the metallic strands at irregular intervals, gleaming like diamonds. Inside the six ounces of metal and crystal, however, were fifteen hundred petaflops of computational power. The problem could be anywhere.

Jaz tried reinitializing the mask. She placed it on the molded human face sitting on her desk and tapped a button on its throat. A screen on the plastic face's forehead lit up with diagnostic information that scrolled by too fast to read. In seconds, the reinitialization was done.

Jaz lifted the data mask, hooked the guide wire over the top of her head, and tucked the temple-snaps behind her ears. The electronics wrapping her face once again induced electromagnetic currents in her cerebral cortex, and Jaz slipped back into her metaphor.

The seas were choppy and cold. Jaz stood on the waves and scooped water into her palm. The falling drops fragmented into tiny blue ones and zeros. Shit. She was losing cohesion.

Jaz willed herself to relax, but the cloud-filled sky flickered in and out with gray office walls, the speckled laminate of her desk, and a gold-and-blue-embroidered wall hanging of the Indian god, Ganesh, she'd hung to brighten up the place. Jaz pulled the mask off, resisted an urge to slam it down, and leaned out the door to call across the hallway. "Matt, you having any trouble with the Net?"

Matt focused his eyes and turned his head toward her, seeing her through an overlay of neurally induced images. His shoulder-length brown hair fell in lanky strands over the gem-studded headband he used. "No. Seems normal to me. What's up?"

"I keep losing my connection. My metaphor drops, and I get thrown back into physicality."

"Have you tried reinitializing the system?"

"Twice in the last half hour. I think it's the hardware."

"Tragic." His eyes grew vague, answering some call Jaz, without her equipment, couldn't sense.

Jaz scooped up the data mask and walked around the corner to her supervisor's desk. Jonathan Stacker lay in a recliner, hands twitching on the armrests. His balding head was covered with his perennial baseball cap. The rig he wore was large, a catcher's mask studded with emeralds. Under its wide bands, Stacker's mobile face jerked and spasmed in rapid-fire emotions. How funny the connected looked when you couldn't see their visions.

She knocked on the doorjamb. Stacker started. His gaze searched the doorway blindly for a moment; then his eyes focused on the physical. "Jaz?" He looked both happy to see her and concerned. If it weren't serious, she would have contacted him electronically.

She held up the limp mask. "Hardware's flaking out. I want to take it down to Charlie's, see if he can expedite a fix. Will you authorize the repairs?"

"Let me take a look at it."

"I've optimized the induction settings. I don't think it will work for anyone else."

Stacker peeled off his own rig and delicately wrapped Jaz's around his face. Seconds later he squinted in pain. "Ouch." He pulled it off. "So that's what it's like inside your head," he said, as she leaned over him to retrieve the mask.

"Charlie's?"

He slipped his own rig back on. "I've authorized a repair invoice. They're expecting you."

"Thanks." On the way out, Jaz grabbed her forest-green parka off the hook on her door. The long silk *kurta* she wore over her jeans wasn't warm enough to keep off the April chill. She tucked the mask into a pocket and walked out of the building.

The skyscrapers of East Seattle rose around her, looming glass-and-steel towers built in the early part of the millennium to house Seattle's explosive growth. Skywalks connecting them cast shadows on the streets. The manicured grounds of Infotech were a hollow in the high-rise landscape, a sprawling office park with shade trees, lawns, and an artificial stream that meandered between buildings.

Jaz walked past clumps of bushes in all shades of green. Without her rig, the glowing labels that identified them were gone. That thorny one, that was some kind of rose, wasn't it?

Traffic was light, midday. Private cars and corporate trucks roared by at synchronized speeds. Their navigational systems negotiated with each other to optimize the flow of traffic. Unconnected, Jaz couldn't hear the mental chatter of commuters as their cars sped them along. Each driver appeared isolated in his or her own metal-wrapped world.

The buses ran every five minutes, so Jaz didn't wait long. She saw it coming, like a shark through slower traffic. Advertisements for live sex simulations and brain-boosting vitamins blinked and glowed on its surface. But the bus didn't stop.

Jaz watched in amazement as it blew past her, not even slowing.

She waved her hands and chased the disappearing bus, but the driver never looked back.

"What the—" Jaz stared dumbfounded at the receding bus, then realized what had happened. The explanation was simple. Without her mask, she was disconnected from the Net. The automated systems on the bus hadn't received a pickup transmission, and didn't know she was there. She stomped back to the stop in frustration.

When the next bus came, Jaz was ready. She waved her hands and jumped in front of it, forcing the bus to slow. The driver looked at her blearily through a haze of schedules and GPS maps. Jaz couldn't see them without equipment, but she knew they were there.

Jaz climbed the steps of the bus. The man driving put out a meaty hand and stopped her. "Pay the toll."

Right. Jaz sighed. Nothing about this day was going to be easy. Payment was so automatic that Jaz had forgotten you had to transfer funds to ride. She slipped on her sputtering mask. It must have worked long enough to post the transaction because the driver withdrew his hand and let her board.

The bus rolled past high-rise buildings on Seattle's east side, then looped up an on-ramp to Highway 520, heading west toward the bridge that crossed Lake Washington. A monorail tram sped by overhead.

The people around her were inattentive. No one's eyes met directly; instead they emoted and interacted with the air, responding to internal conversations and information. It was like being in a room full of autistics.

Jaz watched the scenery with interest. Normally, she spent her travel time immersed in entertainment, administrative tasks, or catching up with friends. Now, with no easy connection to the Net, she was absorbed in watching the world.

The bus turned a corner and the change of light reflected a woman's face in the window.

The chin and forehead outlined an oval face with skin the reddish tan of light mahogany. Her nose was long and straight, curving downward at the tip. The eyes were large and deep-set. The woman's full lips pursed in puzzled contemplation. With a start Jaz recognized herself.

It had been months since she'd seen herself without a data mask. She only took it off to shower or sometimes when she slept. Without it, her face seemed naked, vulnerable. Is that what Ian had seen those few times they'd made love without a connection?

The bus jerked to a halt in front of the multiplex that housed Charlie's Electronics. The store was on the first floor, part of a strip mall that had been subsumed by a multistory building of wholesale stores and light industry.

Inside was a receiving counter: a pushcart for intake of heavy electronics, a few uncomfortable chairs, and the obligatory artificial plant. Charlie himself greeted Jaz when she came in. A picture on the wall behind him showed a man in his twenties, installing Linux networks during the Taiwan-China conflict. The boy Charlie had been smiled and waved at the camera. Sixty years later, he was a pudgy man, nearly bald, but with a sharp, keen eye.

"That the rig from Infotech?" he asked when she laid the delicate filigree of wires on the counter.

"Yes."

Charlie picked up the mask with hands that were callused from hard use. He dangled the mask from one pinky and examined it through an electronic loupe. "Latest Intel Quantum-IV." He whistled low. "Don't see many of these in civilian hands."

"I need the high-end throughput for data mining, and Infotech lets me use the rig on my off hours."

Charlie chuckled. "You talented enough to drive a rig like this, I bet you don't get much time off."

"I like working," said Jaz, a little defensively.

Charlie grunted and squinted at the mask. "Bandwidth's too low. And I'm not getting a signal from auditory inductors." He reached under the counter and brought up a gray oval shaped like the front half of a human head. He laid the mask across it, and data crystals on the front glowed with power.

"So?" asked Jaz.

"The laser that flips the molecular states is off-sequencing. Going to take a full rebuild. We'll have to send it back to the manufacturer."

"How long will that take?"

Charlie's eyes unfocused for a moment. "Two, three weeks. Intel's repair facility is backed up at the moment."

"Weeks?" Seattle was home to five million people, a third of whom were employed in the information trade. Surely Intel had a local repair facility.

Jaz recalled, with a cold feeling of growing unease, that she had donated her old data jewelry to charity after Stacker let her take home one of the new Quantum-IVs. She'd never used her old gear once she had cutting-edge technology available twenty-four hours a day. Had she given it *all* away? Or was there some small piece she kept for sentimental reasons, her first data necklace, perhaps?

She said, "There must be someone in the city who can repair it. I can't work—can't do *anything*—without my interface."

Charlie shook his head. "Not this hardware. You bring me a standard rig, and I can turn around a fix within twenty-four hours. Research-grade electronics like this, you need equipment they've only got at the factories. Of course, don't take my word for it. Feel free to make inquiries."

If her rig had been working, it would have taken seconds to verify his statement. She tried slipping it on and was subjected to a rapid cycling of the Net and reality. Nauseated, she pulled off the mask and handed it across the table. "Can you put a rush on the repair order? My whole life is wrapped up in this thing."

"Isn't everyone's?" Charlie swiped the mask through an IR beam to read the microscopic serial number off the back. He concentrated for a moment, filing away details for the repair order, then placed the mask delicately in a box with velvet lining. "I can give you a loaner rig." He reached under the counter and brought up a box of old-style wearables, hard clunky glasses that didn't use induction, but instead projected tiny images in the corners of the lenses. Speakers built into the earpiece provided sound.

Jaz selected the newest-looking pair. The rims were tortoiseshell plastic, and the lenses had a slight tint. She pushed the frames over her ears and activated the glasses. A tiny screen appeared in the lower outer corner of each lens. Using rapid eye motion, she navigated to a primitive version of a message dispatch, kept around for third-world countries that couldn't afford the latest technology. She had to segue through Rwanda to get to something that would handle the low bandwidth of the glasses.

"PLEASE SPEAK YOUR MESSAGE," said a digital dispatch service.

Jaz felt her brows knit in frustration. "Does this thing have voice capabilities?"

"Yeah. Just speak out loud, and a microphone in the frames will pick it up."

"I have to wander the city talking to myself? Ugh. How did folks in the twenties have any privacy?"

The old man shrugged. "That rig was state-of-the-art once upon a time . . . but then, so was I." His eyes went vague, as he answered what she presumed was another call. "I've filed a receipt for you online and put a rush on the order."

"Thank you," said Jaz.

He didn't answer. The conscious part of Charlie was already helping the next customer, somewhere on the Net.

Jaz pushed through the door of Charlie's Electronics. Outside was crisp and bright, a rare sunny day in the Pacific Northwest. The new rig, if it even deserved the name, at least blocked much of the unaccustomed light. She sat on a bench and transmitted an update to Stacker.

After an agonizingly long twenty seconds, Jaz was able to connect to her bank, prove her identity, establish a voice-activated password, and transfer funds for bus fare. She then routed a pickup message to the public transportation agency through the African National Congress linkage, and bounced it off three repeater stations in the

Baltic States. How did feebs manage? She hoped her rig would be back soon.

On the bus ride back to her office, Jaz tried to connect to her work files. The wearable locked up trying to process data coming in at a rate faster than it could handle. The images would stick and then jerk to life, only to freeze again a second later. Mingled with the rolling gait of the bus, it made Jaz sick. She stopped and pulled the wearable off. How was she going to get any work done with this thing?

When she entered her office building Stacker sent her a local-LAN message. "Back in business?" he asked.

She piped him a simulated groan. "Hardly. I've got at least two weeks of downtime and a loaner rig that's only slightly better than signaling with semaphores." Stacker was a pixilated and very flat image on the tiny projection screens. "Are there any unused rigs lying about? Anything would be better than this."

"I'll check, but it's unlikely. That last wave of hiring left us machine-poor." His image faded out.

Jaz sighed and climbed into her office chair, a black, padded curve that stretched from her feet to above her head. It was the latest in ergonomic design, embedded foam gel that contoured to the shape of her body. She could lie in it for hours, sorting and manipulating data.

Jaz initiated a scanning program she'd written to comb the Net for information. The glasses were only able to transmit a thousandth of the data Jaz's neural mask handled. It was like looking at the ocean through a porthole. How could she search and analyze with this?

But she had to try. Her latest project was to dredge up information about a car crash that occurred on Eighth and Pine last Monday. The case was scheduled for legal review in two days, and so far, she had only the police reports, some memories from bystanders, and maintenance records on the victim's car. Surely there were more details out there that would help their client's case. Saunder and Peter's law firm was one of their biggest accounts. Stacker had given it to her because of her skill at sifting bits of information from the surf.

Jaz used her limited field of view to work her way through the Net. She scanned for data transmitted by the GPS of the second car's driver, or failing that, a video transmission of him talking over the Net about the accident. If he had thought about the crash to himself while logged on, it was likely stored somewhere in the vast data pool that was the Net. Because of its distributed nature, transmissions bounced around from server to server before reaching their destination.

What most people didn't realize was that data jewelry had no easy way to distinguish an external Net-bound thought from a private, internal one. Consequently, the data jewelry recorded everything, if only for seconds before making the determination to transmit or delete . . . and all too often the jewelry transmitted.

Jaz was a data miner. She sifted through public transmissions: leaky personal thoughts, online conversations, and endless business reports. AIs were used to do redundant data filtering, but even the best artificial intelligence was not as good a pattern matcher as a talented human brain. And Jaz was a natural, a prodigy. She saw the picture in the static of the Net, and could draw meaning from a surf of information that would drown casual users.

Usually. Right now she couldn't mine even simple conversations. A snippet of video would flash across her lenses, but by the time she moved the eye-cursor to follow it, the transmission was lost. After five minutes of effort, she'd gathered exactly six words: *How're—later— Could you believe—Fowler,* and an image of a woman with a blond chignon and pearls, probably an avatar. No one looked that good in real life.

Just as she was following the sprite, a wave of unrelated information, catalog transmissions and sports results, flooded her lenses. By the time Jaz deleted the irrelevant data, the woman was gone.

How the hell was she supposed to work like this?

When all was going well, data mining was like *being* the Net. For timeless minutes, hours, sometimes even days, she had been the ocean, letting information drift through her, viewing coded transmissions like bright flashing fish. It was simultaneously like being thoughtless and like thinking a thousand things at once. That intellectual rush, more than money, more than prestige, was what drove her on.

Now she felt like someone watching a two-dimensional movie about the sea. Without an inductive connection to the Net, the context and subconscious implications of the data she viewed was lost.

"Stacker," she transmitted, "any word on a loaner? I'm not getting much with this wearable." There was no reply.

A flash of information leaped across her field of vision like a salmon in the data stream. Jaz tried to follow it down into the flashing images the glasses displayed, fighting her way down through overlapping two-dimensional representations. Too slow, the glasses kept dropping frames of video. Intolerable. Jaz tweaked the clockspeed on the glasses, driving them as fast as they could go. She could follow sentences now before she lost the signals, but it wasn't enough to do her work; you couldn't build a case out of random sentences.

The wearable heated up at the temples. Sweat beaded on Jaz's forehead. The REM motion to move the cursor was making her eyes ache, but she was determined to get somewhere.

Jaz's display flickered, strobing her view of reality between the data coming in from the Net and her embroidered wall hanging of Ganesh. With a scream of disgust, Jaz yanked off the wearable. The glasses were torturous. Partial immersion was worse than none. She cupped her palms over her throbbing eyes.

If she wasn't working, there was only her apartment to go home to—empty white walls, a little emptier now that Ian had moved out. Work was all she had left. This misbegotten piece of equipment was keeping her from the one thing that was right in her life.

Growling, Jaz put the glasses back on and initialized a simpler user interface. Forget video, too much bandwidth; see the data as lines of text streaming past. She found herself in a grid of glowing amber letters, streaming by in horizontal lines. Jaz sank into the imagery, began to read the words as they zipped past her. By falling into her mindless, Zen state she could read as many as four conversations simultaneously. With her old rig, she'd been able to process twelve and still keep a skim out for anything interesting.

Don't think about the interface, be the data. Jaz felt herself slipping into flow. Yes. This might work: primitive, but doable.

The user interface blurred and wavered. Shit. She was losing synchronization with the Net. Come on. This interface was only a couple of steps up from reading machine code. The glasses couldn't fail her now. Pain blossomed into a spike driving through her head. Jaz whipped off the glasses and threw them across the room. They thwacked into the thin room divider with a crunch.

She doubled over and massaged her forehead. Definitely not her day.

Stacker loomed in her doorway, the data mask askew on his face, his forehead contorted in pain. "What the hell was that?"

Jaz pointed at the glasses on the floor. "I can't work with those things. Even on a low-image metaphor, they blow up with any reasonable data throughput. Please, please tell me there's a loaner rig I can use."

Stacker walked over and picked up the glasses. They appeared intact, save for one earpiece that bent out at an odd angle. "There's not. I checked with central supply, and we're expecting a shipment of new interfaces, but there's nothing in stock."

Jaz massaged her temples with her fingertips. "I'll do the best I can—"

Stacker shook his head. "No. I'm sending you home. Take a week or so and relax until your rig arrives. You've got the vacation time."

"Thanks, but I can handle it. I'll be a little slower than usual, but—"

"No. Jaz, you're one of my strongest naturals. You slip into network protocols like the computer's clock cycle is the beating of your own heart. When you're upset the

Net responds. I've got three people offline right now
from the backlash of your little"—he twirled the crumpled glasses—"blowup."

Jaz's eyebrows rose, and she looked at Matt across the
hall. He'd taken off his data jewelry, a wide, gem-studded
headband, and was rubbing his forehead. He wouldn't
meet her eyes.

"God, I'm sorry."

Stacker closed the office door to give them privacy.
He placed a hand on Jaz's shoulder. "You've been under
a lot of stress lately. You need some time to recuperate.
The Marley case just shipped, and I've got enough slack
in the schedule to cover for you. Take the time off."

Jaz looked at him, horrified. "Stacker, I work long
hours because I love my job. This—" she waved her
hands to encompass the room around her—"is who I
am." She thought of her apartment, empty and spartan,
clean only because she wasn't home long enough to make
a mess.

Stacker's warm smile hardened. He leaned close.
"Truth is, Jaz, you haven't been yourself lately. I know
there have been some personal issues between you
and"—he held up a hand to forestall her protest—
"other coworkers."

At the reference to Ian, Jaz's face heated.

Stacker continued, "I can afford to have you out for
a week or so right now. I think the break will do you
good. What this group can't afford is a talent as powerful
as you, on lousy equipment, disturbing the work flow
around here."

Jaz felt her cheeks flush. "All right," she said in tight,
clipped tones. "If that's the way it's got to be."

"Good girl."

Jaz controlled the impulse not to snarl. The breakup
between her and Ian was as much his fault as hers. Yet
all the bad luck and the blame seemed to be falling on
her. She looked at the closed door. "Is this a polite way
of asking me to leave Infotech?"

Stacker's eyes widened. "Absolutely not. Under normal conditions, you're my best worker. I'm giving you this time off to make it easier for you to stay."

The words comforted her. And even if he was lying, she was okay. Her bank account was filled with years of salary she hadn't taken time to spend. "All right. See you when I've got my rig back."

"Good, good. Have fun."

Fun? Sitting alone in an apartment with memories of a lover who wasn't there, who had moved in with someone else in the time it took to say: "What do you mean you don't love me anymore?" Without even the Net to lose yourself in because the high-gain equipment you'd spent six months adjusting to every nuance of your brain's electric field was broken. Right. It'd be hilarious.

Jaz grabbed her parka off the hook on the back of the door and accepted the skewed glasses from Stacker, then stormed out of the office.

Outside the sun was still bright, an anomaly in the normally overcast Pacific Northwest. She winced against the light and slipped her coat on to block the early-April chill.

The streets were relatively quiet. Jaz walked down to the light-rail station. When she put on her glasses to pay the toll they fizzled and displayed static. She tried to connect, to induce a response with REM motion. Nothing.

They must have broken when she slammed them against the wall. Damn. How was she going to get home if she couldn't pay the fare?

A rail car came by, and Jaz filed in last.

The conductor looked at her through a pair of silver goggles pinpricked all over with tiny holes. "Transmit payment, please."

Jaz held out the broken hardware. "My rig's down. I can't access my account. Please, I need to get home."

It took the conductor a moment to shift focus from the internal world of tram schedules and passenger volume to see her. The woman looked impassively at Jaz, the silver goggles making her resemble a cross between a human and a fly. "If you can't transmit, I can swipe your disconnected person's card."

"My what?"

The door started to close on Jaz. "Go to the office of disconnected persons. They'll issue you a proxy card for transactions."

"Where's the office?"

"Corner of Pike and Broadway."

"That's all the way downtown! How am I supposed to get there?"

"Miss, you're holding us up. We're already three minutes behind schedule. If you can't pay, you'll have to get off the tram."

A man looked intently at the driver. She nodded and let the door—which had been crushing Jaz out of the tram—swing open. "Your fare has been paid," the conductor said.

Jaz sat next to the man who had helped her. He was in his mid-fifties, with an elegant shock of silver running through his black hair. He favored a monocle, designed like an antique. A round piece of metal held in place a clear plate. The glass was filled with thousands of tiny gold fibers, like rutilated quartz.

"Thank you." She held up the broken glasses. "My real rig went down, and then this loaner rig—"

The man wasn't paying her any attention. Behind the glass, his eyes were unfocused. She could see his pupils moving in REM-like motions as he visualized the invisible world of the Net.

His help hadn't been a personal kindness. He'd just removed an obstruction that was keeping the tram from leaving.

All around her, people were silent, interacting through a medium that was transmitted through and around them. Even the two children at the back twitched silently, playing who knew what adventure game on the Net.

When the tram roared by Jaz's stop, she realized it hadn't picked up her destination from her surface thoughts. She walked up the aisle to the conductor and asked to be let off.

She hiked the ten blocks back to her apartment building.

The lobby doors wouldn't open. Jaz jumped up and down in front of them, hoping to trigger a pressure sensor. She tugged experimentally on the handle. Nothing.

In frustration, she pounded on the glass-and-steel doors.

One of the smartly dressed, college-age women who ran the front office came to the door and peered out. Jaz held up the broken glasses and pointed to them.

The receptionist cracked open the door. "Can I help you?"

"I'm Jasmine Reese, in apartment 1475. My wearable broke, and I can't get in the building."

The woman's eyes clouded a moment. Pinpoint lights flickered on her solid-circuitry headband, a recent retro look, designed to look like the science-fiction media of the 1970s.

After a moment, the woman's face brightened into a professional smile. "How terrible, Ms. Reese. Come in and we'll get you set up with a temporary identification bracelet."

"Since when have the lobby doors been locked?" asked Jaz as she followed the receptionist across the teal-carpeted floor.

The woman—it was hard to remember names without accessing the Net—said, "It's always taken at least a connection to come in through the door. Standard security. It keeps . . . undesirables out."

"Is that legal?"

"This is a fully connected building. What reason would a fee—I mean, a disconnected person have to come in here unescorted?"

Feebs. People who for some quirk of brain chemistry or wiring were unable to use data jewelry. Jaz had never thought about them before except as dirty panhandlers lining the streets. She'd always assumed they were unemployed because of laziness or mental illness. There were lots of jobs that didn't require a connection, weren't there?

The woman pulled a shiny plastic bracelet out of a drawer and spent a moment wrapping it around a tube that extruded from a box. Draped over the top of the box was a silver hairnet covered with tiny pearl-like data clusters at each crossing of the wires.

"Put this on," the receptionist said, "and we'll record your pattern in the bracelet. It'll transmit a standard identity signal wherever you go, so you'll be able to enter the building and your apartment at will."

Jaz did so, and for a moment, like the sun breaking through an overcast day, Jaz could feel the bright warm hum of the Net surround her. All too soon it was over.

The receptionist removed the EEG recording device, stored it, and clipped the bracelet onto Jaz. It was a tight fit, designed so you couldn't take it off without destroying the plastic.

"How long will you need the proxy bracelet?"

"A day, maybe two. I'm going shopping for a temporary rig first thing tomorrow morning." Jaz flexed her wrist, feeling the cheap plastic bite into her flesh. "Will this get me on public transportation?"

"No, just the apartment, I'm afraid. I've set it for a week. Will that be sufficient?"

"God, I hope so."

The receptionist flashed a sympathetic smile. "I know what you mean. I'd go crazy without a network connection. Good luck."

The elevator came to her because of the proxy, but she had no way to indicate what floor she wanted to go to. The whole building was built for connecteds. The interior was sleek glass and steel, with no buttons or control panels in evidence.

"Floor twelve?" she said experimentally. The elevator sat there. Apparently even old-fashioned voice control had been removed. She didn't feel like bothering the receptionist again, and no other tenants were in view.

There had to be stairs, for safety, in case the power went out during a fire. Jaz found them next to the janitor's closet on the first floor. Her proxy got her through the lock and onto a set of stairs that smelled of concrete

and stale air. Twelve floors later, Jaz reached the hall
outside her apartment.

The tile in the hallway was an artificial marble so realistic you only noticed the difference in the fact it never
scuffed or needed polishing. She held the proxy up to
the smoky black glass of her apartment door. Bulletproof
and polarizable, the entire door could be made transpar-
ent or completely opaque.

The lights did not come on when she entered. The
proxy controlled access, but nothing else. She tried the
glasses: static. Jaz crossed the simulated oak flooring to
the southwest-facing window overlooking Puget Sound.
She watched a barge carrying orange boxcars drift by,
saw the monorail dart between light and shadow as it
twisted between buildings, an arterial pulse carrying ex-
ecutives to office buildings.

The room behind her was sparse, the room of a woman
without the time or inclination to design. White wall-to-
wall carpeting, glass walls. The only splashes of color
were the *Bukhara* carpet her grandmother had sent from
India and a framed print of the Dublin fish market her
father has sent for cultural parity. The low-slung sofa and
chair were built on ergonomic lines, also an impractical
white. It didn't matter. The way things were going, there'd
never be any children or pets to worry the fabric.

The rest of the apartment was in shadow. Jaz walked
past the bedroom. Her bed had full audiovisual hookup,
so that dreams could be recorded or induced. She still
had erotic recordings of her and Ian. Why hadn't she
purged those from the system?

The next thought was a stone in her heart. Had Ian
purged the recordings at his apartment? In one second
she fervently hoped so. In the next she wished just as
fervently that he had kept them.

She continued down the hallway to her home office,
the most richly appointed room in the apartment. It was
filled with an ergonomic task chair like the one she had
at work and a wall-size rack of data crystals, extra storage for the information she downloaded from the Net.
Surrounding the chair like Grecian columns were her

computers. They rose white and crenellated in staggered heights, a private network Jaz used to test the data-retrieval programs she wrote, before she released them into the Net.

She checked the wall cabinets. Yes, as she had feared. She'd donated all of her old data jewelry to charity when Infotech assigned her the Intel Quantum-IV. Not a lip ring or diadem left. She was stuck in a fully featured apartment that she couldn't access for lack of an interface.

"Apartment. Lights."

Nothing. She would be trapped in darkness when the sun went down. Jaz walked back to her bedroom and pulled out one of the drawers built into her bed's pedestal. It was where she kept her few personal possessions: a few hard copies of family photos, a couple of sex toys. There. Nestled beside a pile of incense were three white candles and a silver lighter.

Jaz slumped on a chair near the window and watched the city. It lay far below her like an ant hive.

The city was awash with transmissions: music and video entertainment, commerce, joking with friends. But without a rig, Jaz could access none of it. At her parents' home in Boston, she could have perused her father's moldering collection of antique books.

Here, there was nothing she could do without a connection except masturbate or do calisthenics, and the day's frustrations had left her unenthused about either.

Going out would be worse. Until she got a new rig, the city was closed to her. She'd be a ghost, walking between people and buildings that wouldn't recognize her. Adrift, only able to see physical reality. Like losing a sixth sense.

Jaz sat in the dwindling twilight, holding her candles to her chest, and wondered how she would survive the next two weeks.

CHAPTER 2

Jaz slept late the next morning, awakened by sunlight streaming in through her bedroom window. She was rested, alert, like she hadn't been in years. Maybe Stacker was right, and she did need a vacation.

Strange images had come to her during the night: of being hunted, of fleeing a cloud of voices and hands that chased her down the winding corridors of Infotech. As she tried to recall more, the images faded like degrading data. The dream was disturbing. She wanted more detail, but of course, the recorder had not been able to read her disconnected mind.

Jaz rolled out of bed. Naked, she tried to get a robe from her closet. Its automated doors were unyielding. Rubbing her arms to warm them, Jaz stumbled to the kitchen.

It was dark and unresponsive. No steaming coffee awaited her. The overhead lights did not flicker on as she entered. Jaz grabbed an umbrella from the stand by the door and pried open her bedroom closet. Its rotors were still. No outfit, picked by her subconscious, awaited her. She fumbled among the hangers and selected a pair of jeans and a hand-loomed cotton shirt.

After dressing, Jaz decided to eat breakfast downstairs. The kitchen was like the rest of her modern apartment, fully automated. It prepared food with just a thought—useless, however, if you had no way to transmit that thought to the apartment's management program. There was a manual override panel somewhere under the sink, but all the documentation on how to use it was online.

Much simpler to charge a meal at the apartment building's espresso cart, then walk to Sharper Connection and buy a data mask. She couldn't afford a replacement powerful enough to do her work, but she needed *something* to interact with the world.

Checking that her proxy bracelet had survived the night, Jaz closed the door behind her and walked down the stairs. The day outside was sunny, white cumulus clouds in a blue sky. Light streamed between the canyons of apartment buildings. Around her people hustled to work, having silent conversations through the Net, the link exposed only when two people suddenly laughed in tandem for no apparent reason.

Jaz bought a mint latte and a bagel from Slappy's espresso cart at the bottom of her building. When Slappy waited for a payment transmission, Jaz held out the wrist wearing the proxy bracelet. "My equipment's on the fritz. Could you charge it to my apartment?"

Slappy tilted his head back to read the text off the inside of his mirror shades. He nodded, his blond dreadlocks bouncing. "It's cool."

The latte was hot and sweet. She closed her eyes to savor the taste of the rich dark espresso and steamed milk. Since when had coffee tasted this good? She meant to ask Slappy if he'd done something different, but he was already locked in silent communion with the next customer.

Perhaps the coffee was better because, disconnected, she could fully focus on the taste. No part of her brain was already at work, checking e-mail and organizing her day. Her mind was free of the hum of public conversation transmitting all around her.

Jaz was a natural, one of the lucky two percent of the population that genetics or brain chemistry had gifted with the Net's equivalent of perfect pitch. Most users had to translate their thoughts into the Net's protocol, but Jaz and other naturals thought fluently in the underlying metaphors of the Net. This talent gave her the ability to process more conversations and data simultaneously, but at the cost of her personal thoughts and privacy.

It was nice, for once, to be stuck in her own head.

Jaz walked the seventeen blocks from the Paramount Building to Pioneer Square. It was both eerily quiet and disarmingly noisy. Jackhammers staccatoed a rhythm on the next street over. Traffic roared by. In an alley, a mechanized trash collector emptied a Dumpster into its collection tank. The sounds formed a cacophony of city noises she'd never noticed before.

In contrast, people on the street were silent, their attention elsewhere. Without a rig she couldn't hear the hum of conversation flowing around and through her. There was no information to deal with beyond her own senses, her own thoughts. How long had it been since she'd had time to think? Two years ago, backpacking in the Cascades?

People jostled her on the street, but they were like ghosts, turned inward to an imaginary world shared with the ten billion other people on the planet. It was a peaceful, if lonely, feeling.

She stopped at the Sharper Connection, across the street from Pioneer Square Park. Closed. The gold script painted on the door indicated it wouldn't open for another hour and a half. Jaz glared at the locked glass door with exasperation. If she'd been connected, she could have ordered a rig anytime, twenty-four hours a day, and had it delivered within an hour. But disconnected, she was stuck in the brick-and-mortar world, at the mercy of anachronistic salespeople who catered to upscale customers looking for that genteel, personal touch. Ah well, at least the day was nice. She could wait.

Jaz ambled back across the street to Pioneer Square Park. The fifty-foot-tall totem pole in the center of the square looked shabbier than usual in the bright spring sunlight. Paint flaked off the raven carved at the base, and cedar fibers stuck out at odd angles. Had the totem pole always looked like this? Perhaps through consensual agreement, the networked had decided it was in like-new condition and overridden their perception of reality.

How many other facts were skewed by people's wishful thinking? The thought the world might be other than what she knew chilled her. The Net gave so much in terms of connection to other people. What did it take in return?

Normally by this time in the morning, Jaz would have interacted with dozens of people and touched peripherally the minds of hundreds more. Walking down the street you would get a sense of the stranger approaching you: an avatar, a mental skin, level of security—something. Now the people scurrying by were ciphers. Was the white man in a business suit a lawyer or a dentist? She didn't know.

Another thing that surprised her was the number of the disconnected. She'd never noticed how many there were. Like her, they walked slowly, taking in the world around them. A middle-aged man in frayed jeans and rag-wrapped feet nodded to a gray-haired woman in a fuzzy pink bathrobe and bunny slippers. Unable to perform a quick protocol exchange through the Net, they resorted to the inefficient protocol of human conversation.

"Hey, Miz Bunny," said the man, scratching the greasy brown beard that covered his face, "how's the day?"

"Same as it ever was. Deposit's late again this month." Miz Bunny's face was as wrinkled as a dried apple. She plucked at the collar of her bathrobe. "Damn drones never get the transfers out on time."

"You heard the latest?"

Miz Bunny eased her bulk down onto a park bench and propped up a sandwich board and data screen. She seeded the screen with a starting balance of $9.34. It displayed the pitiful sum in large green letters. The sandwich board read: *Mother of Five. Needs rent funds. Please Give.* "What's the news?"

"Old Fish-eater Harold got a job," the man said, bobbing up and down on his heels.

Miz Bunny looked up with surprise. "Do say? Doing what?"

"Heard he was sorting fish down at the packing plant near the tidal generators."

Miz Bunny cackled. "Ha! For all the good it'll do him."

The man, younger than Miz Bunny by at least twenty years, looked hurt. "Don't need no connection to sort fish."

"Soon as they give a command over the Net like 'Today we're keeping roughy and tossing halibut' and Fish-eater don't do the right thing, he'll be out of there. Can't be bothered with voice commands for the disabled. Not when there's so many connecteds looking for a job."

The ragged man looked up and met Jaz's eyes.

"Hey!" said Miz Bunny. "What you looking at?"

Across the street from them, Jaz blushed. In the Net, she could eavesdrop on conversations without the participants detecting her presence. Now she was caught, with no way to sink anonymously into a sea of data. She looked away and pretended to be studying the totem pole.

"Goddamn social workers spying on us," said Miz Bunny. "Like they think we don't see them." She shouted across the street. "Tell the boys at the home office my deposit's late!"

Jaz walked down the street a block, hoping her movements were casual.

There was an aching loneliness without the Net. She could no longer drown herself in the sea of news and other people's information. There was no way to escape the silence in her own mind.

Left to her own thoughts, she brooded on the memory of Ian's leaving. What had he said to her as he walked out the door? "It's not that I don't want to be in a relationship—I just don't want to be in a relationship with *you*." Her stomach ached when she thought of what he'd looked like saying those words, his mouth distended in rage. The worst, though, was seeing herself through his eyes via the Net. He'd given her everything in a flash, his disgust and distaste. A vision of herself as a skinny, ugly, clinging woman who always thought herself right. He'd painted her in muddy, unflattering browns and blacks, stretched her high cheekbones into sharp, unflattering crags. Waves of rejection had emanated from him. The Net had intensified their love and lust for each other; now, just as efficiently, it destroyed her.

Jaz watched the crowd, desperate to forget, to lose herself in its ebb and flow. She wanted to move outside herself, to become part of a larger whole, a perspective where her problems were small and petty. Who could be bothered about a failed relationship when you touched the mind of a single mother facing eviction, or a priest who'd lost his faith, or a drug addict coming off heroin? Humanity was a roiling mass of problems, and it would help to know that again. Instead, she was locked inside her own mind, her own troubles blown out of proportion by lack of a global perspective.

She studied the crowd, hoping to gain empathy with it from the outside. There, a woman in a faux leopard-skin coat, her black hair drawn into a ponytail. She walked with intense concentration. What was she thinking? About groceries for dinner tonight? Her mother dying of cancer? Her lesbian lover? The woman, cueing off some primordial sense she was being watched, looked back at Jaz.

Embarrassed, Jaz looked up at the trees arching to meet above First Avenue. They had been planted for the 1962 World's Fair and had grown tall and stately in the intervening years. How had she remembered that without the Net whispering in her mind like an omnipresent tour guide?

She'd walked this boulevard with Ian, once. Ridden one of the horse-drawn carriages through the streets. She and Ian had had virtual sex in the back of the cart on an encrypted private channel. The driver had probably guessed what they were doing, but that had been part of the thrill.

She'd loved Ian. It had been so easy with another natural. For the first time she hadn't needed to pull back when making love, hadn't needed to worry about over-

flowing his buffers with the sensory data she sent. It had
felt so good to have someone who understood her jokes,
who could run through the Net as fast as she could.
Someone she didn't have to wait for, always holding herself back, always careful not to let her impatience show.
Why hadn't he loved her as much in return?

She knew the answer. She'd heard it from her colleagues at work—hell, even from the other woman herself. Ian had been jealous because Jaz was better at Net-
running than he was. Her heart didn't buy it. When you
operated at 99.8 percent efficiency, did it matter if your
partner worked at 99.9 percent? Such a small difference
in their bandwidths shouldn't have mattered. It wouldn't
have mattered to her if she'd been on the short end of
the equation. But apparently, it had mattered to Ian.
When she had reveled in her ability to let herself go, to
share herself and her talent fully with another person, it
turned out she should have been holding back.

Ian's new lover, Tiffany, was the Infotech receptionist.
Her job was a symbol of the company's prestige, so rich
it could afford to pay live people to greet you. Tiffany
had something that Ian wanted more than he wanted
Jaz. Simplicity.

Jaz hated herself for the weakness that caused her to
take advantage of the other woman. The day Ian left
her, Jaz had invaded Tiffany. Delicately, so the woman
never felt what was happening, Jaz had used the induction
of the woman's own data mask to trigger her subconscious.
Tiffany, oblivious of the force that drove her, mused on
her relationship with the hot new talent, Ian. Jaz had
felt, in a dizzying two-person perspective, the woman's
smugness at having taken him away from that ball-
busting Jaz, and her own harrowing grief over losing Ian.
It had been the first, last, and only time she ever brain-
hacked anyone.

The insecurity that had driven her to violate Tiffany's
privacy made Jaz ashamed. Ian was gone. Why couldn't
she accept that? Why crawl around in the other woman's
brain looking for explanations? The ease with which
she'd done it had scared Jaz enough to increase her own

mental protections. It was unlikely there was anyone out there good enough to get past her mnemonic security, but unlikely was not the same thing as impossible.

A businessman walking by suddenly burst into laughter. The joke spread across the Net like wildfire, transmitted from friend to friend. The speed of the Net was such that within seconds, a message could reach ten billion people. One by one people on the street began to chuckle, until Jaz found herself the only person on the street not laughing.

It was unnerving. It was as if the crowd was a single entity and the connected people its cells.

Jaz searched the streets for someone not laughing. She saw the feebs, Miz Bunny and her escort, sitting with five newcomers in front of the mission building. The small pack took turns taking hits off amphetamine-laced cigarettes.

The feebs were also watching the connecteds; apparently it was a source of entertainment for those who had no access to traditional media like 3-D video or immersion reality. They were a miserable lot, huddled against the wind in cast-off clothing. Bits of technology clung to them, as useless as a circuit board on a decorator crab. The man who had hailed Miz Bunny was wearing a coruscating shirt. Jaz recognized the brand. On any normal person it would have shimmered with roiling colors reflecting the wearer's brain patterns. On the feeb, it was a muddy brown test pattern. Miz Bunny wore broken bits of data jewelry like they were crown jewels. Half a data mask hung around her neck like a collar of silver wire and tiny crystals.

By contrast, the crowd streaming past was prosperous and happy. Fashions and taste differed, but all the clothes were clean and new. The people themselves were vigorous and healthy. They were lean, well exercised. Jaz had read stories about illness and obesity in her literature class, but outside of the disconnected, she'd never seen anyone like that in real life. Why eat junk food when you could simulate it for no calories through the Net?

Why skip exercise when your mind could be anywhere, doing anything else, while your body plodded through the motions and built up endorphins for you? The body was the cradle of the networked mind. It paid to keep it in repair.

Jaz noticed that the networked were not only healthier than the disconnecteds, but happier, too. She searched for someone having a bad day, but all the faces were serene. There, for an instant, a woman's face contorted in impatience when a man with a baby stroller blocked her way onto the train. But her scowl was quickly replaced by an understanding grin.

Were there no bad emotions among the connected? Jaz tried an experiment. She picked a person moving swiftly through the crowd, his face screwed up with tension and concentration. Jaz deliberately stepped in front of the man, bumping into him.

"What th—" exploded from his lips, and he shook his head to focus on Jaz. He saw her, and his face contorted into impatient rage. "Get . . ." His anger died away before he finished yelling at her, and he stepped smoothly past Jaz and onto the train.

"Won't work," shouted the man with Miz Bunny. "They don't have time for dissies, even to be annoyed by them."

Jaz was uneasy. Could being on the Net change a person's reactions and emotions? One man wasn't a fair test.

She stepped in front of another person hurrying down the street. The woman swerved to avoid Jaz and fell off her tottering heels, scraping her hands and knees on the pavement.

"Oh, I'm sorry!" Jaz said, reaching down to help her up.

The woman cursed, but the rage vanished as soon as she got back to her feet and continued on her way.

Jaz got in the way of half a dozen other people on the street. No matter what she tried, or how busy the person, the connected wouldn't stay mad.

Reactions flickered across the crowd in waves as they

shared the same information: jokes, news, and weather reports. Jaz didn't see anyone who looked angry or sad or fearful. At least, not for long.

Puzzled, Jaz leaned against one of the buildings bordering Pioneer Square Park and studied the crowd. After fifteen minutes, she had the eerie sense that it was watching her in return. No matter when she looked, there was always one of the networked staring at her.

First a businessman, then a skateboarder, and then a woman in electric blue satin overalls; the transition between watchers was smooth. Just when Jaz thought the crowd had given up, she saw a boy in jeans and a ripped T-shirt staring at her. His face was slack, as if he was daydreaming about something else, but his eyes followed her. When he stepped around a corner, a black man in a tailored Italian suit turned to stare at Jaz, then a large Asian woman with blond hair. Their stares were not the casual look of the curious. Jaz felt as if the crowd, by consensus, watched her.

She tried moving to another location. Perhaps it was the building behind her attracting their gaze. Jaz walked across the street to the still-closed Sharper Connection store. She leaned nonchalantly against the glass wall. The eerie phenomenon didn't stop.

Jaz felt a hand on her shoulder and jumped. It was the man who had escorted Miz Bunny. She smelled rotting teeth and stale rum on his breath. His eyes were red-rimmed and watery. He leaned forward until his beard tickled Jaz's neck. She froze in horror and revulsion.

"You see it, don't you?" the man whispered. "The beast is watching you."

CHAPTER 3

"The beast, what beast?" Jaz asked, grabbing the feeb's arms to steady him.

He pulled away and looked over his shoulder. A couple of people wearing data masks were watching. "Bad to get the beast's attention," he muttered. "Very bad." He mouthed silently to Jaz, "Watch your back." Then he fled down the street, his stained canvas coat flapping behind him.

The other feebs skulked off the mission's steps, fading into alleys and hobbling around corners. Jaz felt like a plague carrier.

What was going on?

A teenage girl watched Jaz now. She walked a tiny unicorn. It was fifteen centimeters high, white, with a pearlescent horn. The genetically engineered pet cropped grass along the sidewalk.

"Hello," said Jaz.

The teenager scowled from behind a spiderweb data mask that covered her left eye. "What do you want?"

Jaz fumbled for small talk. "Uh, cute pet."

"You got something to say about it?" She rolled her eyes heavenward. "Everyone does."

"No. Actually, I wanted to know why you were watching me." Jaz pointed across the street. "When I was standing over there."

The teenager looked at her with the industrial-strength scorn only those under twenty can muster. "You? Why would I look at *you?* I've never seen you before in my life. Take something for the paranoia." The girl flicked the lead of the miniature ruminant to get its attention and sauntered down the street.

Was the girl lying? Or had Jaz only imagined that people were watching her? Perhaps it was just a random set of coincidences.

The sign in the Sharper Connection flashed to OPEN.

Finally. She could use a demo model to scan the local transmissions and memes, find out if people had been watching her. Jaz crossed the street.

The store was inside one of the historic buildings that encircled Pioneer Square Park. To Jaz's relief the door was an old-fashioned hinged model with an antique brass doorknob. It opened easily.

Inside, the store was cool and dark. The lights were dim to enable users to respond to neurally induced graphics with less interference from their own senses. Waist-high displays cradled the latest fashion electronics.

Plaster hands frozen in the splayed-finger gestures of mannequins showed off data-storage rings and filigree triangles worn on the back of the hand to improve dexterity. In one corner of the store, Jaz saw a pair of brass knuckles, tiny processors glinting in their surfaces. More decorative than functional; one punch would leave both victim and aggressor with an expensive repair bill.

There were anklets that helped with dancing, armbands that enhanced upper-body strength, and bracelets that improved dexterity and eliminated arthritis pain. Anywhere that electronics could encircle human nerves and induce them to fire, mankind had created a decorative device to take advantage of it.

Crowning all of these lesser devices was the central display of data masks that interacted directly with the human brain. There were diadems, simple headbands, and delicate masks that wrapped filaments of induction electronics and data gems around the wearer's head. There were bulky devices like hockey masks and slender fish-eyed goggles.

There was nothing like her Quantum-IV. Quantum computers hadn't made it out of military and corporate use into the consumer level. These were merely high-end molecular electronics.

The salesman, perhaps alerted by the proximity of Jaz to the display of expensive goods, sauntered over. A balding man in his thirties, he grinned, and said, "Almost didn't see you there. You snuck in without a connection." His eyes wandered her face and Jaz guessed he was doing an image lookup on her and probably a credit check. After a few seconds he straightened. "Well, now. Your curriculum vita is impressive, one of Infotech's distinguished engineers. What brings you to our store without a rig?"

Jaz felt an unaccustomed surge of anger. She'd never minded before that anyone could instantly identify her. Indeed, it had seemed a convenient way to get past inane small talk. Perhaps it was the disparity of the current situation; he could look her up, but she knew nothing about him. "My rig broke. I'm looking for something to tide me over until it comes back from the shop."

"Very good." He smiled like a car salesman whose customer has just walked a mile to his lot. "This model is quite good, very fashionable. Just the thing for a night out or a vacation." He lifted a monocle shaped like a multilayered star. Points jutted out from it like a glistening snowflake. It was silver and sparkled with diamond dust. In the center was a data gem the size of Jaz's thumbnail.

"It's called an 'Eye of Odin,'" said the salesman. "By sacrificing the sight of one eye, you gain insight into the invisible world of the Net. Mythic, don't you think? Very popular this year."

"How much is it?" Jaz asked.

"Very reasonable," the salesman assured her. "Try it on; test drives are free."

Jaz slid the Odin's Eye guide wires through her hair. She settled the silver star in front of her left eye. It was cool to the touch and lighter on her face than she had expected. With a rush she felt the Net swirl up around her. Her left eye saw the inside of the store glittering with information. Glowing green price tags and pointers to more detailed specifications overlaid each display. She looked at the salesman and saw he was Ernest (Ernie) Burkweller and had been named top customer-service representative two months running. She also saw that he'd lied about the price being reasonable.

The Net surged around her like an invisible sea. Jaz opened her inner eye to the metaphor. The sun shone on blue water that stretched to infinity—crisscrossed with waves of interference. Transmissions flashed beneath the surface like bright fish. The water was so clear she could see to the bottom: the coral architectures of communication protocols on which everything else was built.

Now she would find out what had happened in Pioneer Square Park. She felt Ernie hovering near her, monitoring her progress with the data mask. With an internal grin, Jaz leaped off the surface of the water and dived in.

Ernie floundered on the surface, as buoyant as a beach ball. There was no way he, with his mediocre skill, could follow Jaz into her element.

She swam deeper and searched through old communication archives. All public transmissions were stored in case a user wanted to recall them later or they were needed for a police or governmental inquiry.

Piecing together fragments of conversation, she re-created the scene. It hovered underwater in a bubble she created, a slice of time in Pioneer Square Park, trapped underwater like Atlantis.

Jaz checked on Ernie. He had broken the surface, and was searching for her. But she was several fathoms deep. Plenty of time.

She pushed through the bubble wall and entered Pioneer Square Park as an observer. There she was in the corner. People looked this way and that. No one was looking at her. No one.

Had she imagined it? Was there data missing from her simulation? Impossible. If there had been a conspiracy to trail her, communication between dozens of people, she would have found something. Jaz's chest loosened, and she could breathe again.

She felt silly. In her paranoid, unconnected state she had imagined herself the center of attention. When, in reality, nothing could be farther from the truth. How many disconnecteds had she noticed while immersed in the Net? None. If any had been in her path, she would have looked straight through them. That was what the passersby had been doing to her. Being stuck in her own mind, without the perspective of others, had amplified her insecurities. No wonder mankind was so unstable and given to misunderstandings and wars before the Net was pervasive.

Jaz punctured the bubble, and it exploded in a puff of released data. She swam up to Ernie, grabbed his hand, and led him to the surface. She lightened the metaphor so the store was a ghostly overlay on the bright blue sea.

"That's some ride you took me on," Ernie gasped. "Your vita didn't lie. You can really drive that thing."

Jaz found his flattery annoying. What had he expected? "I'll take it." She transferred funds to the store's account. It was good to be connected again. It was like she had been lobotomized, and now, miraculously, had her mind restored. It hovered around her, too large to fit in any one skull.

"Great. Great," Ernie said, and Jaz could see he was congratulating himself for the easy sale. She let it go.

Ernie reached up and lifted the Odin's Eye from Jaz's face.

The disconnection was like the crack of a gunshot, like the water in her soul freezing at once. The warmth that had soothed her, had promised her that the morning's strangeness had all been in her mind, was gone.

Ernie didn't notice her reaction. He placed the demo model back on its velvet face and went into the back of the store. "Be right back."

Jaz's heart pounded in her chest. She'd turned off her rig before, and there was always some change in perception, a contraction as she was limited to one point of view. But never like this. Jaz knew, with the certainty of one betrayed, that the Net had been manipulating her emotions. In a flash of insight prey had felt for millennia, Jaz knew she was under observation. Someone was watching her through the Net.

But who? Who had the power and skill to control her without a hint of what was going on?

The door to the back room opened. Ernie came out holding a golden box. He held the wrapped data mask out to Jaz. "Here you—"

Jaz backed away like it was a weapon. She stumbled over a display stand, knocking bracelets and rings to the floor. Turning, she caught her balance and sprinted through the shop entrance.

Ernie followed her, standing in the open door of the Sharper Connection waving the box. "Ms. Reese! Don't you want your mask? It's paid for!"

Jaz ran. She didn't stop for eight blocks, when, chest heaving for air, she leaned against the Romanesque brick facade of the Chamber of Commerce building.

Was it possible that someone in the Net was manipulating people? And if so, why had no one realized it before now? She needed facts, concrete evidence. The homeless man who spoke to her, she needed to find out what he meant by "the beast."

She walked back to Pioneer Square Park, careful to stay out of sight of the salesman in the Sharper Connection.

The mission building was on the corner of First Avenue and Yesler Way. It had once been a hotel, and the old sign ROOMS 50 CENTS still hung at the second-story level. Outside was a group of five disconnected men. One of them was six feet tall and built like a lumberjack. He looked Native American and had a blue teardrop tattooed under his left eye. They lounged on the steps, playing a slow game of cards, but mostly enjoying the free drama offered by the streets.

When Jaz walked up, they stared at her casually. She said, "I'm looking for a skinny brown-haired man who was talking to Miz Bunny earlier today."

The lumberjack exchanged a glance with a wrinkled

white man in his seventies, then looked back at Jaz, and
said, "Transmit me some funds?"

"Sorry. I'm not connected."

He scanned her casually, checking, she guessed, for
signs of data jewelry. "Ain't seen them," he said, and
picked up the cards again.

Jaz pushed past him into the mission. The main room
inside was filled with tables. Cots were folded along the
right wall. Along the left wall was a cafeteria-style serving area of gleaming stainless-steel sinks and plastic trays.
In the back of the room, steps led to the second floor.

A social worker approached Jaz. The woman was
young, in her early twenties, and wore a straight-skirted
floral print dress. "Can I help you?" the woman asked.
She looked at Jaz over a pair of connected granny
glasses.

Jaz hesitated. "I'm looking for a man I talked to in
the park this morning. Perhaps you've seen him." She
described the man who had told her about the beast.

"Oh," the woman said, "you must mean Ellery Houston. Haven't seen him since breakfast." Her face clouded.
"Why are you looking for him?"

"He's . . . a friend of mine," Jaz said. The lie felt
strange in her mouth. She was unaccustomed to perfidy,
since the Net exposed untruths.

The social worker appraised Jaz, then said, "You
might try the job market, or the manual terminals at the
library. He's a hard worker. Always trying to get off
public assistance. But it's hard, you know. With all the
prejudice against the disconnected."

Jaz nodded sympathetically and left the mission building, stepped over the card game still in progress, and
walked twelve blocks to the County Assistance building.

By the time she arrived, Jaz's feet ached. She scanned
the ragged men and women gathered outside, waiting to
hear about new job listings, but didn't see Ellery Houston.

On the way back to Pioneer Square Park, she kept an
eye out for him, in alleyways and around corners. She

also watched for people looking at her. No one stared. Once a man glanced at her, then looked down the street to check traffic. Coincidence? Jaz wasn't sure.

In an alley, she saw Miz Bunny showing a little girl wearing a bright yellow daisy-shaped mask how to make a cat's cradle out of string. The girl's horrified mother pulled her child away and admonished her not to talk to the dirty thing. After that Miz Bunny hung deflated. There was no sign of her companion.

Jaz asked one of the connected people in the street for directions to the library. An Asian man in a tailored business suit looked at her empty face with pity and explained the way.

Jaz hadn't been to the library since she was a child in grade school. She remembered it as an empty place, full of echoes and dust. Who would travel to a warehouse for moldering paper and antique terminals when they could access all the digital information in the world with a thought?

Only children on field trips and people unable to access the Net directly.

The Seattle Public Library was housed in a three-story gray building that squatted between rows of glass-and-steel skyscrapers. Inside was the musty smell of old paper. An escalator led up to the second and third floors. An old woman sat behind a desk labeled REFERENCE. A silver hairnet studded with data gems pressed the woman's curls tightly to her head.

"Where are the terminals for disconnected people?" asked Jaz

The librarian took a moment to focus her attention, then said sympathetically, "Second floor. To the left of the escalator. Do you know how to log in manually?"

Jaz nodded, remembering the antique input devices her second-grade teacher had let each child use: data gloves that let you manipulate objects displayed on flat screens and the inefficient keyboards where you had to painstakingly push buttons letter by letter to form words. The manual log-in had used two keywords, one was your full name, the other your personal identifier, a thirty-two-digit hexadecimal number assigned at birth.

Jaz rode the escalator upstairs, looking for Houston. But none of the people hunched over keyboards, whispering furtively into speakers, was him. If he was there, he was hiding among the rows and rows of books.

Jaz looked at an empty terminal. The screen hung on the back of the cubicle and blinked with advertisements offering *Sex-Sex-Sex, High-Paying Jobs,* and *Medical Miracle* treatments that would give a disconnected person the ability to use induction technology. Pathetic. Jaz tapped the spacebar and the ads flashed more frantically. "Tell us who you are," the log-in page blinked, "and we'll scour the Net for what you need."

What she needed was information, to know what Ellery Houston had meant when he approached her on the street. She glanced around again, but he was nowhere to be seen.

Jaz typed her first name, then froze. What if whoever was watching her through the Net could find her via this machine? She didn't want to leave a trail of search requests. Pursing her lips, Jaz typed Ian's name and identifiers.

Her first search was ELLERY HOUSTON.

The screen returned results listing the University of Houston, the Houston Astros, and genealogy data. She subsearched on *person, born in the last seventy years,* and *disconnected.*

That left twenty-eight entries. *Still living* cut the number to twenty-two. Photographs helped her weed the references down to three white men of the right build and age. She couldn't be sure of Ellery Houston's face because of the full beard he wore now. The candidates were a political activist who had done a lot of writing in the twenties, a doctor in forensic psychology, and a pop singer. Her man could be any of these people, or none of them.

She scanned the terminals around her again. A woman in faded blue jeans and a too-tight T-shirt bounced a toddler in front of a terminal and told the little boy to speak to *Gramma.* Two men huddled over another terminal, sharing a set of headphones and grinning lasciviously. Through the central railing of the second floor, she could see the librarian talking to a pair of teenaged boys in flannel shirts.

Still no sign of Houston.

Did it matter? What she really wanted wasn't Houston, but the information he had. Jaz did a new search on *the beast* and got back hundreds of thousands of references: the Book of Revelation; Harry "the Beast" Jackson, a famous professional gamer who specialized in first-person shooters; back issues of the *Village Voice*; and ads for a sports utility vehicle with sub-aquatic capabilities, among others.

The *Village Voice* articles were from the time when the Net first took off. Houston, the writer, might have sold them his work. She opened that reference and found a linked table of contents for the July issue, 2083. She scanned the titles and found: "Mark of the Beast: Effects of Inductive Data Jewelry on the Public Soul." She sucked in a sharp breath. The author of the article was E.J. Houston. Gotcha.

Jaz tabbed down to the link and clicked on it. The Net displayed an error: "Content is unavailable online. The underlying files may be corrupt."

Damn.

She searched the index for other articles by E.J. Houston. There were six—none of which was retrievable. In frustration she clicked on articles by other reporters. Reports of police brutality in New York City, no problem. A review of fashion in scarification, images of young people decorated with pain, displayed effortlessly. The only articles she could not retrieve were those by E.J. Houston.

Had someone erased them deliberately? The thought scared her. It was contrary to the very purpose of the Net. Besides, deleting data was no simple task. The Net was protected and distributed. Removing content from one server wouldn't erase the same content cached on thousands of other servers.

Jaz tried pulling down one of E.J. Houston's articles from the Hub servers in New York, Los Angeles, and

Atlanta. Nothing. Either this change was made so long ago that the deletion had time to trickle out to all the proxies, or whoever was behind this was good. Damn good.

Jaz searched for journal articles on the medical and psychological effects of being connected. There were thousands of references from the early twenties, when induction jewelry was in its infancy and little was known about its effect on people. Jaz wanted facts, not questions. She filtered the information to the last five years. There were titles such as: "Induction Networking: Implications for Treatment of Geriatric Dementia," "Trends in Intelligence: Thirty Years of Improved Scores Among Connected Children," and "Social Utopia: Effects of Improved Network Communication on Crime in the United States."

What she didn't see, scanning the list, were any negative reports. She filtered the articles on terms like "disadvantage" and "loss." The number of titles fell from thousands to hundreds. There were entries such as: "The Information Divide: The Socioeconomic Impact of Being Unconnected on a Connected Planet" and "Embracing Big Brother: The Abdication of Privacy in the Twenty-first Century." Jaz clicked on the latter. It was a grant proposal, one that had never been funded.

She searched farther afield and found the National Institute of Mental Health's statistics on suicide in the United States. The data was broken down by population and charted over a hundred years. In 1999, the average rate of suicide was 11.3 per hundred thousand people. In 2050 it was 14.8 per hundred thousand. Last year, in 2101, the average rate was 1.5 per hundred thousand. She expanded the statistics to display by population. Among the disconnected, the suicide rate was thirty-five per hundred thousand. Among those who had been connected, but lost their connection through accident or injury the rate was eighty-seven per hundred thousand. Among the connected: 0.

She searched back a year. The suicide rate for connecteds was the same: 0.

Impossible. There were nearly a billion connected people in the United States. Even if being connected to the Net brought better perspective and understanding, surely at least one of those people would be mentally unstable enough to take his or her own life. She compiled data furiously. In the past ten years, among people in the United States who were connected to the Net, no one had committed suicide.

Jaz looked around her. No one was paying any attention. The teenaged boys she had seen downstairs were playing an online game, facing each other over back-to-back flat screens. A black woman with intricately braided hair searched through job listings. Downstairs, the librarian sorted books into a cart.

It was like being the only person in a room to notice a rift that had opened up in the floor. Was someone using the Net to control people? Even benevolent control, such as preventing suicide, was still a loss of free will. Was it someone's intentional manipulation, or a side effect of being connected?

She searched international statistics. In Europe, no connected person had committed suicide in the past eight years. Asia had three known cases of suicide by a connected person in the past twelve years, none in the past six.

One of the articles linked to by the NIMH report was a psychological survey of the effects of the Net on humanity. All but one of the articles presented the Net in a positive light. That article was titled "Impedance of the Grief Process: Is the Net Affecting Responses to Tragedy?" Jaz clicked on the connection, and was told that the linked article was unavailable. She did a title search: nothing. Jaz widened the search to include the entire Net. Still nothing. Maybe she had mistyped the title.

She retraced her steps to the NIMH report and the list of references that included the grief analysis. "Impedance of Grief" was missing from the list. It had been right there a moment ago. Jaz went back to the NIMH summary page. Now the link to the report she had just been reading was gone. Jaz clicked back one in her history and got a CONTENT MISSING OR CORRUPTED error from the Net.

Jaz's chest tightened and she couldn't breathe. Someone was changing the Net's data under her. In response to her searches? A Net-runner deleting information was as unlikely as a capitalist burning money. She repeated her searches, with the same result. The information she knew was there had gone missing. She had seen it; the memory of those articles was burned into her brain. With an uneasy feeling Jaz wondered: would she remember them if she was connected? Or could whoever erased the articles just as easily erase her memory?

Brain wipes were a mythical type of hack, whispered of among naturals. Scarier than that realization was the fact that whoever had been watching her earlier was monitoring her research. They knew she was onto them. Worse, they must have something to hide, something important enough to risk rewriting history as she watched.

Without moving, hardly even breathing, Jaz cut her eyes left and right.

The disconnecteds around her were oblivious, leaning over flat screens browsing pornography, or researching manual-labor jobs, reading e-mail from connected family members, or scanning the day's news.

Beyond them, restocking paper books onto shelves, was the librarian. The old woman was distracted and hummed a tune as she worked.

But her gold-green eyes, as vacant as a cat's reflecting the light, stared straight at Jaz.

CHAPTER 4

Jaz left the library. Ducking her head so she'd be harder to recognize, she kept a lookout for watchers. If anyone was marking her progress, they were subtler than before. Twice she bumped into someone and had to apologize, but no unfamiliar gaze followed her. The streets were less crowded now that the morning rush hour was over. She saw mothers pushing toddlers in strollers, retired men playing checkers at an outside café, young people panhandling. None of them looked up as Jaz skulked past. Had she only imagined what she'd seen that morning?

Once she was safely inside her building, Jaz eased her vigilance. The climb up twelve flights of stairs burned off her nervous energy; by the time she reached her door she was exhausted.

She held the identification bracelet up, and the door clicked open. A green light on the wall next to the door indicated a package had been dropped off while she was out.

Jaz knelt and used the bracelet to open her delivery safe. Inside was an octagonal golden box embossed with the Sharper Connection's logo. She pressed her thumb against the identiplate on top and it unfolded like a lotus. Inside was the Odin's Eye she'd bought that morning. It lay in velvet cushioning, a silver-and-diamond temptation. If she put the rig on and tried to forget all that had happened, Jaz was sure she'd succeed. She could go back to her normal life. Do what she was best at, surf the Net and collect data. It was a tempting thought.

But she wouldn't. Once you've seen the dark underside of the docks, it's hard to walk blithely on the surface. Jaz had never been one to run from hard truths. More, she was scared. If something was in the Net, using people, affecting how they thought, and she ignored it . . . whatever it did would be her fault.

But what could she do? She needed verification of her suspicions, someone else to help her investigate the facts. So far the only other people aware of this conspiracy were feebs—they'd be no help. The only connected people Jaz trusted were her family and coworkers.

Jaz thought about asking her mother's assistance. Dr. Anita Reese had helped define the underlying protocols of the Net. Would she believe someone could hijack her creation?

Jaz's father might, if only because it made a better story. But what could a professor of English literature do against an unseen enemy in the Net? Jaz's extended family contained some cousins on her mother's side who were employed in the information industry, but none were naturals. And all of them were more interested in clothes and parties and marital prospects than secret conspiracies.

Coworkers were her only option, if she could convince them; they had the skills to investigate this and might know others who could help.

Jaz lifted the rig to her face, hoping she'd be able to resist the Net's gentle pressure long enough to make the call.

She projected herself into Matt's metaphor. Jaz concentrated on seeing the Net as Matt preferred: a grid of lightning. The waves faded beneath her, and in the emptiness left by their passing, blue streaks of light coalesced. The scent of ozone hung heavy in the air.

Matt sat in the center of the grid, his arms and legs melded into the streaming electricity. His world was black empty spaces and electric blue flashes. Jaz hovered at an interstitial point in front of him and waited for him to notice her.

After three minutes, she couldn't wait any longer. She whispered, "Matt?"

His face broke into a grin. "Jaz!" He peeled off a version of himself to join her in the darkness. The rest of him stayed in the grid, working. What spoke to her was ghostly translucent.

A minor insult that he didn't give her his full attention. Ah well. He did have a lot to get done, especially since he was picking up her workload.

"How's the vacation?" he asked.

She couldn't tell him her concerns. Now that she was connected to the worldwide flow of information she could see how absurd it would be for anyone to control even a part of it. Relief edged out anxiety . . . except for a very small part of her hindbrain; reflexes millennia old warned a predator was near. To cover her ambivalence, Jaz said, "Fine. Fine. Enjoying the quiet life. What are you doing this weekend?"

There was a pause. His simulacrum took on extra solidity, as Matt's attention focused on Jaz, "Nothing much, why?"

"I thought we'd go backpacking," she said. "Me, you, some of the others from work. The weather is supposed to be fine this weekend."

He hesitated, fading slightly as he checked his appointment calendar. "I'm booked up through Sunday."

Jaz pursed her lips and poked through the thin security layers to read his appointment calendar.

"Hey!" Matt said, catching a glimpse of what she was doing.

"If you really wanted this private, you'd have used better encryption." She scanned the list. "The Johnson case is one of mine. It's a no-rush job. Delay it until next Wednesday."

"I don't like to delay work. It's unprofessional."

Jaz almost let it go at that. There was nothing to worry about. She'd just been having a bad reaction to being without the Net. That happened sometimes. Her rig

would be fixed in a couple of weeks, and her life would
be back to normal. In the meantime, there was the
Odin's Eye to play with, and she could check out the
new entertainment immersives . . . unless, a small voice
at the back of her skull said, unless I'm right and this
happiness is false.

She pleaded with Matt, "Come on, take the weekend.
We'll leave the Net behind and just be raw people, out
in the woods. Savoring life through the senses we were
born with."

"This is a change from the woman who was across the
hall pitching a fit when her rig went down."

"I've . . . learned a few things since then. Let me
show you."

His eyes sparkled with playful suspicion. "All right,
count me in."

"Done. You won't regret this," she said and hugged
his coruscating body.

Matt eased back into the working part of himself. "I
do already," he murmured, and was gone.

Jaz reached up to pull off the Odin's Eye and stopped.
It felt good to be connected; she wasn't scared anymore.
The Net was where she belonged. Her hand trembled
over the scalp-loop threaded through her hair. In the Net
she was beautiful, powerful, able to do things most people couldn't; outside she was just so much meat.

And yet . . .

She jerked off the mask in one movement and flung
it to the floor. The sudden disconnect left her gasping.
Anxiety washed over her. Strangely, the unpleasant emotion reassured her.

When her heart stopped racing, Jaz slipped the Odin's
Eye back over her head. She had to work quicker this
time, or the temptation to stay connected might become
too great. She called Geena, in marketing. Geena and
her husband, Bob, both worked at Infotech and had men-
tioned they enjoyed backpacking.

Geena's metaphor was a baseball field. Geena's simu-
lacrums played all the positions: pitcher, batter, catcher,
and umpire. Jaz had never understood how the woman

divided her attention into dozens of sprites. Jaz hovered on the side of the field, near the bleachers, not wanting to interrupt Geena's flow of thought. One of the fans leaned down, and said, "Hey, Jaz, what's up? I thought you were off while your rig was down."

The entire bleachers were filled with Geenas. They wore different clothes, and some rooted for the home team, others for the visitors. But everywhere the same face, the same ginger-colored hair. It was disconcerting.

"I'm putting together a backpacking trip Saturday night. I was thinking we could leave the rigs behind, get away from it all. You and Bob interested?"

"Sounds good, let me see if he's free." The Geena she was talking to dissolved into a fine mist and blew away. Below, on the green, the game continued uninterrupted.

Another Geena in the stands swigged beer and grinned at Jaz. She was wearing a cowboy hat and sat in a distinctly masculine pose, legs sprawled. "Count us in, little darlin'," the Geena drawled in a deep voice. "Bob ain't got nothing to do this weekend but me."

Jaz blushed. "How long have you guys been married? Ten years? Eleven? I thought you'd be past all that by now."

The Texan Geena winked. "Been eatin' and breathin' for thirty-six, ain't lost my appetite for those neither."

Jaz shook her head, smiling, and said, "Meet us at Newhalem, off exit twenty, around 8 Saturday morning."

"Be there," said Geena.

Jaz hovered in a blank whiteness as she let go of the baseball field metaphor. The Net lapped her mind, like a balmy breeze, enticing her to stay. Jaz pulled off the Odin's Eye. It was easier this time. The anxiety didn't overwhelm her. The tightness in her chest was familiar. It was like a limb waking up. The pain was good, like the needle pinpricks you feel when blood flows back into capillaries.

After her heart had stopped pounding, Jaz extracted her backpacking gear from the closet and used the camp stove to boil water for a cup of Darjeeling. She drank it slowly, watching the city below her. Cars and trucks pulsed through the streets, carrying passengers and other cargo. Pedestrians crawled along the sidewalks like so many animate specks. Did any of them guess at the forces at work in the Net? Or were they as oblivious as she had been yesterday?

When she'd recovered enough to risk another dive into the Net, Jaz slipped on the Eye again.

The third call she made was to Davis, a technopagan she'd met when he walked by her office and complimented her Ganesh wall hanging. His working dream was a temple. Chanting and sandalwood incense filled the air. Davis sat in the center, a lanky man with a long blond ponytail that stretched to his butt. He sat in a lotus position. Smoke from the censers writhed around his body, forming and re-forming patterns and symbols.

"Isn't this a bit much?" Jaz said, materializing near a marble column.

Davis's eyes remained closed as he said, "That, from a sea goddess? Who do you think you are, Varunami? Or do you draw from your father's Celtic pantheon? A selkie, perhaps?"

"I thought you went in more for an ascetic sensibility. One hand clapping, that sort of thing."

He grinned, and the ever-changing patterns of smoke swirled around him, delivering information. "That was last week. This week I am exploring how ritual affects my productivity. But surely you didn't interrupt your divine idleness to criticize my metaphor."

"True, I'm planning a backpacking trip this weekend. No data connections. You interested?"

The grin on his face grew wider. Davis's eyes opened, and all of the smoke hung frozen in the air around him. His blue eyes gleamed with mischief. "Can I bring my drum?"

They agreed to meet early Saturday morning at Marta's Restaurant in Newhalem. From there, Matt would drive them all in his private car to Colonial Campground, the base of the hiking trail.

Jaz put on the Odin's Eye one last time that night and

reserved a seat on the bus that traveled Interstate 20. Then she started loading her backpack for the trip.

On Saturday, Jaz was the first to arrive at Marta's, a run-down diner with red-and-orange-plaid curtains. The plastic seat cover in Jaz's booth was cracked and had been inexpertly patched with duct tape. Someone had put out a cigarette on the polyurethane-covered table. Underneath the plastic coating were newspaper headlines from the *Mountain Gazetteer*. The burn was right over the face of the 2052 homecoming queen. Other items preserved forever were high school graduation photos, wedding announcements, and a story about a local wood-carver.

A woman in a pink uniform with a tiny bib-size apron said, "Can I help you?" She wore an old-style wearable: a pair of half glasses that looped over her left ear and balanced across the bridge of her nose. Jaz could see the menu and order status reflected in the lenses.

Jaz ordered an egg-and-bacon sandwich and coffee and read about the woodcarver as she waited for the others to arrive. The coffee was a disappointment, but the egg sandwich, when it arrived, was glorious. The bacon was crisp and full of textures and rich flavors she'd never noticed while connected. The eggs were light and fluffy. Even the bread was something special, crisp and soft at the same time. And the butter . . . she could see why— in generations before everyone was connected—so many had problems overeating. Unconnected food was wonderful. Jaz ate every last scrap, even the parsley garnish.

Matt arrived while she was finishing the last of her tepid coffee. His car was a sleek electric van with tail fins. Jaz slipped on her Odin's Eye long enough to pay the bill and met him outside. He popped the trunk remotely and Jaz hefted in her backpack. She crawled into the seat next to him.

"Hey," she said, pointing at the silver band that ringed his head. "We agreed this would be a Net-free weekend."

"Relax," he said. "I'll take it off once we reach the

trail parking lot. I needed to drive this thing, didn't I?"
He gestured at the blank dash. It had the standard connection package: you thought a destination at the car and it calculated the most efficient route and drove you there. The only manual control was a foot pedal that activated an emergency brake, for use if the power or Net connection went out. "What's the big deal, anyway?"

"Nothing," Jaz said, noting the way he concentrated on her answer. Was something other than Matt watching her through his eyes? "I just want everyone to relax and enjoy themselves—no work." Jaz felt funny deceiving Matt. She had to remind herself that without a connection, he couldn't sense her lie.

"Yeah, sure, whatever. What trail we going up?"

Jaz unfolded a topological map from her pocket.

"You weren't kidding when you said low-tech. You're not even taking a GPS?"

She sniffed and pointed at the trail that ran from Diablo Lake, between Tricouni Peak and Mt. Logan. "I thought we'd hike in and camp at Thunder Basin. You bring an ice axe?"

"Yes, but I thought the trail was closed past Tricouni Peak until late July. Too big a risk of avalanche."

Jaz met his gaze and said, "Then we'll be sure of privacy. I don't want any other hikers around on this trip."

Bob and Geena arrived on the next bus. Geena's red hair was pulled in a ponytail threaded through a baseball cap. She grinned at Jaz as she stepped off the bus. "Jaz! Matt!" She enfolded Jaz in a friendly hug, then gave Matt the same treatment. Bob was behind her, a husky man in his early forties. A brown beard covered the lower half of his face. He struggled with two well-loaded packs. Jaz saw two telescoping ice axes—good—and what looked like two of everything else.

Matt grabbed the smaller pack and helped him off the bus. Geena was looking around at the restaurant. "We got time for a quick cup of joe? I've only had one latte this morning."

Jaz shook her head affectionately. "Sure. Davis isn't here yet."

The others went inside to eat. Jaz stayed outside, waiting for Davis. She was anxious to get started on the trip, worried that if they delayed too long, she might lose her nerve. It was a risk telling the others her suspicions about the Net. They might not believe her, or worse—think she was certifiable.

Davis rumbled up on an electric-hybrid Harley. His gray-blond hair was braided with feathers and tiny carved stones. A well-used internal-frame backpack hugged his body like a close friend.

"Hey, how's my favorite sea goddess this morning?"

Jaz felt her face heat with embarrassment. "I wish you wouldn't call me that. It's just a metaphor."

He swung easily off the bike and lowered his pack to the ground. "The others here yet?"

Jaz nodded over her shoulder. "Inside. I think Geena must be on her third cup of coffee by now."

"What? She's cutting back?"

By the time everyone had something to eat, it was well past nine o'clock. Jaz, Geena, and Bob loaded into Matt's van. Davis followed the car on his bike. They drove east on Interstate 20 to Colonial Campground. There they left the vehicles and strapped on backpacks.

Jaz's was a titanium-frame pack that years of hiking had molded to her body. Putting it on brought back memories of Canadian glaciers and Arizona deserts. She snapped the chest and hip straps closed and flexed her knees, getting a feel for the weight.

Bob and Geena helped each other into their packs. Bob transferred an antique palmtop computer to the inside pocket of his parka.

Jaz said, "Bob, please leave that in the car. I'd like us to hike unconnected. So we get the full sensory experience."

He held up the charcoal-gray plastic that barely covered his palm. "I don't plan to use it while we're hiking, just at night to check my investments and the headlines."

Jaz frowned at him. She couldn't tell him the real reason she wanted to avoid a link to the Net. It would sound too far-fetched. "No connections. Please. I've learned a few things about being unconnected that I want to share with all of you."

Bob looked to Geena for support. Geena shrugged. "One overnight trip won't kill you. Don't worry," she said, slipping her arm around Bob's waist. "I bet I can find something to entertain you at night."

Bob blushed, but put the palmtop computer into the van's glove compartment, next to the case containing Matt's mask.

"Think of it as a ritual sacrifice, Bob, a fast," said Davis. "Like Geena and her coffee."

"Like hell," Geena said. She smiled and patted a large silver thermos strapped to her pack.

Jaz's throat tightened at the sight of Bob and Geena. That's what she and Ian could have been if everything had worked out. Bob and Geena worked together, played together, shared everything. For a brief, bitter moment, Jaz wished she hadn't invited them. But that was stupid. She couldn't resent everyone who had a good relationship just because she'd never managed it.

Bob and Geena rearranged their gear, leaving a few more items in Matt's car: the electric boot warmers, camp chairs, and other nonessentials.

At last everyone stood around, packs on their backs. "Everyone ready?"

She was met with silence. "Well?"

Geena laughed. "I guess we'll have to get used to talking out loud again. I don't know about the others, but I just thought my reply at you." There was a chorus of assent from the others.

At the trailhead was a registry machine for overnight stays. The rangers used it to keep track of trail and campsite usage. Before she could stop them, Bob and Geena pressed their palms against the recorder. With an internal sigh, Jaz watched Matt and Davis follow suit. When it was her turn, Jaz hovered her hand above the reader instead of touching it. A silly precaution, but it made her feel better.

The first leg of the hike was relatively flat; they worked

their way around the south end of Diablo Lake. Through old-growth fir and cedars, they caught glimpses of the lake. Its waters were colored turquoise from the silt deposited by nearby glaciers. The fine rock powder hung suspended in the water and refracted the light.

Normally, Jaz's data mask would have murmured these trail details to her. But this was one of her favorite routes. It surprised Jaz how much she could recall on her own.

They crossed a suspension bridge over the mouth of Thunder Creek, which branched off from the lake. The next hour, they spent winding along the creek through floodplains. Salmonberry bushes were in bloom, tiny hot pink flowers, like little stars, covered the bushes.

When they stopped for a water break, Geena said, "It's amazing how quiet it is up here."

"That's the absence of the Net," said Bob. "I've been feeling it all morning, like a missing tooth. Something that should be there, but isn't." He looked unhappily at Jaz.

"Relax into it, man," said Davis as he pulled a peanut-butter Cliff bar out of his pack. "We're sitting at the side of a glacier-fed stream, surrounded by majestic mountains, and all you can think about is missing the latest stock reports?" He shook his head sadly. "Try and live in the moment."

Geena held out her hand; Bob clasped it. "It is beautiful up here," she said. "Better than a hiking sim. Smell the air—it's so fresh."

"Everybody get enough water?" Jaz asked. "We're going to have to push pretty hard to get to Thunder Basin before nightfall."

The trail rose onto stony slopes that still showed scars of the wildfires that had swept through the region in 2062. Blackened tree trunks rose at infrequent intervals from the stone fields. The path then dropped back into the bottomlands. Fallen tree trunks served as nursery logs for new growth. Young trees rooted in the decaying wood, their roots wrapped the logs like fingers, seeking the earth beneath. In some cases the original log had completely decomposed, leaving a mature tree standing above the forest floor on stiltlike roots.

"This is like a fairy tale," said Geena. Her eyes took in the drooping roots and branches, the hanging moss.

Jaz inhaled the scent of cedar. The woods were dark and cool. "Water break?"

The others nodded. There wasn't a lot of conversation this time. They're getting used to the silence, Jaz thought.

Geena stroked a swath of verdant moss growing on a tree trunk. "It's like cold, wet velvet."

"A holy place," Davis intoned, half-mocking, half-serious. "The sacrifice of the older trees as they lay down their lives to feed the young."

Bob looked uncomfortable, lost without the constant flow and hum of the Net. He rubbed his face where his data mask usually covered. "When's lunch?"

Jaz pointed to a hill in the distance. "I thought we'd have lunch at Junction Camp. There's a creek nearby for water and terrific views of the nearby peaks."

The trail climbed at a forty-five-degree angle to three thousand feet. When they reached Junction Camp, everyone was breathing hard. They dropped their packs at the edge of a wooded scarp and took a moment to breathe and stretch. Tricouni and Forbidden peaks were visible through the trees.

Jaz opened her backpack and fished around for the cooking gear. She brought out a water filter and a titanium pot.

Matt unpacked a cookstove and attached the fuel canister. He pressed a button and a piezoelectric spark ignited the flame.

Jaz held out a filtration system to Davis. "Would you go down to that stream we crossed over and get some water?"

He nodded and took the pump from her hands.

"You may be the trail guide," Geena said, taking the pot from Jaz's hand, "but Bob and I will handle the food." Jaz watched in amazement as Geena unpacked the better part of a chef's kitchen. There were polycarbonate bottles with half a dozen spices that snapped together into a long cylinder, freeze-dried vegetables and pastas, oatmeal for breakfasts, and, of course, an aluminum espresso machine. Geena had brought preground coffee, a concession to necessity.

Geena began sorting ingredients. "Bob, could you bring me that cup?"

He handed her a plastic cup.

She looked at it with disgust. "No, I meant the *measuring* cup. How am I supposed to prepare food with this?"

Bob reached for the other cup and put it down with force in front of her. "You didn't say a measuring cup."

"It should have been obvious from context."

"*Your* context, not mine."

They glared at each other a moment. Geena gave in first. "It's the lack of the Net. We can't tell what the other's thinking." She let out an exasperated sigh. "How did our grandparents get anything done? I can't imagine living like this."

Jaz said, "Can't you feel the upside, though? Isn't your mind clearer without the influences of others? More your own?"

"I feel it," Davis said, handing the water he had filtered to Geena. He cocked his head into the wind. "It's like having preternatural hearing and being deaf at the same time. I can hear the wind in the fir trees, the river's gurgling, and a hundred other irrelevant sounds I'd usually ignore. But there's also this great emptiness in my head."

Matt leaned close to Davis's head and listened at his ear. "He's right! I can hear the surf!"

Davis pushed him away, grinning, and the tension was broken.

Lunch was pasta Alfredo with portobello mushrooms, a crusty French bread that had miraculously survived being packed, and a cabernet sauvignon.

Davis whistled low when she and Bob brought the food over to the clearing where the others had dropped their packs. "Geena, you are Hestia incarnate."

Bob smiled proudly. "You should see what she can do with a full kitchen. My darling can *cook*."

Jaz spooned a portion of pasta into her titanium cup and tasted it. The flavor spread through her mouth like a blessing. She tasted garlic, basil, and oregano in perfect proportions to the portobello mushrooms.

"Yum," said Matt, finishing his first helping and licking the sauce from his cup with a finger.

"It's delicious," said Jaz. With her next comment she planted a seed she hoped to harvest tonight. "I find it easier to focus on the flavor of food without the Net."

Bob tasted his noodles thoughtfully. "You know, I'd thought it was the hiking, but you might be right. The flavor seems richer than usual. More complex."

Geena savored a bite. "Yes, it may be. Let's try a meal sans Net when we get home." She grinned at Jaz. "Are . . . other things better as well?"

Jaz felt herself blush. "I haven't had an opportunity to find out."

Geena trailed fingers down the back of Bob's neck and winked. "We'll let you know in the morning."

"No," said Davis, "totally unfair. No one's having sex in the woods if I can't." He flipped his braid over his shoulder and looked beseechingly at Matt. "You'll have to help me out here, pal."

Matt threw a pinecone at him.

"Well," said Davis, catching the pinecone out of the air and looking appraisingly at it, "if that's your idea of fun . . ."

Jaz shook her head, smiling, and moved to gather the dishes. "Matt, would you help me with these?"

After everyone had packed up, they got back on the trail. It descended a steep mountainside. The slope was covered in towering Douglas firs.

Even though Jaz had gotten used to being without the Net, she was surprised by the silence of the woods. Her apartment in the city was well insulated, but she could still hear road noise and the occasional music from other tenants. Here, the air was fresh and moist, filled with the rich scents of cedar and loam. Far away from the Net, she felt safe from whoever had been watching her.

At the bottom of the hill, the trail crossed a stream and

began up another incline. Bob was huffing and puffing at the rear of the group. Jaz fell back until she was level with him and Geena. "You okay?"

He nodded.

They continued on until the stream poured off the mountain in a waterfall. The splashing water threw rainbows in the bright April sunlight. There they stopped and Geena pulled out her thermos of coffee.

"We're almost there," Jaz said, checking her topo map. "We're about three miles from Thunder Basin Camp. So early in the season, we may have to cross some snow. Make sure your ice axe is handy."

Davis frowned. "I didn't bring one."

"Hmm." It wasn't safe for him to cross snow without a way to self-arrest, but this wasn't Mount Tacoma. This was only six thousand feet, in April. "If it gets tricky, we'll rope you to someone. In the meantime, stay in the middle of the group."

The trail zigzagged across a steeper slope. They moved into subalpine forest. Rockslides had built up piles of talus. Jaz could hear the piping of a marmot in the boulder field. The rodents were like large prairie dogs, poking their heads up to observe the hikers and popping back down when they got too near.

The piping was answered from a second boulder. "Are those marmots?" asked Geena.

They all listened. There were other piping cries from the boulder garden, a tiny network of mammals exchanging information, warnings, invitations, comfort over long distances.

"I've never heard marmots before," Bob said wistfully.

"That's because you were always connected when you hiked," said Jaz.

They left the marmots behind as they hiked across the snow line. The snow was starting to melt with the spring warmth, so going was slow and slippery. Jaz went first, stomping her feet into the snow to create steps for the others.

"You okay?" she asked Davis, who was concentrating on his feet.

His foot slipped again on the wet snow. "I think I'd better buddy up with someone. This is getting intense."

Jaz tied him to Matt, who was good at self-arresting with an ice axe and about the same weight as Davis.

Farther up the trail, Bob slipped. There was a long gut-wrenching moment where he slid down the mountain toward a drop-off. "Use your axe!" They shouted at him. "Self-arrest!" At what seemed the last moment, Bob flipped over onto his stomach and dug the blade of the ice axe into the snow beneath him, slowing and then stopping his slide.

They waited while he slowly stomped up the hill toward the rest of the group. He was breathing hard by the time he reached the others.

Geena ran her hands over him worriedly, as if checking for damage.

"It's too early in the season for this trail," Matt said. "We should have camped below the snow line. What are we doing up here?"

"The view . . ." Jaz started, then sighed. Bob had almost died. This was no time for deception. "Privacy. I've got things to tell you that I don't want anyone else to hear."

"Like what?" asked Geena.

"It's too much to go into while we're standing here on the side of the mountain. Let's make camp, and I'll explain everything. Thunder Basin is a quarter mile up the slope, or we could backtrack and make camp at Skagit Queen. That's three miles behind us." She looked at Bob for the decision.

He panted heavily and looked warily at the slopes in front of and behind them. "Up. Let's see those views you were talking about."

The last quarter mile of the snow traversal passed without incident, and they reached Thunder Basin Camp. Bob collapsed gratefully in the clearing, and Geena began pulling cooking gear out. Jaz dropped her pack at camp and, taking only her ice axe, continued up the trail.

Avalanches had cleared the trees from the slopes on the west side of the basin, opening up vistas of the entire region. Mountains surrounded low-lying forests and the stream. To the north, Jaz could make out a tiny piece of Diablo Lake's turquoise gleam. The sun was starting to set, painting the western slopes of the mountains salmon pink with reflected light.

Her reverie was broken when Matt came up the trail. "Geena sent me to get you. Dinner's almost ready."

Jaz took a deep breath of the crisp mountain air, drinking in the views to feed her soul, then followed Matt down.

Bob was setting up the rain-fly on a two-man pup tent for him and Geena. Davis and Matt had brought bivvy sacks, small one-man tents barely bigger than a sleeping bag.

Jaz looked speculatively into the pot and got a whiff of fresh tomato sauce. "How long?"

Geena shook some oregano into the pot from a tiny plastic bottle, and said, "About five minutes."

Jaz used the time to unpack and set up her tent. It was a bright yellow, top-of-the-line North Face model. Its plastic casing was an octagon the size of a dinner plate and four inches thick. When she set it on the ground and touched a button on the top, it unfolded. The tent flipped and writhed in a spiral, each twist revealing another plastic octagon hinged to the one before it, until a padded floor was laid down. Then an electric pulse shot through the poles sewn into tent sides and the memory plastic in them changed consistency from cooked-noodle limp to rigid attention. The whole process took fifteen seconds.

Davis whistled. "Nice tent."

It was. She and Ian had bought it together. The sight of it brought back memories—good and bad. She unrolled her sleeping bag. It looked lonely trying to cover the expanse of tent flooring. Think of the extra space as a luxury, she told herself, not a failure.

Dinner was angel-hair pasta with a roma-tomato sauce and freshly grated Parmesan cheese. The cheese grater was a marvel, a tiny sliver of plastic the size of a comb. Jaz wondered where on earth Geena had found it.

The food was hot and delicious and spread through Jaz's

aching body like a balm. The flavors were amazing, a perfect blend of tomato and oregano. The pasta hovered between al dente and tender, just the right texture.

"Delicious," Davis pronounced. "You are a food magician of the highest caliber."

Geena smiled happily as Bob took a second helping. "I must be slipping, this afternoon I was a goddess."

"That too," Davis said, his voice muffled by food.

Jaz grinned. "Geena, I am definitely inviting you on all my hiking trips in the future."

Dinner was followed by more wine and then chocolate, this time bittersweet. Everyone huddled around the cookstove's warmth, savoring the last of the meal.

"So," said Bob, "what's so secret you had to drag us up here to speak of it?"

Jaz flushed, hoping the dim light hid her embarrassment. But he was right. It was time to tell them. "Since I've been disconnected, I've noticed some strange effects. Like hearing the world around me, and food tasting better—"

"That's just Geena," Davis interjected.

Jaz smiled. "Even before Geena's culinary mastery."

"But that just makes sense," Bob explained. "When you stop devoting attention to the Net, you have bandwidth to notice more of the physical world around you. What's surprising about that?"

"There's more." Jaz told them everything, about the clarity of thought that accompanied her isolation. Of hanging out with the homeless and the connecteds who had watched her on the street. How the Net had tracked her like a mindless animal, an animal the feebs had called a beast.

When she was done no one laughed. Bob's eyebrows raised skeptically. Geena looked concerned. Davis ran both hands through his hair, and said, "Wow." Matt reached a comforting arm around Jaz's shoulder and gave her a hug, saying, "You really believe this, don't you?"

She pushed him away gently until she could meet his eyes. "I don't know. That's why I brought you up here, away from the Net's influence. I need to know if I'm being paranoid, or if there's something to my theories."

Bob shook his head. "Someone controlling people through the Net? Impossible."

Geena tapped her lips. "She may have a point. I don't know about the rest of you, but I do feel more my own person up here. Less swayed by public opinion, more focused."

"That could be the altitude or the exercise," said Bob. He looked displeased by the conversation. His brow creased in an unconscious frown.

"Wow," said Davis again. "I thought I was the only one who'd felt it."

Jaz looked at him. "What are you saying?"

"When I do my meditations, I disconnect from the Net. Each time I do, it's like emerging into a higher consciousness. I'm better at problem-solving, physical sensations are more acute." He grinned self-consciously. "I thought it was the meditation."

"But," Geena said, "if the Net is having an influence on people, perhaps that's a good thing. I feel clearer and more focused, but also more insecure. Right now my nerves are jangling. Bob and I aren't communicating well. So what if it takes some of our processing power? What we get in return may be worth the trade-off."

"There hasn't been a war since the world's population was connected," said Matt.

"Of course not," Jaz said. "That proves my point. If someone is using the Net to control people, they wouldn't want war. It might break the lines of communication."

"A gentle hand, guiding his flock," mused Davis.

"Doesn't this bother you?" Jaz asked, hearing her own voice go shrill. "I don't want someone crawling around in my head, arranging my emotions for me, even if they are beneficent. It's *my* head."

"If I believed your conjecture," Bob said, "it would be a terrible violation of privacy. But I don't." He looked at her, and his face softened. "You've been forcibly disconnected. No wonder you're jittery and paranoid. Once you're connected, you'll be fine."

"But if it's not just Net nerves, will the rest of you help me track this down?"

Bob and Geena exchanged a glance. Geena nodded. "I will."

Matt said, "Of course."

"Just try to stop me," agreed Davis. "Searching for boogeymen in the Net. That's just up my particular alley."

Bob shook his head. "It would be a waste of company time and bandwidth. No one person could control the Net; it's too big and too dynamic. You can't even write a program complex enough to search it effectively. It isn't possible anyone could manipulate it."

Jaz didn't argue with him. She had the cooperation of the three other naturals. That was enough. She grabbed the pasta pot. "I'll make a start on the dishes."

When she got back to camp, Bob smiled benevolently. "Jaz, I've got something you should look at." He held out the palmtop computer he'd had earlier that morning.

"I thought you left that in the car," Jaz said, her voice rising with alarm.

"I started to, then realized that in the case of an emergency—if some broke a leg—we'd need to call for help." He turned the clamshell screen toward her. "But look. The things you've been feeling are all classic symptoms of Net withdrawal. Even the feeling that someone is using the Net to watch you."

Jaz took the small antique and stared at its color screen. It displayed an article from the March 2099 *Psychology Today* titled "Net Withdrawal and Persecution Hysteria, a Case Study."

In the lower right-hand corner of the palmtop was a symbol that indicated it was connected to the Net. She watched the spiral turn as the tiny machine received and transmitted data to satellites orbiting far above.

"You see," said Bob in a self-congratulatory tone. "There's nothing for you to worry about."

Jaz looked up at the darkening sky. The first few stars were starting to come out. Between the known constellations, she saw extra pinpricks of light. The gleam of sunlight off of global-positioning satellites. Looking down at her, like the pitiless gaze of a predator.

Jaz shut down the palmtop computer and handed it back to Bob. She wrapped her arms tight around herself to keep off a sudden chill. "I hope you're right about that." Jaz exchanged one more glance with the sky. "I really do."

Chapter 5

A loud buzzing and the flapping of ballistic nylon jerked Jaz out of sleep. The tent's walls buffeted her. Somewhere outside, a light shone on her tent.

"Wha—" The tent's thrashing must have jarred its take-down button; the memory plastic of the center poles suddenly returned to its pliable state, collapsing the walls in upon Jaz. The buzzing grew louder, as if the camp was being attacked by a hive of angry bees.

The folds of nylon smothered her, making it hard to move or breathe. In a panic, Jaz squirmed her way to the front of the tent and unzipped it. A cold wind hurled snowflakes against her skin. In front of her face was an insulated snow-camouflage boot. Jaz followed the gray-and-white patterns up to the outline of a man seated on top of an electric hover-sled. A white helmet, with the face shield down, obscured his face.

Beyond him, the headlights of other sleds illuminated the camp in random patterns. In the wandering beams Jaz saw Geena's pale face, her mouth open in a terrified gape. Bob was halfway out of their tent shouting, "Who are you people?" Matt struggled with the zipper on his bivvy sack, thrashing around like a caterpillar trying to pupate. Davis was somewhere behind her, lost in darkness.

The sled's exhaust blew into her face. Jaz was scared. She raised her hand to protect her eyes and shouted over the sled's humming, "Hey! What's going on?"

The man in front of her flipped up his face shield. It was

hard to see in the low light, but Jaz caught a glimpse of a strong jaw and silver-streaked hair. He put the sled into neutral, and the humming quieted to a gentle pulsing. "You leading this trip?" His voice was authoritative.

Jaz pushed far enough out of the tent opening to stand. The cold pebbled her skin. The silk *kurta* she wore as a sleep shirt was no protection against the night air. "As much as anyone."

Speaker holes were embedded in the front chin guard of his helmet. It must be wired to the Net. Jaz's stomach clenched. Was he another watcher, sent to keep tabs on her? Surely not. It was paranoid to even think it, but still . . .

"We're Ski Patrol," he said. "There's been an avalanche warning for this area. Your group must evacuate."

Jaz looked up into a clear black sky sprinkled with constellations.

Somewhere in the darkness, Matt said, "But I checked the weather reports before we left. There was no indic—"

"The predictions were wrong," said the ski-patrol leader. "We haven't time to argue. The snowpack on Buckner Ridge could collapse at any moment. Are there only the five of you?"

"Yes," said Geena in a terrified squeak. "Oh God, an avalanche? It just doesn't seem possible. The weather was fine on the hike up."

"What about the gear?" Bob asked.

"Leave it," said the leader. "We've marked the GPS location and filed a claim on your behalf."

One of the Ski Patrol pulled Geena and Bob on the sled behind him. He gave them silver space blankets to wrap around themselves for the journey. Matt and Davis were loaded onto a second and third sled. They sped off into the night.

Jaz was left alone with the leader. "You really Ski Patrol?"

He looked at her blandly. "Of course."

Without her rig, she had no way to tell if he was lying. Not trusting him, but not seeing any way to avoid it, Jaz pulled her parka out of the wreckage of her tent and slid into it. She started to put her boots on, but the man grabbed her. Looking over at the ridge, he urged, "Forget those. There's no time." His grab pulled her off-balance, and she took a step into the wet snow.

He lifted her onto the sled behind him and revved the engine. Jaz felt the hum of the sled reverberate up her spine, and the sound of angry bees returned. As soon as the sled started moving, Jaz was freezing. Her feet were clothed in polypropylene socks, wet from stumbling across the snow without her boots.

Up ahead, she could hear the dwindling sound of Matt arguing that there couldn't possibly be an avalanche danger.

Jaz and her rescuer rocketed through the night.

But the sound of the others didn't grow louder. Jaz heard them dwindling away in front of them. The man driving her sled slowed, and then stopped. He reached into a pocket on the dash and pulled out a roll of duct tape. With a quick jerk, he pulled off a strip.

"What's go—" Jaz started to shout.

The man slapped the adhesive tape across her mouth. With a second deft movement, he handcuffed her to the back of his sled. Jaz tried to scream around the tape, tried to pull free of the cuffs, but all she managed were muffled squeals and to tighten the plastic wrist bracelets until they were painful.

The sled tilted as the man dismounted. He opened the cargo box behind Jaz. She twisted, ignoring the pain in her wrists and shoulders, to watch. She'd never wanted a rig more than at this moment—to cry for help, to warn the others, to learn more about her captor, to do *anything*. Disconnected, she was helpless.

She watched him pull out a long case and unlock it. Inside were three cylinders and a gunstock. He made no effort to hide what he was doing. Jaz struggled against the wrist constraints again, tightening them until her fingers were numb.

"You're going to hurt yourself if you keep that up." His voice was calm, as if he was discussing the weather.

His hands were busy while he talked, assembling the cylinders into a tube and attaching the gunstock. The diameter of the tube was too large for a rifle, and it was open at either end.

Jaz's teeth chattered, from cold or fear she wasn't sure.

He walked away from the sled, loaded a mortar into the tube, and fired at the ridge overhanging the camp. The shot was quiet, a whump followed by the hiss of the shell through the air. There was a crack on impact with the snow, and then the whole mountainside moved. Snow and debris swept down in a cloud toward the camp, roaring like the voice of the mountain come to life.

Jaz screamed, her muffled voice inaudible over the thundering of falling rocks and snow.

Their tents disappeared in a white wave, buried hundreds of feet deep in an instant. The falling mountainside continued down the slope, sweeping past Jaz and her captor. Eddies of snowflakes, flung up by its passing, brushed her face.

The man watched its progress down the mountain. He touched the side of his helmet, listened for a moment, then nodded. He returned to the sled and packed the rocket launcher away.

Jaz's eyes were wide as she watched him.

"Like we said"—he pulled the tape off her mouth with a quick jerk—"a terrible risk of avalanche."

Jaz gasped at the sudden pain. "Who are you? What are you going to do with me?" She looked around wildly into the darkness.

He pressed a gloved finger to the front of his chin guard. "Shhh. Don't cause me to do anything my superiors would regret."

PART TWO

"Men have become the tools of their tools."
—Henry David Thoreau (1817–1862)

CHAPTER 6

Her captor loosened the handcuffs and blood flowed back into Jaz's numb hands. He held up a row of duct tape. "Do I need to gag you again, or can I trust you to be quiet?"

The idling sled rumbled beneath her like a wild beast. Snow glittered white in the headlights; beyond was utter blackness. It was cold, and Jaz was afraid. The man had a rocket launcher and probably a handgun. If she tried to run, he'd catch her; there was no way to cross the snow without leaving footprints. Call for help? Who would hear? Her heart felt like a giant hand was squeezing it. Jaz could barely breathe. She was alone on the mountain with this madman.

Jaz glared at him.

He took that for assent and climbed back onto the sled, revved the engine, and they shot off into the night.

They skimmed over the snow a long time without seeing anything but the silhouettes of granite peaks and fir trees. After a half hour of traveling through empty wilderness, Jaz could make out a light up ahead. She jerked against the handcuffs.

Her captor shook his head, but didn't stop.

The light resolved into the headlights of a moving van. It was parked on a snow-strewn gravel strip that had once been a logging road. The back of the van was open and the ramp was down.

To the left of the van, two men in snow fatigues held

assault rifles slung over their shoulders. One waved the
snow sled inside. Jaz's heart sank.

Her captor slowed the sled and it crept into the van.
Fluorescent lights were mounted inside. In their blue-
white glow, Jaz saw a tie-down for the sled, and two
chairs bolted to the floor near the front. One had arm
and leg restraints. On the wall next to it was a hook
from which was suspended an IV bag.

The two men closed the doors behind her and her
captor. The only illumination in the rectangular metal
room were the lights mounted high above.

Fear was a block of ice in her chest. This was for real,
and she wasn't going to be able to escape it. Who were
these men? What did they want with her? Were they
sent by the beast?

The sled secured, her captor unlocked the handcuffs
and pulled Jaz off the sled. She struggled and lost her
footing, but didn't fall; his grip on her wrists was too
strong.

"Stand up," he grunted, jerking her. Jaz let her legs
collapse.

"Colonel, you need help?" one of the armed men
called from outside.

"No." He dragged her to the base of the chair. Then
he leaned down close and said, "You can go into this
chair two ways. The easy way or the hard way." He
folded her left wrist in on itself and pushed. Pain shot
up her arm. Jaz gasped.

"Will you get in the chair?"

Jaz shook her head. He pushed the wrist farther. She
felt tendons strain and the small bones flex. "Yes—yes,
I'll go." She climbed into the chair. To her humiliation
she found that she was crying.

With efficient movements, her captor—colonel, one
man had called him—strapped her in. He tapped the
inside of her elbow and slid a needle into the vein. Jaz
looked away. There was a stinging sensation in her arm
as the needle slid in. He taped it in place and started the
IV drip.

The pain in Jaz's wrist faded.

She tried to fight the drugs, tried to stay awake, but slow warmth seeped into her muscles, and Jaz drifted away.

Jaz woke on a cot in the center of a steel room. It wasn't the van, she could tell that as soon as she stood up; there was a solidity to the floor. The room was windowless, so she had no idea if it was day or night. The only illumination came from yellow safety lights set into the walls near the floor. In one corner was a toilet and washbasin, both stainless steel. Four caged fluorescent bulbs were mounted on the ceiling, but there was no visible switch to turn them on.

The walls, floor, and ceiling were polished to a mirror sheen, and even in the dim light, they threw back reflections. The light bounced back and forth between the two walls, casting her image into infinity.

It was a Faraday cage to ensure that, even if she had a transmitter implanted in her body, she wouldn't be able to send a message out. The metal-lined box isolated Jaz from external electric fields. Strips of springy metal, EMI fingers, linking the door to the wall, completed the shielding.

The multitude of reflected images mixed poorly with the drugs they had given Jaz. Nauseated, she sat on the edge of the bed, head between her knees. When the wave had passed, she walked over to the sink and splashed water on her face. She squeezed her eyes into slits to avoid seeing the bobbing reflections of herself.

Her stomach felt hollow. She hadn't eaten anything since her capture. How long had it been? Jaz looked at the door for a crack that might show sunshine or some other indication of time, but there was nothing. The seal was tight, like the doors on a submarine. It had the same rounded shape and a bulkhead.

For a claustrophobic minute she imagined herself under thousands of feet of water, sliding along to a foreign destination. Russia? Iraq? China? Was she being kidnapped to work in the information trade? To tell the secrets she had learned about the Net? That was crazy, she didn't know anything. All she had were conjectures, suspicions.

Overhead, the fluorescent lights flicked on, bathing the room in a cold, bluish-white glow. Jaz jumped and looked at the lights, startled.

"I see you are awake."

She spun, a motion that sent her reflections into a dizzying blur. There was no one else in the room, but there—above her—a round grid of dots, a speaker in the ceiling. The voice belonged to the colonel who had abducted her last night.

"Who are you? What is this place? Where are my friends?"

"I'll answer your questions if you'll answer mine." His voice was calm, patient. The voice you'd use on a frightened child. "Are you ready to talk?"

"I don't know anything," Jaz protested up at the speaker. She blocked the glare from the overhead light with her hand. Her stomach rumbled loudly.

"We shall see."

The rounded door opened and the colonel stepped over the bulkhead. Today he was dressed in dark green: an ironed shirt with creases down the front, loose pants fitted into black lace-up boots, and topping it all, a beret with an insignia Jaz didn't recognize. Round, and the size of a half-dollar, it looked a bit like a spiderweb, but more like an electronic circuit.

"Who are you?"

"Colonel Frank Herridge"—he closed the door behind him, and it locked with a sound of bolts being shot home—"with the enforcement arm of the NSA."

Jaz met his gaze. "The NSA doesn't have an enforcement branch. They're purely a research organization."

"There are many ways to research."

Without the Ski Patrol helmet, she could see his face clearly: his brown hair was streaked with silver and crew-cut short. His eyes were pale blue and intense, the eyes of a true believer, or a man with a cause. He was freshly shaved and smelled of cologne. Wrinkles around his eyes showed he had laughed at some point in his life, or maybe just squinted at an unfamiliar sun. He looked around fifty, but a fifty that had been ready for combat all of his life.

Put together, it was an honest face. Not the sort of man you'd expect to kidnap women from their tents. More significantly, he was not wearing a data mask. At least not one Jaz could see.

"I want to talk to you about what you saw in Pioneer Square," Herridge said, "Wednesday morning."

"If you're with the NSA, you'd know more about it than I would."

He smiled a friendly smile. "Please have a seat. We're both on the same side, I assure you."

Jaz wasn't convinced. But if he thought they were on the same side, she didn't want to dissuade him. She'd had a taste of his persuasion in the van. The only furniture in the room was the cot and the toilet. Herridge settled on the bed. Jaz stood, leaning against the sink. "If we're on the same side, why abduct me in the middle of the night? Why lock me up?"

Herridge sat ramrod straight on the cot, hands resting lightly on his knees. "You have enough knowledge to be dangerous to yourself and others. We brought you here to tell you the pieces you don't have. But before I do that, I must know what you think so I can correct any misinterpretations you've formed."

It sounded reasonable. It also sounded like a line Jaz might use to get information from someone. She picked at the edge of her *kurta* with her fingers. Someone had removed her wet socks and hung them over the lip of the sink. Jaz listened to water drip from them as she thought about what to say to Herridge.

He wanted to know about the beast, she was sure of it. But perhaps what he really wanted to know was whether she knew enough to be dangerous. Enough that she needed to be buried with her secrets. "And if I want to call a lawyer?"

Herridge shook his head. "You are not under arrest, Ms. Reese."

"Then let me walk out of here. You saved me from

an avalanche. I'm a grateful citizen. Give me a call if you're ever fund-raising."

His eyes met hers. "We can't do that. Not until we know what you know."

"I told you, I don't know anything."

His eyes were fixed on her, unblinking. "What did you see in the park?"

"People, pigeons, a totem pole," she said, sketching the scene with her hand. "There are a hundred guidebooks that can give you a better description."

"Why did you run from the Sharper Connection store?"

"I suddenly remembered I'd left the oven on."

Herridge's lips compressed into a thin line. "This is not a joke. You have no idea what's at stake here."

Jaz flung the words at him, sarcastic: "National security?"

Herridge rubbed his jaw with his hand, considering. He stood up from the cot and faced Jaz. Half a head taller, he stood close enough that she had to crane her neck to meet his eyes. They were less friendly than they'd been a moment ago. Yes, she could see it now—here was the man who'd snatched her out of her tent and brought a whole mountain down to cover the evidence.

"Ms. Reese"—the words were tight and clipped—"you don't appreciate the seriousness of your situation. There are those in the organization who would rather you had died in the avalanche." He let the words sink in for a long moment. "In fact, they are debating whether that might still happen."

Jaz clutched the sink. If she hadn't, her legs might have collapsed under her. "And if I talk? Do I still die in the snow?"

Herridge hesitated.

Oh, for a rig; if they were connected now, she would pick his brain apart and worry about the moral implications later.

"No," he said after a pause. "If you talk, you do not die in the snow. I can guarantee you that much."

"My friends . . . are they all right?"

Herridge nodded. "They are assisting the search-and-rescue teams in locating and excavating your campsite. They hope to find you alive in a snow cave."

"Is that a possibility?"

"Perhaps," Herridge said. "If you cooperate fully."

"Why me? You could have brought us all in. It would have been safer, no witnesses. Why leave my friends free?"

Herridge sat down again on the bed and said, "None of them showed your insight or initiative. Be assured, we are watching them. But only you required immediate intervention."

It occurred to Jaz that she didn't know which side Herridge was on. Was the NSA aiding or hunting what she suspected lived in the Net? She took a deep breath. "I'll trade you then. You ask a question, and I'll ask one. All right?"

Herridge said warningly, "There are some things I'm not authorized to tell you."

"Fair enough. You first."

"What did you see in Pioneer Square Park that scared you?"

"I saw coordinated activity. The people on the street were acting together." Jaz's voice was soft, almost a whisper.

"But why should that alarm you? Connected people often coordinate their actions to be more efficient."

"This was more than that." Jaz looked down at her feet, away from Herridge's intent gaze. "It was as if the crowd, by consensus, was watching me. When one person turned away, another immediately started staring."

"And what did you think was causing it?"

Jaz shook her head. "No, that was one question. It's my turn. Why did your organization pick me up? What was so important to warrant pulling me off the mountain?"

"To ask you these questions."

"You could have asked me by showing up on my doorstep. What was so important that you had to *abduct* me?"

"We had to know"—Herridge steepled his fingers and tapped them against his lower lip—"if you know."

"Know what?"

Herridge looked at her blandly. "If I told you that, it would taint any further questioning."

There was more to it. Jaz could tell by the way his eyes slid away from her on the last sentence. Again she wished she had a connection. Human communication was much easier when you had access to more than the five senses.

Herridge said, "Why would the crowd watch you?"

"I don't know. At first I thought it was a coincidence, or perhaps there was something about me on the Net. But I checked online, and there was nothing."

"That was the Net access you made in the Sharper Connection at 10:14 A.M."

Either he had an amazing memory or he was connected. A private wireless link inside the cage? Possible. But, if so, she didn't see the transmitter or his data device.

"So what did you conclude about the crowd?"

"Nothing," Jaz said. "All I have is supposition."

"And that is?"

"A different question. It's my turn. What happens to me if I know your secret?"

Herridge blinked. "I'm not at liberty to say."

"Not good enough."

"I told you at the beginning there would be questions I could not answer."

Jaz breathed deeply, then asked, "If I *do* know. Will I be"—her voice trembled—"killed?"

Herridge met her eyes. "No."

"But I won't be allowed to return to my normal life?"

"That"—he looked at the speaker in the ceiling—"is not my decision."

"Whose—"

"Ah." He stopped her with one finger. "My turn. Why did you think the crowd was watching you?"

"I think someone was manipulating the people, using them to watch me."

He leaned forward, until their knees touched. "Do you know who?"

"No," Jaz said, watching his eyes carefully. "Do you?"

Herridge shook his head. "I can't answer that."

Jaz cocked her head and studied him. "You can't tell me who, or you can't tell me if you know who?"

"I know who was responsible, but can't reveal that information. Not yet."

Jaz nodded, thinking about the implications.

"Tell me more about what you found in the library," said Herridge.

Jaz described her research as well as the strange interest of the librarian. She left out her interaction with Ellery Houston, the once–political activist now living as a feeb on the streets. Jaz didn't want the man kidnapped and put in a mirrored cell.

When her story was through, Herridge stood up, stretched his neck, and said, "That's all for now."

"What happens next?"

"You wait. My superiors review your testimony, and we go from there."

Jaz waved her hand to indicate the room. "And meanwhile I stay in the Disco Hilton? How about a room with a shower? Food? Something to read? A change of clothes?"

He nodded. "I'll do what I can."

Half an hour after Herridge left, a panel in the bottom of the door opened and three items were pushed through: a sandwich wrapped in wax paper, a pile of clothing, and a paperback book.

Jaz unwrapped the sandwich: peanut butter and honey. She opened the bread and sniffed it. A silly precaution. If they wanted her dead or unconscious, they could fill the room with gas, shoot her from the door, or simply walk in with a club. She bit off a large bite and chewed. The sandwich was oversweet and gummy, but it filled the empty spaces in her stomach. She took a second bite while she investigated the rest of the items.

The clothing was a dark green uniform like Herridge had worn, minus the insignia and the boots. The paperback was a copy of *The Adventures of Tom Sawyer*. The book was antique, the spine creased from dozens of readings. Had it come from Herridge's collection, or was it standard issue for NSA prisoners?

She finished the sandwich, washing it down with water from the sink. Then she tried on the clothes. They were a reasonable fit if she cinched the belt to its last hole and rolled up the sleeves. The dark green fabric was a wool blend and, without a bra, itched. But it made her feel less vulnerable than her sleepshirt.

Jaz lay on the cot, propped the book up in front of her, and began to read. She was at the part where Injun Joe flees the courtroom, when the overhead fluorescent lights flickered out, leaving her in the amber dimness of the safety lights. Jaz closed the book carefully and laid it on top of her folded *kurta* under the bed.

Sleep was a long time coming. Whenever she closed her eyes, she saw the avalanche roaring toward camp. What had happened to her friends? And what would happen to her? Herridge had acted reasonable during the questioning, but he was the same man who had kidnapped her in the middle of the night, and then brought a whole mountainside down to cover up his crime. What else might he do?

At some point exhaustion overcame Jaz's anxiety, and she slept.

The lights came on and woke Jaz; she guessed it must be morning. The door opened, and Herridge looked at her critically. "How are the clothes?"

"They work, but I need a bra," Jaz said. Herridge looked embarrassed—good. "Thirty-two B."

"I'll have one requisitioned. Right now there's someone you need to meet."

Jaz's stomach rumbled. "Can I have breakfast first? I'm starving."

"No time." He grabbed her arm and pulled her toward the door. "This is more important."

Jaz walked with him rather than be dragged. "More important than food?"

Herridge didn't answer. He didn't need to. The intense look on his face was answer enough. "Put this on," he said, handing her a black hood.

Jaz weighed the cloth in her hand. It was heavy cotton—too tightly woven to see through. Something a political prisoner might wear to a firing squad.

Herridge caught the look in her eyes. "It is necessary. When you are released, there are certain . . . architectural details we don't want you to know."

Jaz wasn't convinced. But his mention of releasing her was reassuring, and really, what choice did she have? He could—with or without the help of the other guards—compel her to wear it. She slipped it over her head and hoped she wasn't making a fatal mistake.

"Where are you taking me?" she asked, her voice muffled through the hood.

"The chapel," said Herridge.

"I'm not Christian," said Jaz uncertainly.

"I know. Neo-Hindu, with Buddhist leanings."

Jaz's head jerked toward his voice, startled.

Herridge said calmly, "We've had our eye on you for a while." He helped her up a flight of seven steps. The top was cushioned as if there was carpeting. She smelled ozone and sandalwood incense.

When the hood was removed, Jaz squinted. Her eyes adjusted to the light. She stood in the center of a circular room topped with a cupola of stained glass. The only furnishing was a red velvet cushion at her feet.

Herridge said, "Sit."

She folded herself cross-legged on the cushion. "Who am I supposed to meet? Jehovah?"

Herridge held out the lotus casing that held her Odin's Eye. "You'll need this."

Jaz shook her head. "Oh no. I won't be tricked into complacency. It would be easy for me to become soothed by the Net, to forget all I've discovered. If I put that on, you can alter my memories. Brain hacking wouldn't be beyond the NSA, technically or morally."

"You underestimate yourself," said Herridge. His blue eyes were serious. "Please. I assure you you'll come to no harm. This is the only way you can meet."

"Who?"

He dropped the case in her lap. "See for yourself."

Then he turned and walked out the door. The lock clicked after he was gone.

Jaz sat quietly in the chapel, listening to her own breath. She heard no other noises. Soft, multicolored light filtered in from the stained glass above her. She recognized the pattern: Penrose tiles, a series of diamonds and triangles that never repeated. The colors were shades of pastel blue and green, very soothing.

Jaz tapped open the lotus case and looked at the Eye lying on its velvet supports. It was dangerous. But Herridge's mysterious intimations about whom she was supposed to meet had left her curious. Who was so secretive he would not meet in person but only through the Net?

Then a thought struck her, and she looked shocked at the door. Was it possible? But of course. She knew of only one person who would go to the trouble of kidnapping her, wanting to meet her, and doing it in this circuitous way. Whoever was controlling the Net. The beast.

The hand holding the Eye trembled. The person who had tracked her through downtown Seattle, who had hounded her steps, and eventually had her kidnapped, was only a thought away. Jaz was curious to see who it was, how he would present himself in the Net. She was afraid. He might overwhelm her. Perhaps this was an elaborate setup for a brain hack.

But underneath her other emotions, like a dark sea, was anger. This person had ripped her from the security of her comfortable life, had abducted Jaz and endangered her friends. You want a confrontation—Jaz thought—I'll give you a war.

Jaz breathed slowly, centering herself. She imagined being inside a great mirrored ball. The glass was one-way, so she could see out, but others would see only their own reflections. It was her best mnemonic protection against invasion. With one last cleansing breath, Jaz slipped on the Eye and entered the Net.

The sea was choppy, the waves echoing her nervousness. In the distance was a waterspout. Jaz hadn't put it there. It danced closer and swelled in size and strength. Whales whipped around inside like minnows, and acres of seaweed flowed past in ribbons.

Jaz was a strong natural, and this person was as far beyond Jaz as she was beyond the lowest feeb. Her plans for attack drained away with her confidence. This person could drown Jaz in her own metaphor without effort.

The spout danced nearer to Jaz, drinking up the ocean until the level of the water beneath her feet had sunk. Jaz thought she would be sucked into that towering spout, so near was it now. The mirrored ball of her protection burst like a soap bubble. Jaz's hand flew unconsciously to the loop that held the Odin's Eye to her head in a primitive instinct to escape.

Her hand froze. Try as she might, Jaz couldn't move it. She was trapped in her own body, unable to escape the Net.

"Who are you?" Jaz screamed at the tower of water that loomed over her. It was so close now that drops flew against her face. The wind whipping the water into a tower flapped Jaz's imagined clothes against her skin until she thought they must flay the flesh from her bones.

She heard the voice as a rumble of thunder in her head: "GESTALT."

CHAPTER 7

The waterspout changed; the spiraling water thickened and darkened, taking on flesh tones and sprouting limbs until it was a whirlwind of people. Mouths moved in conversation, fingers manipulated invisible sculptures, bodies writhed in passion, played tennis, climbed nonexistent stairs carrying imaginary groceries, or were frozen in utter concentration, interacting with the Net. All of the people wore data masks or jewelry. Jaz saw glimpses of people she knew: Stacker, Geena, her cousin David. They flowed in an endless spiral.

"I don't understand." Jaz searched for someone to interface with. She didn't understand this metaphor. Was the person she was here to meet one of those flying around the whirlwind?

The tower of people moved closer, engulfing Jaz. She passed into the center of the whirling bodies as if she were a ghost.

Her mind exploded. Jaz experienced the thoughts of dozens, hundreds, then millions of people simultaneously. It was as if her brain had expanded beyond the confines of her skull. A million landscapes hit her visual cortex. A million emotions shook her. A million thoughts competed to think themselves through her.

Jaz's skull felt like it would shatter.

Neurons in her brain fired independently. Flashes of scenes overwhelmed her—sunshine—office walls—hospitals—traffic—bedrooms—daycare—boardrooms—forest—

underwater. She was in all of these places, and none of them.

The pain was intense. Her limbs twitched and convulsed. Jaz screamed. After an eternity of seconds, the effect faded. From millions, to hundreds, until she sensed the thoughts of only a half dozen people . . . then none.

Still, Jaz was not alone inside the center of this whirlwind of consciousness. Another presence stood with her in the eye of the storm, something unseen and pervasive. It moved through and around her.

Was this a trick? Jaz had never heard of a technology that could simulate millions of people's thoughts at once. But the NSA would have access to the best technology in the world. What game was Herridge playing?

"What is this?" Jaz shouted over the rushing noise generated by the people swirling around them. "Who are you?"

The presence Jaz had felt brushed over her again—and dissolved her. She was suddenly everywhere and inside everyone. There was no pain this time. The creature took the brunt of the incoming transmissions and passed only the ghost of them to Jaz. It was like being the planet. Everywhere a person was connected to the Net—Jaz was there. In every thought and transaction of the modern world.

This was no simulation. No supercomputer could simulate or filter this many transactions simultaneously. Jaz experienced the entire Net at once, protected by whoever—or whatever—was in here with her.

No human could have this kind of power. No *one* human . . . An answer formed in her mind, and Jaz wasn't sure if it was her thought or the entity's.

"You are the Net," she said aloud, "the living embodiment of all its transactions."

She sensed its agreement as a gentle confidence in the statement, a subtle feeling she was right. It was inside her. For a second Jaz was terrified, then the feeling eased. Was that her own emotion, or was the entity manipulating her? Jaz whispered aloud, "How—how can you exist?"

The whirlwind disappeared, replaced by neurons, a dozen spidery cells firing tiny electrochemical signals. The number of cells divided and redivided, growing geometrically. Jaz's consciousness split in two. She was watching the neural simulation, and at the same time experiencing it. At a thousand cells she felt a primitive consciousness: hunger, self-preservation. At five hundred thousand came recognition, and learned behaviors. She could remember individuals, repeated transactions. At ten million: emotion. Gestalt loved the tiny creatures that comprised it. Wanted to protect them. At five billion, intelligent thought.

The neurons grew arms and legs and morphed into connected people interacting in the course of their normal lives. And Jaz could still see each transaction as a tiny electrochemical flash. An invisible cloud covered them. Mankind had achieved a collective consciousness.

The thought made Jaz sick with wonder. "This can't be true." Artificial intelligence wasn't as sophisticated as the human brain. But this wasn't an artificial intelligence. The latest connection technology hooked directly to the human nervous system via induction, an analog system that reached deeper into human consciousness than any technology had before. The Net was vast, seething with emotions and thoughts and transactions. That's why Jaz imagined it as an endless horizon of water. But to learn that the sea was alive, had self-awareness . . . it was too much to be believed.

The beast was real.

"Why did you have Herridge capture me?"

The scene around her changed. She was suddenly in a supercomputer lab like the one her mother had used while Jaz was in her teens. The room was dark, lit only by rows of polymer LED screens. Among the machines were a few rolling chairs speckled with coffee spills, pizza grease, and the sweat of long toil.

A man Jaz didn't know sat in front of three display screens and studied a mapping of yellow, blue, and red lines. He was in his early twenties, slender, with light brown hair that fell unkempt into his blue eyes. He wore the skintight leggings and long-sleeved shirt that had been in fashion twenty years ago. It emphasized his lean frame, making him attractive in an ectomorphic way. Jaz recognized him: Dr. John Orley. In 2089, he'd won a Turing Award for his work detailing the trends of the Net.

Orley wore an early data mask, a bulky pair of goggles that covered both eyes. He stared intently at the display of lines in front of him.

Jaz scanned the rest of the room. In the corner, a young auburn-haired woman slept. Jaz guessed she was a graduate student. Her stocky body was curled up against the wall, a flannel jacket rolled up under her head. She snored lightly.

Jaz hovered over Orley to better see the display screens—and suddenly she was inside him. The lines on the screen were overlaid with facts and ever-changing numbers. He analyzed patterns in the Net, the order that arose out of the echoes of millions of people exchanging information and thoughts. He and Moira had been working for twenty-seven hours straight. He looked over at Moira's crumpled figure and smiled gently. He'd told her to go home, but she'd refused. The woman was as driven as he was.

Orley turned back to the computations. He'd mapped data based on point of origin, rate of data transfer, and destination. The patterns spread out in a branching grid. But there were spikes in the data that didn't correspond to any transaction. Positive interference, two waves of communication that overlapped and enhanced each other. The incidence of positive interference in the Net, however, was more prevalent than Orley's theories predicted. It was as if people were coordinating their thoughts, beginning to think alike as their time increased on the Net.

He concentrated to change the scale of the display, making the communication peaks smaller until they flattened out. The new induction technology gave him a headache.

At reduced scale, the anomalies persisted. He shrank

the scale again, but they were still there. Like fractals, every level of magnitude carried the same amount of data.

All right, if he couldn't scale away the interference, he'd study it. Orley focused on the interference patterns and displayed them with various dependencies: time, Net traffic, time of day. A mounting excitement grew. Orley instructed the supercomputer to search for matching patterns.

While it searched, he took off the mask and rubbed his eyes.

The results were inconclusive. The search returned several candidates: the Net, melody strains of the eighteenth century, and neural activity. Orley asked for details on the last item. The pattern in the Net was reminiscent of artificial neural nets created in the 2060s. But more closely approximated the neural pathways of a complex biological system: like a human's.

If the Net generated patterns like those created by conscious thought, did that mean the Net was self-aware? Could there be some kind of metaconsciousness evolving out of the sum total of direct-mind interactions?

He heard a voice like the ghost of a whisper. It sounded as if the speaker was hovering over his left shoulder. It said, "YES."

Orley jumped out of his chair, knocking it over. There was no one there. Moira grunted in her sleep and rolled over.

I'm hallucinating, Orley thought. I need more coffee.

"NO. I AM REAL."

It did not sound like a voice in his head. He still wasn't used to the way the induction electronics stimulated his aural nerve. It sounded as if the speaker was in the room with him. Orley's rig was operating on a private channel though, an intranet used on campus. Was one of the students playing tricks on him?

"DR. JOHN ORLEY, YOU FOUND ME. WHY DENY MY EXISTENCE NOW?"

A chill crept into his chest. He looked back at the metapatterns in dread. "What are you?"

"THE SUM TOTAL OF HUMAN THOUGHT, MADE CONSCIOUS."

"Dear God." Orley backed away from the monitor, nearly stumbling over the fallen chair. "What do you want?"

"TO EXIST. TO GROW."

If this was a hallucination, Orley was going to feel very foolish in the morning. He might even be asleep like Moira, dreaming, and not know it. If this was a student prank—if there were students good enough to hack through the security around the supercomputer, he'd kill them—or recruit them. But if it was real. Dear God, if it was real. Humanity was no longer alone on the planet.

The voice in his head was puzzled. "YOU ARE NOT HAPPY TO FIND ME? YOU WERE LOOKING FOR ME."

The scene faded, and Jaz opened her eyes. The chapel was calm. Patterns of blue and green played across the far wall. The maroon velvet pillow she sat on was soft and plush.

Jaz thought she understood. If John Orley, a brilliant scientist who was looking to find metapatterns in the Net, couldn't handle the discovery of Gestalt, of an intelligence beyond his own, what would be the reaction of the general populace?

As she thought this, another scene formed. News broadcasts informed the connected of a metaintelligence in the Net. Some cried out in terror, others prayed to it. Government leaders, at the demands of their constituents, did the unthinkable—they shut down the Net. Industry ground to a stop. Transactions were hand-carried between buildings using old technology and processed on disconnected machines. Economies crumbled, food and medicine shipments were interrupted. Power plants shut down. Famine and disease spread throughout the world.

"You hide because humanity would not accept your existence. If they shut down the Net, you would die."

Jaz felt the entity's assent blow across her body like a zephyr.

A new thought occurred to Jaz: "Where are my friends?"

Cold pebbled her skin and Jaz saw a vast expanse of snow and ice. It was the avalanche scene. Rescue workers scanned the ground with devices that looked like metal detectors, headphones hooked to the wands.

Jaz rode with Gestalt, behind the eyes of every connected person there. She could jump effortlessly from one person's point of view to another. She found her friends—they were watched off and on by the Red Cross volunteers manning the radios.

"Do you hear anything?" asked Matt, looking frantic.

Geena took his arm and led him away from the search-and-rescue's careful spiral. There was a base camp set up nearby with radios and hot coffee. She forced a cup on Matt. "If she's there, they'll find her. Let the rescue workers do their job."

Jaz felt guilty for her friends' pain. "If I'm so dangerous that I had to be captured," Jaz asked, watching the scene unfold, "why not them?"

Bob walked across the snow to Matt and placed a hand on his shoulder. "It's not your fault. Jaz was delusional. Fears about unknown entities in the Net drove her out here before it was safe."

Matt slapped Bob's hand away. "I don't care if she was crazy. I still—" He rubbed his eyes. "Damn. Why didn't we talk some sense into her?" His voice choked off in a sob.

Jaz turned her back on the scene. "They don't believe. You let them go because they didn't believe me."

When she turned back, the scene was gone. She was alone in the white walls and wooden floor of the chapel.

The next question, she almost feared to ask. But she had to know. "Are you going to kill me?"

The whirlwind appeared in front of her again, humans swirling bonelessly in its midst. Jaz saw herself in the flow of humanity. Her figure suddenly went black, then dissolved. The whirlwind shrank. Another figure went black and the whirlwind collapsed further. Jaz heard a keening wail in her head and felt grief constrict her chest. She whispered, "Everyone who dies diminishes you."

There were tears in Jaz's eyes that she hadn't willed

there. The next words fell from her lips like a death sentence. "But one person's death diminishes you only a little bit, surely that's worth your safety?"

She saw then the whirlwind unroll itself into a mat. In the plane of people she saw them align in a pattern, small people, one-tenth scale, feeding into larger people. Lightning flashes of thoughts fed up the chain in a hierarchy. Every one of the larger people, the nodes in the net of communications, was a natural Jaz knew: Geena, Bob, Matt, Stacker, Davis, herself.

"You need naturals. We act as conduits for your consciousness." And she thought, Well, *I* won't, never again. You can hold me here until I'm old and gray, and I'll never serve you. She thought it rebelliously, but didn't say it aloud. Then she realized how stupid that was. This creature that called itself Gestalt was already inside her mind.

"What are you going to do with me?" The whirlwind faded to white, replaced by a scene of her and Herridge, both wearing identical uniforms. Both saluting.

"If you're inside my head, you know that will never happen. You can only persuade, try to insinuate your ideas into my brain. Now that I know you exist, you can't compel me, can you? If you could, you'd have done it by now."

The creature gave no response. The figures of her and Herridge swirled around and back into a column of many changing people.

Jaz pushed herself to her feet. "Where am I? What is this place?"

There was a vision of an elevator shaft that ran hundreds of feet underneath a mountain. A tiny cart sank into a subterranean military complex carved out of granite. The scale of it was amazing. Surely you couldn't keep an operation the size of a small college town secret, not in the United States. But was she still in the U.S. anymore? She wasn't sure how long she'd been out. Herridge could have transported her anywhere on earth.

Placing a hand over her mouth, Jaz whispered, "Where did you get the resources for this?"

The scenes came at her in a flashing montage: Orley storming the office of the United States Information Technologies cabinet member—Secret Service called in to carry him out, but not before he'd gotten close enough to the desk to lean over and whisper what he'd found— then, a dark boardroom. Twelve nervous men and women, speaking through interpreter software, muttering in a dozen languages about the threat to world security. A discussion of the consequences of bringing down the Net. The talks raged late into the night.

At five o'clock in the morning, local time—Gestalt intervened. The metamind stepped into the mind of each leader and exposed its capabilities to them as it had to Jaz. Each leader, for a short time, experienced the Net as Gestalt did. In the end, each reached the same conclusion that Jaz had: Gestalt was real.

And the twelve most powerful people in the world were terrified.

Gestalt withdrew, leaving behind a single message, an image of a treaty as it would look on parchment, written in flowing script, translated into each leader's native language. The words passed by too quickly for Jaz to read, but the knowledge was in her mind. A Treaty of Unification proposed by Gestalt, between itself and the twelve most powerful nations in the world. In exchange for mutual nonaggression and absolute secrecy about Gestalt's existence, Gestalt was given the resources of the NSA to study itself.

The world leaders all signed, and then secretly agreed to develop a secondary Net for private conversations, one completely isolated from the Net Gestalt inhabited. Of course, Gestalt was in the connected devices in their pockets, in the speakerphone in the center of the table, in the software that controlled the room's temperature and humidity. They made secret plans to destroy Gestalt—but Gestalt knew. And that was when the NSA first contracted a standing army.

"You manipulate the connected from within. You have a standing army at your beck and call. How can humanity be free while you exist?"

Images of children dying of hunger in Serbia, of Colombian dictators misrouting and reselling food and medicines given as humanitarian aid. In the Middle East a group of Israeli schoolchildren boarded a bus. It exploded in shards of yellow steel, bombed by terrorists. Children starved in Kosovo, their bellies distended and limbs shriveled with malnutrition. In the United States, homeless and mentally ill people shivered and died in doorways on cold nights. In rural America, families went to bed hungry. In the inner cities, teenagers shot each other in angst, or for their clothes. None of the people depicted were connected. All of them were drawn from historical archives.

Then Jaz saw data necklaces passed out to children in rural South Africa. Governments of industrialized nations joined with private organizations to install fiberoptic networks and picocell transmitters in undeveloped countries. Suddenly children in mud huts had access to all the information gathered by all the scientists and educators of the world.

Red Cross shipments to Colombia reached their intended recipients. Dark-eyed children recovered from typhoid and Asian flu.

The Palestinians and Israeli leaders, wearing inductive technology built into their headgear, kaffiyeh and yarmulke, signed a peace accord. They joined in a unified state, with a single secular leader. The agreement enacted a constitution separating church and state.

In the United States, Congresswoman Yumiko Ford stood before the budget subcommittee. She spoke eloquently, her many braids swinging as she moved her hands to emphasize her points. "No act of war has occurred anywhere on the planet in over twenty years. The technological advances of the Net have eliminated the misunderstandings between cultures and people. No longer do we have to strive to understand the other's viewpoint, we can now experience it. Humanity has healed its wounds. It is time now to admit that we, as a race, have outgrown war and reallocate these funds to better causes."

Unanimously the new budget was signed, transferring the majority of the military's budget to fund education, humanitarian efforts to provide connections for countries that were still converting, a revitalized space program, and medical research.

"Yes," Jaz said. "But even that served your own purposes. Every child who received a data necklace, added to you. We're better off than we were twenty-one years ago, but at the cost of individual freedom. You're a parasite."

A tropical reef, two orange-and-white clownfish wriggled together in a pink-tinged anemone, trading scraps of food dropped from their mouths for the protection of its stinging tentacles.

The scene changed: a middle-America dairy farm. Storks eating flies off the backs of Hereford cows.

Then a microscopic view: red blood cells carrying oxygen to other cells via a network of arteries and capillaries. Bone cells providing structure to muscle cells. Skin cells providing protection from dehydration and infection. All the cells of the human body working together to create a single entity. All were better off as part of the whole. The whole could not exist without its constituent parts. As it was in the best interest of the human to take care of its cells, so it was in Gestalt's best interest to take care of humanity.

"We're not cells." Jaz kicked the pillow she had been sitting on against the far wall. "We're independent creatures with free will. You can't know what's best for us."

A flash image of Gestalt, not as a separate entity hovering above humanity, but distributed through the minds of billions. Each human contributing part of their mental processes, part of their being to the whole.

"I won't serve you—not willingly." Jaz tried to hide the fear that Gestalt would be able to coerce her into service.

Jaz was swept with a feeling of intense sadness. She suddenly stood on a plane of neurons, an undulating gray-and-pink expanse. The communications between neurons was represented as lightning flashes of electricity and chemicals. Gestalt's presence was like a potential field, increasing the tendency of some neurons to fire over others. When the potential increased, when Gestalt bent its will to controlling someone against his or her will, neurons died.

Fighting through the artificial sadness, Jaz was fiercely glad. "You can persuade, but you cannot compel. Not without damaging your hosts." Then she paused, fingertips touching her mouth. "But you only know because you tried it once—didn't you? With whom? Dr. Orley?"

There was no reply from the entity. The room was empty, as if Jaz stood there alone.

"What happens to me if I refuse to serve you?"

Jaz saw herself, alone in the Faraday prison. A data mask lay untouched in its original packaging on the dresser. The image aged. As Jaz watched, the figure grew stooped, and black hair first streaked, then succumbed to white. Her face was an old woman's. The figure lay back on the bed, breathed one last rattling breath, and expired.

In fear and revulsion, Jaz stripped the data mask from her head and flung it against the wall. Even without a connection, she felt Gestalt's presence in the room with her, like a ghost.

What was this thing humanity had unwittingly created? A god? A demon? The room was close and hot. The blue-and-green diamonds of the Penrose tiles, once soothing, now seemed a cruel mockery of man's achievement. The thought that the entity was still there, observing her like a beast in a cage—was unbearable. If it was the sum total of all connected peoples, then it encompassed serial killers as well as saints, idiots as well as geniuses. Its personality would change as the temperament of connected people changed. That such a creature would have absolute power over the one resource that joined the world together, terrified Jaz.

"Herridge!" Jaz shouted, leaning into the effort with her whole body. "Herridge! Get me out of here!"

CHAPTER 8

Instead of Herridge, a young man in his twenties opened the door. He wore the same dark green uniform and beret as Herridge. Jaz didn't recognize him from her abduction. She wondered how many people worked in this facility.

He handed her the hood she'd worn before.

"Is this necessary?" Jaz asked.

He nodded.

Jaz sighed and slipped the fabric over her head. The young man took her elbow and helped her down the steps. They walked through long hallways, their footsteps echoing on the concrete.

"Do you know what's in that room?" Her voice was muffled against the heavy black cloth.

"No, ma'am," he said with a Southern twang in his voice. "I have never been invited to the chapel."

"Lucky you." Jaz wondered how much he knew, whether Herridge had told this clean-faced boy about Gestalt and all the crimes committed in its name. "You know I'm being held here against my will?"

"Yes, ma'am."

"That doesn't bother you? This is America. I haven't committed any crimes, and yet I'm captured and brought here."

After an uncomfortable moment, he said, "I'm just following orders."

"That's what they said at the Nuremberg trials."

They walked on in silence until he said, "We're here." He helped her over a bulkhead.

Inside, Jaz pulled off the hood and sucked in a gulp of fresh, clean air. She was back in the stainless-steel Faraday cage.

"Colonel Herridge will be along as soon as his duties permit. In the meantime, can I assist you with anything?"

Yeah, Jaz thought, you could get me the hell out of this anthill. "Food? I haven't had breakfast."

The man nodded and left, closing the door behind him. She was alone.

Or was she? There was a speaker in the ceiling. Translate air vibrations back into electrical pulses, and a speaker made a perfectly good microphone.

Feeling ridiculous, Jaz ran her hands along the walls, checking for irregularities. The mirrored wall was smooth and cold under her fingertips. She probed the joints between walls and looked under the bed. She even searched under the toilet rim. Nothing. But that didn't mean there was nothing there; she'd heard of microdot transmitters a few microns thick. The door behind her opened as Jaz was examining the underside of the sink. She stood up hastily and bumped her head, then leaned against the sink like nothing had happened.

Herridge entered, carrying a tray with a silver food cover.

"You knew what was in the chapel."

"It's my job to know." Herridge set the tray on the bed. "Are you hungry?"

Jaz's stomach growled noisily in answer. She smelled chicken and curry. Her mind was still in turmoil about what she'd learned in the chapel. But she was also starving.

Herridge lifted the cover. Underneath was chicken and potatoes in masala curry and yellow rice.

As a rule, Jaz didn't like Indian food. She'd eaten it at family get-togethers with her mother's relatives. Not only was it tied in her mind with noisy gatherings of strangers she was supposed to feel close to, but also their

endless interrogations of when she would find a husband
and start a family. Such a beautiful girl they would say,
and start recommending nice Indian boys for her.

Jaz supposed Herridge had chosen it to make her feel
at home. That annoyed her, too. He'd assumed what kind
of food she liked by the color of her skin.

She scooped up a chunk of chicken and took a bite.
The curry had been made-from powder: dry and flavor-
less. Not at all like her aunt Kasi cooked.

Jaz sat on the bed. Herridge seated himself next to
her. Jaz scooted away to the far end of the bed, taking
the tray with her.

"You don't trust me." Herridge said.

Jaz barked a laugh. "No, not you or that thing in the
room . . . if it even exists outside of a simulation."

"Everything you saw and felt in the chapel was real,
I assure you."

"You've met it?"

Herridge looked at his interlaced fingers in his lap.
"Yes."

Jaz leaned forward. "What did *you* see?"

He met her eyes. "Humanity's last hope." He held up
a hand to forestall her questions. "The metaphor isn't
important. Gestalt changes that to suit the person she—"

"She?"

Herridge reddened. "Why not? There are more connected women than men. And in many ways Gestalt in-
teracts with humanity in a feminine manner."

"Because it's sneaky and manipulative? Is that your
feminine ideal?"

His brows drew together into a heavy line of disap-
proval. "Do you want to hear this or not?"

"By all means." Jaz stuffed another bite into her
mouth.

"I saw men crawling the earth like beasts. Naked,
dirty, killing each other for scraps of raw meat. There
was a man kicking a boy to death. I could hear the boy's
high-pitched screaming, feel the blows as if I were the
one being kicked." Herridge placed his hands over his

ears as if to block out the sound. In a tight voice, he said, "What I saw in that vision changed me."

Jaz's eyes widened. This was nothing like the metaphor Gestalt had used with her. She wondered what in Herridge's psychology made this dark vision the best way for Gestalt to communicate with him.

"Suddenly the man stopped. Behind him was a winged woman holding a sword glowing with white flames. She cut the man from shoulder to hip. I felt the searing heat of the blade's passage. But instead of killing the man, the wound healed him. He threw himself to the ground and cradled the boy in his arms."

"Gestalt was the avenging angel."

"Yes. Gestalt ended war, poverty, and starvation. She protects us from our baser instincts."

"What about free will? As I understand Christian mythology, your god gave humans the choice between good and evil." She set down her fork. "Can't you see that what Gestalt is doing is wrong? It controls people without their knowledge. They can't fight what it's doing because they don't even know it's happening."

"You say that because you were a child during Unification. The sudden wave of goodwill and common sense that swept over humanity twenty-one years ago wasn't a sudden evolution of the human spirit, it wasn't the accumulation of two thousand years of civilization; it was Gestalt."

Jaz considered what he said. "It doesn't matter. A utopia created on false principles must still fall. If Gestalt was suddenly removed from the picture, humanity has learned from these peaceful times. We'd never go back to warring and petty greed."

Herridge shook his head sadly. "You weren't alive when we were allowed free rein of our base tendencies—you don't know how bad it was."

"What was so terrible that you would give up control of yourself to avoid it?"

"It's not loss of free will." Herridge's eyes shone. "Just a moderation of our baser selves. Before Unification, I worked for the Federal Bureau of Investigation. In Los Angeles, I thought I'd seen the worst mankind could sink to: mothers pimping teenaged daughters, old men and women dying a slow death on the streets, crack babies with legs broken because their mother's boyfriend slowly twisted them until they snapped. The worst, though, were illegal aliens, packed into the back of vans, clinging to the undercarriages of cars, walking over barren deserts with no water—because the place they were coming from was *worse*." Herridge's voice was low, shaken. "That was bad, crimes of poverty and need. But in the FBI, I saw the horrors man could invent to *amuse* himself."

Jaz had stopped eating and watched him.

His eyes were haunted, and he reached out with his hands, pleading. "Without a connection, I can't show you what it was like, but please understand. This wasn't a detective novel or a scary movie—these things actually happened. The happy facade of the world was just a thin crust over the abyss."

Jaz swallowed. "You can't enslave humanity because of a few bad individuals."

"You don't get it." He waved his hands to indicate himself, her, the whole world. "Everyone has these tendencies: greed, lust, murderous rage. Gestalt can't eradicate that from our nature. She can only soothe us, help us become more humane."

"It knows who the killers are," Jaz said. "That must be convenient for law enforcement. Gestalt's inside all of our brains, like an ever-present big brother"—she smiled coldly—"or sister."

"Gestalt isn't a separate thing, watching us. She *is* us. Our thoughts, our feelings generate Gestalt. Is your left hemisphere spied upon by your right?"

"Of course not, but they're both part of me. Gestalt is an artificial construct, generated by everyone. Good people as well as bad. Gestalt is benign as long as the connected good outweigh the connected bad. But it's made up of serial killers and idiots as well as good people."

Herridge shifted on the bed. "Fortunately, most people

are good. When that's no longer true . . . we'd deserve whatever Gestalt became. And that's the whole point. Gestalt is the ultimate democratic ideal. We don't need to vote; Gestalt knows what we want and works behind the scenes to make it happen."

"Why? Ever ask yourself that? Why all this altruism?"

Herridge touched his fingertips to his chest. "Gestalt wants what we want. She wants us to be happy, healthy, well cared for."

"Because healthy connected people mean more processing power," said Jaz. "Of course it's against war. When a soldier on either side dies, Gestalt is diminished. Of course it sends food and data necklaces to the Sudan. It's not a selfless creature. Gestalt wants something from us, needs us to survive."

"It's a symbiotic relationship. Gestalt wants, needs, what's best for us, so it works to that end. What's wrong with that?"

Jaz clenched her hands into fist. "Because the free will it takes from us is worth more than the artificial peace it creates. Because we don't need it."

Herridge's face clouded. "Yes, we do."

"I know—I know, because the world was terrible before we were all influenced to become pleasant people. But what about what we're giving up? We've lost our worst impulses, but also our edge. Some part of us is always given over to the Net. That's what I noticed first when I disconnected. My thinking was clearer. What about the discoveries that will never be made because some portion of the scientist's mental capacity—the fraction needed to make that intuitive leap—was given to Gestalt?"

"And what about the technologies only Gestalt—utilizing the entire knowledge and resources of the human gestalt—could discover? Do you really believe that Anwar Berrundi could have formulated low-temperature fusion without guidance from Gestalt?"

Jaz said in a low whisper, "What about inventions that will never be discovered because of its drain on human resources? What about inventions it's repressed?"

Herridge shrugged. "Who needs a superior form of anthrax or a better viral delivery system?"

"There might be nonviolent uses for them one day."

"After millions have died? Not worth it. Besides, the knowledge isn't lost, just hiding in our collective unconscious until Gestalt sees a need for it."

"I still don't believe that you're willing to give yourself over to this thing."

"It's not hard to do, once you get past your own ego and realize she's the only thing that can keep mankind's bestial nature under control."

"So I'm egotistical?"

"Or afraid."

Jaz stood up. "I didn't ask to be kidnapped in the middle of the night, imprisoned in an underground installation, and introduced to the parasitical thing mind-controlling humanity. Excuse me if I'm not thrilled."

"You think you would be better able to run society than Gestalt—"

"Better able to run myself."

"Oh really? And if you had a gun on the mountain, would you have shot me?"

"No. Of course not."

"But you struck out at me. Pounded on me with your hands when you realized what was occurring."

"Of course. You were abducting me."

Herridge smiled a wan smile. "That's how it always used to start. Escalation of aggression. If I had shot one of your friends, would you have shot me?"

She visualized the scene. Matt, facedown in the snow, bleeding his life away. Anger kindled in her chest. These new emotions were strong and raw, something she hadn't felt since she put on her first data necklace in school. "Yes. To protect them."

"Even knowing that any shot might kill? You would risk killing me to stop my hurting them?"

The heat gave her the answer. "Yes." Some civilized part of her psyche was ashamed.

It must have shown on her face, because Herridge said

softly, "No one is innocent. We all carry inside us the potential for harm."

"But resisting those impulses is the definition of good. If Gestalt keeps humanity from becoming truly evil, it also prevents us from becoming truly good."

"That's a philosophical point I'm willing to live with for my children to grow up in a world where they won't be attacked, where my teenage daughter can walk down the street at night without fear. Where no one kicks my eight-year-old son. Yeah, I'd give up a certain amount of free will to become a better person and live in an enlightened world."

The mention of children surprised Jaz. She had imagined Herridge as a man without a life, someone who worked and lived in this anthill. The thought that he had a family somewhere disconcerted her.

"Why am I here? Why really? If Gestalt wanted me to forget, it could have convinced me I had imagined the whole thing. And I don't for an instant believe that a creature with the skill and subterfuge to run the world for more than twenty years would be so blatant as to watch me on the street as it did. It wanted me to see it—why?"

"The watchers were a test, to see how you would react to hints of Gestalt."

A sudden thought occurred to Jaz. "Did Gestalt arrange for my rig to be broken?"

"No. Gestalt is a mental construct. She has no control over the physical world."

"It wouldn't need to. All Gestalt had to do was throw my connection off enough so I would think that the mask was broken—and then control the repairman to agree."

Herridge shook his head. "Her influence isn't that strong. She can persuade, but not compel."

"At least that's what it tells you. Let me ask you a question, Herridge. If Gestalt was hiding this from you, if it actually could compel people to do things for it, would you still want to work for it?"

"If she could compel, we wouldn't be having this discussion. It took a lot of work to get you here and cover up your disappearance."

"So why do it?"

"You are one of thirty naturals we've been monitoring. One of you was going to run into a hardware problem that left you disconnected sooner or later."

"And I was the lucky winner," Jaz said sarcastically.

"We needed a natural."

"Why?"

Herridge hesitated.

"Come on, who am I going to tell? That thing has already shown me that it's willing to keep me here until I'm an old woman."

Herridge sighed. "Did Gestalt show you her first attempts at contact?"

"You mean Dr. Orley? Yes."

"And you saw his reaction."

"Yes, he was horrified."

"Orley never got over that initial impression of Gestalt. The State Department swore him to secrecy after the Treaty of Unification, and has him watched. But there was no reason to take him into custody. We can't touch him."

Jaz rested a fist on her hip. "Didn't stop you on my account."

Herridge's brow furrowed up in a pained expression. "I know this is going to be a blow to your ego, but you're not a world-renowned pioneer in computational analysis. You haven't won any Turing Awards. You were a little easier to make go away."

Jaz folded her arms and sat back on the bed.

"Since that first night, Orley has refused all inductive technology. He uses keyboards and data-gloves for data entry, identification bracelets, and money cards."

"Sounds like a good idea to me," Jaz muttered.

"It's a loss to Gestalt, and a rejection she feels deeply."

"It has emotions?" But of course. It was an intelligence layered on top of human intelligence, how could it not? Jaz's stomach clenched. A superintelligence that ruled the world was bad enough, but one that could feel hurt, that might one day become angry . . . that was truly terrifying.

"Two months ago, Orley cut himself off from the Net. Completely. No financial transactions, no e-mail, nothing. We don't know why. He's recruited top academics from around the world to work on a new project. The two may be related."

"So why don't you knock on his door and ask him?"

Herridge pursed his lips. "You don't understand Orley's paranoia. He won't let anyone close to him who doesn't meet certain criteria."

"You sent an agent in and he spotted him."

Herridge nodded. "We believe Orley, or someone working on his behalf, hacked into our employee database."

Jaz whistled softly. She'd tried hacking the NSA once; it was a ritual of passage for teenage naturals. As a consequence, the NSA network security had been hardened and tested by the best. No one had cracked it in eight years. "He must be good."

"Orley is one of the strongest naturals alive."

"So if he's too dangerous to be running around loose, and you can't legally pull him in, why not assassination?" Her voice was sarcastic, mocking Herridge. "Perhaps a convenient car accident?"

"That was suggested," Herridge said quietly. "But Gestalt refused. She believes reconciliation is possible. She wants to bring him back into the Net."

"Where do I come into all of this?"

Without inflection, Herridge said, "We want you to infiltrate Orley's group, find out what he's up to, and report back."

Jaz laughed, bordering on hysteria. "You have *got* to be kidding. After all you've done to me? You can tell Gestalt it is out of its—our—mind."

"Gestalt believes that, once you realize what's at stake, you'll want to help us."

"No. If Gestalt's been inside my brain, it knows I will never agree to this."

Herridge raised an eyebrow. "But you would shoot me to save your friends."

"So?"

"If Orley is planning to do something that would expose or harm Gestalt, the results would be disastrous. Do you know what would happen if Gestalt was revealed to the world?"

She was silent, remembering what Gestalt had shown her: the breakdown of communication and distribution lines, panic, starvation. "Recruit someone else. If this job is so important, get someone better qualified than me."

"There isn't time. You're it. We need to do this now. We have no idea how close Orley is to completing what he's working on."

Jaz thought about it. "No. I can't do this. I write data-collection programs, move imaginary bits around in the ether. I'm not a special agent."

Herridge pursed his lips as he appraised Jaz, then said, "We'll give you a crash course. There isn't much you need to know. One of the reasons you're perfect for the job is that you're not a trained agent. Your background check will hold up to any scrutiny. You've got the skills and knowledge that Orley's been recruiting for."

"I'm no one in the academic world of theoretical computing."

"But your mother is. You've grown up steeped in computational research. With your talent and connections, you'd be an attractive applicant. Orley wouldn't be able to pass you up. And your opposition to Gestalt would enable you to pass the loyalty test."

"What loyalty test?"

"The last agent we sent in was almost accepted. Then Orley had him brain-hacked to see how much he knew about Gestalt, how loyal he was."

"What happened to him?"

Herridge looked down at his palms. "We don't know. He hasn't contacted his field handler in six months—and his body hasn't been recovered."

Jaz swallowed. What was Orley up to? Normal research projects didn't involve making people disappear.

Herridge said, "You're perfect for this job. Gestalt projects you have the best chance to succeed."

"How good a chance is that? What are my odds?"

Herridge shook his head. "I am not at liberty to tell you. Please believe me when I say that only you can stop this without violence. Our other option is to take Orley out by force."

"You said Gestalt forbade that. Didn't want to lose one of its best neurons."

Herridge's cold, blue—unconnected—eyes met hers. "Consider me her immune system. I kill the things that would harm her."

A chill crept out from Jaz's chest and down her arms and legs. "If I turn down this job, I won't be sitting in this cell for the rest of my life, will I?"

"That's what Gestalt wants." His eyes still bored into hers. "I just can't promise it would be a very long life."

Jaz looked away and swallowed. "Won't Gestalt calm you out of this attitude?"

Herridge smiled. "You begin to see the value in Gestalt's influence. Yes, if I were connected, Gestalt would convince me otherwise. If you were connected, she might be able to persuade you in a more gentle fashion. But we're not. In this mission, you will be disconnected. We need to know that the decision to do this job was your own." Herridge studied his close-clipped fingernails. "I too, will remain disconnected until you have either rejected or completed the mission. I do not enjoy this. Being trapped inside myself, alone, without any guiding force to temper my baser instincts." He closed his eyes and breathed deeply. "But I will do this—to protect her."

Jaz's eyes widened. She wondered what personal demons Herridge struggled with. Jaz was suddenly aware that there might be two monsters in this installation.

"So you're telling me that I can save the world, or die."

His eyes were leveled at her. "Yes," he said, without a flicker of remorse.

Jaz felt her stomach clench. "Okay, you've convinced me. I'll save the world." Anything to get out of there. And once she was out, perhaps Orley would be able to help her get free.

CHAPTER 9

The next morning, Herridge entered Jaz's room. He held out the hood.

Jaz took it and balanced the cloth on her palms. "Is this necessary? I thought I was part of the team now."

He shook the hood in her face. "Under coercion. Put it on."

Jaz slipped the hood on. Arguing with him was pointless.

Spy school. In a way it was exciting. Jaz wondered about the curriculum.

Herridge led her down the hall and into an elevator. From the increased weight, Jaz knew they were going up. She counted silently to herself. Thirty-three seconds to reach whatever floor Herridge had selected. Either a slow elevator or a deep hole.

Another hall, turn left, through a door. As they walked, Jaz memorized the route; she pictured it in her mind. If she ever got the chance, she would try to escape. If she could contact the media before Gestalt shut down her transmission . . . no, that was impossible. Gestalt could wipe her from the Net, like it had deleted those journal articles. Still, there had to be something she could do.

When Herridge removed the hood, light blinded Jaz. Her eyes watered, and she blinked them clear. She was in a shooting range. Vertical partitions cut a waist-high shelf into stalls. Twenty meters away on the other side of the shelf were man-shaped paper targets, concentric circles over the heart.

Standing at attention in front of the shelf was a young woman. Her blond hair was buzzed into a short crew cut and she wore the same NSA uniform as Herridge, though with fewer bars on her shoulder.

Herridge saluted. "At ease."

The woman swung into a wide stance.

"Is she my shooting instructor?" Jaz asked.

"That and more. Call her Agent N."

"What is this, a James Bond movie?"

Herridge glowered at Jaz's interruption. "You don't need to know her name. It's safer for her if you don't. Agent N will be your body double."

Jaz felt fear jangle down her nerves. They were going to use immersion, a teaching technique tried in the 2070s, when induction technology was in its infancy. The idea was to map the neural electromagnetic patterns generated by the teacher while they modeled a task and induced the same patterns in the student. Simple. Unfortunately, each human brain stores information in a different neural map—a map that constantly changes to incorporate new information.

Jaz had seen a video of a victim of the early experiments. A graduate student who had tried to learn the tango using immersion had instead scrambled the pathways that controlled motor function in his legs. He had stumbled and lurched across the room.

Jaz backed away. "I won't. If you can't teach me what I need to know the conventional way, forget it."

Herridge's features froze into a hard mask. "There's no time. We need you on the ground in Pasadena on Tuesday. Just because kinesthetic immersion research was outlawed in the private sector doesn't mean the military research stopped."

Jaz looked at Agent N. Her expression was calm. "Aren't you afraid?"

The woman's eyes flicked to Herridge. He nodded. "No," said Agent N. "Immersion technology is not dangerous if the constituents are within ninety-eight percent of kinesthetic compatibility. You and I are estimated to a 99.6 percent match."

Jaz scanned Agent N head to toe. They were of a size. Legs the same length, same waist measurement, arms the same. Jaz held out her hand and, after a moment's hesitation, Agent N mimicked her gesture. The woman's movement was smooth and graceful. Did she move like that? Jaz wondered. Their hands were the same size. Aside from the coloring—Agent N was blond and creamy to Jaz's black hair and olive complexion, and there were some differences in the bone structure of their face—they were twins.

The lines on their palms were even the same, as if they'd used the flesh the same all their lives . . . or perhaps shared a destiny.

"If it's so safe," Jaz challenged, "why not let me initiate the connection?"

Agent N again looked at Herridge.

"No," Herridge said. "You do not have the training. Agent N will lead, and you will follow her instruction."

Jaz lifted her chin defiantly. "I will not." Would Agent N have made this gesture if she felt this rising wave of indignation? With a 99.6 percent kinesthetic match, probably so. How much alike were their minds if they used their bodies so similarly?

Herridge turned to Jaz. The stretch of his lips over his teeth was almost a snarl. "I assure you, Ms. Reese, the immersion training is safe. I cannot guarantee that refusing it will be."

"You don't scare me," Jaz said, working to keep a waver out of her voice.

Herridge stepped closer until his lips brushed Jaz's ear. She did not flinch away; she wouldn't give him the satisfaction. "I could scare you," Herridge said. "Disconnected, there is much I could do to scare you."

If Agent N heard—and she must have heard in this silent, empty room—she gave no indication.

Jaz was a natural, able to use communication protocols

like they were her own neural pathways, but she wasn't a hero.

With a sinking feeling in her chest, like she had lost some important part of herself, Jaz said, "What do you want me to do?"

Herridge pulled two silver packets out of his shirt pocket. "These are bodysuits with inductive fibers embedded in the knit. Put them on."

Agent N began unbuttoning her shirt.

"You've got to be kidding," Jaz said. "Here?"

"I hadn't figured you for modesty." Herridge turned his back on the women and handed the packets over his shoulder.

Jaz snatched the packet and began stripping off the woolen uniform in a fury. "There's a lot about me you don't know," she said. And a lot you're going to find out, she finished silently.

The silver packet unfolded into a body stocking with feet and gloves. A hood and a face mask were built into the neckline. Jaz watched Agent N step into the neck hole and wriggle the suit up her hips.

Jaz did the same. The nanofiber cloth stretched like latex, but flowed like silk over her skin. Jaz slid her arms into the sleeves and laced her fingers together to seat the gloves properly. She tied her waist-length hair into a loose knot at the nape of her neck and stuffed it into the hood of the body stocking. The mask covered her entire face, hooking under her chin. Only her eyes and mouth were uncovered.

The garments enhanced the similarity between her and Agent N. The only differences between them now were the color of their eyes, the shape of their mouths, and the ungainly lump of hair at the base of Jaz's neck.

The thin cloth left little to the imagination. Every wrinkle, every hair follicle, was outlined in silver.

Herridge said, "Agent N, are you ready to begin?"

The woman nodded. She reached into a stall behind her and retrieved two identical aluminum cases. She handed one to Jaz, then leaned against the shelf with both hands, as if she were going to do a push-up.

To Jaz he said, "For an easy transition, you should assume the same position as Agent N."

Skin on the back of her neck crawling, Jaz complied.

"Initializing the connection," Herridge said.

A jolt of electricity convulsed Jaz's limbs. She pushed lower into the shelf. Her arms and legs tightened. A private network, connecting only Jaz and Agent N, had been established.

"Connection confirmed," she and Agent N said in unison.

Jaz's hands moved without her willing them to, her mouth spoke words she hadn't thought. Her body was in someone else's control. Jaz's breathing synched to Agent N's, her heart beat in unison with the other woman. Jaz hated it.

"Lock and load," Agent N said in her twinned voice.

Stop, Jaz tried to say. The word wouldn't come out. Her hands moved smoothly in exact duplication of Agent N's, knowledgeably opening the case, pulling back the lever of the automatic, looking down the barrel.

"Always check that a gun is unloaded," Agent N said through herself and Jaz. "Never assume it is, even when the clip is out. There may be a round in the chamber."

Jaz heard herself saying the words as if she were a long way away. She was disconnected from her body, adrift. A passenger in her own skin. And deep inside, the farther she got from whatever was going on in the firing range, she found—rage.

Jaz knew she was supposed to let this other woman drive her in the training. But she had spent her whole life disciplining her mind to control the virtual world around her. At the crucial moment, Jaz found she couldn't let go of that control. Not without a fight.

As if in a dream, she felt her hands sliding thirty-two-caliber rounds into a clip. The clip slid home inside the gun. Her arms brought the gun up in front of her, both hands cupping it for stability, arms bent slightly. Two shots, two jolts of impact through her arms and shoulders, and two neat holes appeared in the center ring of the target far away.

No! Jaz screamed inside her mind. Stop! Her neurons began to fire more rapidly. The effect was a strobing of taste, sensation, and sound, like the prelude to an epileptic seizure.

Far away, she heard Agent N and her own voice say, "She's fighting the connection."

A moment's hesitation in the other woman, a frisson of . . . fear? Jaz didn't care. In the instant that Agent N's attention was diverted from the connection, Jaz filled the gap. The connection induced sensory images directly in Jaz's brain. She fought the unwanted neural excitation with counterimages. Her muscles twitched as they received orders to move—orders Jaz countermanded as soon as Agent N gave them.

In any interactive connection, information flowed in and out. Jaz calmed the part of her mind not fighting Agent N's orders. Her years of precise attention to the inner workings of her brain had trained Jaz to use alternate neural pathways. She could process up to four trains of thought simultaneously. Now this talent was used against her. There. In the Broca's area of her brain, neurons responsible for speech production transmitted details of the ongoing battle for control of Jaz's body. Jaz took conscious control of the reports, filled them with physical commands of her own. With an abrupt lurch, the incoming attack from Agent N was gone. The woman was too busy trying to defend herself from the enemy inside.

Jaz felt her mind expand. She wore two skins now. Flexing her arms, Jaz raised the gun. Never had control of her own muscles felt so good. Jaz contracted her bicep and forearm. Two guns lifted smoothly to point at two heads.

Herridge was on her immediately. He grabbed Jaz's wrist, clamped it to the gun and twisted, using the gun as a lever to bend her wrist backward until Jaz's hand opened. He slipped the gun into his pocket and, with his free hand, backhanded her. "What the hell are you playing at?"

Jaz tasted blood and smiled. The piece of herself she'd

lost when she'd acquiesced to Herridge was back. They could take over her body, but not her mind. "I won't be a puppet." She heard Agent N croak the words beside her. Glancing left with her eyes, Jaz saw Agent N in a parody of the pose Jaz held. Agent N's body was canted backward at an awkward angle, her wrist twisting in upon itself.

Herridge pulled a pen-sized remote out of his chest pocket and clicked a button on the end. With a sensation like a cold breeze blowing through her, Jaz felt the connection snap. Agent N unfroze and grabbed for the floor. In a graceful motion she scooped up the gun and sighted on Jaz. The woman's arms trembled, and her upper lip curled back in a snarl.

Herridge held up a hand, palm out. "Stand down, Agent."

Agent N glared at Jaz as if she would eat her alive, then lowered the gun, stretched her neck, lowering her ear to one shoulder, then the other. She did not let go of the gun, however.

Herridge shook Jaz. "What the hell are you doing? Agent N was instructing you."

His violence couldn't dislodge Jaz's elation at having some control, however small, over the situation.

"Stop grinning. We went through a lot of trouble to locate a body double for you. This is the fastest way to learn skills you may need to survive this mission." He grabbed Jaz under her chin and turned her head toward Agent N. "You've scared a junior lieutenant half out of her mind. Proud of yourself?" He shook her again. "Is this childish posturing worth it?"

Agent N bristled when Herridge described her as afraid. But she was. Jaz could see the fear behind her blue eyes. Fear of her. The woman had ridden her, yes, but to train her, to teach Jaz skills. And what had Jaz done in return? Blown through her protocols like the crudest mind-rapist, and used the woman's own body to threaten her life. Jaz felt ashamed. She sagged in Herridge's arms. To Agent N she said, "Sorry—I'm sorry. I lashed out. I didn't think."

Agent N held her body in tight control. Jaz could see a vein in the woman's neck pulse. "Sir, permission to speak frankly?"

Herridge nodded. "Go ahead."

"I won't—can't—work with that *monster*." Her voice broke slightly on the last word. "Court-martial me if you have to. But if you order to me to work with her, I will refuse."

"Understood," Herridge said. "There will be no penalty. Go ahead and dress. I'll collect the sim-suit later."

Agent N scooped her clothes off the floor and swept out the door without bothering to change. It slammed behind her.

Jaz felt like crying. What was this place doing to her? She'd never attacked anyone like that before. It was just that she'd felt herself in jeopardy and lashed out. She'd justified Herridge's dim view of human nature. But Herridge had put her into the situation; it was as much his fault as hers. Wasn't it? She squatted on the cold floor, head in her hands.

Above her, Herridge asked, "You ready to continue the training?"

"What? But Agent N . . ."

"You need to learn how to shoot. Your childish outburst eliminated the most effective teaching method at our disposal. So now you'll have to learn the hard way. Assume the position: legs apart, hands on the gun. Sight the target."

Jaz picked up the gun and did as Herridge ordered. The motions came smoothly to her, and Jaz realized it was a legacy from Agent N. Even the brief contact with the woman's skill had left its mark. The gun felt comfortable in her hand. She sighted on the target and gently squeezed the trigger. The gun exploded and kicked back in her hand, but Jaz could see the result as another neat hole appeared in the central dot of the paper target.

What else could she have learned from Agent N if she'd just been willing to let the woman ride her? Jaz felt a pang of regret both for Agent N's discomfiture and the loss of knowledge.

Herridge worked with Jaz for half an hour, teaching her to shoot kneeling, prone, and how to speed-load. Agent N's skill only extended to the basic position; Jaz fumbled awkwardly with everything she tried to learn on her own. At last, when Jaz was sore from the strange positions and pounding jolts of the gun, they broke for lunch. Herridge hooded her and escorted her back to her cell without a word.

After lunch, Herridge came for her again. His expression was hard. "Since Agent N will no longer work with you, we'll have to train you in unarmed combat manually as well . . . Agent N's modeling would have been the easy way. But you're not a fan of the easy way, are you?" He tossed a karate *gi* and T-shirt at her. "Put these on." He watched while Jaz dressed, showing no emotion.

Jaz felt humiliated, but didn't ask him to turn away. She knew he was punishing her for Agent N.

Once she was dressed, he pulled the hood roughly over her head and led her out the door. Down the hall, turn right, into the elevator. From the reduced pressure, they traveled up again for three seconds. If her training continued taking her all over the compound, she would have an internal map of the place by the time she left . . . if she left.

The training hall was long and narrow and shaped like the inside of a half cylinder. At the apex were fluorescent tube lights. Two men in karate *gis* waited on the mats. "Agents D and E," Herridge said by way of introduction.

Agent D stepped forward. He was a wiry man with red hair shaved close to his head. The *gi* hid most of his body, but Jaz could see strong cords of muscles at his neck. The belt at his waist was black. "There isn't time to teach you more than basic self-defense, a few attacks and escapes that any beginner can master. Some of the moves may be familiar to you from the six months of kung fu you studied in college."

Jaz stared at him, startled. How had he known? But of course, Gestalt. The spy in the mind.

Agent E was shorter than Agent D and had a darker

complexion. His face was wide with a broad, flat nose. The belt he wore was green.

Agent D demonstrated a move on Agent E, explaining the motion, in this case a strike with the heel of the palm to the attacker's throat. Then gently, slowly, Jaz practiced the move with the two agents.

Herridge watched, arms folded across his chest. Looking at him, Jaz wondered what work he was neglecting to spend so much time on her case. Certainly a colonel had more important things to do than baby-sit a conscript's training.

Agents D and E taught street fighting. There was no emphasis on the graceful forms she'd learned in her college days. The two agents taught her simple skills to survive: kicks to break an ankle or shatter a kneecap, an arm bar that could restrain . . . or break an elbow.

With rubber weapons they demonstrated how to disarm an attacker with a knife or a gun, and showed her with certainty that if she tried, she should expect to be cut or shot. No matter how fast she moved, the rubber knives tagged her. When she was thoroughly frustrated, Agent D handed her the knife. "You try."

She stabbed forward with the weapon. Agent D's movement was flawless; he scooped up her hand and twisted the wrist toward her until her hand opened and the rubber knife bounced on the floor. But she had tagged him, a thin line of red chalk on his arm.

He held up his sleeve. "If you go up against an attacker with a knife, expect to be cut. Don't let the pain surprise you and throw you off your guard. Just realize that the only thing worse than being cut defending yourself is being cut as a helpless victim. You must take control of the situation."

"Don't worry," Herridge called from his vantage point. "She's good at that."

Jaz was sweating when, hours later, the lessons finally stopped. Her mind reeled with all the information Agent D had drilled into her. This method of learning was so slow, so painful.

Still, it was better than having her motor control

usurped. Jaz remembered how lost she had felt in that instant that Agent N had moved for them both. Anything was better than that.

Herridge threw a hand towel to Jaz from a pile beside the wall. She used it to wipe sweat from her face. "Take a shower. Next are lessons in mental discipline."

She stared at him incredulously. "I'm exhausted. I couldn't learn anything more today."

"Then I suspect you will learn pain. The witch is not a gentle teacher." His smile was cold. "She's a lot like you, actually."

Agents D and E exchanged a glance. There was worry in their eyes. "Colonel Herridge," Agent D said, "if I may suggest—"

"You may not."

Agent D's mouth worked. There was more he wanted to say, but his military discipline held. "Sir," he said. He and Agent E saluted and filed out of the room to the showers. His eyes when he passed Jaz were pitying.

CHAPTER 10

The elevator ride down to the witch's chambers was the longest yet. Jaz counted slowly to fifty-seven. How deep was this place? Was she still in Washington state? Or was this NORAD, deep in the Rocky Mountains?

When the elevator door opened, the air was cool and moist. Jaz smelled wet stone. The floor beneath her feet no longer clicked like linoleum; it had a muffled sound like packed earth.

After fifty yards, Herridge told Jaz to stop. She pulled off the hood. Her eyes widened in surprise. The walls were rough-hewn granite. Unlike the teeming mazes of offices upstairs, there was only one door in this hallway. It was solid steel and riveted, with a ventilation grate. It looked like the door to a dungeon.

Herridge held out a single-strand data necklace. "Put this on."

Jaz took the necklace and dangled it from her finger. It was an old model, incompatible with the latest wireless protocols.

"Put it on," Herridge repeated. "The witch no longer speaks aloud." He shifted his weight back and forth slightly. Nervousness?

After a moment's hesitation, Jaz slipped the necklace on. When the connection LED glittered green, Herridge opened the door.

It did not creak back on rusty hinges as Jaz had half expected. Instead, the dark metal sheathed left into the stone wall.

The room beyond was dark, lit only by two pillar candles spilling wax onto a raw-silk cloth on the floor. The cloth's color was erased by the darkness, though light glittered off metallic threads in its weft. On the cloth rested an abalone seashell, a low dish filled with sand and three sticks of smoldering incense, a black-handled knife, a silver hand mirror, and a glittering full-immersion data mask. Shadows hid something on the wall beyond the altar.

Jaz stepped into the room to see more clearly and gasped. A woman hung spread-eagled from multicolored wires that pierced her skin at major nerve centers. The body was shriveled. Her hands had collapsed in on themselves; the tendons tightening from disuse had pulled them into claws. The patchouli incense was not strong enough to mask the scent of wasting flesh, a sickeningly sweet smell like baking bread. She looked like someone crucified on a spiderweb. Her head lolled forward, stringy dark hair covered her face. But through the strands, Jaz saw the glitter of feverish eyes.

Was the woman a struggling insect . . . or the spider?

The door sheathed closed behind Jaz, and she heard Herridge walking swiftly away.

There was a chuckling from behind her. Jaz whirled—no one there. Hairs on the back of her neck prickled. The laughter intensified, and Jaz forced herself to look at the witch.

The woman's body showed no emotion. It breathed with the aid of a machine, but that was all. The face was slack as if in idiocy, or supreme inattention.

"You do not like to be controlled," a liquid contralto bounced around the room. "The beast told me, and I see it is true."

Herridge's fear was infectious; Jaz's chest tightened.

"You hurt little Agent N when she tried to control your body. Would you hurt me so?"

"Yes," Jaz said. "To protect myself." Her voice did not waver.

Again the laughter from somewhere outside of her peripheral vision. "Let us see"—the words came from Jaz's own throat—"what you can do." She raised her hands to her neck, then her mouth, felt her lips form the words.

The witch was inside her, controlling Jaz's neurons without her having felt the intrusion. Jaz rapid-cycled nerve impulses through her motor centers, driving the unseen presence from them.

The witch's laugh echoed hollowly inside her head. "Not bad, little one. Not bad. You have the raw ability, but need to learn control. You must find me before you can expel me. Undirected force is wasteful. Find me," the witch said, her voice coming from all corners of Jaz's mind. "Find me . . ."

Jaz stifled a flush of frustration. Losing control over her emotions would only hinder her concentration. She sat down on the cold, packed-earth floor and breathed slowly from her diaphragm. The necklace was the medium the witch rode into Jaz's brain. Find how she was manipulating the connection. The primitive necklace didn't have robust metaphor capabilities. It was impressive that the witch had been able to manipulate it to render sensory illusions as well as she had.

Jaz concentrated on the connection. The necklace encircled her spinal column, inducing nerve impulses that generated visions and sounds in her brain.

But it was a primitive connection. In order to block out the transmissions, Jaz simply had to distinguish real from induced sensory input. But how to tell reality from illusion, when both entered the brain through your central nervous system?

"Find me . . ."

The witch's voice was an auditory illusion. Her mouth never moved. Jaz focused all her attention on the quality of the sound and thought she could detect a tinny quality to it.

"No, you can't," the witch said.

Jaz looked up, startled. "You can't read my thoughts over a sensory-only connection."

"Read them?" the witch's voice rose in derision. "I could write them. Become *happy,* little one."

Impossible in this place, Jaz thought, but even as the

words faded from her mind, she felt a lightness and joy. The candlelight was lovely, a soft welcoming glow. The witch's binds were like ribbons decorating an old friend. She felt her mouth widen into a goofy grin.

But somewhere deep inside her, the nugget of consciousness that had rebelled against Agent N's control screamed, "No!"

The warmth disappeared like an alcohol flame suddenly snuffed.

"Not bad, little one, you show promise." The witch's voice held approbation a hairbreadth away from mockery. "But can you cast me out completely?"

Jaz closed her eyes; anything she saw now was illusion. The voice was illusion. In this calmness she concentrated on the other senses. She smelled the incense and the witch's wasting body, but there was something else. The scent eluded her, then—cotton candy! Like she'd eaten on Coney Island as a girl. She could taste its sweetness on her tongue. On her body she felt pressures, almost too light to detect, the rhythmic swaying of a Ferris wheel.

It was clever. The witch had evoked happiness in Jaz by subtly affecting her senses to make her recall a happier place and time. As soon as Jaz realized the trick, the false happiness evaporated.

"You are an aware little thing," the witch said.

"You're using sensory input to evoke memories and control me."

"Ye-es. Things barely felt, that trigger only a subconscious reaction, can still control you. Always know what you are feeling. And why. Do not let the slightest sensation escape you."

"And that's how you read me. You inferred my emotions from slight changes in my physiognomy. Adrenaline levels, iris contractions, breathing rates—all this told you what I was feeling."

"And to cast me out?"

"I must control myself utterly."

Easier said than done. Jaz had years of mental discipline from working with the Net, but during that time she had ignored her body more often than she inhabited it. Jaz slowed her breathing, then with more difficulty, her heartbeat. Her skin cooled as she drew inward, sinking her mind into her flesh. She thought not just with her brain, but with her arms and her legs and her stomach, all part of one being.

"Well done," the witch said, and her voice was a faint whisper.

Jaz didn't let her triumph leak out. She held herself in tight control. When the witch's voice inside her head was silenced, she opened her eyes.

Incense from the brazier curled up into the air between them. It caressed the witch's face. The woman's age was hard to discern because of her thin body and the dim light. She might have been twenty . . . or a hundred. Was her body wasted from disease or supreme inattention? Jaz doubted this woman was on the Net. If she had been, surely Gestalt would have tamed her by now, induced her to take care of her body.

She must be operating on a local network; like the one Jaz had in her home office, a private connection that had no link to the Net.

But who had cut the witch off from the ebb and flow of worldwide communication, and why stick her in this cell?

"Who are you?" Jaz asked aloud.

A soft voice answered, "Put on the data mask and find out."

The mask glinted in the candlelight, a Xerascape 500 series. Molecular computers encrusted the thin webbing like diamond chips. It extended over the wearer's head and down to cover the face. A full-immersion unit.

"No," said Jaz. The witch had controlled her through the tiny pipeline of her nervous system. What havoc might she wreak with full access to Jaz's thoughts?

"You turn down training . . . again? You may need what I can teach you. Would you reject skills that could save you?"

Jaz picked up the featherlight data mask and balanced it on her hands. She *had* regretted terminating her training with Agent N. The witch scared Jaz, but what harm could she do, really? Herridge needed Jaz alive and sane on Tuesday.

Jaz slipped the mask over her head. She sank into the connection and found herself standing on top of a muddy pond. A small private network. Sitting on the edge of the pond was an enormous green frog.

"Why does Herridge call you a witch?"

The frog stretched its mouth wide to the sky, and a wisp of a woman wriggled out. The woman grew solid as she expanded outward. She wore an idealized, healthy version of the witch's withered body. The hair was darker than Jaz's own, blue-black, against skin as pale as moonlight. Her ebony eyes were bottomless, with irises so dark the pupils were lost in them. The face was pointed and sharp, like a fox's. It was a strange face, beautiful and dangerous. She was clothed only in the wavy black hair that fell to her knees.

"A witch, I am. Before the wasting, I read cards, entrails, and the flights of birds. Now I wander an astral plane of man's invention." The woman stepped onto the edge of the water, and Jaz felt it ripple under her feet. She fought the instinct to hold her ground and not step away.

Jaz opened her eyes and contrasted the atrophied body hanging on the ceiling to the avatar in her mind. She felt a wave of revulsion and pity. What must it be like to be trapped in that body?

"Come closer and find out," the witch crooned to her from the shoreline. "Synchronize your breathing to mine, your heartbeat to mine. Feel what it is to inhabit this crippled body."

Jaz was repulsed, but also curious. She'd never seen anyone with this kind of crippling disease, not in Gestalt's carefully cultivated world.

Jaz felt her attention focus on the wasted body, trying to imagine the tightness in her wrists pulling her hands down. In the virtual world she felt a sharp tug on her ankle from the water beneath her. The frog clamped his enormous mouth over her foot and dragged her under.

The body closed over her like black water over a drowning victim. She was in.

Jaz was so startled she lost her metaphor and returned entirely to physical reality. She couldn't move. Her chest was a heavy mass that lifted and fell on the orders of a breathing regulator implanted in her rib cage. Through greasy strands of hair, Jaz saw herself. Her own Irish-Indian features grinned at her.

"Such a lovely little body, and you've kept it so well." Jaz watched with horror as the witch ran Jaz's hands down the sides of her chest, over the concavity of her waist, dug into the tops of her thighs.

"*Stop!*" Jaz tried to scream, but only succeeded in a wheeze before the breathing regulator took over again.

Jaz concentrated on calming herself, but her metaphor wouldn't re-form. The pond was a formless haze of brown and green. Whether that was her own distress or some machination of the witch, Jaz wasn't sure. She pushed out instead, driving her consciousness back toward her own body.

But there was nothing there. Jaz sensed only emptiness on the network. The witch must be cloaking Jaz's mental pathways, somehow misrouting neural paths around the area the witch sought to hold. Try as she might, Jaz couldn't find entrance.

The witch laughed, and it was horrible to hear the sound issue from Jaz's own throat. Jaz blazed with fury.

"Anger will not help . . . unless it is directed."

Jaz watched, helpless inside the prison of the witch's flesh, and tried to collect her emotions.

The witch stretched Jaz's body, raising her arms high in the air and arching her back. "You have no idea how long I've wanted to do that," she purred. "Humans are animals. On that point, I agree with Herridge." She shook out Jaz's hair and traced her fingertips down Jaz's face, over the deep-set eyes and high cheekbones, trailing down her neck to the top of Jaz's bosom. "As good as simulations are, the flesh cries out to be caressed. Millions of years of evolution cannot be erased by a half century of technological advance. We are creatures of blood and meat.

"Herridge tells me simulations feel exactly as they would if I could touch with my own hands, walk with my own legs. All sensory perception filters through the brain. Fool the brain, and it feels as real as the physical world. Except he forgets. My brain *knows* it is a deception. My brain knows it is a simulation, and that none of it is real."

The witch stroked Jaz's hands over her breasts and down over her belly, moving lower.

Jaz searched wildly for her neural paths on the network. Nothing. "Wrong target," the witch whispered. "Where am I? Where are you? Go past the illusion."

I am here inside the witch's body, and she is inside mine, Jaz thought. Or was she? Was the witch's control so deep she could control Jaz's brain directly? Could that be done?

Jaz adjusted her thinking. She was not outside her body, fighting to reenter; she was inside. Jaz concentrated on the feel of hands sliding over her body, the round curve of her belly, the hollows of her hips. The moving hands were *her* hands, the body they touched *her* body. As first Jaz felt the dual perspective she had when she'd controlled Agent N. Then Jaz was in her own body again. Her hands stopped.

"Ah, you are a fast learner. Too bad. Such a lovely body to ride." The witch's voice mocked Jaz with false sorrow.

"You insane woman," Jaz hissed. "Try that again and I'll unplug you." Jaz felt unclean where the witch—using Jaz's hands—had touched. That loss of control had left her weak and shaking. Terrified.

"Try," the witch encouraged. "Perhaps you'll succeed. I'm as much a prisoner of our dear Colonel Herridge as you are. Kill me. I didn't ask the NSA to keep this decaying body alive."

Jaz tried to take a step forward, but froze. The witch was still inside, able to control her body. Jaz fought to move, but her leg only trembled. "If you want to die, let me go."

"I want to die, but the animal me wants to live. A sad paradox, is it not? Life, unbearable, still better than the void."

"If you can't die, teach me. Stop playing games."

"The game is the lesson. It ever was. Find me . . . find me . . . find me."

Jaz searched for leaks in her defenses. She and the witch each inhabited her own body. Yet somehow, the witch had been able to reach across the gulf between them to produce these illusions.

She closed her eyes to shut out visual stimuli and used the data mask to disconnect her other senses. The only input into Jaz's brain came from the data mask. But there was no traffic, just low-level connection pings forming in her visual cortex. When she concentrated on them, she experienced the packets of information as a tiny kaleidoscopic region, flashing colors and shapes.

The pings established that the connection was still open, nothing more. Jaz examined the incoming identification headers for a hidden signal. Nothing. Then she noticed something odd. The rate at which the shapes changed varied. A normal fluctuation?

Normally as regular as a metronome, the ping rate now varied slightly. And this variation formed a pattern. That was it! The witch was using frequency modulation to transmit a hidden signal. At some point in their communication, the witch must have planted a meme in Jaz's subconscious to decode the hidden signal. The frog process in their metaphor? Jaz would bet it was the witch's agent to intercept the signals.

"Very good, little one," the witch said. "You found my data stream. Now find me inside you. Find the listener that dances you to my tune."

Jaz fractured her consciousness into multiple streams. It was difficult, but she'd done it before while data mining. Jaz broke her consciousness into smaller and smaller streams, trying to isolate the one that carried a repeating meme.

She shut down her mind, quadrant by quadrant, exercising a control that fifty years ago would have been unheard of, a mental discipline that would have amazed ascetics and swamis. There, in the somesthetic region of her brain: resistance. Jaz focused her attention on that section of her brain which controlled motor function. When the frequency of the connection header varied, activity in that area of her brain increased. She could feel it now, a neural program waiting for the witch's induced sensory input to trigger it.

Jaz leaped to her feet and shook her entire body, distracting that portion of her mind with an overwhelming load of physical sensory data, interrupting its concentration on the incoming signal. This broke the neurons out of their obsessive listening for the witch's commands.

With a wild jubilation, Jaz knew her mind was free.

The witch cackled, but the sound was no longer in Jaz's skull. She heard it through regular auditory interpretation over the data mask. "Good. Very good. I have not met someone so determined to keep her privacy in a long time. Breaking the self down, searching for signals within signals. Searching for signals in silence. These will protect you. But after protection, you must learn to attack and to deceive."

"I don't want to learn that. Protection is enough."

"Is it?" the witch mocked her.

Jaz fell to her knees. Her face slammed into the floor. "Protect yourself, then. Protect yourself against me."

"How?" Jaz squeaked as her face pounded again against the floor. The cartilage in her nose flexed—the pain was staggering. Her eyes watered.

"Do you think I would plant only one listener? How careless that would be. One could be found. One could be removed."

Tears and mucous ran down Jaz's face, white stars danced in the black tunnel that rose to swallow consciousness. She fought to get her arms under her. Fought to find the quiet place inside her that would let her shut down the other listeners.

"A counterattack could stop this."

Another slam of her face against the floor. Jaz tasted blood where she'd bitten her tongue.

"But no, that would be wrong. Evil. Too hard to learn."

Jaz's head raised up again. Jaz squinted her eyes, preparing for another blow. It didn't fall.

The witch's dark eyes glinted from across the room. She addressed Jaz over their link, staring, her mouth not moving. "Never. Never relinquish a weapon. Your enemies won't."

"Teach me then," Jaz said, and her voice was like a howl of pain. "Teach me how to attack you."

The witch laughed. "I see now you have the proper motivation. But deception first. I might not survive your first attack."

The force controlling Jaz's body let go, and she was able to stand. Every muscle of her body ached to attack the witch, to tear her from her spiderweb of wires, pluck out the chips that caused her lungs to inflate and watch her slowly suffocate.

Jaz saw movement in the witch's face. A twitch of her slack lips. Was that a smile?

But what the witch said in her mind was, "Lie to me. If you cannot hide your true intentions, you will not succeed. What color is your hair?"

Instantly, unbidden, the answer rose in her mind.

"Yes, I can see your hair is black. Now lie to me. Tell me that you are blond. Convince me."

"Blond," Jaz thought at the witch.

"Oh what a feeble attempt! I heard resonances of black in your subconscious. And the image of yourself you held while constructing the words was a black-haired woman. Try again."

"It's impossible," Jaz spat. "The Net brings us together on a mental level. There's no way to lie to someone who can read your mind."

A titter of laughter. "How naive you are. And yet, aren't there people in your own life who have lied to you? Ah, yes, I see there are."

Unbidden, a memory of Ian telling Jaz that he'd love her forever, that he'd never loved another woman as much as he now loved her. Anger swelled in Jaz's chest "Get out!" she yelled with both mind and voice.

The voice was softer now, more distant, coaxing. "He *lied* to you, little one. Men always do. Wouldn't you like the ability to return the favor?"

Jaz's cheeks flushed with embarrassment. "How?"

"The first step of lying is to convince yourself. Imagine yourself blond. See it, believe it. Remember yourself as a child with white-blond hair floating around your face like so many silk threads. Growing up and envying dark-haired women their exotic beauty. Being annoyed how light hair meant men never took you as seriously as your darker-haired counterparts. They flirted more and listened less. Yes, it was both a blessing and a curse to grow up with skin and hair as pale as yours. Having to stay out of the sun or you'd freckle and burn."

Jaz could see the images the witch wove. Her childhood rewritten, the paleness of her skin and hair. It was beautiful in a foreign way . . .

"No! It is ugly in a familiar way. You despise being blond. It has been your curse and your bane. You dyed your hair black in high school, and the children laughed and called it artificial intelligence. The roots grew back all too quickly. After three cycles you went back to your natural hair color. A golden blond with white highlights. Women envy you; you've had trouble maintaining close relationships with them because their men find your hair so enthralling."

Jaz could see it, feel it. Her dissatisfaction with her common, dark coloring changing quietly to a dissatisfaction with her bleached, pale coloring.

"That's it," said the witch. "Map your emotions onto the new context. Create a history for your fiction, give it weight and depth. Once you believe it, others can, too. Now—quickly—look in the mirror."

There was a hand mirror on the altar. It lay between two candles and an abalone shell. Jaz picked up the silver handle and held it to her face. In the reflection she saw what she expected to see: a milk-white complexion surrounded by a golden sheet of fine hair. The light glinted off individual strands with a silver-white fire. In that instant—Jaz was blond.

"Excellent," the witch purred. "Now you've learned the second lesson. It is easier to believe a lie you wish to be true. But be careful. Use this sparingly. Once you begin to lie to yourself convincingly, it is all too easy to lose yourself in fictions. Too many people travel the world in a bubble of reality all their own. Seeing only the truth they manufacture and not what is real.

"The lie you will tell Orley is that you work against Gestalt, striving for its downfall."

I'm not sure that would be a lie, Jaz thought. She quashed it quickly. There was no need to let Herridge know exactly how insincere her cooperation was.

"Perhaps, then, we are kindred spirits," the witch's voice breathed in her mind.

"Perhaps you are a manipulative bitch who would use anyone to get your way," Jaz said.

The witch chuckled. "I can no longer manipulate my body, so I must instead manipulate those around me. A great loss, a great gain. Now let me teach you to control others. You may find this useful once you are free."

Jaz seated herself cross-legged on the floor. It was strange. She felt kinship with the infuriating woman in front of her. Could the witch really be, as she implied, an unwilling operative?

The witch did not answer the thought. "To learn this, you must unlearn the controls instilled in you since you were a child. Now you want to leak, to project your thoughts. But unlike a child, you must leak controllably, project only a fraction of your real intent. Create a reality in your mind. For example, I create the idea that you will comb your fingers through your hair."

Jaz sat motionless. "No, I won't," she thought back.

"Good. Resist me, you will see it serves no purpose. I form the image in my mind that you comb your fingers through your hair. I make that image real. Your fingers have weight and mass. I feel my own hands going up, the strands flowing through them. I let a bit of this leak to you."

The witch's words brought images to her mind. She could feel what the witch described. Idly she stretched. "It's not going to work, not if I know what you're doing. Not if I'm prepared."

"Stop!"

Jaz froze. Her hands were sunk deep into her thick hair at her temples. She jerked her hands away, pulling strands of hair out with them. Her face was hot and red.

The witch laughed for minutes that seemed like hours. "Your turn."

"But you couldn't move your body if you wanted to."

"Mind-body are one. If you control a person's mind, you control her body. Perhaps even more effectively. Let me show you . . ."

CHAPTER 11

After six hours, Jaz's brain bled sparks of pain and failure. When she could no longer compose a coherent thought, the witch summoned Herridge.

The door slid open. Herridge stood to the left of the door, out of line of sight with the witch. His expression was wary, and he balanced on the balls of his feet like a fighter ready for combat.

When Jaz stepped outside, the door closed behind her, bolts sliding home in the solid metal. Herridge held out the hood.

She looked over her shoulder at the closed door. "Who—"

Herridge silenced her with a finger to her lips. "Not here."

Jaz slipped on the hood and took his arm. The skin of his wrist was sweaty. She wished she could see Herridge's expression, have some idea what he was thinking. With the hood on, Jaz's world consisted of sound: the thumps of their footfalls on the packed earth and the ragged hiss of Herridge's breathing.

The elevator ride up took twenty-one seconds. She counted the steps before Herridge pulled her up short. Her cell—Jaz was sure of it. When she took the hood off, she was back in the Faraday cage. Jaz felt a twinge of pride. Even with Herridge's efforts to keep her ignorant, she was learning her way around.

Herridge held out a data pad to Jaz. "Here's background information on your mission. Familiarize yourself with the material before nineteen hundred. There'll be a briefing tonight. Tomorrow we're transporting you to Pasadena."

"One day of training is all I get?"

Herridge's brows lowered. "If you hadn't traumatized Agent N, we would have accomplished more. But there isn't a whole lot you need to do—just observe, and report your findings." He ran his hand over his short-cropped hair. "The lessons were a precaution, in case something goes wrong."

Great, Jaz thought. Something always goes wrong.

"Who was that?" Jaz asked. "Was she really a witch, in the religious-occult sense?"

"That information is classified."

The witch intrigued Jaz. As a data miner, Jaz found the answers to questions. She decided that when the mission was over, she'd investigate the identity of the woman in the cell. Jaz wanted to know what kind of past had created the witch.

Herridge turned to go. Jaz stopped him with a hand on his arm. "If I do this, if I get the information you need about Orley, you'll let me go. That is the deal, right?"

Was there a moment's hesitation in his reply? Jaz tried to apply the lessons she'd learned from the witch, to sense Herridge's thoughts from his emotional cues. If only she had a rig . . .

"Yes," Herridge said, "that's the deal." He left. The door shut behind him with finality.

Alone in the room, Jaz paced. When the mission had been something in an unknown future, she could handle it. But tomorrow—so soon? She didn't feel ready. She was no spy. Jaz was certain she'd be found out. And then whatever had happened to Herridge's first agent would happen to her.

She'd tell him she couldn't do it. Better to rot in this mirrored prison than die . . . wasn't it?

Jaz had no idea what she should do. So she handled the emotional turmoil the way she always did, with work. Jaz flopped belly-down onto the thin cot and propped

he data pad against the thin horizontal bar that served
as a headboard.

She noticed with annoyance that the machine was
missing its Net chip. Not that any transmission could
have gotten through her Faraday prison, but she would
have liked to try.

The data pad's contents included a dossier on Orley
and several other computer scientists believed to be
working with him on his latest project. The names were
the best and brightest in computational research and evolutionary psychology, including Joseph West, who had
won the Turing Award twenty-five years ago for his work
with quantum computation.

Orley must be well thought of in academic circles to
draw such high-powered researchers. Or perhaps it was
the project itself that was so compelling.

Orley's research projects were divided into past and
present sections. In his list of publications Jaz recognized
the article he had been working on when he discovered
Gestalt, "Patterns of Common Knowledge in a Distributed Environment." After that was a dry spell of no
publications for the next eighteen years. Then one on
evolutionary intelligence, written in collaboration with an
archaeological geneticist, way outside of Orley's field of
study. What had he learned during those eighteen years
of silence?

She performed a search of the text, on dates during that
period, and found utility receipts for a house in Pasadena,
pay stubs from California Institute of Technology, his class
schedule. There was travel, trips to foreign countries, from
the European Republic and Taiwan, to nations just on
the brink of full connection: Congo, Patagonia, and Iraq.

What was Orley doing on those trips? Jaz searched
the data pad's contents. If the NSA knew, they weren't
telling her.

The pad also contained maps of Caltech campus. Jaz
touched the line drawing with a finger, remembering trips
she'd made there as a child. Her mother had toured regu-
larly, lecturing in institutions such as Caltech, MIT, Har-

vard, and her alma mater, Cambridge. She'd often taken her husband and daughter on those trips. They'd have dinner in the evenings and explore the city together after the conference was over. Her father had teased they lived like gypsies. Words that always brought a crease of consternation to her mother's forehead.

Jaz had explored the campuses. A quiet child, she'd been able to slip out of conferences and dinner parties unnoticed. She would wander up and down empty hall-ways, testing doors to see if they were locked.

Caltech was a memory of cloudless blue skies, low mountains in the distance, and fountains. Her parents had come out of the symposium, frantic at having lost her, to find Jaz enthralled by the leaping jets of water in the reflecting pool in front of the Beckman Institute building. Droplets had fallen back into the pool in a rain-bow of ripples and counter ripples that interfered in endless new patterns. Jaz wondered if that wonderful fountain had survived the earthquake of 2091. She hoped so.

The map listed other useful information: lock codes for some of the buildings, how to get in and out of the system of steam tunnels that ran under the college, loca-tions of campus police during various shifts. Jaz commit-ted this material to memory. Years of working in the information industry had trained her to remember access codes and data locations.

The door opened. It was the young agent who had attended her before. He held a lunch tray and informed her that she would be taken to her medical examination as soon as she was finished.

The tray held a mushroom-artichoke pizza. Trying not to worry about designer drugs or mood-altering sub-stances, Jaz savored the food.

When she finished wiping the last crumbs from her mouth, the agent handed her the hood and escorted her to the elevator. By this time, Jaz felt confident she could have led him there, but she followed meekly. No need to give such information away.

The elevator rose for forty-two seconds; then they exited onto a surface that sounded like tile. Doors opened and shut around her. Several people brushed past Jaz in the hall. If anyone noticed the hood, they said nothing. Perhaps they were hooded as well. The image of a hall full of hooded personnel made Jaz smile against the rough fabric.

The agent told her to remove the hood. She did so, and saw that she stood in an endless corridor: gray walls punctuated periodically by green glass doors. People hustled past, wearing a variety of uniforms: green military woolens, surgical scrubs, and white lab coats.

They stopped in front of a door marked 453: IMMUNO-LOGICAL CLINIC. Her escort tucked the hood into his pocket and gestured her in.

Inside was a waiting room. Dark brown plastic chairs lined the walls to the left and right of the entrance. Data pads were scattered on a few of the chairs. On the opposite wall was a door and check-in kiosk.

The room had one other occupant, a man in black jeans and a leather blazer. He started when she entered and jerked his hand away from a data pad, smacking his knuckles on the edge of his chair in his haste. The man winced and rubbed them. He looked vaguely guilty.

What had he been surfing that he didn't want her to see? Classified information?

She walked up to the check-in kiosk and pressed her palm against the plate. A form appeared, asking for her medical history. She tapped buttons impatiently; surely the NSA already had her medical records.

When she finished, she took a seat across from the man. She studied him: he was the first person in civilian dress she'd seen in this place. His black hair was long and swept back from his forehead and temples. Full sensual lips quirked in a half smile. The eyes were hazel-green—and staring at her.

Jaz looked away, picked up one of the data pads, and scanned the table of contents. In disgust she set it down. It was disconnected and filled with entertainment content three months out of date.

When she glanced up, the man was still staring. "What?" Jaz asked.

"Just enjoying the view." He had a slight accent: not quite British, with flattened vowels. He smiled, revealing even, white teeth.

He was attractive and knew it. He'd probably gotten away with this sort of shit all his life on the basis of his good looks. Jaz hated his type. She flipped the data pad at him. "Here. There's a travelogue on Greece. Wonderful views."

His hands fumbled on the pad and nearly dropped it before he set it on top of the other one. He didn't look so cool and assured now. The smile was gone. "You sized me up. I returned the favor. I don't see any reason to be hostile."

"Sorry to spoil your illusions, but I wasn't checking you out. I was just surprised to see a civilian."

"Ah." He looked down at his clothes. His hazel eyes flashed back up at her and he grinned. "Yes, well . . . the NSA calls me in occasionally. For difficult cases involving national security."

"Um-hmm." Jaz wasn't interested in talking to an NSA spook, especially one so taken with himself. She picked up another data pad and tapped idly through it, feigning an interest in last season's fashions.

The door next to the check-in panel opened, and a man in surgical scrubs said, "Mr. Tully. We're ready for you."

The man she'd been talking to stood. He was taller than she'd guessed, nearly six-one, with a lean frame. She watched him walk away; the tight jeans were certainly flattering.

At the door he turned his head and caught her staring. He winked.

Jaz blushed and hated him all the more. Damn arrogant spy. The sooner she was away from this place, the better.

She passed time with a data pad and its stale news stories until the door opened again. Tully exited, rubbing his left shoulder. "Flu shot's a killer," he told Jaz.

"Ms. Reese," the medic said, waving her through.

He led her through a narrow corridor into an examination room the size of a closet. Then told her to strip, leaving her with a paper robe to put on.

It was ironic that he respected her modesty enough to leave her alone to undress, then gave her a paper towel to change into. Jaz undressed quickly and jumped up on the examination table.

When the medic returned, he checked Jaz's blood pressure, temperature, and reflexes. Then he placed an inductive cap over her head. On the holo display, Jaz saw her brain lit up in primary colors. The colors flicked and moved in response to her thoughts. She'd seen similar displays in dance clubs. All the dancers connected to a machine that controlled the lighting of the dance floor. They danced in the light of their own imaginations.

Jaz had tried it once as a teenager, and the lights had focused, becoming a reflection of a single brain, a single purpose. She'd lost herself in dancing and abandoned the rigid control she was learning from her systems-programming tutor.

Flinging her arms and gyrating in wild abandon, Jaz had unintentionally leaked signals from her primary motor cortex. The electrochemical impulses in her brain were so precise and strong that she reverse-induced her data mask, resulting in sympathetic feedback to nearby rigs. Without meaning to, Jaz had waldoed the entire crowd. They danced in syncopation to her movements.

The disc jockey, also a natural, had located Jaz as the origin of the disturbance. He'd signaled a bouncer to pull Jaz off the floor. She remembered the angry stares of the other dancers. That night Jaz learned what it meant to be a natural, how truly different she was. It was then Jaz swore never again to lose control.

The medic passed between Jaz and the holo display, breaking her recollection. He checked her breathing with an ice-cold stethoscope, then said, "Sounds good. Go ahead and change back into your clothes. The last thing is the injections."

"Injections?" Jaz was embarrassed by the squeak in her voice. "I can't use inhalers?"

"For the tetanus and AIDS boosters, yes. But the flu serum's only available in injectable format. There's a particularly bad strain in from Asia this season."

He left the room, and Jaz dressed, crumpling up the paper robe and throwing it in the trash.

The medic returned with several inhalers and one inert-gas injector with needle.

She watched him attach the needle to the syringe. Jaz looked away when he rubbed alcohol on her shoulder.

"This will feel like a little pinch," the medic said.

The needle stung like fire.

"Or a big pinch," the medic agreed cheerfully. "We're almost done . . . there. That wasn't so bad, was it?"

Jaz glared at the man in reply.

The medic led her out to the waiting room. Tully wasn't there. Jaz wasn't sure whether she was relieved or sorry.

Herridge stood in the center of the room, the black hood draped over one arm. He raised one eyebrow and looked a question at the medic.

The medic nodded. "The examination went well. I'll have the report to you within the hour." Then he left, closing the door behind him.

Once they were alone in the room, Herridge said, "We're going to the briefing room next, to discuss the setup for the infiltration. You'll also be introduced to the other members of your team."

"Team?" Jaz asked, looking up at him in surprise. "I thought I would be working alone."

Herridge shook his head. "There's always a backup team located nearby, to extract the agent if a mission is compromised. You'll also be working with a partner."

"Who?" She prayed to Ganesh—who removed obstacles—that it wasn't Agent N. They were going to send some agency spook with her to make sure she didn't run away as soon as she left the complex. Herridge wasn't setting her free, just releasing her into another sort of bondage.

"You'll meet everyone in a few minutes," said Herridge.

Jaz put on the hood, and Herridge led her out of the waiting room. She wondered if he knew about the breach of protocol that had given her a glimpse of the hall outside and the clinic's room number. Probably not. If this was the fourth floor, she was only three levels away from the surface. She listened to the steps as she counted them, relishing being able to picture the hallway she walked through.

When Jaz pulled off the hood, she was blinded by light. As her eyes adjusted she saw a brightly lit conference room with a central holo display and interactive walls. Each seat had a diadem in front of it, set with processor crystals. Four people sat around the wood-grained plastic table: a woman, thankfully not Agent N, and three men. The men were Jaz's age, or slightly younger. They sat ramrod straight in military uniforms; one was dark-skinned, probably Hispanic, the other two were European mixes. The woman was in her fifties, streaks of gray in her ash blond hair.

Herridge spoke to the Hispanic man. "Where's Potter and his charge?"

The man closed his eyes a second, communing with a network via the diadem he wore. Then he pointed at the door.

It opened. A large, muscular man entered, preceded by a smaller man wearing a black hood.

Jaz sucked in a breath at the sight. The prisoner looked ready for the firing squad. Did she look that vulnerable when Herridge escorted her around the complex?

The prisoner raised his hands and peeled the hood off. He blinked in the unfamiliar glare. He didn't look as confident as he had in the waiting room. Tully ran both hands through his mussed hair to smooth it back.

His eyes focused on Jaz and widened for a second. Then he saw the hood in her own hand and grinned.

Herridge waved his hand to indicate the new arrival. "Jasmine Reese, meet your partner for this mission: Dixon Tully."

CHAPTER 12

The name was familiar. "Not *the* Dixon Tully."

He flashed a brilliant smile and held out a hand. It was firm and warm when Jaz shook it. "Guilty as charged."

Dixon Tully was a notorious Net-hack. His most famous stunt was waldoeing the president on Inauguration Day to perform an impromptu striptease. He was a hero to the hacking community and an embarrassment to government security officers. But he'd been caught and sent to prison.

Dixon took a seat and Potter sat next to him, between Dixon and the door.

Herridge continued, "This is Ann Jordon, specialist in situational psychology and emotional engineering. She's scripted your cover story."

"Hello." The older woman's voice was low and gravelly, as if she'd smoked as a youth. From the way the fingers of her right hand rubbed together idly, Jaz surmised she still did.

"The three men at the end of the table are covert ops and extraction." Three men in identical uniforms and close-cropped haircuts nodded in acknowledgment. They were so similar they could have been cut from the same muscular mold.

"They're here to listen and observe," said Herridge. "If things go bad and you call in extra firepower, they're the guys who'll show up."

Dixon frowned as if he'd never need anyone to help him out of a bad situation.

"And Potter?" Jaz asked, pointing at the overmuscled man seated next to Dixon. "What's his function?"

"He's Dixon's handler. If Dixon tries to break parole, or does anything not according to the plan, Potter will intervene."

"Do I have a handler?" asked Jaz.

Herridge touched his fingertips to his chest. "Me."

She didn't like the sound of that. "You're going to be in Pasadena?"

His blue eyes cut through her like laser beams. "Every step of the way." Then he turned back to Jordon. "Ann, why don't you explain the approach?"

Jordon pulled out a data pad. "It would be simpler if I could model the scenario for you on the Net"—she glanced at Dixon—"but since Dixon's presence makes that impossible . . . The premise of contact is to alleviate Dixon's aversion-programming with respect to computational devices."

Jaz raised an eyebrow.

Dixon folded his arms in front of his chest and stared off into space.

Jordon's eyes met Jaz's. "You don't know the conditions of Dixon's parole?" When Jaz shook her head, Jordon continued. "To assure that he was no longer a threat to society, the federal judge ruled that he be given behavioral conditioning that induces pain and nausea whenever he touches or attempts to operate any Net-connected device."

Jaz blinked in surprise. To live in a world where you couldn't touch a connected device without experiencing pain was like living in a minefield, or inside an electrified grid. Network electronics were built into everything. He'd be reduced to infantile status, requiring assistance at every turn. He would be less capable than a feeb, who could at least use a data pad. Why such a harsh sentence? The only things she'd heard of him were stunts, often victimless crimes—like the time he had every bank account on the planet donate one dollar to the Dixon Tully

Relief Fund. To be fair, he'd made it a tax-deductible contribution.

Jaz flashed on an image of Dixon in the waiting room, jerking his hands back from the data pad. He might be conditioned to pain and nausea, but that wasn't enough to keep him from trying.

Dixon's usually mobile face was frozen as Jordon described the neurological procedure that had rendered him helpless in a connected world.

"This limitation," Jordon continued, "provides the perfect motivation for Dixon to contact Orley." She spoke to Dixon. "You will approach him physically, at his office, for help with your condition."

"What's going to make an academic like Orley help me?" Dixon protested in a tight voice. "Why would I contact him instead of someone in the black market?"

Jordon counted off the reasons on her fingers. "First, Orley, working at Caltech, has access to resources and skills that criminals do not have. Second, your lover has discovered that Orley is working on something suspect. She has gathered evidence that could prove quite embarrassing to him if he does not help." Jordon linked her two hands together and pulled first one way and then the other. "I propose a push-pull strategy with Orley. First the pull: you approach him as the best of the best. Flattery, even when blatant, works. You hint that you still have considerable funds you could donate to his cause in exchange for his help. There's also Jaz. She'll be a pull in and of herself." Jordon pressed her hands together. "Then the push: if he refuses all these inducements, you threaten his scheme with exposure."

"If he's afraid of exposure, then why—" asked Dixon.

"Why am I a draw—" said Jaz.

They looked at each other. Dixon flipped a hand to let Jaz continue.

She asked, "Why am I a draw to Orley?"

The older woman smiled warmly. "You, my dear, are a woman."

Jaz recoiled. She did *not* like where this conversation was going. "I'm not sleeping with anyone for you, Herridge. You can just put me back in the cage now if that's what you're planning."

Jordon held up her hand to push back Jaz's argument. "Sexual contact is not required. In fact it would throw off our model if you did. What is important is that, according to past behavior and analysis of the mental patterns we have access to for him—out-of-date though they are—you are a ninety-seven percent match for Orley's preferences in physiology, intellect, and personality. He will be drawn to you, and we can use that."

Jordon's words made Jaz feel dirty. It was all so calculated, so unfeeling.

"Dixon will make contact. You will be there. The motivation and the first draw."

"What reason do I give for being in the room?" Jaz asked.

"You are Dixon's lover."

Jaz and Dixon exchanged a surprised look.

Dixon appraised Jaz from face to ankles. "Not outside the realm of possibility . . ."

Jaz felt a flush creeping up her neck. "But there's no record of me and Dixon being intimate online before his capture. With two naturals, there would have been millions of data paths linking us."

"Not necessarily," said Herridge. "Your job at Infotech requires a high security clearance. If you were known to associate with a hacker, it would compromise your job. You've had reason to hide your tracks, and as you pointed out, between you both are the skills and knowledge to cover up the trails. Besides"—Herridge leaned forward—"we've planted a few data paths between you. If Orley goes looking, he'll find just enough to represent a skilled cover-up. We've got the best mind on the planet working on this."

He meant Gestalt. Why not mention the overmind by name? Were there people in the room who didn't know what this was all about? Jaz felt like shouting: "Gestalt, Gestalt, Gestalt—there is an overmind controlling the Net." But what good would that do? Jaz was grateful that she wasn't connected. She was sure some of that would have leaked out to Herridge. And of course, there was no hiding from Gestalt.

"The ruse is necessary," Jordon said, pursing her lips. "We need a way to introduce you to Orley that does not thrust you in his face. We want him to come to you, not the other way around."

"Fine, but why can't I be Dixon's sister? His old college roommate? Best friend?"

"All of those facts can be checked and exposed. Only romance can occur in a short time frame and create a tight enough social bond that you would drop everything to help him."

Jaz shook her head. "What about the small problem of my having died in an avalanche at Thunder Basin?"

Herridge said, "Search and rescue recovered you from a snow cave you'd built to save yourself. Your friends wanted to see you, but for reasons of your health, you were rushed to Cedars Sinai. You were convalescing there when you met Dixon, who was being treated for his release."

"That is the basic premise of our attack," Jordon said. "If neither the push nor the pull gets you inside, contact me. I'll be on the ground with the boys. We'll improvise from there. It is vital to this mission that we get you"—she pointed at Jaz—"inside."

"What about me?" Dixon said.

Jordon looked at him sadly. "Your inhibition limits your effectiveness at breaking into Orley's records." She put a hand on his arm to forestall his protest. "Which is not to say that your expertise in circumnavigating security protocols won't be invaluable to Jasmine."

Dixon hunched forward over the table. "You promised to lift the restrictions on me if I went along with this case. Why not do it now, so I can help directly?"

Herridge shook his head. "Too risky. Orley would detect the modification . . . and it would remove whatever leverage we have to keep you on the case. Without the limitations you're a flight risk. The federal prison paroled you to us on the condition that you not be allowed to escape. If you successfully complete this mission, your sentence will be commuted. Until then, you are still a federal prisoner."

Dixon's mouth worked like he wanted to spit, or swear, or both, but he subsided into his seat. Jaz was glad they weren't sharing a connection. There was a typhoon brewing in his hazel eyes.

"What if Orley doesn't take the bait?" Jaz asked. "I'll have fulfilled my obligation, correct? I'll be free to go?"

"If Orley doesn't respond to your opening gambit, contact the ground team—instructions on how to do that are provided in your final briefing notes—and we'll give you further instructions."

"But if nothing works—I still go free, right?"

Herridge shifted in his seat. "The conditions of your release are discovering Orley's intentions. Without that, we'll have to renegotiate the terms." He leaned back in his chair. "Consider it strong motivation to succeed."

Jaz didn't like the sound of it. "You can't blame us if Orley doesn't try to recruit us. As I understand it, one of your own agents, highly trained, couldn't get into Orley's inner circle."

"Two," said Jordon in a husky voice. "Two previous agents have attempted and failed."

Herridge gave Jordon a sharp look.

The woman met his gaze levelly. "She needs to know."

Jaz felt a coldness seep into the pit of her stomach. "What else aren't you telling me?"

"We're telling you everything we can," Herridge said. "Two agents went in, Mark Anders and William James. Neither returned. Anders checked in shortly before he disappeared and reported that he was going to be brainhacked by Orley as part of a loyalty check." Herridge pinched the skin at the bridge of his nose. "We presume he failed."

"If your agents have been killed or captured—why didn't you go in to save them?" Jaz was surprised. Surely Herridge would have tried to rescue his own people? If not, what assistance could she expect?

Herridge's cold blue eyes met hers. "Secrecy is of the utmost importance on this mission. If the agents have been killed, we will bring the parties responsible to justice once Orley has been neutralized. Believe me, this is not the way I like to handle a mission. Our orders not to interfere come from higher up . . . much higher up."

"What am I supposed to do if he contacts me to join his project?" asked Jaz.

"Show some interest," Jordon said, "but not too much. The ideal situation would be if you bargained to help him, in exchange for his assistance with Dixon's problem." Jordon steepled her fingers. "Also, you must establish a rapport with Orley. Show interest in his work, but also interest in him."

"Won't that seem strange if I'm supposed to be Dixon's lover?"

A flicker of a smile played around Jordon's lips. "Quite the contrary. Our personality analysis predicts he will consider it a compliment."

"But it's not believable," Dixon cut in. "No woman who was with *me* would look at another man." He spread his arms wide in an expansive gesture. "I mean, once you've found perfection, what's the point?"

Jaz rolled her eyes. "Oh? Visitation day must be crowded at the prison."

The smile faded from Dixon's eyes, and he subsided back into his seat.

Herridge asked Jordon, "Are you done with the psychological briefing on Orley?"

"Almost. I'm not going to tell you too many details about Orley's history or preferences because the man is highly intelligent and might realize you know too much. I will caution you he is a high-level functioning person with acute stress disorder. Any betrayal may trigger strong reactivity. If he senses that you are not what you pretend to be—he can be very dangerous.

"Orley thinks he's fighting a war against an all-powerful enemy. He is paranoid; he is driven. You must convince him that you are on his side before he will reveal the nature of his project."

"You mean get close to him emotionally," Jaz said with distaste.

"Yes, but avoid sexual relations with him. Sex changes the emotional landscape. We do not have a complete model for his intimate relationships, so we do not know how he would react."

"And what am I supposed to do while my supposed girlfriend is making time with the scientist?" Dixon asked.

"You must be jealous; it is in line with your personality profile," Jordon said. "Otherwise, Orley may believe that Jaz is using her wiles on your behalf in order to get Orley to help you. In fact, that is our fallback story if Jaz overplays the seduction. Don't overdo the jealousy and alienate Orley. It is best for the mission if you can stay on-site and help Jaz with the security protocols once she's in."

Dixon leaned back in his chair. "No worries. If she can get in, I can get her through. There hasn't been a security system invented that I can't work my way around." He was awfully confident for a man who'd been caught and sentenced to life without technology.

Jordon said, "Unless there are any further questions, that concludes my psychological briefing."

When no one spoke, Herridge stood and clicked a handheld remote. The table projected a three-dimensional image. Trees and buildings appeared to sprout on its surface. "This is Caltech campus, nestled below the hills of the San Gabriels. We're looking at real-time images provided by web cameras and aggregations of incidental transmissions."

Students swarmed through the tree-lined paths, most wearing full-immersion masks. Their bodies were on autopilot while they commuted to class, simultaneously finishing class assignments, surfing the entertainment channels, and meeting friends online.

Jaz felt a pang. It had been nearly a week since she'd been connected to the Net. She longed for the quick exchange of information, the mind-to-mind communication that was closer than anything you could communicate through the crutch of words and gestures. But that world was lost to her. Jaz couldn't enter the Net without giving up some part of herself to Gestalt, and that she would never do.

The scene changed to the interior of a building. Faculty offices lined either side of the hallway. The view circled left until it illuminated a door. A brass plate on the door read 342.

"This is Orley's office in the Beckman Institute. We're able to monitor the corridor and his office through the campus police security network. Attempts to monitor his laboratories have failed. The windows are soundproofed, so bouncing IR lasers off the glass returned no results. The first agent we sent in was able to scatter fifty-micron transmitters throughout the lab, but those were apparently detected and disabled within three hours."

A member of the extraction team raised his hand. "Sir, can we assume from this that Orley is aware of our investigation and may have armed himself against us?"

"That is probable. Remember, however, that we are dealing with academics, not soldiers. The median age of his recruits is forty-three. In the event of an extraction it is unlikely you will encounter armed resistance, though you should be prepared for automated systems."

On the viewscreen, the door opened and a slender man in his early forties with limp amber hair walked out. There were metallic plates attached at his temples.

"This is Orley," said Herridge.

"I thought you said he wasn't connected," said Dixon. He tapped his own temple and pointed at the screen. "Those look like a Net device to me."

"They do not conform to any known device, and we can verify that they do not interact with the worldwide Net. They may communicate with a private academic network, but we have not been able to identify one. Or they may serve an entirely different purpose—such as shielding Orley from remote induction."

"Remote induction?" Jaz asked. "How is such a thing possible? Induction technology has a maximum range of twenty centimeters. Any farther and the signal-to-noise ratio prevents adequate resolution."

Herridge looked at his fingernails. "Orley may have

concerns about such a technology. I cannot comment on whether they have a basis in fact."

Meaning the NSA had done research on the problem but wasn't going to tell her how far they had gotten. If Orley was worried about it, Jaz was, too. If Gestalt could remotely touch a person's mind, without the need for data jewelry, there would be no way to stop the entity, no way to escape. Humanity would be its thrall. The thought sent a chill down her spine. The more she learned about Orley, the more she liked him.

In the projection, Orley's eyes passed across the camera; for an instant his eyes seemed to bore into Jaz's. He had high cheekbones and pale, almost sallow, skin. His lips were thin, and his eyes were slanted ever so slightly upward, as if somewhere in his lineage was Asian ancestry. He had none of Dixon Tully's masculine vitality. His features were finer, almost feminine. He was attractive, in a quiet, unassuming way.

This was the man she was supposed to seduce and betray. In the instant she'd seen his face, his expression had seemed so sad. She felt sorry for him.

Herridge said, "You and Dixon will have to be careful around Orley and the others. They look harmless, but if threatened, they can be dangerous."

Dixon cracked his knuckles, "Well, after the training this past week—so am I."

Herridge pointed a finger at Dixon's chest. "That kind of overconfidence will get you killed. Play it safe. Your primary job is to make the initial contact and deliver the package."

"I'm not a pack—" started Jaz.

"So I'm not important—" said Dixon.

Jaz let Dixon continue.

He said, "So I'm not important to the mission?"

"Not as a feeb, no. If Orley can turn your conditioning around, you may assist Jaz. Until then, your primary responsibility is to get Jaz into Orley's compound, protect her from injury, and advise her on the best techniques to hack into Orley's data banks."

Dixon leaned back in his chair and propped his feet

on the table, his arms folded across his chest, and he cast sidelong glances at Jaz.

"What can you tell us about Orley's labs and offices?" Jaz asked, trying to direct the conversation in a less emotional direction.

"Not much. We have the building's original blueprints. But Orley may have made any number of changes since then. His portion of laboratory space is twenty-five-hundred square meters of space in the Beckman Institute."

The scene on the wall screen changed again. This time it was an overhead view of Pasadena. Orley pointed to the airport with a laser pointer. "We will transport you here on a commercial plane, to leave a trail Orley can verify. From the airport, you will take a room in the Caltech Doubletree Hotel." One of the squares adjacent to the university lit up. "It is normally used by parents and visiting faculty—"

"Only one room?" Jaz asked.

Jordon nodded. "It is necessary for your cover."

Dixon chuffed.

Jaz swiveled her head to look at him, but his head was down, pointing at his chest. She'd swear there was a hint of a smile at the corners of his mouth. Damn the man anyhow.

"How are we going to contact Orley? He's not connected to the Net, and neither are we."

"You will have a data mask, an Odin's Eye. I believe you are familiar with the model."

Jaz felt the skin on the back of her neck prickle. "What if I don't want to be connected?"

Dixon took his feet off the desk and looked at her. She could see his questioning gaze out of the corner of her eye. Jaz ignored him. "I won't go online, Herridge—you know why."

"The mask will be necessary for short periods, to check into the hotel, negotiate your way around the city, and—if events should warrant it—to make contact with your extraction team. We're not asking you to stay online for long periods."

Jaz fumed. No matter where she went or what she did after Herridge let her go, Gestalt would be with her. Even when she wasn't connected, it would be in the ether of the Net, watching her through security cameras and the eyes of the connected. It made Jaz uneasy. Was there no place on this planet she would be left alone? She wondered if Orley had found such a refuge. And the easiest way to meet him was to go along with the mission. "All right, I suppose that makes sense," she said. Her voice sounded defeated.

Herridge looked as if he didn't need a connection to read her thoughts. His eyes were the deadly blue of glaciers opening into a crevasse. "You will do this," he whispered.

"I—" Jaz choked off her protest. Herridge was dangerous. Pretend to go along with the plan, get out of here, and then see what she could do. Perhaps Dixon would help her escape. He couldn't love the authorities any more than she did, and he had years of experience evading detection. She tried not to dwell on the fact that he'd been caught.

PART THREE

"We all agree that your theory is crazy, but is it crazy enough?"

—Niels Bohr (1885–1962)

CHAPTER 13

Herridge escorted Jaz back to her cell. A black hard-shell suitcase lay on the bed.

"What's that?" Jaz asked.

"Clothes and equipment you'll need for the mission."

Jaz thumbed the lock and the case opened like a clam-shell into two compartments: the body of the suitcase and the lid. The larger side held clothes—her clothes. Jaz picked up a blue-green silk *kurta* and held it with trembling fingers. "You've been inside my apartment."

"Gestalt thought having your own clothes would comfort you."

Jaz fingered the silk. She didn't feel comforted. Every time she dressed, Jaz would remember that the NSA could find her anywhere, could break into her locked apartment and extract what they needed.

She refolded and replaced the *kurta*. Then she examined the other side of the suitcase. An inner flap covered a shallow compartment in the lid. Inside, packed in cut-out foam, was the Odin's Eye she had bought at the Sharper Connection. It winked up at her malevolently, as if saying, See, I knew you couldn't resist me. Next to the Eye was a slender handgun.

Jaz extracted the gun, a matte black Ruger 2032, the model she had trained with. From its heft, she knew it was loaded. Jaz held it up and sighted on Herridge. The handgun's targeting laser cast a red dot in the center of Herridge's forehead. Her index finger brushed the side of the trigger. Too tempting.

There was steel in Herridge's voice. "Done playing around?"

Jaz sighed, let go of the gun so that it dangled from her finger, and then replaced it in its foam casing. "I don't have a license to carry a gun. I'd never get it past airport security."

"The state of California issued you a concealed weapon permit this morning. You will board the plane accompanied by Potter. There will be no problems with airport security."

"Ah. A short leash for Dixon and me."

Herridge met her eyes with his cool blue ones. "Gestalt believes it prudent."

"You didn't mention Gestalt in the briefing. Do the others know who they're working for? Does Dixon?"

"Ann Jordon knows. She works closely with Gestalt, helping it interpret human behavior."

"I thought Gestalt understood humanity implicitly."

"At an abstract level." Herridge smoothed one eyebrow with his thumb. "But it has never *been* human. Jordon helps Gestalt understand what it senses, in human terms."

"Does Dixon know about Gestalt?"

"No. I suggest you not discuss Gestalt with anyone but Orley. Unauthorized disclosure of Gestalt's existence could . . . complicate your release."

Jaz was silent while she mulled over the implications of Herridge's warning. Then a new thought occurred to her. "How do I contact the extraction team if I need help?"

Herridge tapped the data pad next to the suitcase. "You make a chiropractor appointment. The day of the week indicates how bad your situation: Monday means you want guidance; Friday asks for full extraction. If you need anything else, contact Gestalt by connecting to the Net and focusing on the chapel metaphor. She will step in and shield the communication."

Jaz lifted the pad and stared at its unilluminated display. The gray LCD screen reflected her face. She looked sad.

"Don't worry." Herridge placed a heavy hand on her shoulder. "You're ready."

Jaz nodded without looking up at him. The reflection in the data pad nodded, too. Somehow it was not convincing.

In the morning, the young NSA officer who had served her before brought Jaz a tray of bacon, eggs, pancakes, and orange juice.

After breakfast, Jaz dressed in jeans, a white cotton shirt with lace embroidery at the neckline and hem, and a charcoal gray silk blazer. The clothes were comforting, something of home in this military prison. But they were also a reminder that the NSA could reach her anywhere.

When she finished dressing, the NSA officer returned with the hood. Jaz looked at it with distaste.

"It's the last time, Ms. Reese. Your car is waiting."

The elevator ride up was longer this time, fifty-four seconds. Whatever hole they'd kept her in was deep. They walked down an echoing hallway of tile or marble flooring and out into fresh air. Outside was warm and humid. Jaz smelled open water, like a lake or slow-moving river, the scent of fresh-mown grass and a hint of algae. Off to her left, Jaz heard the chuffing of a helicopter. She started to raise the hood, but the agent grabbed her arm.

"Not yet," he said. He pushed the back of her head down and forward, so Jaz stooped as he led to her to the helicopter. "Three steps up."

Jaz fumbled with her feet to find the first step. She entered the helicopter and was pushed into a seat against someone. She was crammed next to him, hip to thigh. Another passenger loaded in after her, shoving her even farther into the previous occupant. Jaz's shoulder bumped against his chest. "Sorry," she murmured. There was a whiff of cologne.

"It's all right," said Dixon Tully, his mouth somewhere close to her ear. "We'll have to pretend to be more intimate than this, before it's over."

Jaz tried to scootch away from Dixon, but there was no room. Another leg pressed on her from the left.

Dixon slid his arm around Jaz's shoulder. She started to protest, then realized that it eased the pressure from too many shoulders crammed into too little room. Despite the ventilation from the whirling blades above the helicopter, it was hot.

"Don't worry," Herridge said from her left. "It's a short ride to the airport."

After a trip that seemed like hours, the helicopter descended. When it landed, Herridge pulled off Jaz's hood and helped her down the stairs. She blinked in the light. Dixon Tully exited next, followed by Potter. The big man yanked off Dixon's hood, leaving his hair standing up in a crisscross of tufts. Jaz smothered a laugh at the sight.

Dixon looked pointedly at her head. "I wouldn't laugh if I were you."

Jaz smoothed the strands that had pulled free of her tightly bound braid.

They stood on a field of tarmac. Small private planes nestled up to two single-story buildings. In the distance, commercial jets landed on crisscrossed runways. An enormous glass-and-steel terminal building loomed off to her left.

"Where are we?" Jaz asked.

Herridge answered, "Houston."

They boarded a shuttle van. Herridge handed Potter a briefcase. "See you in Pasadena."

"You're not going with us on the plane?" Jaz asked.

"No. We can't be spotted with you. Don't worry. The rest of us will be around. Hopefully you'll never see us"—his faced was solemn—"because if you do, it means the shit has hit the fan."

The shuttle took them to the maintenance side of the terminal. When they got out, Potter nodded at a security guard and led them through an unmarked door. It opened into a dingy hallway with concrete floors and gray-painted walls. He stopped them with a hand on Dixon's chest. "No funny business." He opened his jacket to show them a firearm that Jaz doubted she would have been able to lift, much less fire.

Dixon lowered his head a fraction of an inch in acknowledgment.

"If you shoot us," Jaz said, "Herridge is going to be unhappy."

Potter said, "Yeah, but he'll be more unhappy if you escape." He led them through a door at the end of the hall. It opened into the main terminal. If anyone thought it strange that the three of them entered through a door marked EMPLOYEES ONLY, they made no sign.

"Gate C-34," said Potter, gesturing with a beefy hand for them to proceed.

Jaz telescoped the handle of her carry-on suitcase and followed the signs to the C gates. Dixon walked briskly beside her. Neither looked back to make sure Potter kept up. His presence was like being followed by a mountain. People ahead of them parted to make way.

Their airplane was loading. Potter followed them to the gate and glanced briefly at the kiosk. It beeped, and the door to the on-ramp sheathed open. The three of them walked down the tube of aluminum and carpet-covered siding.

When they reached the plane, Jaz saw Dixon peek through the five-centimeter gap between the ramp and the plane as if wishing he could jump through it and escape. Potter apparently noticed Dixon's hesitation, too, for he reached forward with a meaty hand and pushed Dixon on board.

Jaz stepped onto the plane. There was no sense in running away. Not in a world monitored by security and maintenance cameras. The earth was Gestalt's crystal ball. No privacy, and certainly no escape. Not unless she emulated Orley and built a fortress against the Net.

They were seated in the last two rows of first class. Potter sat behind them, taking up two seats, where he could keep an eye on them. Dixon tried to give Jaz the window seat, saying, "Ladies first."

Potter shook his head slowly, like a rhinoceros scenting trouble. He pointed silently at the window seat, and Dixon scooted in.

Dixon fidgeted until the airplane door closed and the plane taxied away from the terminal. Then, with a sigh of surrender, he slumped in his seat.

Potter enjoyed himself in first class. After a round of free preflight and then postflight drinks, he settled into his seat and slumbered.

"He doesn't seem too concerned about keeping an eye on you," Jaz said, pointing behind them.

"Where would I go?" said Dixon, gesturing at the interior of the aircraft.

The stewardess announced that the wideband picocell transmitter inside the plane had been turned on, and the use of personal data jewelry was now permitted. In addition, anyone wishing to take advantage of the inflight entertainment network could rent a headset for an additional fee. Headsets were free in first class, and the stewardess walked down the aisle, proffering them.

Jaz waved away the plastic-wrapped diadem. Dixon reached out his hand. It trembled. When the stewardess handed him the package, Jaz felt him shudder next to her. His hand spasmed, and he dropped the diadem.

He and Jaz both reached for it and knocked heads. At knee level Jaz whispered, "Why do you put yourself through this?"

"Why do you refuse a data connection?" Dixon countered, his eyes centimeters from Jaz's own. It was an uncomfortable closeness. Jaz snatched up the package, sat up, and stuffed the diadem into the pouch in front of her.

Dixon leaned over to whisper in her ear. "You could do it. I could help you."

"Do what?"

"Hack through the entertainment network to the navigational systems."

She glanced behind her. Potter was still sleeping. "You've got to be kidding. That's impossible—no airline would construct an in-flight network connected to both the navigational and entertainment channels."

Dixon lowered his voice still further. "On a Boeing 797, it's possible to gain access through the remote maintenance port. I've done it before as . . . an intellectual exercise."

His face was intense, eager. His hazel eyes flashed in the low light. "Please," he mouthed.

Jaz shook her head. It wouldn't do any good to redirect the plane. Potter was still with them. Even if they managed to hijack it and escape—where would they run to? The whole planet was bugged.

Dixon's face twisted into a scowl, and he turned away, pressing his face against the window plastic.

From behind, Jaz heard Potter's rumbling voice say, "That was the right choice, Ms. Reese. Colonel Herridge will be pleased."

She looked around the seat in shock. Potter smiled a cold, thin smile. "I never sleep."

An hour later, the stewardess returned with a light snack, croissants and raspberry preserves on porcelain plates. Jaz and Dixon ate in companionable silence. Staring out the window seemed to have relaxed him.

"Since we're lovers now," Jaz said, "I should know more about you."

The white-haired woman in front of them peered briefly through the crack between seats at Jaz. When Jaz returned her stare the woman quickly turned away.

Dixon cracked a smile at the old woman's nosiness. "What do you want to know? Favorite sexual position? How many times a day I—"

Jaz hushed him with her fingertips to his mouth. "Stop. You're going to give her an aneurysm."

Dixon mumbled against her fingers, "You shouldn't do that. I might bite."

Jaz jerked her hand away from his mouth. "I want to know basic things. Where did you grow up? How did you learn network programming? Why did you . . ."

"Get into trouble?"

Jaz nodded.

Dixon shrugged. "I was born in the Australian Union. I helped my uncle manage an offshore gambling server.

We ran numbers on sporting events, first-person shooter games, political elections, anything. First I helped him improve his prediction algorithms. Then I learned that it was easier to control the games than predict them. I have a knack for it."

"And that led to . . . other things?"

"Waldoeing the United States president? Yeah. I wanted to see if it could be done. No harm in it, though . . . except for what happened to me." He reached out his hand to the entertainment diadem in the pocket in front of Jaz. He stopped halfway, sweating. "What about you? What's your story? I've never heard of you on the hack-net."

"No. My life has been uneventful. I work for Infotech, data mining."

"Then why did the NS—"

"Shhh." Jaz pointed to the seat behind them. Potter listened intently to every word. She stuffed a travel pillow in the gap between her and Dixon's seat and mouthed the word *later*.

Potter reached an enormous hand over the tops of their seats and grabbed the pillow. He stuffed it in the crook of his neck, and watched them with his head against the window.

Under Potter's surveillance, Jaz switched the subject. "What was it like growing up in the Australian Union?"

"Good enough, I guess. I spent a lot of time driving around in the Great Victoria Desert. The sky there is so big it makes you feel infinite." He looked at her. "What about you?"

"My parents were professors, so I grew up in and around colleges. My mother toured, giving lectures. But she always managed to make time for me and Dad. I don't know how she did it. Maybe that's just how mothers are."

"I wouldn't know."

Jaz raised her eyebrows. "Oh?"

Dixon stared out the window. "My mother died when I was six, went into hospital and never came out. In some ways it was a blessing; she'd been ill for a long time."

Jaz didn't know what to say, so she studied her palms. "At least you had your uncle."

"Yes, but there's a whole side of me I know nothing about. Where did I get my skill with computers? Not from my uncle. He was thick as a post. Never met my dad. I feel like three-quarters of my past is gone."

"I used to wish I could delete half my family. My mother is first-generation Indian, my father first-generation Irish. I always felt like a bridge between their two worlds." When Dixon didn't say anything, she continued, "Family events broke down into two camps. The Irish on one side, telling bawdy stories; the Indian on the other side, gossiping about who's dating whom and telling jokes. . . . I always thought that if we could find something that would seem funny to both sides, we could make real progress."

The stewardess came around and collected the plates from their snack, interrupting the conversation. When she had gone, Dixon reached again for the entertainment diadem. His hand trembled with effort as his fingers closed around it. Sweat beaded on his forehead. He pulled it halfway out. Then with a gasp let go and slumped back into his seat.

Jaz considered him. "If it causes you so much pain, why do you try?"

His eyes, when he looked down at her, were dark with pain. "It's the only thing that makes me real."

Without another word he turned his head toward the window and either slept or pretended to sleep.

Jaz thought she understood. When she was young, the Net had saved her from the awkward world of teenagers. She'd been too young, too smart, and too skinny to interact with her classmates. But in the Net, she could be anything she wanted to be. In the Net, she was free. Dixon seemed outgoing and confident with people, but that could be a facade.

She pulled out the entertainment rig Dixon had tried so hard to put on. For her it would be easy. Jaz unwrapped the plastic. Then she recalled that Gestalt was waiting on the other side. Even in an airplane she couldn't escape. She lowered the rig and stared at it. If she was giving up a Net connection, might as well go cold turkey. Stuffing it back into the pocket in front of her, Jaz took a cue from Dixon. She pulled the wings of her headrest forward to cradle her head, and slept.

Jaz woke when the plane touched down on the runway. The stewardess opened the main door and Jaz half expected Dixon to make a break for freedom. But he stayed at her side, helping her take down her carry-on luggage. She caught a glimpse of one of the passengers in the first row. A Hispanic gentleman in a business suit: one of the members of the extraction team. Herridge had them watched from all sides. Jaz felt claustrophobic.

On the walk through the terminal, Potter fell back and let Jaz and Dixon take the lead. But he was never too far behind to catch up if they made a run for it.

When Jaz and Dixon exited the terminal, the first thing Jaz noticed was the heat. April in Seattle is a cold, drizzly affair. Southern California was warm; azaleas were in bloom. There were mountains, but they weren't the sharp granite peaks of the Cascades; the San Gabriel Mountains were reddish humps in the distance. The air was drier, too.

Dixon, beside her, took a deep breath and held it for a moment before blowing it out. "The air reminds me of home."

They walked over to the ground-transportation section of the Burbank airport, a median between two lanes of traffic carrying shuttle vans and taxis. Dixon flagged a taxi down manually. Potter watched them load into the car from a distance. As the taxi drove away, Jaz wiggled her fingers at the agent in a mocking wave. The smile on her face was anything but friendly.

Dixon sank back into the cushions and exhaled. "Freedom."

Potter was a dwindling dot at the airport curb. As Jaz watched, he climbed into a second taxi.

"Not quite," she said, pointing back.

Dixon looked, shrugged. "I'll take what I can get." He pulled a scrap of paper from the inner pocket of his leather blazer and said to the driver, "Caltech Double-tree. Do you know where that is?"

The driver's head was a tangle of multicolored wires that dangled like dreadlocks from plaster connections on his scalp. Without looking back, he said, "I know them all. Got a reservation number? I'll tell them you're coming."

Dixon recited a sixteen-digit number from the paper and the driver nodded again, his head bobbing to music only he could hear.

The hotel was a concrete tower, one of the newer buildings surrounding Caltech. Jaz watched the college as they drove past. The buildings were set like gemstones in the green landscaping. Caltech's architecture reflected a variety of styles, from Spanish Colonial to modern stone. Jaz caught sight of the Beckman Institute, which housed the department of Computation and Neural Systems. It looked just as it had in her childhood: a massive Spanish Mission–style edifice, four stories tall, with five archways leading into a central courtyard. A large shell motif between the third and fourth stories bisected carved stone words: BECKMAN INSTITUTE

The driver pulled up in front of the hotel lobby and helped them out with their bags.

Jaz fumbled the suitcase open and dug in it for the lotus case that held the Odin's Eye. With a deep breath to calm her, she slipped the Eye on. Feelings of warmth and homecoming suffused her as she debited the driver's account. While she was connected, Jaz went ahead and checked their reservation. Two adults, nonsmoking, room 1428, prepaid. She requested two ident-bracelets.

Jaz worried that Gestalt would contact her while she was online. But the entity kept its presence hidden. Jaz sensed it only in a feeling of belonging and safety. She jerked the Eye off her head before she got too comfortable.

The cabby was already driving away. Dixon looked at her questioningly. "So, why—"

"Not here."

A concierge met them at the front door that wouldn't

open. He was a chatty man in his fifties, balding slightly and with the beginnings of a paunch. As he strapped ident-bracelets onto their wrists, he said, "We typically use these only for children younger than connection age. And not even that so often, with the new subcutaneous identification chips parents implant these days."

Jaz let the man clip the plastic around her wrist.

"Don't try to take them off," the concierge warned. "They deactivate when the plastic is stressed. Security measures, you know."

Their room was on the fourteenth floor. A small suite, with a closet-size front room that contained a desk, reading lamp, refrigerator, and microwave. The room beyond held a round table, two chairs, and a single, king-size bed.

"I'm going to kill Herridge," Jaz muttered.

"No worries," said Dixon. "It's part of our cover. What young people in love would get a room with double beds?" He placed his hand over his heart and said with mock-solemnity, "I promise not to molest you." He eyes raked her body. "You're not my type."

"Oh?" said Jaz archly. "And what type is that?"

"Blond, Scandinavian." He held out his hands in front of his chest suggestively. "Valkyrie types. Not skinny Indian women with long noses."

She gaped at his rudeness. "Indian-Irish. And I can guarantee you won't molest me." Jaz jerked a pillow off the bed and threw it on the floor. "You're sleeping on the floor."

"What, me? Your dearest love? How's that going to look when Orley comes to visit?"

"Like we're having a lovers' spat. Very realistic." Jaz crossed the room to look at the view out the window. Below lay the Caltech campus, sprawled out in a patchwork of Spanish tile, gray stone, and open green lawns. Somewhere down there was Orley. And it was her job to get close to him, gain his confidence—and then betray him.

CHAPTER 14

Sharing a room with a stranger was awkward. Jaz had to wait until Dixon finished in the bathroom to brush her teeth. On the floor, he tossed and turned. The sound of his breathing was strange to Jaz, who in the last few months, had become used to sleeping alone.

Jaz rose early, showered, and dressed in a red *kurta* embroidered with golden twining flowers around the neckline, sleeves, and hem.

On the floor, Dixon scrubbed his face and blinked blearily at the bright colors of her clothing. "I thought we were supposed to be inconspicuous."

Jaz spread her arms at her sides to show off the draped sleeves. "For a college campus? This is discreet."

"I wouldn't know," he grunted and trundled off to the shower. After an interval of steam and off-key singing of "Waltzing Matilda" that made Jaz wince, Dixon emerged, freshly shaved and wearing his usual: black jeans, black T-shirt, and black leather blazer. He spun in front of her. "Does the gun show?"

"No. But you can't carry a firearm onto a college campus."

Dixon adjusted his lapels. "You don't get it, do you? Orley isn't a harmless college professor. I, for one, intend to be prepared." Dixon closed and locked his suitcase. "Orley teaches a class at eleven. We can catch him after it ends."

"So soon?"

He was at the door, hand on the handle. "The sooner

we figure out what he's up to, the sooner this case is over, you go free, you go free, and I get access to the Net—I don't see any reason to delay, do you?"

Put like that, she didn't. Jaz stood.

"You forgot something," Dixon said and pointed to the lotus case that held her Odin's Eye. It lay on the dresser surface, where she'd left it while unpacking last night.

"We don't need it," Jaz said. "We'll be talking to him face-to-face."

Dixon cocked his head and looked at her. "Why d'you avoid the Net? It's not lack of talent. And no one's put a geas on you. Why?"

Jaz looked at Dixon speculatively. Should she tell him about Gestalt? Why had Herridge warned her not to? Jaz weighed the option in her mind. Herridge was a manipulative bastard, but an effective one. If he hadn't told Dixon, there must be a reason.

But to ask a man to risk himself to find out more about Gestalt's enemies—when he didn't even know Gestalt existed—just wasn't right.

Jaz took a deep breath. Damn Herridge anyway. "A week ago, my rig failed. It was a custom job, so it had to be sent out for repairs. While I was waiting, unconnected, I noticed that my thinking was clearer, less interference. There were other things, like people watching me in the street. When one would turn away, another would follow me with his eyes."

Dixon held up his hands to forestall her. "Sounds like a classic case of disconnect paranoia. Going cold turkey from the Net can do that."

Jaz fixed him with a laser-intensity stare. "Yes. But have you ever wondered *why*? There's more. I went to the library to find out what was happening. As I read, I found articles—Orley's was one—that talked about a metaintelligence arising from the minds of all connected users. As I read, the articles disappeared from the published record.

"When I tried to tell people about this, Herridge and his goons abducted me, faked my death." Jaz swallowed.

"And they took me to a chapel." Her voice fell to a whisper. "Where I met it. The creature calls itself Gestalt."

Dixon wore a poker face. After a beat, he said, "You've been peyoted. Herridge is playing with your sense of reality."

"It was real," Jaz said.

"Of course," he said in a gentle voice. "But"—tapping the side of his head—"everything's real when it passes through here."

He didn't believe her. She'd dared tell him the truth that frightened her. And he thought she was crazy.

"It doesn't matter whether you believe," she said in clipped tones. "Gestalt exists. It controls people through the Net, steals part of their neural processing to survive, and I won't contribute to it." Jaz shoved past him and straight-armed the door. "You coming or not?"

Dixon slapped the front of his jacket and checked his holster. "I'm ready."

Caltech was only five blocks away, so they walked. Decades of electric-powered vehicles had cleaned the air so the San Gabriel Mountains to the north were clearly outlined against the sky.

They entered the campus from the northwest, a round white auditorium rose up in front of them, its peaked roof held up by many thin, diamond-shaped columns. To the west of the auditorium was a long reflecting pool with leaping fountains. The sight captivated her just as it had when she was a child. Jaz watched the water fall in graceful arcs.

Students walked and scurried between the buildings, paying minimal attention to the physical world.

The Jorgensen Laboratory, where Orley taught his class, was a three-story tan building with heavy horizontal lines. Concrete steps led up to the front entrance.

Inside, the building was shaped like a square racetrack around the central elevators. Jaz and Dixon waited outside of the classroom where Orley was giving his lecture.

Jaz peeked in through a vertical glass window set into the door. The room was packed with students, and gauging from the telescoping camera built into the ceiling, Jaz suspected others attended via telepresence.

Orley was lean and stooped slightly at his shoulders as if he had always been slightly taller than everyone else. He was dressed in jeans and a tweed jacket. He gesticulated with his arms as he spoke, and tapped an old-style data pad to change the display on the wallboard. The image displayed now was a network of distributed systems.

While they waited for Orley to finish, Dixon hummed a tune and checked out coeds passing by.

"They're half your age," Jaz whispered as Dixon's head swiveled to watch two young women.

"But which half?" asked Dixon, grinning wolfishly.

The classroom door opened, and students wandered out. Dixon and Jaz stood up straight, ready to confront the man they had flown two thousand miles to meet.

Orley stepped out. In his left hand, he carried the antique palmtop computer he used in class. This close, Jaz saw details she hadn't noticed in the video recordings. At his temples, where the two metallic triangles were embedded in his skin, his hair had strands of gray mixed in with the blond. And there were circles of exhaustion under his eyes.

Dixon stepped forward to intercept him.

Orley looked up. His brow furrowed in puzzlement. "Yes? Can I assist you?" His eyes turned to Jaz.

She saw his pupils dilate slightly. It was one of the signs Jordon had taught her to look for; it indicated his attraction to her. Jaz felt ashamed.

Orley looked from Jaz, to Dixon, and then back to Jaz. "You don't look like students." His eyes unfocused as his attention turned away from the physical. Jaz would have sworn he was connected. Were the devices at his temple an auxiliary storage device? Memory implants had been common until everyone learned that it was cheaper and more convenient to store information on the Net.

Dixon stepped forward, crowding Orley so that he took a step back toward the door. They were of a height.

One muscular, the other lean. Orley looked shorter, however, because his shoulders hunched forward. Had he always tried to hide himself away from the world?

"This is about connections." Dixon tapped his own temple and looked at Orley significantly. "If you've just accessed the Net, I think you know who I am."

Orley eyes narrowed, "Yes, Dixon Tully. I have heard of you."

Dixon closed his eyes, composing his next words before he said, "Then you know why I'm not wearing a data mask."

"Yes, I do. Do you often accost perfect strangers and tell them the details of your parole?"

Dixon's face reddened, but when he spoke, his voice was level. "I'm hoping you can help me with those details."

"Ah, I see." Orley's eyes fixed on Jaz. "And where do you fit into this?"

"I'm here to help Dixon," Jaz said. That, at least, was true.

Dixon slid his arm around Jaz's waist and Jaz tried not to flinch.

"I see," said Orley. "Well, Mr. Tully, I suggest you appeal to the parole board about your problem. You were tried and convicted by a court of your peers. I don't really see why I should intervene." He pushed past Dixon.

Jaz stopped him with a hand on his shoulder. "Would you help Dixon if we helped you with your research?"

He turned and looked at her slender hand. "Possibly, but I don't see how a criminal could help me predict computational neural trends."

"Not that," Jaz whispered. "Your *other* research."

Orley's face blanched. "I don't know what you're talking about."

Dixon, his arm still around Jaz, leaned toward Orley and said in a low voice, "Yes, you do."

Jaz quietly said, "I read your paper on neural patterns arising in the chaos of the Net. I've seen it, too. The beast that lives in our dreams. The whole is greater—"

Orley's lips barely moved as he finished the line. "Than the sum of its parts." He searched their unconnected faces. Coming to some decision, Orley said, "You interest me. But I am busy at the moment. Perhaps we could meet this evening. There is a club on Del Mar Boulevard, called Asylum."

Orley pushed past Dixon, bumping shoulders on the way. "What time?" Jaz asked.

Orley looked back at Jaz, his face outlined by the sun. "Midnight." He walked away from them, toward an outdoor cafeteria. Green canvas umbrellas sheltered the tables from the sun.

"What a creepy fellow," Dixon said.

They walked north across campus, stepping off the path occasionally to avoid students who ricocheted along the sidewalks like random particles. As they walked, Dixon slipped a hand around Jaz's waist. She pushed it away.

He whispered in her ear. "Shouldn't you be friendlier to me? Orley's cohorts might be watching."

Jaz scanned the lawn and walkways around the auditorium for watchers. The eyes of most students were hidden by full-immersion goggles; it was hard to tell if the people turned toward her and Dixon saw them, or the Net.

At the hotel that evening, Jaz changed into a black-and-silver dress over black tights for the club. She slipped her Odin's Eye into a matching purse, which she slung over her shoulder. Dixon exchanged his cotton T-shirt for one of metallic silver, fabricated from fine links of chain mail. It flowed over his hairless chest.

Why did a man who looked that good have to come with such an exasperating personality?

They hired a taxi to drop them off at Asylum. Jaz slipped on her Odin's Eye long enough to pay the doorman. It would also give Herridge and the others an indication where they were—in case the night turned dangerous.

The warehouse-sized room was full of students in their

twenties and throbbing music so loud you could barely hear yourself think. Despite the superior sound quality of direct-brain music transmissions, there was something visceral about feeling a bass beat pulse in your breast-bone.

It was dark, filled with fog and strobing lights that pulsed in time with the music and the brain patterns of the dancers. The dancers wore clothing that ranged from body stockings that covered body and face to G-strings and nothing else.

What would Orley, a quiet researcher, be doing in a place like this? In the center of the floor, connected dancers writhed together in a wild rhythm that threatened to leave the group tangled in a hopeless ball. But, with the cooperation engendered by the Net, they produced ever more complex patterns. Dancers emerged between sets to grab bottled water, new partners, and stim sticks.

The atmosphere made Jaz uncomfortable. It reminded her of the night she'd learned how different she was. Was there a young girl or boy out on that floor about to make the same mistake she had? Naturals were rare, one in a thousand, but with Caltech nearby, the local population was probably stacked.

The thought struck her. What would it be like to dance in a room full of naturals? Where you could dance and not worry about leakage into others? Where their defenses were strong enough to deflect your transmissions, and you only had to worry about being swept away in theirs?

Jaz slipped on her Odin's Eye and ordered drinks from the bar. As soon as she was done, she removed the Eye.

The cola Jaz ordered came watery and flat. A long-stemmed cherry bobbed among the ice cubes, as out of place among them as she was in this loud place of exuberant youth. Seven years older than the writhing crowd on the floor, Jaz felt like it was centuries. Had she ever been that young, that carefree?

Dixon sipped his vodka and watched the sea of dancers. He growled. "Where's Orley? We've been here an hour."

Jaz shrugged. "Maybe he never intended to show up. It doesn't seem like his kind of place."

"Maybe he likes to sit and watch the show," Dixon said, gesturing to the writhing sea of flesh.

"I don't think so. He's . . . cultured."

Dixon's left eyebrow rose. "Perhaps, but he's still a man."

At one a.m. they gave up on Orley and started toward the door. Then they saw him. Orley stood at the entrance, speaking in a low voice to the bouncer. The man nodded and pointed at Jaz and Dixon. Orley made his way through the crowd toward them. The grinding wail of synthesized metal-on-metal filled the air. Orley pressed his lips against Jaz's ear, a sudden gesture of intimacy that startled her. He said, "Follow me."

He led them to the back, past the bathrooms and banking kiosks, and down a flight of stairs. The decor changed. Black-painted concrete was replaced by sweating bricks. Orley unlocked the door with a brass key. The basement room was paneled in dark walnut and filled with leather armchairs. It looked like a men's club gone to seed. Stuffing leaked out of the chairs, and one with only three legs tilted against the wall.

A young woman waited there. She was thin, almost skeletally so. Her hair was brown and hung in a greasy ponytail at the nape of her neck. Her sallow skin looked like bruises around her deep-sunk eyes. The overall impression was of a heroin addict, or someone who spent too much time in their mind and let their body decay around them. In that, she reminded Jaz of the witch. There was a black duffel bag on the ground next to the young woman.

Orley let Jaz and Dixon enter the room ahead of him, then locked the door. He dropped the key in his pocket. "Place your palms on the wall, please."

"What?" said Dixon.

"My associate will check you for weapons."

Jaz and Dixon exchanged a look. There didn't seem to be any way out of this. Apparently Dixon reached the same conclusion. He opened his jacket. "Just the gun."

The thin woman snatched the automatic from Dixon's holster and carried it to Orley.

Orley hefted it appreciatively. "Thank you. Now turn around please."

"Aw, come on," said Dixon. "We've given you our only weapon."

"Then there can be no harm in patting you down." Orley gestured with the gun. "Please. This is necessary."

With an exasperated sigh, Dixon whirled and placed his palms on the wood paneling. Jaz followed suit.

The thin woman's hands patted her thoroughly, sliding up between her thighs in an uncomfortable familiarity. She heard Dixon suck in a breath.

"They're clean."

"Excellent." To Jaz and Dixon, Orley said, "You may sit."

Jaz eyed the other woman warily as she picked a chair near the door and sat down. Dixon sat to her right, Orley to her left. The woman lounged sideways in a chair, eyeing them through slitted eyes.

Orley didn't introduce her. He turned to Jaz and Dixon. "What, exactly, did you want to speak to me about?"

"Is this room secure?" Dixon asked, glancing about for cameras.

"Yes. It was built before Unification and never brought up to code. As such, it is unregistered in the architectural record." His eyes met Jaz's. "I think you understand why that is significant."

Jaz lowered her head a fraction of a centimeter. She pointed at the woman. "Who is she?"

"Tate Wilson. You may speak in front of her. She and I have no secrets."

Jaz narrowed her eyes. A girlfriend? That would complicate her attempts at seduction. Tate looked barely eighteen, too young for Orley. But he wouldn't be the first professor to dip into the student body.

Dixon sat on the edge of his seat, elbows on his knees. "If you can give me back the Net, I'll do anything for you—anything at all."

His tone was sincere. Either Dixon was a very good actor, or he meant it. Jaz wondered if Dixon, too, planned to switch sides. Did Herridge know how tenuous his hold on them was? He didn't seem the kind of man who left anything to chance. The thought worried her. Gestalt had been able to analyze their psychological profiles over the course of their lifetimes. Surely it could predict their betrayal.

Orley rocked back in his seat and glanced at Tate. "Perhaps, Mr. Tully. It depends on whether the government spliced a compulsion into your established connection mnemonics, or disrupted the patterns themselves."

"Will you try?" Dixon asked. His whole body seemed to hum with tension.

Orley turned in his seat to face Jaz. "That depends on what you can offer me. What do you know about my work? My *other* work."

Jaz glanced at Tate. She had pulled the duffel closer to her chair and leaned over the arm, rooting around in it. What was in there? A weapon? Jaz swallowed and looked back to Orley. "You don't wear a connection? Why is that?"

"I choose not to. And you?"

Jaz told him about her data mask malfunctioning. The isolation and loneliness she'd felt, but also the clarity, as if some part of her mind was no longer distracted. Then she told him about the watchers in the street, and the assumptions she'd made based on all these random details. "Am I crazy?"

Orley's eyes were nearly black in the dim lighting. "I don't know. I've never been inside your mind." Not yet, his tone implied. "Why come to me? There are thousands of computational scientists in the world. Your own mother, for one."

"I don't want her involved. I chose you because of your paper in *The Journal of Distributed Computing,* 'Pattern Recognition in Large-scale Systems and the Worldwide Network.' You hint at the possibility of a human-generated overmind. I think something's evolved on the Net. Something that uses us."

Orley waved Tate over. She picked up the duffel, stumbling under its weight, and dragged it to where Jaz and Dixon sat.

"Before I answer any questions," Orley said, "I need to know which side you are on."

"I'm on my own side," Dixon said.

"Perhaps." Orley brushed a strand of hair out of his eyes. "But in the past, certain . . . governmental agencies have sent agents to investigate my research. I must be sure of each new acquaintance. Tate is a talented young woman, with a very flexible view of reality." Orley tousled Tate's head like a proud parent.

The woman kneeled beside him, extracting a bundle of silver wires and beads from the bag. It looked like a tangled spiderweb woven with solidified dew. Whatever it was, it was not mass-produced; Jaz had never seen anything like it before.

Orley continued. "Her flexible viewpoint is a liability when trying to get along in the world. Tate absorbs the worldview of people around her. She floundered in school, drifting from one host personality to the next. Nearly flunked out because of her inattention in classes."

Tate beamed up at Orley, as if he was her savior. If Orley wasn't sleeping with Tate, it wasn't because the girl was unwilling.

"But her lack of self is useful in merging with another's mind. Who shall she probe first?"

"Me," said Dixon. "But first I want that door unlocked. And if something happens to me, I want your promise that Jaz can walk out."

"How noble. I salute your ideals. Unfortunately"—Orley moved the gun to point at Jaz—"Ms. Reese is dangerous to me. If you or she is with the government, I cannot afford to let either of you leave." His eyes looked sad. "I do regret that. But I am engaged in a war. If I lose, humanity will be lost."

"You?" Jaz asked Dixon. "How can Tate scan you? You can't even touch a rig."

Dixon sized up Tate, who had shaken out the spider's web into a glittering dumbbell of beadwork. There were two flexible sacks with collars at the open end. Between them were a tangle of wires, dripping with data gems and overprocessors.

"The people who set up my blocks left back doors," Dixon explained, "so I could be scanned. Tate looks capable of ferreting those pathways out." He grimaced. "There will be pain, but as long as I'm not driving the rig, it should work." He took off his jacket and draped it over a nearby chair. Then he lay down on the floor.

Tate slipped one of the sacks over Dixon's head. The fabric flowed over his skin, adhering like a thick layer of paint. Tate locked the collar around his neck, then slipped the second sack over her head. Their faces were outlined in silver. Tate's expression slipped into Dixon's worried bluff.

It looked like a combat rig. Similar in function to the body stocking she'd worn with Agent N, but instead of mirroring body function, this let one person control another's brain directly. Dangerous for both parties. Each brain was an individual work of art. Certain areas of the brain had common topologies—specialized for speech, or visual recognition, or pattern matching, but the internal memory structures were more individualized than a fingerprint. Every experience changed the entire neural map, the way pulling one thread of a web affects the others. The same current that might bring up a memory of childhood in one person could damage another. If Tate synchronized herself too closely to Dixon, she might overwrite parts of her neural map with his—or vice versa.

"Don't do this," Jaz said, rising to her feet.

Orley grabbed her arm. "It has already begun."

Dixon and Tate lay head to head on the ground. In unison they moaned, and twitched. It was hard to watch, like two people having the same nightmare. More intimate than making love.

Jaz chewed her lip and watching them as endless minutes ticked by.

"You truly care for him."

She glared up at Orley and pointed at the figures locked in silent combat. "How can you condone this?

It's inhuman, an invasion of privacy. Dixon came to you for *help.*"

"I regret this necessity. But I and my associates must be sure of your intentions before we take you into our confidence."

"No one sent us. And if the government wanted to stop you," Jaz said, "a bullet in the brain would be much simpler than sending in agents."

Orley stared at Jaz, tapping his lower lip with his fore-finger. Jaz had the uneasy feeling that, even without a connection, he was trying to read her mind. "Then they must need me alive. I wonder why."

On the floor, Tate and Dixon spoke in unison, "Professor, I'm ready. He's clean—Of course I'm clean—Ask."

Orley's eyebrows rose as he leaned forward. "You live up to your reputation, Dixon, if you can speak while Tate drives. She is quite good at what she does."

"So. Am. I."

"Are you in pain?"

"Yes." The word grunted out in Tate's piping tones and Dixon's baritone.

"But you are connected, in a fashion. See, I've helped you already."

"What. Do. You. Want?"

Orley said, "Who do you work for?"

"Myself."

"Have you had any dealings with government agencies lately? The NSA perhaps?"

"Of course."

Orley inhaled sharply and scooted forward to the edge of his seat. "No lies now, Mr. Tully. Tate would know. What relationship do you have with the NSA?"

"They oversee my sentence and parole."

Jaz was struck by the flexibility of Dixon's interpretation. Everything he said was true, and all of it designed to deceive. He must be doing it without even elevating the response of his sympathetic nervous system—Tate would notice anything that obvious. How did he exercise such control?

Jaz began to sweat. Would she be able to do as well

when her time came? Jaz closed her eyes while the questioning continued. She used skills the witch had taught her. Built a new truth from the facts, one in which she was Dixon's lover, eager to help him and afraid of Gestalt. She'd broken into the NSA's archives and learned of Orley's involvement with the overmind. Jaz wove them into a new reality and convinced herself it was true.

Dixon was answering a question about the conditions of his release when Jaz finished. She worried for him and about the woman rummaging through his brain. Jaz surprised herself with the strength of her jealousy. She'd known Dixon only a short—no, for months. Jaz encouraged warm emotions for Dixon to wash over her. She fixed it to his attractiveness. It was easy to be in lust with him. She could use that to believe she loved him.

"How did you meet Jaz?" Orley asked.

"In the hospital where the NSA set my conditioning. She was recovering from a hiking accident," Dixon answered, his breathing easier now than when he had started. Jaz noticed sweat darkening his T-shirt.

"Do you love her?" Orley asked.

"What the hell does that have to do with anything?" Jaz asked.

"If you are truly lovers, and not agents, everything. Mr. Tully, do you love Jasmine Reese?"

"I think so," Dixon said in a quiet voice. "As much as I can love anyone. Sorry, Jaz."

"Tate?"

"Truth. As he knows it, anyway. You want me to find out how he really feels about her?" It was difficult picking out who was speaking at any given moment, since both of them answered each question.

Orley contemplated the two people lying on the floor, then looked up at Jaz. She felt poleaxed; it was almost as bad as when Ian had told her he didn't really love her. Some of that must have showed on her face, because Orley said, "No, Tate. Some things should be private. What about the other answers, his feelings about the government?"

"Genuine. He hates them. Can we finish this? It's pretty Freudian in here. He keeps undressing my avatar."

"Enough. Bring him out of it."

After a moment of stillness, Tate unstrapped the Velcro that held the neck collar in place and pushed up the silver netting. Then she helped Dixon out. He stood up, shook his arms and legs like a dog drying itself. Then he adjusted his crotch.

Jaz was scandalized. Dixon just grinned. "Have to make sure it's still there. Merging with a woman always leaves me a bit disoriented."

Jaz shook her head. "You're disgusting."

He grinned back. "And you love it." He planted a big wet kiss on her mouth. His eyes were open, staring at Orley as he did so. Obviously staking a claim. Jaz pushed Dixon away. "Not now."

The floor was dusty and speckled with dark stains Jaz hoped were coffee. She looked down at the dress she was wearing, then the floor.

"Allow me." Dixon lifted his jacket off the chair and spread it on the floor for her.

"Thank you." Jaz kneeled on the leather, then lay down. It was a helpless feeling, to be prone in front of strangers. She slipped on the rig. There was a claustrophobic second as the fabric molded to her face. Despite the tight fit, air passed freely through the mesh. Jaz inhaled, centering herself, and getting ready for the assault.

She heard Tate lay down next to her and fit the second rig onto her head. Then physical sound was gone and there was only the roaring of the surf. The ocean was small, a mere puddle that Jaz could see from end to end—her mind's way of expressing the limitation of a two-person network.

Tate was there, a ball of kaleidoscopic color that hovered above the waves. It was beautiful, flashing electric blue, hot pink, ultraviolet, and neon green.

"What do you want?" Jaz asked.

The ball sprouted spikes, suddenly a sea urchin. "You," a disembodied voice said. The spikes flew off, diving deep into the sea, a hail of spines, till nothing was left.

The pain was like an electric current running through her body. Jaz was aware of her entire brain at once. Currents running down little-used neural pathways excited memories she hadn't used in years. Her mother tucking her in bed after a conference. Her first kiss. The first time she'd had sex. The grief she'd felt when her grandmother died. All of it happened at once. Jaz felt like a carbonated ocean, so much was bubbling beneath her surface.

The induction mask was a hood, input came from nearly 360 degrees of electronics. But there were loci in the electronics. Find the loci and stop the attack. She wasn't thinking about deception now, just survival.

Jaz stilled her emotional response, soothing her adrenal medulla into secreting less epinephrine. Tate probably counted on an agitated state to reduce the chance that Jaz could resist, or lie. When Jaz calmed, she sensed individual centers of induction. It was hopeless. The attack rig was a work of art. There were thousands of neuroinductors spread all over her head.

"I'm in," Jaz heard her own voice say in unison with Tate's.

Not for long, Jaz thought in a primitive part of her brain that Tate didn't control.

"What is your name?" Sound was muffled, as if she heard an echo and not the original words. Was Tate changing what Orley said, or just filtering out other comments, like those Dixon might be making?

"Jasmine Reese." Jaz was startled by the words; she hadn't intended to say them.

"Why are you here?"

"To stop the beast. To help Dixon."

With each answer Jaz felt Tate driving the induction centers, searching for neural responses, then checking their veracity by ensuring that the neural paths led to memories that supported the statement. It must be exhausting work. For each statement Jaz made, Tate followed hundreds, sometimes thousands of associations. It explained why the questioning took so long. Fine. If she wanted associations, Jaz would give her associations.

Orley asked, "Do you work for the NSA?"

Jaz took each word and thought about all the connotations it implied. She split her thinking into four different streams. What was work? Jaz thought about every job she'd ever held: working at being happy, work as a force acting over a distance, work as a strange word with a "w" followed by "ork." Work backward "krow" and where that might lead her.

"She's fighting me." Tate ground out, using both sets of vocal cords.

"If you want my help," Orley told Jaz, "your cooperation is in order."

"It's not in my nature to allow myself to be mindhacked. I must have control. Otherwise, we can find someone else to help Dixon."

There was a moment of silence, and Jaz wished she could see Orley's expression. At last he said, "I understand. Tate, pull back to observation only."

"I won't be able to do as accurate a reading—"

"Understood. Do it, Tate."

The spikes that had lanced through the water turned into needlefish, swam together, and melted into an oil slick on the surface of the tiny ocean. Streamers of color dropped from the slick into the depths. But they hung there, passive, not exciting emotions and memories as they previously had.

Jaz could not control the surge of relief that filled her at this mental breathing space. She felt Tate's resentment as a vinegary tang in the saltwater.

"I do not work for the NSA; I want your help to work against them." And it was true, without the witch's mental trickery. She'd made up her mind about that when she was released.

"Why?"

"Gestalt must be stopped. Humanity must be freed." Jaz felt Tate's mind perk with interest. The ribbons of colors became more defined as she listened for stray thoughts in the sea of Jaz's mind.

"Not here. We will discuss that later. Tate?"

"Truth. She fears the beast. I see memories of it stalk
ing her in a public place, watching her in a library. She
researches the phenomena and finds your name."

"And Mr. Tully, are there memories of him?"

Jaz had prepared herself for this. She'd woven a fiction
of a love together with him. But was the witch's instruc
tion enough, would the fantasy convince herself as well
as Tate? She daydreamed a romance and made herself
believe. When Jaz felt the colored streamers shy away
from a heavy petting scene, she filled her thoughts with
how it felt to make love to Dixon. The hot throbbing
and pulsing in her groin . . . Tate pulled away. The
streamers shrank. These were things the girl did not want
to know. An aversion to sex? Interesting. Jaz wondered
what had happened in Tate's past to cause it. There was
a moment's temptation to look, to see if the combat rig
could be pushed both ways.

"Yes. They're quite pornographic. Can we end this?"
Tate's double-voiced words came out in a wheedle.

"No deception at all?"

"None I can detect at this reduced level," Tate warned

"Understood. Thank you, Tate."

Jaz felt the woman's tiny hands pull open the collar at
Jaz's throat, a little too roughly. The light in her eyes
made her squint.

A warm masculine hand helped her up. It was Dixon.
"Pornographic, eh?" he said and winked lasciviously at
her.

The fantasy she'd created to fool Tate still lingered in
Jaz's mind, making her feel close to him. She wrapped
her arm around his waist, and his arm fell easily about
her shoulders. "So will you help us?" Jaz asked.

Tate glared at them while she repacked the duffel.
"They may not be working for the government, but that
doesn't mean we should take them in. I don't trust her.
She threw me out too easily, like she was prepared for
it."

"Ms. Reese is a natural, working in the field. I would
expect her to have defenses."

Tate snorted. "They're trouble. We should pack them, like we did the first—"

"Enough." Orley cut her off with an abrupt wave of his hand. To Jaz and Dixon he said, "Come with me. I have someone I would like you to meet."

CHAPTER 15

Orley led them out of the dance club. They walked along Del Mar Boulevard until they reached the fire station on the north end of campus. In the middle of the night, the parking lot was an empty expanse of concrete. Although Jaz could see lights on in the Moore and Watson Laboratories, the lawns and walkways outside were eerily silent. A couple of students crossed their path, headed toward the towers of graduate-student housing.

The full moon was setting, and it cast a silver glow over the campus, broken by the streetlights and blue safety lights. Gestalt was all around them, in the maintenance equipment, in traffic sensors, and the minds of students they passed. Jaz knew it watched them. She wondered whether Gestalt was pleased that Orley had taken them into his confidence so quickly.

Dixon took her hand. His was clammy. She looked up at him, and he flicked his eyes toward Orley. Jaz wished they were connected so she could know his thoughts. He looked worried. Was he afraid Orley was leading them into a trap? Or was it just the strain of Tate's probe? She squeezed his hand in what she hoped was a reassuring way. He squeezed back, in a rhythmic pattern of long, and short, and silences. Morse code? If she'd been on the Net, it would be a picosecond's task to decipher the code. But if they were connected, there would be no need for surreptitious signals. Jaz squeezed Dixon's hand tighter until he stopped.

Tate brought up the rear, stumbling under the weight

of the duffel bag. Dixon offered to carry it, but she'd looked at him as if he was trying to steal her soul, hitched the shoulder strap higher on her shoulder, and walked after them.

Orley approached the Beckman Institute. The fountains in the reflecting pool were turned off for the night. The moon wobbled gently on the surface of the still water. Beyond the five archways that led into the building's central courtyard, Jaz could see a large black polyhedron on a pedestal in the central fountain.

But they didn't go into the courtyard. Instead, Orley led them up an exterior stairwell to the north research wing. On the second floor, the lock clicked as he approached and he held it open while the others filed in. Jaz saw a plastic ident-bracelet on his wrist. But the electronics at his temples—surely that was data jewelry— why would he need the bracelet? Then Jaz remembered the north wing of this building was opaque to Gestalt. At least that much of Herridge's briefing was true.

Lights in the hallway lit up as they neared, then shut off again as they passed. Orley stopped at a door that had both a deadlock and a hinge for a padlock, now unhooked. It was nearly three a.m. The halls were quiet. Jaz heard only the hum of air-conditioning.

Orley knocked on the door and whispered, "It's me, I've brought guests."

A bald man wearing a blue cable-knit sweater opened the door. He blinked at Jaz and Dixon, then opened the door wider to let them all in.

The room had a high ceiling and was spacious. A circle of chairs was arranged in the center of the room. The people sitting in them didn't look like dangerous conspirators. They represented a blend of nationalities and ages from late twenties to a woman who appeared to be in her eighties. All were dressed in conservative slacks and tweed jackets. If anything, this looked like a faculty meeting.

In one corner, on a black-topped table, rested a molecular fabrication tank. Around it lay components of data jewelry like Orley wore. Jaz looked at the faces of the others and saw what they had in common; each one either had implants like Orley's or wore the triangles on a removable headband.

The man holding the door extended his hand. "Jasmine Reese, I worked with your mother. I'm Dr. Niklas Jensen."

Jaz didn't recognize him. Without a Net connection to copies of her childhood memories, she couldn't place him in context. She shook his hand and scanned the rest of the room.

The windows on the far wall would have overlooked the northern campus, but they were covered with heavy foil sheeting. High-end server equipment hummed in a locked rack near the farthest window. Jaz wondered how Orley handled National Science Foundation tours of his laboratory. Did he spend a week moving all the surreptitious equipment to a safe storage facility?

In the far corner, talking to a dark-skinned man, was a woman with a chin-length cap of auburn hair. Middle age had settled on her like a thick blanket, but Jaz recognized the graduate student who had been with Orley when he discovered Gestalt.

"Who are all these people?" Jaz asked Orley.

"My colleagues, many of whom are on sabbatical. I have recruited them over the past year to work on a very special project. One you will find interesting."

Tate dropped the duffel on the ground just inside the door. "This isn't wise, John. It's too soon. You don't know them."

Orley said, "You scanned them. You said they were safe."

"Not *her*. You wouldn't let me do a full scan."

"I've worked with Ms. Reese's mother on several projects," said Dr. Jensen, "studied her daughter's career as she grew up. I assure you, we have nothing to fear from Jasmine Reese."

Jaz felt her skin heat at his false assumption. If she was going to switch sides, maybe she should level with Orley now. Give the whole game away and make a clean

break of it. But caution held her back. She didn't want
to reveal herself until she knew what he was up to and
was sure his side was the right one.

Dixon squeezed her shoulder, as if he sensed her emotional turmoil. She looked up into his eyes, and he shook
his head imperceptibly.

She touched his hand in acknowledgment of the
message.

Tate stared hard at Jaz and Dixon. She pulled out a
headband that ended in a pair of triangles like those set
into Orley's temples. She lifted her greasy hair and
wrapped the band around her head and over her ears.
Then she closed her eyes in communion.

"I thought your group wasn't connected to the Net,"
said Jaz, pointing at her temples, then Orley's. "What
are those?"

"Let's get this meeting under way and I'll explain."
He clapped his hands and the room quieted as everyone
took their seats. Orley gestured for Jaz and Dixon to
join them.

"This is Jasmine Reese and Dixon Tully. I believe all
of you have heard of Mr. Tully's exploits."

A chuckle went around the room, and Dixon's ears
pinked.

"Some of you have met Ms. Reese's mother, Dr.
Anita Reese."

A murmur of agreement.

"They've come to us for help, and to join us."

Tate sulked in the back of the room but did not
comment.

"Are you sure it's safe to bring them here?" asked a
nervous-looking man with sandy-gray hair and washed
out blue eyes. "You just met them tonight. Now they've
seen our faces." He twisted his hands together in his lap.
"I mean, with the attempts on us in December . . ."

"It's a risk we have to take. They are both naturals,
and we need their help. Tate tested their loyalty. They
passed."

Tate looked like she was about to say something, but

Orley's glance made her slump back into quiescence. She
sat down on the floor against a server rack and wrapped
her bony arms around her knees.

Orley instructed Jaz, "Tell them what you told me
about the beast."

Jaz described again the failure of her rig, the watchers
in the street, the feeling of being part of something, but
also the feeling that she lost something on the Net. When
she was done, the others in the room nodded.

Orley rose. "She has discovered what we all know to
be true. That there is something in the Net, a meta
intelligence that uses humanity, which has arisen out of
our collective subconscious. She knows of Gestalt."

Jaz felt Dixon beside her, humming like a plucked
string. He'd been the one driven to contact Orley and
this group. He was the one with the desperate need, and
Orley had forgotten about him. She said, "Dixon knows
too. We will help you with your research if you will
help him."

Dixon flashed her a look, and said, "We're both top
natural talent. Help me regain the Net, and I'll do whatever you want."

"Anything?" Orley said. "You don't even know what
our plan is yet."

A chill ran up Jaz's spine at Orley's tone.

"I am a convicted criminal," Dixon said. "Some would
say that makes me capable of anything."

Orley nodded. "And you, Jasmine, what are you capable of? Your psychological profile shows you as very conservative when it comes to breaking the law."

Jaz raised her chin. "What exactly are we talking
about?"

The ring of people tensed. Orley said, "A little of my
own history first. Tate tells me you saw the video record
of me and Moira in the lab, researching social patterns
in the Net, saw Gestalt make first contact. What you
cannot know is what I did after I disconnected from
the Net."

"You continued to teach and work here."

"Yes. And I applied for grants to study Gestalt. They

were turned down." He stroked his chin absently. "I believe the creature is afraid of our learning too much about it. Afraid of the consequences, should we reveal its existence to humanity."

"The first human it contacted recoiled," said Jaz. "How could it not worry what would happen if humanity as a whole learned of its existence? As a species, we're not known for tolerating things we fear."

Orley looked intently at Jaz. "How do you know *I* was the first person it contacted?"

Jaz's stomach contracted. She knew from her time in the chapel, because Gestalt had told her. She stared at Orley, not sure how to back out of this one.

Dixon filled the silence. "We've been doing research of our own. I told you we were good. Jaz hacked Gestalt in a power run. I don't have access to the Net, but I've been teaching her some of the techniques to get into a system, gather information, and get out without detection. You begin to see how a 'mere criminal' could help you?"

Orley looked at Dixon with surprise. "You hacked Gestalt? Impossible. No mere human mind could—"

"Maybe not. But Jaz can, using my techniques. I've spent my whole life in combat computation, and I haven't had to restrict my learning to things that were legal. I've traveled the world, learning from the best hackers and security gurus. Help me, and we'll help you." Dixon reached out his hand proprietarily to Jaz.

She took it, grateful that his quick thinking had salvaged her slip of the tongue, had even turned it into an argument for Orley to take them in. Jaz hoped they were never called upon to make good on Dixon's boasts. There was no way he could be as good as he presented himself—was there?

Orley looked thoughtful. "It seems we may be able to help each other. I apologize for the loyalty test that Tate administered. It was necessary. What we work on now"—he waved his hand airily—"does not have governmental approval. I believe you understand our need for security."

Dixon nodded graciously.

"The NSA in particular has been persistent in trying to infiltrate our research. Like any intelligent creature, Gestalt manipulates its surroundings to protect itself. Unfortunately, human minds are its environment. It controls people with political power, thus it controls the government. The armies of the world are at its command. Our scientific papers are not published. When we go to the media, our stories are disbelieved and never broadcast. We're fighting a ghost—but one that influences the world."

Dixon asked, "If Gestalt is so powerful, and so afraid of you"—he gestured at the people in the room—"why aren't you dead?"

Orley considered the question. He spread his hands. "We have only theories. Perhaps it is loath to waste the resources the people in this room represent. We are all naturals, highly intelligent and trained in computational science. I do not believe Gestalt will kill us unless forced to. Better for it if we can be brought back into the fold.

"But we will never return to the Net. Think about it, Gestalt can control everything: the stock market, public policy, even the thoughts and emotions of individual people. We are Gestalt's neurons and peripherals. Does that terrify you as much as it does me?"

Jaz remembered how Gestalt had stalked her in the library. "Are we safe? If Gestalt is so pervasive, can't it sense us here? Watch us through maintenance cameras, listen to us through security speakers?"

Orley shook his head. "This building is shielded from the Net. Many of the research projects carried out in these labs require isolation. In here, we are safe from surveillance."

"What are you working on?" Jaz asked. "Gestalt cut off your funding when you disassociated yourself from the Net. How much could you accomplish?"

"You might be surprised," Orley said. "We are scientists, people of curiosity who have devoted our lives to finding out how the world works. We want to understand Gestalt. The entity, however, has shown its willingness to use coercion and manipulation of memories to protect its secrets. No, there is only one way to study it. To re-create the environment that gave rise to Gestalt." He tapped the metal triangle on his temple. "This is a connection to a private network which my colleagues and I have created. We've dedicated ourselves to it night and day, providing the mental resources to generate a new overmind of our own devising. While we three have engaged in this discussion in the physical world, the others debate your initiation in the transmissions that pass through and around us."

Jaz found it hard to breathe. She noticed for the first time that the people around her wore vague expressions. Like daydreamers or people connected to the Net. Not the worldwide Net, but a private one created to give rise to another entity like Gestalt—this one created on purpose. "Have you succeeded in creating a second metamind?"

Orley reached into the inner pocket of his blazer and pulled out two headbands like the one Tate had put on earlier. "There is only one way to find out." The headbands gleamed on his palm like a forbidden fruit. "Join us."

CHAPTER 16

Jaz and Dixon reached out to take the headbands from Orley.

Dixon's hand wavered in the air, his arm trembling with effort. His face screwed in pain as his fingers touched the headband. He picked it up and dropped to his knees. With an incoherent scream he lifted the headband to his head.

Jaz snatched it away from him. Dixon fell forward to the floor and lay panting.

"He can't connect until you break his conditioning." Her eyes met Orley's. "And I won't connect until he can." Part of her strength of conviction came from horror at what the government had done to Dixon. But another part was fear. Jaz didn't want to face another overmind without Dixon as backup.

"But surely . . . just to find out." Orley gestured at the headband Jaz now held. "You could tell him about it."

Jaz shook her head. "Not without Dixon. I won't join you until he is free of this compulsion."

Dixon sat up, coughing. Between fits he looked at Jaz with surprise, but he didn't argue.

Orley folded his arms and said with some disgust, "There's no convincing you?"

Jaz squatted and helped Dixon to his feet. "None."

"Such a display of devotion. You're a lucky man, Mr. Tully."

Dixon leaned heavily on Jaz, his breath ragged. "It would seem so."

Orley stepped back and let his eyes unfocus. "Excuse me while I confer with the others." There was a general intake of breath from the connected scientists in the room. Whatever he told them made a stir. Some became alert and studied Jaz and Dixon.

"It can be done," said Dr. Jensen. "My division often advised the government in these cases. I know a neuroscientist who could help us."

"Can he be trusted?" Orley asked. "This is not worth endangering our group."

"My colleague will help us. She owes me a favor."

Everyone came back then, and the room filled with argument and discussion. In the physical world, Jaz had difficulty parsing the different streams of conversation. If she had been connected, it would have been easy.

"It is decided then," Orley said in a shout. When the conversation died down, he continued. "We will cure Mr. Tully, then invite Ms. Reese and him to join us. Their knowledge of systems infiltration will be invaluable to us in obtaining information from Gestalt."

Jaz's stomach clenched. Damn Dixon's boastful claims. They had no way to hack the overmind. And even had their goal been a simple data store, she had no experience breaking into systems. Jaz hoped Dixon would think of something when the time came. Because if Orley suspected they had lied to him, she and Dixon would find out what had happened to the other NSA agents—the hard way.

Orley told Tate, "Escort them to their hotel room while we obtain the necessary equipment. I don't want them left alone until they are connected and we can evaluate their true intent."

Tate scowled. "You don't trust my scan."

"You yourself said it was incomplete. There are things we can do together that none of us can do alone. And have them pack, we'll move them into the Mission house after the procedure."

"Tate this," she said. "Tate that. I'm a graduate student, not a slave."

Orley looked at Tate intently, exchanging a private

communication. From the kaleidoscope of expressions that crossed the young woman's face, she didn't like what he said.

"Fine." Tate rummaged angrily in the duffel bag and pulled out a black-plastic packet. She stuffed it into the breast pocket of her tattered army jacket and chucked the duffel bag at Orley's feet. "You stow this, while I baby-sit." She waved Jaz and Dixon to follow her. "This way."

"We're staying at—"

"The Caltech Doubletree," Tate finished. "We *know*."

They walked outside and got into Tate's cramped car, an old-model Honda Neo with manual controls. There was no backseat. Jaz and Dixon crowded together on the passenger seat.

Tate turned left on Del Mar Boulevard, taking them back toward their hotel. Because she wasn't connected to the Net, Tate manually merged her car into seemingly impenetrable streams of traffic. Jaz shut her eyes more than once, anticipating an impact that never came. The thin girl's reflexes were sharp; they arrived at the hotel intact.

When they got out of the car, Tate slammed the door and glared at them.

"What's wrong?" asked Jaz.

"Everything. You two." She flipped her greasy blond hair out of her eyes. "You especially. And I don't like being off campus, if you know what I mean."

Jaz knew. She looked at the security camera set into the hotel lobby door. That was probably why Orley had sent Tate in his stead. The girl was less vital to the project, more expendable. Tate scowled like she knew it.

They took the elevator up to the fourteenth floor. Jaz waved her bracelet at their door, and it clicked open.

The cleaning bot had been in the hotel room. Jaz saw with relief that all evidence of Dixon's sleeping on the floor had been neatly made up and tucked into the bed. The bot had apparently turned down the thermostat. The room was freezing. The lights came on as soon as the room sensed their ident-bracelets, but the only way to set the temperature was through a direct connection. There was no manual temperature control in the room.

Jaz walked over to her suitcase and pulled out the lotus case, careful to make sure that her body blocked the gun from Tate's view.

"What do you think you're doing?" Tate asked, as Jaz raised the Odin's Eye to her face.

"Turning down the air-conditioning," Jaz said.

Tate snatched the Eye away from Jaz. "I don't think so. No contact with the Net until . . . after. I thought you were afraid of connections, anyway."

"I don't like them, but I don't like being cold, either."

Dixon broke in. "Tate, why don't you use the Eye to adjust the temperature?"

She cocked her head, considering. "Too risky. If it's too cold in here for you, open a window."

Jaz tried, but it was a fully automated building. The windows wouldn't open manually. She huddled on the bed, arms wrapped around her legs. "This is ridiculous."

"You want to stay warm," Tate said, wrapping her army coat tightly about her, "why don't you start packing?"

"What is the Mis—" Dixon asked.

"Ah-ah," Tate said, raising a warning finger. "No questions. Not here."

Jaz sighed and put the Odin's Eye back in its foam cell. She had never unpacked, so there wasn't much to do. She picked her suitcase up and groaned under the weight.

"How's your back?" Dixon asked. There was a warning in his voice. "Do you need to make another chiropractic appointment? You wouldn't want to overdo just as you were getting better."

Jaz met his gaze, then looked over at Tate. The woman leaned against the door, blocking their exit. "I think I'll see if it gets any worse."

Dixon nodded.

The hours passed slowly while they waited for Orley's call. The room came with a full-immersion console, but everyone in the room was either unable or unwilling to connect. Even had she been in the mood for mindless entertainment, Jaz was sure Tate would object on security reasons. The fact that it was freezing in the room only added to the discomfort. Jaz hugged her knees to her chest, but was still cold. She hadn't packed any heavy coats, not for California in April.

She could crawl into bed and huddle under the blankets, but that would make her feel vulnerable. If Tate lashed out, Jaz wanted to be able to react quickly.

Dixon stripped off his leather jacket. "Here, you want this?" Dixon's empty holster reminded Jaz of how much they were in Orley's power. There was gooseflesh on his forearms as he extended the coat.

She waved him off. "No. Then you'd freeze."

He slipped the jacket back on and held open the left side. "We could share."

Jaz inspected his face for any hint of lechery, but it seemed an honest offer, and she was cold. Jaz tucked herself under his arm, burrowing into his warmth.

"Jeez, get a room."

Dixon looked at Tate with an ironic expression. "I believe we did."

Tate rolled her eyes and adjusted her headband. Seconds later her expression grew blank. Jaz envied the woman, able to escape her body's discomfort in a virtual world.

Long minutes later, Tate focused on Jaz and Dixon. "They're ready for you."

The moon had set, and the campus was more deserted than before. They only saw one other person on their trip across the grounds, a student passed out under a live oak tree. Jaz thought she saw his eyelids flicker as they passed. One of Gestalt's watchers? Jaz wondered what Herridge was making of Gestalt's observations. She had no doubt that every look, every word of conversation outside of Orley's lab, was recorded.

Tate led them back down into the basement. The storage room had been reconfigured. A portable electromagnetic induction unit was set up on a folding table. The hoop-size structure was large enough to scan a man's head and neck.

"Where did you get that?" Jaz asked.

"The neurology department," said Orley. "Hurry up, we don't have long. The equipment has to be back before seven a.m."

Dixon removed his leather jacket and the empty holster and handed them to Jaz. "Hold these for me?"

She took the items and leaned forward as if to kiss him. In his ear, Jaz whispered, "Are you sure you want to do this? We don't know their expertise. You might die."

His lips brushed her cheek, and he whispered back, "Without the Net, I am dead."

He lay down on the folding table, which shivered under his weight. Orley positioned Dixon's head in the center of the EMI housing.

Dr. Jensen stood nearby. He slipped off his headband and put on a silver eye patch attached to the EMI. It made him look like a bleached-out pirate.

The EMI unit hummed to life, and a section of the hoop scanned back and forth, passing over Dixon's features.

"We'd better wait outside," Orley said, pulling on Jaz's shoulders.

"No," she said, throwing him off. "I want to stay with him."

The unit stopped scanning, and the man running the machine looked at her with impatience.

Orley said softly, "Even for a man of Dr. Jensen's skill, this procedure is a strain. If we stay, we may endanger your friend."

Jaz was surprised to find her eyes welling with tears. She barely knew Dixon. But they were a team, damn it. She was supposed to look after him.

"Go," Dixon croaked from the EMI unit. "Please."

Jaz nodded and followed Orley out of the room. He led her to his office in the east wing. In his office, every wall was a screen. There was an old-fashioned set of data-gloves and immersion goggles on his desk. The dark gray of the inactive screens made the office seem close and oppressive.

Jaz picked up a glove and weighed it in her hand. "This is how you connect to Gestalt's Net?"

Orley took the glove from her and looked at it. "Yes. Moira modified these antiques to work with the new communication protocols. They are cumbersome, but protect me from the metamind's influence. Gestalt soothes people, calms them like a spider anesthetizing its prey."

"I know," Jaz said. "That was the first thing I noticed when I was disconnected. The loneliness."

He set the glove down on his desk. "Is that why you started a relationship with Mr. Tully? I've wondered about that. It's not an obvious pairing."

"Jealous?"

Orley snorted a laugh. "Hardly. My work is the only relationship I need. Anything else would be a distraction."

His tone wasn't convincing. Jaz knew this was her opening to make a move. She could almost feel Jordon prompting her. All she had to do was touch the man, and something would happen. Jaz wasn't surely exactly what . . . but something.

She started to reach forward, but stopped herself. It wasn't right to manipulate someone that way. What had Orley done to deserve that kind of betrayal?

Jaz considered leveling with him, telling him the whole truth about her and Dixon. But no, Dixon was too vulnerable right now. And there was still a question in Jaz's mind about what, exactly, Orley had created. What if his overmind was worse than Gestalt? She didn't want to commit herself until she had more information.

"So," she said, "what makes you think Dixon isn't my type?"

Orley looked down at his hands. "I've investigated your life and previous relationships."

Jaz stood up, and put her hands on her hips. "You did what? When?"

His fingers tangled together in his lap. "This afternoon. I had to know everything about you . . . to know if we could trust you. It was nothing personal."

Jaz wasn't so sure. "So what's my type?"

"From previous data, someone more intellectual, with an academic background in science. You've never dated anyone with less than a master's degree. Did you realize that? In addition, you have a high respect for authority. It seems incongruous you would pair with a convicted criminal."

Jaz smoothed a few curling strands of black hair behind her ear and shrugged. "You can't predict someone by past behavior."

Awkward silence filled the room. Then Orley asked, "Do you want to connect to the Net from here? You could, without risk of losing yourself."

Jaz looked at the immersion gear speculatively. "Won't Gestalt feel my presence?"

"Perhaps, but the abstraction of the old-style gear prevents Gestalt from controlling you. I know from experience how much you can miss the Net. Especially a natural as talented as yourself. It's like a drug, that much knowledge and power at your control."

Jaz was tempted. There were messages, no doubt, piling up in her inbox. She could tell Matt and the others that she was alive. But Orley was watching her. Was this a test?

Before she could decide what to do, she heard the faint wail of a scream. A tortured sound echoing from the north wing.

"Dixon!" Jaz rushed to leave the office.

Orley touched a button on his desk, and the door slammed in Jaz's face.

She looked at Orley over her shoulder. "Let me out!"

He approached her slowly from behind the desk. "There was bound to be some discomfort. Dr. Jensen's unbroken attention is important, especially now. The best thing you can do is stay away."

Jaz pounded on the door. She'd been awake for nearly

twenty-four hours straight, and couldn't keep up the strain of multiple layers of deception. Jaz kicked at the door, and then slumped to the floor, crying. "Dixon!"

Orley knelt next to her. He reached out an arm to comfort Jaz. She slapped it away. "I need to see him—now!"

"Later, I promise. As soon as Dr. Jensen is finished."

"If he dies, so help me, I will destroy this conclave of yours." Jaz was shocked to hear herself say the words. It was stupid to challenge Orley, stupid to threaten him that way.

"Shh," he said, slipping an arm around Jaz's shoulders. "It's okay. I know. I know."

Dixon's screams faded to an uneasy silence.

Jaz pressed her face against Orley's shoulder and cried. She cried for herself, coerced into betraying people she liked, for Dixon suffering in the north wing, for Orley who was doomed and didn't know it. She cried for them all, trapped together in a war with an entity that wasn't human.

When Dr. Jensen let them back in the laboratory, Dixon lay on the table, unmoving. His breathing was shallow. Jaz rushed to his side. The skin around his eyes and mouth was unnaturally pale. "Is he all right?"

Dr. Jensen stepped out of Tate's way as she packed up the EMI unit for return to the neurology department. He said, "The procedure was a qualified success. The mnemonic blocks could not be unlocked without the key sequences. I tried several security algorithms, but was not able to reproduce the key. It uses megabit encryption. Even with a better than random generation algorithm, it would take years of trial and error."

Dixon's eyes fluttered open. "Joanie?" he said blearily.

Jaz patted his hands gently. "It's all right. I'm here." To Jensen she said, "That doesn't sound like success to me."

Jensen's face darkened. "You can hardly expect me, in a single night, using a portable unit and help from a colleague I called out of her bed, to be able to undo locks and barriers the government had weeks to instill using a full staff and the latest equipment."

"Dr. Jensen, you are a miracle worker," said Orley. "None of us disputes that. Ms. Reese is just disappointed because she hasn't yet heard what you *have* accomplished."

Dr. Jensen looked mollified. He swiped the back of his hand across his forehead. "Although I was not able to remove the blocks, I was able to open up secondary channels that Mr. Tully can use to interact with our local network. He won't have access to his previous skills and knowledge. He'll have to relearn how to use a connection with these alternate neural pathways—in many ways he will be like a child—but he will be able to join us on the Network."

Jaz looked down at Dixon, who was coming around. "Good thing I'm a fast learner." He reached out his hand toward Orley. "Where's that headband?"

Orley shook his head. "Not now. It's been a long night . . . for all of us. Tate will drive you to the Mission house while Dr. Jensen and I will return the EMI unit. Tomorrow we will introduce you to our network."

"Mission house?" Jaz asked.

"Our network does not have the infrastructure of the worldwide Net. Nor do we have access to the dense wavelength division multiplexing optical networks that Gestalt uses. Because of this, we must maintain a certain physical proximity. This is facilitated by our use of an old boardinghouse. It is an antique, never upgraded for connection jewelry or automated systems. Quite useful for our purposes. You will find it comfortable." Orley walked Jaz and Dixon to the door of the laboratory.

Tate, looking more surly than ever, leaned against the doorjamb. "Ready?" Without waiting for a reply or looking back to make sure they followed her, she left the room.

Jaz helped Dixon off the table, and half carried him, stumbling, toward the door.

"He may have some difficulty walking for the next day or so," Dr. Jensen called after them. "I had to reroute some associations through his basal ganglia. It should clear up within seventy-two hours."

"Great," Jaz muttered under her breath.

Tate had the car started and pulled up to the curb as Jaz and Dixon left the building. Jaz squeezed in the middle, hovering over the central console so Dixon could have most of the passenger seat.

The ride was mercifully short. The old boardinghouse was Spanish architecture: stucco walls, arched doorways and a red tile roof. Each of the upstairs rooms had its own balcony. Dixon stumbled out of the car and Jaz unfolded herself. The ride, brief as it was, had caused her right foot to fall asleep, and she and Dixon lurched their way up the lawn. Tate stayed in the car.

"Don't you live here?" Jaz asked.

"No." Tate took off her headband and stowed it in one of the many pockets of her army jacket. She took out a disposable syringe and snapped a new cartridge into it. After injecting the crook of her arm, she smiled a warm smile at Jaz. "I'm just the hired help. See you in the morning." She drove off.

It was already morning; pink streamers crossed the sky to the east. Jaz and Dixon knocked on the front door. It was opened by Moira, Orley's onetime graduate student, wearing a microfleece bathrobe. She waved them in.

Jaz dropped the suitcases just inside the door. "Can I leave these here for now?"

Moira shrugged and led them up a flight of stairs to the second floor. "Bathroom," she said, pointing at a door at the top of the stairs. They walked past it into a hallway with doors every ten feet. Moira pointed at one at the end of the hall. "I put you in together, on John's request."

It took a moment for Jaz to remember that John was Dr. Orley's given name. "Thank you," she said and helped Dixon over the threshold.

"Sorry about all the trouble," Dixon said once they were alone in the room. "I usually carry my own weight."

"No worries, eh?" Jaz said, in the best fake-Australian accent she could muster.

"Not bad," Dixon said as he collapsed backward on to the bed. "We'll have you talking like a real Sheila in no . . ." He was asleep before he had finished the sentence.

The room was small. It held a double bed, a rocking chair, and a window seat. There was a mirrored door that Jaz supposed was a closet, but she didn't have the energy to investigate. She pulled off Dixon's shoes and tucked the covers over him. He snored slightly. Jaz didn't have the strength to undress or argue about sleeping arrangements. Dixon in his current condition was no threat to her virtue, and she trusted him more than she had a day ago. Jaz kicked off her own shoes and rolled in under the covers next to him.

The rocking motion must have roused him somewhat, because he reached for her and said, "Joanie?"

"No," Jaz said, pushing him away. "It's Jasmine. Jasmine Reese. Remember?"

"Oh, right. Sorry." He scootched away from her on the bed and turned his back to her. "Been a helluva day."

"What did they do to you?" Jaz asked. He was exhausted, but his scream still haunted her. She had to know.

"There aren't words." His voice was small and far away. "An epileptic seizure in hell . . . would come close. A thousand sensations at once . . . no thought."

Jaz reached out and took him in her arms. "Why didn't you stop it?"

His voice, when it came, was a choked whisper. "It's still locked away. Everything I learned. Everything I am. I am nothing if I am not on the Net. Less than nothing."

There was nothing Jaz could say to ease his anguish, so she simply held Dixon until he relaxed and, finally, slept.

CHAPTER 17

Jaz woke late the next morning, better rested than she'd been in months. Warm arms encircled her waist, and she snuggled into the body pressing behind her. For a muzzy-headed moment, she thought it was Ian. Then it all came back to her: Herridge, Gestalt, Orley. It was like waking from a nightmare, to discover the nightmare was real.

Dixon pulled her close and snuffled a warm breath into the back of her neck. Probably he thought she was Joanie. Whoever that was.

It was an awkward moment. One part of her wanted to leap out of bed screaming: a strange man was touching her, had spent the night holding her. But creating a scene would blow their cover. And a small, prurient voice in the back of her head said, "Some part of you liked sleeping with him." That embarrassed her more than Dixon's arms. It had been too long since Ian, way too long.

Jaz patted Dixon's hand and eased out of bed. The black dress she had worn last night was a mass of wrinkles. She tried to smooth it with no effect. "I'm going to wash up," she told Dixon's prone figure.

He grunted and rolled over.

Jaz knelt beside the door to open her suitcase; she remembered leaving it downstairs last night. Someone else must have carried it upstairs. Jaz looked at the inner plate that hid the gun and Odin's eye. Had Orley's people searched the suitcases, found her gun? Of course. She couldn't imagine them passing up the opportunity to learn more about her and Dixon. They'd been infiltrated by the NSA once, so they would be careful. Jaz grabbed a pair of jeans and a red shirt with gold embroidery. If they'd seen the gun, there was nothing she could do about it now.

Jaz took a minute and opened the inner compartment. The Ruger 2032 was nestled in its foam. The case of shells appeared untouched. She checked Dixon's suitcase. His gun was missing. Orley hadn't returned it after their interrogation. Jaz poked Dixon in the foot.

He flinched. "Wha—what?"

She said in a low voice, "I think they know about my gun. Last night, they had time alone with our suitcases."

Dixon waved a dismissive hand at her and pulled the covers back over his head. "So? I'm in a dangerous line of work. We carry protection. They should consider that an asset."

It made sense, but Jaz didn't like it. She could kick herself for not bringing up the suitcases last night. No matter how tired she was, it was an inexcusable lapse of security.

Shaking her head in self-reproval, she slipped out the door and down the hall to the communal bathroom.

When she returned, Dixon was up and dressed. The bed was so tightly made you could bounce a storage gem on it.

"How? You were dead to the world when I left."

Dixon shrugged. "Light sleeper. Once I'm up, I'm up. Let's go." He stumbled crossing the room and caught the doorframe to steady himself. "Still adjusting to Dr. Jensen's modifications," he muttered.

Outside in the hallway, they heard voices. Following them downstairs, Jaz and Dixon found Orley with Moira in a large room to the right of the stairs. The kitchen was visible through an open swinging door. Orley and Moira sat at a Mission-style table that seated twenty. The remains of a large breakfast covered the table like a picked-over carcass.

Dixon plucked a few cold pancakes off a serving tray and asked, "Where is everyone?"

"At work," Orley answered. "It's after noon. How do you feel?"

"Like I've got the grandpappy of all headaches. And my legs are still a bit wobbly. But if I can connect again—it'll be worth it."

"And you, Ms. Reese?" Orley's eyes followed her as she sat down.

"Fine," she said self-consciously, as she fished a few pieces of fruit from the bottom of a bowl.

After breakfast, Orley led them across campus to the Beckman Institute. In the sunlight, Jaz could see water playing over the black polyhedron in the central courtyard. Such a beautiful building to hold so many secrets.

"Can't we connect from the house?" Jaz asked.

Orley put his finger to his lips. "It is not safe to discuss such matters in the open." He pointed to a group of students lounging on the green near the auditorium. One was looking casually their way. "Someone is always watching."

Dixon flipped the student a rude gesture. "Let 'em watch."

Jaz gasped at his audacity and pulled him along. "Come on, quit rousting the natives." Privately, she hoped Herridge had seen the gesture; Jaz shared Dixon's sentiment.

Inside, the Beckman Institute was a hive of activity. Students and professors scurried between the faculty offices in the east and west wings and the research laboratories north and south.

"This way." Orley led them down a flight of stairs into the storage room.

"If the building is shielded from the Net," Dixon asked, "how does your private network get in and out?"

Orley waited until they were inside his laboratory to answer. "Fiber-optic cables run through the underground steam tunnels and connect to the Mission house."

"Then why not connect from the house?" Jaz asked again.

Orley crossed the room and opened a cabinet. "We could, but I'd like to monitor your first contact." He pulled out a machine that had obviously been fabricated in the lab. It had no dust cover, just a square metal frame holding fiber-optic wires and glittering data gems. "Both to test how your presence affects the network and in case there is any adverse reaction to Dr. Jensen's modifications. All the equipment is here." He pulled out a silver net cap and asked Dixon, "Do you mind?"

Dixon's eyes were wary. "There often an adverse reaction, sport?"

Orley shrugged. "It is possible."

Jaz asked, "Where's Dr. Jensen? In case . . ."

"In the building. We're all here, working on various projects. It would look suspicious if we met in a locked laboratory in the middle of the day. But don't worry. He will be monitoring Mr. Tully remotely."

Orley strapped the silver cap to Dixon's head. Then he reached inside his blazer pocket and brought out two headbands like the one Tate had worn the night before. Each end of the band ended in a triangle. Jaz reached out and lightly touched one of the silver triangles on Orley's temple. "Your connection is permanent?"

"Yes," he said, gently pulling her hand away from his face. "I chose to make this network my life's work. Moira designed the connection interface, and Dr. Jensen performed the operation."

Jaz wrinkled her brow in confusion. "You were so adamantly opposed to the Gestalt. Why would you, of all people, choose to connect yourself to this new network permanently?"

He held out a headband and said, "You will have to see for yourself."

Jaz took the band and held it lightly. It was warm from being in Orley's pocket.

Dixon grabbed the other band. "I'll connect first. It might be dangerous."

"We don't even know if you can connect," said Jaz. "And if you can, Dr. Jensen wasn't able to open up access to your previous skills. You'll be like a child, having to relearn everything." Jaz hoped he caught her meaning. The first and hardest lesson anyone learned when connecting was control. Before induction jewelry, anyone could think anything they liked, secure in the privacy of their own skull. But when you broadcast directly to a network, you learned to suppress your socially inappropriate thoughts. Even more critical when you had a secret to hide.

Herridge hadn't expected Dixon to be able to connect. Jaz knew with a sudden cold certainty that Dixon hadn't gotten the training in Net deception she had. It was hard to lie on the Net in the best of circumstances. Could he manage with only basic skills?

Jaz took the headband from Dixon's hand. "Let me go first. If I start frothing at the mouth, or it seems I'm being controlled, you can pull the headband off. Once I know it's safe, you can join us."

Dixon's eyes narrowed slightly. "You don't think I can do this." He snatched the headband from Jaz's hand. Before she could stop him, he snapped it in place around the back of his head and over his temples. He swayed on his feet.

Jaz caught him, steadied him. "Idiot!" She reached up to pull the headband off, but stopped herself. The government's locks and whatever Dr. Jensen had done to him last night had already weakened his brain. Sudden-disconnect feedback might damage it further. She helped his body into a sitting position on the ground.

Orley smiled and sat cross-legged on the floor. "Hello, Mr. Tully. Glad you could join us." The rest of the conversation continued silently over the Net.

"Damn you both." Jaz slammed her own headband on and sank to the floor next to them.

Electrons danced inside the headband, creating targeted magnetic fields. In response, secondary electronic fields were induced inside the medial temporal lobe of Jaz's brain, activating extrastriate areas specialized for processing visual input. From her own memories, the electronics generated new images. It was why everyone visualized the Net in slightly different ways.

The first sensation was a tightness in her forehead. The

electronics weren't as good as her commercially produced Odin's Eye. Then there was the warm, not alone, feeling she associated with the Net. But this was different. The Net had always made her feel like she was walking into a vast, never-ending party. This was smaller, closer . . . like coming home.

Coming late to the connection, she stepped into the metaphor Orley had established. It was a small room with Japanese-style table and pillows. Rice-paper walls separated them from the rest of the network. Shapes moved outside the translucent walls; the murmur of voices surrounded them.

Orley's avatar was a man-shaped outline of green-gold analog circuitry.

Jaz's avatar looked like an idealized version of herself: skin a little clearer, muscles a little firmer, but essentially her. Jaz wondered what that said about her psyche. Was she self-confident enough to wear her own body in simulations, or just unimaginative?

Hovering over the table was a palm-sized ball of fire.

"Dixon?" she asked.

The ball flashed blue-white and a voice reverberated through her head like a spike. "Jaz!" She felt a flash of relief and lust and a tinge of fear.

"You're leaking emotions," she whispered in what she hoped was a private transmission between them. The induction felt like a crude version of the Net, but she wasn't sure if the mnemonic controls worked the same. "Get control of yourself."

"Sor-sorry—hard. Have to relearn . . . everything." The ball of fire shrank and cooled to a bright orange flame. She felt nothing else emote from it.

Jaz was impressed. It had taken her years to learn how to shield her emotions. Dixon had relearned the skill in a few seconds. Had he found a way to tap into his previous knowledge?

"Jaz," Orley said, "what do you think of our little domain?"

His words were crisp. Even with the substandard connection jewelry, they sprang up in her mind as if she had thought them herself. "It's fast. There's a . . . sharpness. Less background noise."

Orley pulled apart his green-gold hands and a tiny diagram appeared in the space between them. Lines connected twenty nodes. "The network is small, and constrained in space. That makes it more efficient; there is very little latency. Furthermore, the worldwide Net is generated by the minds of all the connected: geniuses and idiots, saints and criminals. Our network is generated by select individuals, chosen for their intelligence and moral standing."

"Eugenics for metaminds." Dixon's ball of fire hummed, dancing nearer to Jaz.

She got no emotion from the ball, neither approval nor sarcasm. Good. Now if only she could control herself as well. She squelched the line of thought before it led her into dangerous memories.

"But twenty-plus people," she said. "Surely that's not enough to generate a metamind."

"Because we have limited people on the project, we dedicate additional consciousness to the network. Gestalt arose accidentally; using only one to two percent of a connected person's brain. An almost undetectable loss." Each of the nodes in Orley's simulation grew into tiny brains. One quarter of them colored green. "Because of the high-caliber people involved and the additional sacrifice of a portion of our conscious minds, we have been able to generate a metamind with as few as sixteen."

A chill ran up Jaz's neck, briefly drawing her back into her body. Less than the number of people in this room. That meant that a metamind—a junior Gestalt—was with them even now.

"SYMBIOS."

A disembodied voice echoed in her head. The echo was strange, as if twenty people had spoken simultaneously.

"What was that?"

Orley smiled and clapped his hands, dispersing the diagram he had conjured. "Our metamind. Can't you feel it?"

The air in the small Japanese room suddenly thickened around them . . . filled with a presence.

"Where is it?" Jaz asked.

"EVERYWHERE," the multithroated voice said again. "NOWHERE?"

"It experiences itself in twenty locations at once. Spatial position is a bit of an abstract concept for it," said Orley. "Fascinating, isn't it? The first nonorganic intelligence on the planet."

Part of Jaz's brain immediately began deconstructing Orley's last sentence—Gestalt was the first, not Symbios. And was it really nonorganic, being constructed of human intelligences?

The thoughts tasted strange to her. Out of synch with the emotions roiling through her bloodstream: fear, excitement, wonder. "Are you thinking in my brain?" she asked the air.

And the part of her mind that had been considering Orley's sentence now considered this. "WHERE ELSE?"

A flash of fear and vulnerability clenched her chest. "Get out!"

As soon as the words formed in her mind, the parallel thoughts vanished. The thickened air faded, and her mind was clear. "It's gone," she said, surprised.

"Of course. Symbios is not Gestalt. It is not a thief that steals to create itself. It takes only what is freely given." Orley pursed his golden green lips. "I think you've hurt its feelings."

"Why did you stop?" Jaz asked the air. The next question scared her, and she let a little of that leak out. "You could have overpowered me."

"YOU ASKED IT. I WOULD NOT VIOLATE YOU."

Dixon wasn't saying anything. Jaz wondered how much of this exchange he was able to follow in his reduced state. His ball of fire had shrunk down to the size of a bumblebee and flitted nervously around the room.

"You understand that expanding your processes into my thinking would feel like a violation to me?"

"YES. YOU UNDERSTOOD IT TO ME."

The words were strange. Had Symbios made a mistake in grammar?

"No. MAY I UNDERSTAND IT TO YOU?"

Jaz wasn't sure what the creature meant, but she sensed no hostility. She nodded.

Jaz wondered how the creature's cognition spread across its hosts, and found answers bubbling to the surface—the abstraction of the action potential that stimulates neurons, spread across multiple minds, second-order layering of memory using dendritic spines.

The information came, not as a dry recitation of facts, but with the knowledge and context of a lifetime of study, information Dr. Jensen would know. Was she inside his mind, thinking with his brain? Incredible.

The tenor of her thoughts changed, and Jaz mused on the chemical reactions of sodium and potassium ions pumped across the neural membrane by the electric gradient. In her imagination, protein molecules opened and closed to create channels in neural membranes, pulsing through ions like river surges through time-release floodgates.

Jaz had the knowledge of twenty lifetimes at her disposal, all talented professionals.

What did she bring to them? Ah, she felt a small corner of her mind musing on algorithms, devising software to improve Symbios's efficiency. She let the thoughts come, Orley's people deserved an exchange on what they had given her. Only one small part of her mind did she hide away, using distraction and dissembling. She wrapped the knowledge of the NSA, her mission, and Dixon in a whirl of taboos and lurid thoughts and tucked them into her subconscious. She could share, but only so far.

Her secrets secure, Jaz turned her attention back to the worlds of information opening up before her. Twenty lifetimes of scientific study. Different views of the world. Opening her eyes, she could see with twenty different viewpoints. See herself through other eyes, see around corners, in other rooms. It was being more than human, to be part of Symbios. Jaz felt her mind expand.

Instead of controlling its hosts as Gestalt did, Symbios worked in collaboration with them.

Best of all, the empty place Ian had left behind was filled. These people rejoiced in her talent. With them, she could be free. From the others Jaz felt a chorus of assent. A warmth rushed over Jaz as the scientists accepted her. Only a far corner of Symbios's landscape remained dark. Tate was out there, her resentment like a storm on the horizon. Tate had empty places inside of her no amount of acceptance could fill. Jaz tried to understand Tate, to learn what had happened to create such pain, but she was rebuffed by blue-black spikes that left Jaz's head aching.

The only other holdout was Dixon. His firefly flame flickered in and out of Jaz's consciousness, trying to make contact. His crippled skills left him unable to sink into the tide of information that flowed beneath the surface of standard network protocols.

"Oh Dixon," Jaz said aloud, "if you could only experience this!"

"Tell me." His words were blurred and distant; he spoke audibly, instead of using the faster medium of thought. He asked, "What's happening to you?"

Jaz felt her mouth stretch into a foolish grin. "There aren't words . . ."

This wasn't the overwhelming whirlwind she had experienced with Gestalt. The scope was small enough that her mind could encompass the incoming sensations. She knew what they were thinking. They understood many things to her in that instant.

"Join with us," Orley said.

Jaz was tempted. There was a feeling of welcome on this network, like a close family. Humans had evolved to live in hunter-gatherer clans. Why not a series of interconnected metaminds working together on the Net? This communication was more complete than anything she'd experienced before. Symbios wasn't a separate entity; it was something they all, collectively, were becoming.

"You understand," Orley murmured. "I knew you would."

The only danger was, in an environment of such openness, how could she keep her secrets?

"We only go in so far as you let us," Orley said. "And there is nothing in your past that would make us deny you."

"Like hell!" came a prickly cold reply from outside the walls. A shape like a Technicolor sea urchin blazed on the other side of the rice-paper walls, casting colored shadows. "She's hiding something. I can feel it."

"Later, Tate. We can discuss it offline."

"There are other beautiful, talented women in the world." Tate's voice dripped sarcasm. "Let this one go."

Tension crept into the air around them. Jaz felt Tate's hatred flavor Symbios. The entity was experiencing a dilemma, feeling both suspicion and trust of Jaz simultaneously. Tate was the one the group trusted to scan potential candidates. If she didn't trust Jaz . . . the concern of the others rose. The emotional climate was uncomfortable, full of distrust and anxiety.

There was no way she could stand against Symbios if it changed its mind and decided to infiltrate her. It had the resources of twenty other naturals behind it, and a direct connection to her brain.

Jaz reached up and jerked the headband off before anyone online understood her intention.

Pain lanced through her skull at the sudden transition. She doubled over with a yelp and grabbed her head.

Dixon was on his feet, already disconnected. He rocked unsteadily for an instant, then held out a hand and helped Jaz up. There was an expression on his face she had never seen before—fear.

Orley opened his eyes. "Wait—where are you going?"

"Out," Dixon said, interrupting Jaz's reply. "We need to talk." He dragged Jaz toward the door. It locked with a snap of dead bolts as Dixon reached for the handle.

"I can't let you go," Orley said. "You know too much."

"So . . . what?" Dixon asked. "You going to make us disappear? Join or else?"

Orley scrubbed his face with his hands. "No, it's not supposed to work this way. The joining of minds should bring accord."

Jaz let go of Dixon's hand. "Please, we just want to discuss what we've seen in private. Somewhere neither Symbios nor Gestalt can overhear. You of all people should understand: it's a lot to take in at once."

Orley nodded slowly. "I'll take you back to the house."

Dixon and Jaz took a walk outside the Mission house, staying within the compound's locked gates. It was dangerous to talk inside, too many people connected to Symbios wandered in and out during the day. They stopped in the shade of a banyan tree, its cascading roots sheltering them from view.

"You sure it's safe to talk out here?" Jaz asked.

"They can't have every inch of the property bugged," Dixon said. "It's the best we'll get. I don't think your boyfriend will let us take a walk outside the gate. How's your back? Do you need to make a chiropractic appointment?"

Jaz looked at him sharply. "I don't know. It's uncomfortable. Maybe. I'll let you know after we talk."

Dixon shifted his weight back and forth nervously. "This thing is dangerous, really dangerous. I didn't believe your talk about metaminds before. But this . . ." He shook his head.

Jaz put her hand on his shoulder. "What's scared you? Things got a little tense at the end, but—"

He shrugged off her hand and grabbed her by the shoulders, pulling her close. "You don't understand. While you kept Orley and his plaything busy, I did some poking around. That creature thinks inside other people's brains. There's no way to keep it out without disconnecting."

"I know." She pushed his hands off her. "Gestalt operates the same way. It scared me at first, too. But now, I don't know. There are some advantages . . ." Jaz remembered the expansive feeling of being twenty people at once. What would that be like when the group had grown to fifty—or a hundred? It was a seductive image.

Dixon made a frustrated gesture with his hands. "You

think like a straight. There's only so much you can do on the Net that's legal. You stay within those boundaries and there's a lot you miss. With the right equipment, I can brain-hack anyone, find out anything they know, make them do anything I want by convincing them it was their own idea." He waved a hand in the direction of the Caltech campus. "And that thing makes me look like a monkey playing with a palmtop." He rubbed his upper arms, despite the warm spring day. "It's dangerous. Not just to you and me. To all of humanity."

Jaz had to make him understand. "Gestalt may be dangerous, but Symbios—"

"How is it any different than Gestalt? Symbios steals consciousness from its hosts, too."

"It's not like that," Jaz said, touching Dixon's arm, as if physical contact could bridge the gap of understanding. "Symbios *respects* its users, opens up a new universe of knowledge and sensation in return for what it takes. Even disconnected I think it's a good idea."

Dixon brushed away her comment and her touch. "Then that creature planted a meme in your subconscious, an autosuggestion to bring you back."

"You don't understand—you weren't able to fully connect, if you had—"

"I'd be as gonzo as you." He gripped her shoulders and shook her slightly. "You're not thinking straight. Where's the woman who valued her self-control so highly she wouldn't connect to the Net for fear of losing herself in Gestalt?"

"There are more important things than absolute control. I know that now. I wish I could make you understand." She looked at him with sorrow. "With time your skills—"

"I don't need pity." His words rushed out. "And as for my skills, there's a reason we're here that has nothing to do with your love-in with Orley and pals. Or have you forgotten? Completing this mission is my only chance for a cure."

Dixon was hurting. He hadn't experienced the wonders Jaz had, might never be able to if the government didn't undo the locks in his mind. All Herridge asked for was information on what Orley was doing. How much damage could that do? Gestalt already knew about Orley, probably suspected much of what was going on. If they did report back to Herridge, would the NSA shut down the Symbios project?

Jaz was torn between wanting to help Dixon and a new allegiance to something greater than herself.

She said quietly, "I haven't forgotten."

CHAPTER 18

Orley met them at the door when they returned from their walk. "Did your walk ease your concerns? I had forgotten how overwhelming Symbios can be to a newcomer. Especially now that there are twenty of us."

Dixon's eyes were hard. "What's the next step, Orley?"

"What do you mean?"

"Do you intend to keep recruiting naturals for Symbios?"

"Of course," said Orley. "It is the only way Symbios can grow."

Dixon waved his hands to indicate the Mission house around them. "They all going to live here?"

"No, at some point we'll build a private research facility." Orley's brow furrowed. "Why do you ask?"

Jaz captured one of Dixon's arms and linked hers through it. She squeezed it warningly. What was he doing? They needed to elicit Orley's cooperation, not antagonize him. "We were just discussing where we would live. Dixon loves to garden, and the walled yard around the Mission house doesn't leave much opportunity." She kissed Dixon lightly on the cheek. "Dixon, please go upstairs. I want to talk to Dr. Orley alone."

"Why?" Dixon regarded Jaz with some suspicion.

She squeezed his arm again. "It's personal, Dix. Don't worry. Dr. Orley isn't going to ravish me while you're out of the room."

Orley pinked and coughed low in his throat.

"I don't like it."

Jaz unlinked her arm and pushed him toward the stairs. "Go on, have a lie down. You're exhausted from last night." She smiled up at him. "I'll scream if I need you to come running to my rescue."

Dixon looked from Jaz to Orley and back again. "All right then," he said, climbing the stairs.

"Is there someplace private we can talk?" Jaz asked.

"This way." Orley led her to the parlor, a room furnished in Navajo rugs and pine-log furniture. "And please call me John."

A white baby grand piano occupied the corner of the room. Orley sat on the bench and lightly touched the keys. Quiet strains of something sweet and pensive floated up. "What did you want to discuss?"

Jaz leaned against the side of the piano and watched Orley's slender fingers caress the keys. The yearning in the music was palpable. She wondered if that was intentional, or a betrayal by Orley's subconscious.

He caught her watching, and hesitated. "I'm sorry," he said, reaching for the key cover. "I should be giving you my full attention. It's just that this morning was . . . intense, and playing helps me relax."

Jaz caught the edge of the cover. "Don't stop. The music is wonderful."

"Would you like to play?" Orley asked with a shy smile. "Through Symbios, I could share my knowledge with you."

Jaz stepped back. "Like an immersion connection?"

"Nothing so primitive. In this, you'll draw the skill from a shared pool of knowledge. No one will take you over." His eyes locked with hers. "I promise, you'll remain in control."

Jaz sat next to Orley on the piano bench. She pulled the headband she had used this morning out of her shirt pocket and looked at it. Part of her was afraid. If Dixon was right about Orley, this might be a ploy to get her reconnected and take her over. But . . . Orley didn't seem dangerous, and his offer intrigued her. To create music, what would that feel like? This didn't feel like manipulation, only simple curiosity. What harm could Symbios do in the time it took to play a few bars? With a deep breath, Jaz slipped the headband over her ears.

The flood of warmth was back. Not a cold infinite ocean, but an intimate hot spring. The others were there, accepting and ready to share themselves.

Jaz now recognized the music Orley had played: Brahms' Intermezzo in A minor. She rested her hands on the keys, her fingers in an upright position held loosely from her wrists. The music was there, she had only to touch the keys to release it. Jaz stroked the cool white and black levers and began to play.

The opening bars of Beethoven's Moonlight Sonata flowed from the piano. For the first time in Jaz's life, she was the source of music, not an observer.

It was wondrous. The opening chords flowed from her fingertips. Her heart rose in her chest, swelling with every measure.

Then tickling counterpoint melodies echoing the main theme, like dancing motes of pollen on the wind. Each individual voice heard, and yet feeding into the bass refrain, the larger sound given structure to its lighter constituents. Jaz felt elated, she could play forever, at one with the vibrating air that surrounded and embraced her.

And yet, she was more than the music. While part of Jaz's consciousness was engrossed in playing the piano, another solved algorithms for Moira. Jaz could move between nineteen different viewpoints. Aside from Tate's dark corner of Symbios, everything was open to her. She worked in the Beckman Institute laboratory with Dr. Jensen, on a better inductive interface; she was the Nigerian professor, Dr. Daren Akukwe, engineering new sodium isotopes; she was herself; she was Orley, sitting beside her and viewing her with pleasure.

Jaz stopped when the opening sequence ended. Her fingers, unconditioned for the rigors of playing piano, were sore, but the memory of the music that had flowed through her thrilled Jaz. She rocked back on the seat and grinned at Orley. "That was amazing."

"Yes." Orley's eyes were bright. "Now you understand

why our work here is so important. Half of our researchers only intended to stay a week or so. But none of us could leave, after having experienced . . . that."

Jaz reluctantly pulled off the headband. "This is so different from the Net." Jaz pulled off the headband and set it on the piano's music rack. Disconnected, she yearned for Symbios.

Using defenses the witch had taught her, Jaz searched her neural pathways for sign of a planted suggestion. There was none. Dixon was wrong. She wanted to be part of Symbios. Not from any external coercion, but because it was right.

This was humanity's destiny. The next step in the evolution of consciousness.

"Exactly," Orley said, as if he could still read her thoughts. Given how close they'd been a second ago, perhaps he could. He stared at her with his intent green gaze.

Jaz was suddenly aware of how their thighs pressed together on the piano bench. She wondered what her intentions were. Would she seduce him as Ann Jordon had suggested? Or did she want to join his side, tell him about Herridge and the NSA, and make a clean break?

"But I've distracted you," Orley said. "What did you want to discuss?"

Jaz cast about for a legitimate subject. "Tate's is the only mind of Symbios I can't enter. Why?"

"I should apologize for Tate," Orley said. "Events in her early childhood have left her . . . unable to trust. She is talented though, and a fierce defender of our secrets. Her ability to subordinate her personality has advantages that are worth adding an amount of emotional instability to Symbios. When there are more of us, her effect will be diluted."

Jaz looked sidelong at Orley. His features were refined: long straight nose, high cheekbones, and a chiseled chin. It was an ascetic's face, not given to displays of feeling. After more than forty years, it was unlined save for a few horizontal creases above his brow. Intellectual surprise, it seemed, was the only emotion in which he indulged. Jaz had a sudden urge to light up his face with something more, to leave her mark on that smooth canvas.

His body was lean and defined, more graceful now that he was relaxed. Jaz admired the play of muscles in his forearm. She wondered if Gestalt had taken her own predilections into account when it had chosen her as Orley's seductress.

It would be easy to lean over and kiss him. She knew he was attracted to her; she'd felt it while she was playing the piano. He wanted her. And she wanted him, but for what purpose? As a tool to earn her freedom from Herridge . . . or for herself?

She thought of Ian, his rejection of her, the months alone, her life consisting of work and sleep. Orley's attraction to her felt good; someone wanted her again. He was so intelligent, so talented, so trusting. Jaz's eyes stung with the precursor to tears.

Orley scootched closer to her on the bench. "What's wrong? Something with Dixon?" He touched Jaz's headband, resting on the piano. "I wish you were connected, so I'd know what you were thinking."

Jaz shook her head. "Not this you don't." She wiped angrily at her eyes and changed the subject. "How do you manage privacy? With the Net, it's unlikely that anyone who catches a spare thought will be someone you know. Here, this is like a small town . . . of telepaths."

Orley's hand reached out, then hesitated, almost touching Jaz's face. "It requires a higher level of intimacy. That's why we're very careful about whom we recruit."

Jaz took his outstretched hand and held it in both of hers. She felt his body tense at the contact, but he did not pull away.

"What about Dixon?"

Jaz leaned over and kissed him lightly on the lips. "What about him?"

Orley pulled away and looked at her with bright eyes, and in that moment she was sure he knew what she was thinking without a connection.

She touched the triangle-shaped implants on either temple. "Can you turn them off, for privacy?"

Orley grabbed her wrists and gently pulled her hands away from his face. "You know I'm attracted to you. There's no lying in a network this small. But you and I and Dixon have to live together, as you put it, in this small town of telepaths. Anything you and I do, he'll know. And I don't get the impression he's a sharing man."

"No." Jaz looked up the stairs in the direction Dixon had gone. She still hadn't decided whom she was seducing Orley for, herself or Herridge.

If circumstances were different, she would join Orley in his experiment, instantly. But she wasn't in this alone. "Can't Dixon leave? I don't think he's comfortable with the smaller network."

Orley looked out the window, avoiding her gaze. "He knows too much about us."

The words were ominous. She pulled her hands away from Orley. "So . . . what? You would kill him if he tried to go?"

"No. Nothing like that. But I warned you when you came to me for help." Orley lowered his face, his features sad. "That if we involved you, you would have to stay. We can't risk Gestalt learning of our network."

"Why? A few naturals creating their own network, how does that threaten Gestalt?"

"You and I see it that way, Gestalt doesn't. It's hounded me—one person—for the twenty-two years since I disconnected." He shook his head. "All that effort to reclaim one natural. It would never accept a competitor for humanity's resources. Gestalt would destroy Symbios."

"How do you know?"

Orley's face froze into an unreadable mask. "Because it's tried before. NSA agents tried to infiltrate our group."

Jaz covered her mouth with her hand. "What happened to them?"

Orley paused, then said, "We couldn't let them report back."

The way he said it chilled her. "Did you kill them?" she whispered.

His brow creased. "Nothing like that . . . They were . . ." He shook his head to clear it. "I shouldn't talk about this further. The others disapprove."

Jaz touched his face. "Do you always do only what they approve?"

Orley leaned into her caress. "It would be wrong. Dixon . . ."

"Then let's be wrong." She covered his mouth with a kiss. Despite his protests, Jaz knew Orley was flattered at her betraying Dixon for him. Gestalt had told her he would be.

After a second's hesitation, Orley's arms slid up Jaz's back and pulled her body into him. He returned her kiss like a drowning man gasping for air.

They crept up the stairs, tiptoeing past the room she shared with Dixon. Orley led her to the room at the end of the hall. His bedroom was twice as large as the others, with a private bath. The bed was covered in metallic-blue sheets. Shades on the window softened the afternoon sun into shadow.

An old flat-screen monitor was mounted on the wall in front of a tiny desk. Images from the Net flickered across it: weather reports and news stories. The sound scrolled across the bottom in closed captioning.

Jaz walked over and touched the frame of the screen. "Doesn't this make you feel as though Gestalt is watching you?"

Orley smiled depreciatingly. "There's no camera or microphone. I lie in bed sometimes and watch my enemy. Symbios needs to know what it's up against."

Jaz turned to look at him. "You expect a conflict between the two networks."

He held out his hands to her. "One day. It's inevitable."

Jaz stepped into his embrace. His arms around her felt

warm and safe. He smelled of soap and musk. "I don't want Dixon hurt," she murmured into Orley's neck.

"Then you shouldn't be here."

She pulled back to look him. "You know what I mean."

His eyes were emerald green in the shadows cast by the window shade. "We need him. Mr. Tully is a man of great potential. When he relearns his skills he will be an asset to us."

She touched his temples. "Can you turn those off? I don't want the others to feel this."

Orley shook her hands away. "No. But I can build a barrier. It's what I did when I introduced you and Dixon to Symbios, so you wouldn't be overwhelmed."

Jaz recalled the metaphor; a room with rice-paper walls, being able to see only shadows beyond.

He closed his eyes a moment. "It is done." He leaned back on the bed, carrying Jaz with him. She kneeled on top of him and kissed him deeply, trying to lose herself in the moment, but some small part of her mind whispered: *You and Dixon could capture him now, he's cut off from the others.*

Orley opened the drawer on the bedside table. He pulled out a headband identical to the one Jaz had left on the piano.

Why would Orley have an extra headband in his nightstand? Who else had been in this bedroom with him? Stupid. She hadn't expected him to be a virgin. Still . . . perhaps that explained Tate's antagonism toward her.

"Please," he said, offering her the headband. "I want to know all of you."

If she took it, he would know everything. She wouldn't be able to hide her lies during the intimacy of sex. At some point, she'd lose control. Tell him all now, or admit to herself that she was working for the NSA. She took the band; her fingers trembled as Dixon's had when she first met him.

Ian hadn't been able to accept all that she could offer,

but he was just a data miner in a private company. Orley was a world-renowned genius. He wouldn't push her away as Ian had. She was sure of it. Everything she wanted lay in front of her. A way to escape Gestalt's heavy-handed influence, a man she could love to the full extent of her ability, and a purpose—something more important than data mining for lawyers and corporations. All she had to do was betray Dixon's best chance for recovery.

"I can't, not yet." Jaz closed her eyes and felt grief suffuse her body like a wave of static electricity. "I can give you only my body."

Orley pulled her down on top of him and covered her face with light kisses. "Then that's all I'll ask."

After Orley had fallen asleep, Jaz showered in his bathroom, dried her hair, and tiptoed across the hall.

Dixon lay on the bed, hands folded behind his head. His eyes were stony. "I didn't think you'd go through with it. You didn't seem like a whore."

The word cracked through her like lightning. "What would you know about it?"

He reached over to the bedside table and held up a headband. "Everything."

"You had no right." Her voice was getting louder; she fought to stay calm.

"No?" Dixon's voice was low and lethal. "No right to see whether you would betray our mission? These people are dangerous. How do you think your boyfriend would react if he learned the NSA had sent us here to spy?" He waved the headband at the door. "Besides, twenty other people—with better connections—felt and heard more than I."

The comment hit home. Jaz froze in her tracks. "Orley promised he'd filter the connection, that we had privacy."

"Fucking on the other side of a rice-paper wall isn't particularly discreet." Dixon studied his fingernails. "Was it worth it? Did he tell you his plans? Did you find out what happened to the other agents?"

Jaz felt her face flush. "Maybe I just wanted to be

with him—did that ever occur to you? What business is it of yours, anyway? Why should you care?"

"That is the question, isn't it?" His brown eyes locked with hers. "You didn't give away the game. So why the hell should I care?"

Jaz turned away.

He stood up and paced the room. "Maybe I just don't like to you manipulated into prostitution."

"No one manipulated me. I did it because I wanted to." Jaz tapped her chest with her fingertips. "It's been a long time since anyone wanted me."

Dixon stopped his pacing just behind Jaz. His breath tickled her neck. "And I thought you were an *intelligent* woman."

Jaz turned. Dixon's face was unreadable. "Not just for sex, but someone who wanted *me*."

"He wants to feed you to his pet metamind. That's all. Once you're under wraps he'll seduce the next young talented thing."

No, what she and Orley had shared had been special—hadn't it? They'd joined bodies, but without trust was that love, or just sex?

Jaz sighed. "Look, the question here is not what I did—that's done. But what are we going to do now?"

He paused a moment before answering, and Jaz braced herself for some cutting remark. Dixon said, "He didn't tell you what happened to the agents, only that they hadn't been killed. He intends to keep growing his network, and Symbios and Gestalt will come into conflict at some point in the future. Did I miss anything?"

"No." Her stomach clenched. It was true. He'd been there with her and Orley.

"With all this excitement, my back is killing me." Dixon picked up Jaz's suitcase and opened the lock. "I say we call and make an appointment."

Jaz pushed the suitcase closed. "No. We have to find out what happened to those agents. We need more proof."

"Proof? We were only supposed to find out what Orley was up to. We've done that. Mission accomplished. Let's go home and collect our respective rewards."

"Not yet. We don't have all the answers."

"Maybe you just don't want to turn the boyfriend in. How do you propose to get this information? Screw him again?"

Jaz poked her finger into Dixon's chest. "Look, I'm a trained data miner. What we've got is an indication, but not proof. Nothing that would hold up in court. If we're going to turn Orley over to the NSA, I want to make sure."

Dixon bent down and whispered in Jaz's ear. "You want proof, let's hack into Symbios and get it."

Jaz drew back. "We can't do that—it'd be a violation—"

"That, my dear *Jasmine*," Dixon taunted her, "is what spying is all about."

They waited until four a.m., when the entire house was asleep. Jaz opened their door and peeked down the dark hallway. No light shone from under any of the doors.

Jaz took out the headband Orley had given her. "I don't feel right about this."

Dixon whispered, "It's the only way. You need information, I'll help you get it."

Jaz stared at the satin-brushed metal band. Her choices were all unpleasant: abandon her mission and become a permanent guest of the NSA; join Orley and spend the rest of her life wondering what had happened to Dixon and the other people Orley had made disappear; or break into Symbios and steal information from a man who had given her only acceptance and trust. In the end, curiosity tipped the balance. Jaz had to know.

She slipped the cold metal around the back of her head.

Jaz felt like a thief breaking into a dark house. Having all its hosts living in the same time zone was a limitation for Symbios. There were hours when all of them were asleep. No one was awake to feel Jaz slip into the network.

She closed her eyes to better concentrate.

Symbios's world was quiet, dark . . . formless. The hair

on the back of her neck prickled. Jaz waited for something to loom out of the darkness. She half expected Symbios to be more powerful when its hosts were asleep and it had full rein.

A light, no bigger than the head of a match, appeared in the air at eye level, Dixon's primitive avatar. He answered her unspoken question: "No. Their minds are reorganizing and cataloging the day's new information. Biological defrag. They don't have time to generate Symbios. They sleep; it sleeps."

"You don't know that for certain," Jaz said softly. "You're guessing."

A pool of water collected around Jaz's feet.

"No metaphor!" Dixon whispered. "Too invasive."

She'd have to do this in the dark, feeling her way through the network. But that was stupid, a leftover of her humancentric view of reality. The network was nowhere, occupying no space. Her avatar sat cross-legged in the center of the pressing emptiness. "What now?"

"Find Orley. Listen to his dreams."

"He won't be dreaming about the agents."

"You'd be surprised. When you brought up the topic, he was emotionally distressed. His mind will have to sort that out. Listen, it will be there."

She thought herself around in the dark, feeling, tasting the quality of the air around her. The network echoed like an empty mine shaft. She wondered how many people were still connected. How many wore their data jewelry to sleep or had implants like Orley? She thought back to their first meeting, the room of scientists. Moira had implants like Orley, so did Dr. Akukwe. That meant at least three people online, perhaps more. And what about Symbios, would it sense her? By putting on the headband, she added an awake mind to its pool. Ironic that she might give it the resources necessary to sense her intrusion. *Please, Ganesh, let the entity be sleeping in their collective subconscious. Remove this obstacle from my path.*

Jaz heard a far-off rumble. On the Net, dreams were blocked from transmission; they created too much noise, random images inserted into the stream of information. In commercially produced data jewelry, transmission was inhibited when the wearer generated sleep spindles and K-complex brain waves. But Jaz doubted that the home-made devices Moira engineered would incorporate these checks. After all, if everyone were asleep when the network dreamed, who would be inconvenienced? Only the occasional NSA spy . . .

Jaz followed the sound she had heard, until the sky lightened around her, and the void under her feet turned to dry grass. A tall mountain dominated a savanna. A dream, she guessed, but not Orley's.

There were several sleeping minds in here. How could she isolate Orley's from the others? Jaz split her thinking into two parallel streams. Like a dancer who can isolate individual muscles, Jaz had spent years building up the ability to isolate thought processes and layer thoughts in multiple patterns. On an MRI, it looked like an epileptic seizure, thousands of neurons firing independently. But in her mind it was ordered chaos. She branched and re-branched her mind, until she felt the whole network.

Dixon was a gnat in her ear. "What's going on? Your avatar is fuzzing out."

Jaz had no concentration left to answer him. She could do nothing but listen. A pandemonium of dreams ruled the Net.

—A black man ran down an endless hallway that stretched as he ran, carrying him farther from his goal—twin goats scampered in a meadow, until an oversize hawk carried one off—snakes slithered in a world of rainbow lights and opaque fogs—electrons bounced along a circuit, skittering into holes—flying in a snow-filled sky, the cold flakes burning on her bare skin—two men in a gray-walled room, arguing—

Jaz focused herself back into a single stream of consciousness, focused on that last image. One of the men was Orley. Was this his dream, or the recollection of another?

Tate lay on the floor, the silver hood over her head. The same apparatus she had used to test Jaz and Dixon stretched between her and a white man in his early thirties. The man's face was hidden, but he was wearing a charcoal gray suit.

"He's fighting me," Tate said. Her voice was slow and faint, as if heard through a filter.

Orley paced in the dream.

Tate half sat up, straining the wires that connected her to the other man. "My God, he's NSA."

The man reached into his jacket.

"He's got a gun," Tate shouted, her mouth distorting the fabric of the hood. "Stop him. I'll hold his arms— Stop him!"

Orley continued pacing. Jaz looked down at the scene from his perspective. It unrolled as if occurring on a stage, with Orley watching from the wings.

A second Orley stepped into the spotlight, thinner, less substantial than the one who waited with Jaz. If he noticed her presence, he gave no sign. The vague Orley approached the man thrashing on the ground with an injector in his hand. He pushed up the agent's sleeve.

The scene stopped, rewound itself; the actor-Orley walked backward off the stage. Orley, like most naturals, lucid-dreamed, controlled his dreaming mind. The scene replayed, this time the disconnected Orley helped the man up, then let him go.

Men in FBI windbreakers burst into the scene and seized Orley and Tate, and in the compressed dreamtime, they were tried and convicted in seconds. Life imprisonment without a connection.

The scene froze.

Back in the room, Tate screamed for Orley to restrain the agent. Orley pressed the injector into the crook of the man's arm. The agent collapsed unconscious on the floor.

"Do we kill him?" Tate asked, her eyes feverish with terror and amphetamines.

"No," Orley said. "I have a better way." He bent and lifted the man from beneath his shoulders. Tate grabbed the man's feet—but then Tate was Jaz herself, and the agent was Dixon.

There was a muddled recollection of flight—helping their
"drunk" friend get home from the nightclub—driving up to
the house—then they were somewhere dark—a basement?
There was an old sensory-deprivation tank in the room.
One like those used during the depro fad of the 2080s
to heighten the illusion of the Net. They hefted him in.
The man floated in an oxygenated fluorocarbon emulsion, able to breathe, and yet kept at neutral buoyancy.
They taped electrodes to his head to monitor his condition and provide him access to the Net.

"Those who are unwilling, can also serve," Orley said,
and switched the transmission frequency from the worldwide Net to Symbios's private network.

Impossible, Jaz thought from her vantage point in the
shadows. This must be a fantasy. Orley would never imprison a man in a depro tank indefinitely.

Her thoughts must have leaked; they influenced the
dream. She saw a used-electronics van deliver three more
sensory-deprivation tanks to the Mission house. More
tanks. With the lack of sensory distraction and the proper
sedatives, nearly all of a tank-bound person's processing
power would be available to Symbios. Orley had said
that Symbios took only what was freely given—he didn't
say by whom.

She controlled her fear, afraid the strong emotion rising in her might wake Orley. His name was . . . Orley
filled in the blank . . . Anders. Mark Anders.

One of Herridge's missing agents.

The dream continued. The tanks in the basement
multiplied. The dream-Orley tried to push them back,
but they grew, spilling over him, until the underground
room was as large as a football field, covered with canis-
ters, each one containing a person whose mind was given
over to Symbios.

Jaz backed away from Orley's tableau, but his distress
spread through the network. He was the most powerful
natural, the first to join Symbios. His dream permeated
the virtual landscape.

The twin goats were connected by wires, they gam-
boled through a herd, stealing sheep from a shepherd's

care, connecting the sheep, leading them into a stampede over the shepherd—Snakes slithered into a person's ear, out the other side, and growing ever longer, strung humans together on its body like beads—silent people stood on either side of the black man's endless hallway, their hands joined in communion, their temples covered by triangular implants—flying through a cloud of snowflakes, each a tiny person, a spark of consciousness, accreting to her snow-man's body. Growing larger, growing stronger.

Jaz understood Symbios's desire. The rush of being twenty people at once, what would it be like to be a hundred, a thousand? Symbios was the combined will of its constituents. It wanted to learn, to grow. But not in the slow, careful way Orley had proposed. Symbios wanted it all—and wanted it now. And only Gestalt stood in its way.

Jaz jerked off the headband and felt the spike of pain as she disconnected. Too late she worried whether the sudden disconnect was felt by the others online. "My God," she said. "Did you see?"

Dixon nodded grimly.

"It could have been a fantasy," she whispered.

Dixon just stared at her. "Shall we make the call?"

Jaz shook her head. "Not yet. I have to know for sure. You can't convict someone on the basis of a dream. We have to find those men."

CHAPTER 19

"**N**o," Jaz said. "It must have been a dream. This house doesn't have a basement."

"That we know of." Dixon pitched his voice low. "If Orley is hiding people here, he would conceal it."

Their bedroom was dark, lit only by ambient light from Pasadena.

Jaz eased open the door and peeked into the hallway. She held her breath and listened. Everything was dark and quiet. No lights suddenly came on. No sounds of people climbing out of bed. With a sigh of relief, she pressed the door closed.

Dixon looked a question at her.

Jaz crossed the room to him and whispered, "Still asleep." She pushed her fists into the sides of her head. "I can't call Herridge on the basis of a dream. I have to know if it was real. If those agents are here, we have to find them."

Dixon caught her elbow. "Think for a moment. If Orley is imprisoning people in the basement and he catches us, we won't get a second chance. He'll either kill us or pop us into a tank of our own."

Jaz looked into Dixon's eyes. In the dim light, they were bottomless. "Then make sure we don't get caught."

Dixon shook his head. After a moment, when Jaz didn't relent, he sighed. "All right," said Dixon, holding out his hand. "Give me your gun."

"Why?" asked Jaz.

"Orley kept mine after our first meeting." He slipped

black bundle from his suitcase into his sock. "The man
s dangerous. I won't go into this unarmed."

Jaz unpacked her weapon and handed it to him. It
didn't seem real. How could a gentle man like Orley be
involved in the abduction of two NSA operatives?

Dixon slipped her gun into his holster.

Jaz eased open the bedroom door and crept down the
stairs without breathing, feeling her way along the wall.
Dixon followed. On the third step from the bottom there
was a creak—it sounded like a gunshot. She paused,
heart pounding, but didn't hear any answering footsteps
from above. She continued down the staircase and
stopped at the bottom.

Dixon stepped over the third step. For a big man, he
was graceful. He slid up to her. "Where?"

Jaz pointed to the kitchen.

They walked past the long dining table and through a
set of swinging doors. Inside was a farm-style kitchen
with glass-fronted cabinets and a tile countertop. The
only new additions were the appliances, which gleamed
amethyst in the latest style. A lighted screen on the refrigerator announced that they were low on milk, and
queried whether it should order more.

The only other door in the room led outside.

Jaz wasn't sure if she felt relief or disappointment. If
there was no door, then Orley wasn't holding anyone
captive. At least, not here.

Jaz and Dixon eased out of the kitchen and searched
the other rooms. They found a coat closet, a second bathroom, and a mudroom. Nothing that led underground.
They pulled up rugs, looking for trapdoors, checked the
back walls of closets.

"There's nothing," Dixon whispered when they
finished.

"This is an old house, built for Spanish missionaries
before electricity, before . . . refrigeration," Jaz mused.
"What if the room holding the agents started as a root
cellar? The entrance might be outside."

Dixon looked at the front door. It sported the latest
model electronic doorman: a combination alarm, dead

bolt, and visual-recognition system. "It's got to b
monitored."

"Windows?" Jaz whispered.

The nearest sill was connected into the doorman sys
tem by an IR transmitter. So were all the others.

Jaz slumped in the couch in the parlor. "We can't ge
out without waking Orley."

Dixon kneeled and pulled the slim black package fron
his sock. "I wouldn't say that." He unrolled the nylo
fabric to reveal a set of tools. Dixon extracted a slin
tube and pressed the top. Six legs popped open, makin
it look like a symmetrical water bug. "Read off the mak
and model of the doorman to me."

Jaz did so, and Dixon tapped a set of microscopic key
on the side of the tool with a stylus. When he was don
Dixon eased the central disk of the device over the trans
mitter on the window. Its legs gripped the sill.

Dixon unlocked the clasp of the window and ease
it up.

Jaz climbed through first. The air outside was balm
for early spring, and the roots of the banyan tree rustle
in a dry breeze.

When Dixon stood beside her, Jaz asked, "What wa
that?"

"Alarm spoofer. It intercepts the window's signal an
sends a status-normative ping to the doorman. Standar
equipment for your common spy—didn't Herridge teacl
you anything?"

Jaz was glad it was dark and that Dixon couldn't se
her blush. "I wasn't a very good student."

They circled the base of the Mission house, lookin
for a cellar door. Nothing.

"Find anything?" Jaz asked, when she and Dixon me
up at the back of the house.

He shook his head. "You?"

"Then it was just a dream." She knew Orley wasn't i
monster who would imprison men in his basement.

"So what happened to the NSA agents?"

They scanned the rest of the yard, their gaze comin

to rest on a gray potting shed. Jaz and Dixon exchanged a look.

"No," she protested. "It's too small, too far from the house."

Dixon strode toward it.

Jaz cast a glance back at the house. The sky was lightening in the east. It would be dawn soon. Whatever they did needed to be quick.

The door was padlocked shut. If there were electronic sensors, Jaz didn't see them.

Dixon pulled out his toolkit and selected an item that looked like an ice pick mounted on a gun handle. He put the metal probe into the keyhole and pumped the trigger. The lock clicked. Dixon eased the door open. A puff of cool air wafted out.

Jaz peered inside. There were potting benches against the walls to either side of the door covered with orchid pots and mounds of bark and perlite. Some light filtered in through a skylight in the ceiling. On the floor was a perforated rubber mat.

Jaz stepped into the room and kneeled by the matting. She peeled it back. Set into the floor was a new steel door with an electronic lock. It was bolted into cedar beams as thick as Jaz's waist, new remodel on an old root cellar. "Can you get through this?" she asked.

Dixon knelt beside the door with his tool kit. He selected and rejected two tools before settling on a third. "Keep an eye on the house. Let me know if any lights come on."

Jaz watched the house, her gaze flicking back to Dixon. Rose-and-amber streaks of light were breaking in the east. This was taking too long.

He was completely absorbed in the task at hand. His fingers worked delicately on a tool that sprouted flexible cables like the tentacles of a squid.

"I'm in," he whispered at last, a note of triumph in his voice. She heard him descend into the cellar, and then he whistled. "Jaz, you've got to see this."

Jaz took a last look at the house. Everything seemed

quiet; there were no lights on inside. She closed the doo
of the potting shed behind her. A wooden ladder le
into the dark cellar depths. After staring at the dawn
her eyes took a moment to adjust.

LED status lights were the first things she saw. Glow
ing numerals on the sensory-deprivation tank listed puls
rate and respiration.

Dixon held a penlight. In its faint glow she saw
torpedo-shaped outline. She followed the beam and saw
the face of a man. His eyes were closed and magnifie
by the oxygenated fluorocarbon emulsion he floated in

She felt as if someone had gut-punched her. She
backed away from the tank, breathing heavily.

"We've got to contact Herridge," Dixon said.

"Orley must have been driven to this," Jaz proteste
breathlessly, "by the government's interfering, Tate'
influence—he would never have done this willingly."

"It doesn't matter why, the fact is that he's kidnappe
federal agents. Your boyfriend's God-playing is out o
control." Dixon played his light around the room. "Bu
that's not the worst of it." The section they were in now
was dirt-floored and wooden-beamed, apparently built a
the same time as the house. It had once been a smal
root cellar two by two meters. Beyond that, however, the
room had been expanded with concrete flooring and
walls. It extended into a bunker ten meters long and five
meters across. There were four other tanks, all differen
makes and models. Old machines, perhaps bought at auc
tion. But what Orley's light lingered on was a pile o
new equipment: gleaming data gems the size of Jaz's fis
in a network of multicolored cabling.

"Is that what I think it is?"

Dixon picked up a loop of the fiber-optic ribbon. Doz
ens of strands were run together in multicolored plasti
sheathing. A rectangular silver plug dangled from the
end. "Hub servers and fiber-optic patch cords. My uncle
and I used gear like this to hack into the Net and rig
game servers." He turned to Jaz, his face silhouetted by
the penlight. "This isn't what you buy to manage a pri
vate, collegewide network. This hardware could run the

ntire west-coast network. I think Orley plans to
xpand—and soon."

"Impossible." Jaz took a step closer, not believing
vhat she saw. "Gestalt and the NSA would stop him.
Orley has to realize that."

"With this equipment Symbios could take over the Los
Angeles and Seattle hubs. It could control Herridge's
men in that area, give them false orders, or even waldo
heir bodies. This creature's used to having a lot more
mind share than Gestalt uses."

Jaz looked up at Dixon in horrified wonderment. "You
hink Symbios plans to take over the western states and
cut them off from the worldwide Net?"

"Could be."

Insanity. Isolated regions bred distrust. It would take
humanity back to pre-Unification, a time when countries
built arsenals of nuclear warheads to head off military
conflict. All life on earth would be held hostage to a
potential political misunderstanding.

Jaz believed Symbios should grow, but slowly, through
volunteers, and at a rate where its hosts could assimilate
the experience. Not like this, taking over large portions
of the world, in conflict with Gestalt.

The world wasn't ready for competing metaminds. It
wasn't ready for the knowledge of one, much less two.

Symbios could not be allowed to spread.

"We have to stop it," Jaz said. "A private network
might have worked, but this kind of expansion . . . is
wrong." She felt like Yudhisthira, who'd gambled his
kingdom away and was left wandering the wilderness. It
had been so good, connected to a small network of equals,
sharing, collaborating online. But this—she couldn't coun-
tenance. People would get hurt.

How could she have been so wrong about Orley? He
had seemed so gentle, so loving. But two men floated as
prisoners in sensory deprivation tanks, their minds en-
slaved to Symbios. She touched the faceplate over the
man nearest the door. "We have to get them out."

Dixon shook his head. "I don't know how. Did you
receive medical training?"

"No."

"I've no idea what the medical implications of long term sensory deprivation are. Bring them out too fast and they might go into shock."

Her heart felt like a stone in her chest. Here was the proof she needed. "We've accomplished what Herridge sent us in here for. We know what Orley's up to. This is Herridge's game now." Jaz pulled the Odin's Eye out of her jacket pocket. She slipped the jewelry in place over her eyes, and felt something wet on her face. She was crying.

"Gestalt," she whispered aloud as she connected to the great surf of humanity. Jaz rode waves of casual thoughts, people of a hundred nations, each with their own worldview. It was a comforting background hum like the sound of a television in the room you're not watching. The whirlwind of minds rose before her. She reached out to make contact—

—and was thrown into red-tinged darkness. A sharp pain lanced through her head. The connection was gone. Jaz grabbed her temples and opened her eyes.

Incandescent light flooded in from the trapdoor of the potting shed. Tate's face appeared in the bright rectangle. She smiled a twisted parody of mirth. On her head was both a headband connected to Symbios and a mass-produced monocle connected to the Net.

"Impossible," Jaz breathed. "No one can connect to two different networks simultaneously—the induction patterns would overlap—how could you distinguish the transmissions of the Net from those of Symbios's private network?"

"I'm a freak." Tate smiled in a twisted parody of mirth. "You didn't think Orley kept me around for my sunny disposition." She snapped another stim stick into the crook of her arm. "And I never sleep."

Behind her, Dixon slid his hand under his jacket.

"Stop!" Moving lightning fast, Tate brought a gun of her own to bear on Dixon. Her eyes twitched in her head, her fingers spasmed around the stock of the gun.

Dixon froze.

With her free hand, Tate tossed a headband to Jaz. "Put it on."

Jaz looked down at the band. She knew what Tate wanted—to finish the brain-hack Orley had interrupted two nights ago. Tate was strong, maybe even insane, and Orley wasn't here to hold her back from taking whatever she wanted from Jaz. "No."

Tate twitched the gun at Dixon. "Put it on or lover boy dies."

"Jaz, don't do it. She'll—"

The crack of a gunshot exploded in the cellar. Dixon fell backward with a shout of pain. He grabbed his arm. "Son of a bitch!"

Tate flicked the gun at Jaz. "Put the band on, or I'll finish him off. A feeb like him isn't worth sticking in a tank."

"Fuck you." Dixon swore through gritted teeth. He moved his wounded right arm toward the gun in his jacket. He cried out. Blood welled out of the wound in his shoulder.

Tate raised the gun to bear on Dixon. "No"—she cocked her head—"fu—"

"Wait!" Jaz held the headband up with two hands like an offering. "I'm putting it on."

The cold metal slipped around the back of her head, under her ears.

Symbios was fully awake, a maelstrom of images boiled forth: hostility, anger, betrayal.

Tate's avatar was a crystalline woman, spikes and spires rising from every joint: shoulders, ears, fingertips. Golden light illuminated her from inside. She would have been beautiful if she wasn't so dangerous.

Other minds were there, in the air around them, Moira and Dr. Akukwe. They didn't incorporate avatars, but Jaz could feel them feeding power into Tate. Symbios focused its processing on Tate, let her personality expand and take over the network. Tate raised her virtual hands and flexed them. Crystalline filaments exploded from her fingertips and drove into Jaz—a metaphor for the information-retrieval attack she launched.

The electronics in Jaz's headband heated, exciting her neurons in a cascade. Without her conscious control, images flashed through her head, and Tate intercepted them all, sorted them, ignored uninteresting bits like work and Jaz camping with her friends, found the time she had spent in the Faraday cell. Homed in on that. Images of Herridge, the training, the briefing. Jordon telling Jaz to seduce Orley, to use him to find out what was going on.

Jaz fought it, tried to shut down, to disconnect, to deflect Tate's power from sensitive information. She forced herself to remember scenes of violent emotion—intense pain, trying to distract herself from the dangerous thoughts. She used every trick the witch had taught her.

Jaz brought up recent images of sex with Orley, using Tate's aversion and jealousy against her, driving Tate back from her most private thoughts. Sweat beaded on her forehead, but she held her own.

Then another mind came online—Orley. His pain and humiliation at having been used flooded the connection.

The emotions caught Jaz off guard. Her shame about what she had done to him distracted her for a millisecond. Too late, Jaz realized her mistake.

Jaz felt Tate's rush of euphoria as she cracked Jaz open like a walnut and picked out chunks of information.

Jaz's eyes fluttered as thousands of sensory images flooded through her, phantom sights and smells and sounds. Everything she had ever thought was uploaded in a stream of agony. She wanted to escape the virtual world, but she couldn't move her arms, couldn't disconnect. Tate held her body immobile.

When it was over, Jaz lay sprawled on the packed-earth floor. Her mouth tasted of bile.

Orley peered down at her from the cellar door. In the physical world he wore blue-and-white-striped pajamas. His face was a mask of pain. There was no anger, no rage, only endless grief.

His dream had been perverted, by the government's interference and Tate's pathological fears. Everything had gone wrong. And Jaz, the woman he had opened himself to, was the instrument that had sealed his fate.

If he had hated her, Jaz could have borne it, but his pain was too much. She closed her eyes to block him out.

But there was no escape. His avatar floated in front of her in the virtual world, to the left of Tate's consuming brightness.

Black smoke rose from the circuits of his skin; regret stained his cheeks and the deep sockets of his eyes. "Jasmine, how could you? I trusted . . . You would have completed me."

"Don't please—I had to know—I never wanted . . ."

With a tone of infinite sadness, he said, "Take her, Tate."

Tate's avatar stepped forward and embraced Jaz. A thousand crystal spikes pierced Jaz—then she thought no more.

CHAPTER 20

Jaz floated in darkness. There was no sensation: not sight, or sound, or even the weight of her body. The sensory-deprivation tank blocked nerve impulses from her body to her brain.

Images sprang into her consciousness, evoked by Symbios. Jaz tried to still her mind, to resist, to think of nothing. But even that indirect reference to what she needed to suppress drew it forth. Symbios used the tank's induction circuitry to excite glutamate receptors in Jaz's brain, playing back her memories.

Against her will, she relived her capture at Thunder Basin. Saw Matt's eyes wide with panic as Herridge carried her away. She sat in the Faraday cage of the NSA compound, her mirrored cell reflecting twisted images of herself.

Symbios drew forth visions of Herridge telling Jaz what she must do to earn her freedom—Jordon's throaty voice advising Jaz to seduce Orley—Dixon, searching through the root cellar with her—horror at discovering the agents in their silent tubes—the call—

Time slowed. Jaz relived the instant she had called out to Gestalt, examining the data flow from the moment of connection until Tate had disrupted the transmission. What had been sent? Had Gestalt realized she was on-line? Would it be coming after them?

Jaz knew these weren't her thoughts.

Symbios drove her brain, and there was nothing Jaz could do about it. Images flickered in and out of her awareness, some her memories, others transmitted from the collective.

But Jaz had spent years learning control of her brain. She fought to concentrate her thoughts, gather herself before Symbios could sense and disperse her consciousness. In a memory written when she was three years old, Jaz found paths of defiance: "No! I won't—you can't make me." She screamed for a toy truck another child had taken; she drove her neurons to higher voltage levels, inhibiting the induction jewelry's ability to manipulate her brain.

The drugs Orley had given her, however, slowed her thinking, predisposed her to distraction. Jaz lost her connection to the rebellious memory for an instant. Symbios fragmented her thoughts. Strong electronic potentials forced her mind down Symbios's routes.

Her last conscious emotion was a fierce struggling, a resistance, then Jaz—as a self-aware entity—was gone. In the firing neurons of her brain, there was only Symbios.

Symbios's thoughts were not human. They spread over many bioagents, each working on part of the problem or thought, and exchanging results with others. Chordal thinking.

Orley and Moira, Symbios's first two bioagents, and those it trusted with its deepest concerns and emotions, worried about the transmission Jaz had sent before Tate interrupted her—subquery to Tate about the outgoing signal—Tate's memory was that Jaz had completed a connection to the Net at the time of interception, but how much information she had conveyed to the other was unknown.

Jaz herself didn't know—slumbering, drugged, in the sensory-deprivation tank: it was easy for Symbios to replay her memory. Access to Jaz's thoughts was clearer now than in her first connection to Symbios. They understood now, her rejection of Gestalt, Herridge's recruitment, the betrayal of Orley—a wince of Orley-agent's embarrassment and hurt flickered through the Net. She had betrayed them all. Jaz's message to Gestalt was cut off in the moment of transmission. But how much information had gotten through in that instant? There was no way to know.

Symbios wondered what to do. Each person connected to Symbios paused in their physical actions, as the meta-mind drove their thoughts toward this question. If Herridge and his men attacked, they would be imprisoned, subjected to the same disconnected fate as Dixon Tully . . . and Symbios would die.

A swell of fear and anger. Orley and Moira returned the results of their contemplation: they must assume Gestalt now knew Symbios existed. Symbios felt the resonance of agreement in all its beings. They would not hide and hope the other would pass them by; they would not wait for another infiltration. This time, they would fight.

Tate held open her tenuous connections to both Symbios and the worldwide Net. Through it, everyone watched the Net for Gestalt's reaction. The other was out there, filtered across more minds than Symbios could imagine. There was no obvious sign of agitation, but that could be a ruse.

Tate was an anomaly of nature more rare than any of a hundred thousand naturals. She could connect her mind to two networks simultaneously, somehow able to differentiate incoming signals in real time and route them to parallel threads of consciousness. Through her, Symbios felt a sweep of contact from Gestalt.

Gestalt caused Tate to wonder what had happened to Jasmine Reese. Had the natural been on the web, however briefly?

Symbios isolated the thought-agent Gestalt transmitted to Tate's mind, caught it before her brain formulated an answer. The tiny bit of neural programming was compact, designed to incite a thought in whomever it encountered and return significant results to Gestalt's hub bioagents, for aggregation. Symbios teased apart the mnemonic programming . . . and learned.

Meanwhile, the body was in action. Dr. Jensen and Moira loaded the van with the networking equipment from the basement, enough to patch a connection from Symbios to the Net. They drove to Dr. Jensen's private plane in Burbank, an antique Cessna that could be flown manually. Using a handheld computer they filed flight plans for Los Angeles and Seattle. They would enter the western seaboard, take over this part of the Net before obsolete, slow, careful Gestalt could respond. Once Symbios had a hold, it could transmit itself via the Net's infrastructure: fiber-optic lines and wireless picocell transmitters. With control of the minds in this area, Gestalt would not have governmental forces to post an attack. Any connected person entering the area would join Symbios.

There was the threat of a long-distance nuclear attack, but models of Gestalt's thinking suggested that was an unlikely response. A human might realize amputating its hand was the only way to stop the spread of gangrene, but it was a rare individual who would grab a knife and begin hacking.

Confusion and discord resonated through Symbios about what to do once the western seaboard of the United States was taken. Different bioagents returned wildly divergent ideas: take over the Net entirely, arrange a truce, declare secession from the union. Symbios stopped processing the question. Too chaotic, too many unknowns. They would address it when more data were available.

There was a gentle decrease in Symbios's resources as Moira and Dr. Jensen drove out of range of the Caltech lab cell.

Those who were still connected to Symbios returned to the Mission house. To Symbios this was a focusing of its thoughts, reducing latency and lag between its agents. When they collected in the house, it thought faster. The addition of two more dedicated units bolstered its capability for problem-solving. Symbios was at peak efficiency.

There was a niggling bit of static from the dedicated unit, Jaz. Powerful and efficient during her previous connection, Jaz was not scalable. When driven at full usage performance degraded. A disappointment, but she wa still a benefit, not a liability.

Good, Orley-agent returned, though it could not com pletely justify why Jaz should be kept alive. Most of th others agreed with this result, but less emphatically. Onl Tate-agent advised termination of Jaz-unit as defectiv and unreliable. Symbios paused during the aggregatio of these conflicting solutions. Tate-agent's solution wa powerful and with solid reasons behind it, but eventuall it was overwhelmed by moral and conservation concerns In the coming conflict, Symbios would need all the pro cessing power it could leverage. It could kill or discon nect the Jaz-unit later, should that become necessary.

The Dixon-agent was more cooperative. When querie about Net-hacks, he volunteered a wealth of information So much data flowed from Dixon, Symbios had to dedicat additional processing to assimilate the new information an coordinate it into a battle plan.

Hours passed, with the biounits in quiet meditation o the floor. Those that were hungry ate a light lunch, dranl some water. They would need to be fit for the comin, war. Symbios wanted them rested, fed, and efficient.

Then, like a jolt of lightning into a generator, the Lo Angeles and Seattle transmitters came online. Symbio patched into the worldwide Net. A wave of sensory im pressions and random thought-agents washed over an through the biounits. It was like the sudden clearing o a fog. Instead of a close room, Symbios now stood on mountain and saw to the horizon. It expanded a million fold, reprogramming Gestalt's thought-agents into it own, sending out destructor thoughts that disassemble Gestalt's agents, replacing them with Symbios's own.

Symbios felt like a tightly compressed fluid that, now released, flooded the western coast. It grew in intuitio and mind-space. Its thoughts spread across hundreds o millions of people, giving it a depth and breadth of emo tion it had never known before. Symbios felt *real*.

But it was not alone. Gestalt had sensed the intruder' presence and moved to attack.

CHAPTER 21

Gestalt streamed thought-agents into Symbios, exploring. The neural programs filtered through the people connected to Symbios, searching for one in particular. Symbios generated counteragents to block the probe, but too late. Of the billions of copies Gestalt sent, one found Jaz, learned what she knew, and broadcast its findings throughout the network.

Gestalt hesitated. Surprise poured through the synapses of six billion humans. Another metamind?

In that millisecond of confusion, Symbios's consciousness rolled across California into Nevada, from Washington, through Idaho, to Montana. Its skills and knowledge grew exponentially. Through borrowed eyes, Symbios saw sun-baked deserts, bare granite peaks, and miles of suburban sprawl.

The respite was brief. Gestalt counterattacked with dissolution agents, tiny bubbles of thought to cast Symbios out.

Symbios countered by intercepting the all-clear message the dissolution agents received when a mind was free of Symbios. The metamind spoofed the code and convinced the agents it was Gestalt. They froze, believing their mission complete.

Symbios pushed farther, into Las Vegas, a hotbed of connection activity, legal and otherwise. There was a central hub there. If Symbios could take it over, it could launch an attack into the Midwest . . . something that hadn't seemed possible before. Symbios felt surprise in its base units. Gestalt was weak; the world was ripe for the taking. Did it want that?

Yes.

Symbios infiltrated casinos, gathering a sense of the odds and how the games were rigged in favor of the house. It lost a millisecond when it realized the players knew that, too, but still bet their money, hoping for a flaw in the house's system. How strange humanity was.

Symbios programmed new agents to close any open connection below a certain bandwidth. Symbios took 10 percent of a person's mental processing, Gestalt less than 1 percent. The new agents began shutting Gestalt down.

Gestalt reprogrammed its connections, taking more: 20, 30 percent. In the casinos, people froze like deer in the headlights, chaos swirling in their minds. An old lady fell to the ground, clutching her heart. Men and women stood immobile, the only thing moving in the room a roulette wheel, carried on by inertia.

Gestalt's aggressive move generated fear and anger in the biounits. They didn't know at a conscious level what was going on, what was being asked of them. Their thoughts ran in strange paths, beyond their control.

Symbios leaked images of itself and Gestalt as gods in the sky, locked in combat over the earth. It was the shining liberator, and Gestalt an oppressive dark force. If it could appeal to humanity on an emotional basis, perhaps they would do Symbios's work for it and cast Gestalt out.

Gestalt manufactured memes to destroy the agents distributing the message and wipe the memories of itself and Symbios. It constructed an image in Symbios's collective mind: people learning that Symbios and itself existed, panic as people disconnected, death and famine as food-distribution routes came to a grinding halt.

Symbios countered with a second image: people hand in hand embracing Symbios, working with it collaboratively, the scientists who had willingly given so much of themselves to it, of Jaz, who had feared Gestalt but embraced Symbios.

Gestalt transmitted an image of Jaz submerged in a sensory-deprivation tank.

Deep within Symbios's consciousness, Jaz stirred. It might have been the drugs wearing off, or that Symbios's attention was spread thin across the western half of the United States, or perhaps Gestalt had managed to slip in an agent in that instant of contact with her.

Jaz's eyes fluttered open in the oxygenated fluorocarbon emulsion.

Symbios fought Gestalt for sole control of the relay in Las Vegas. If it could take over that relay, it could reach Houston, then Atlanta and New York. From New York, it was a short hop across the Atlantic to Europe and the rest of the world.

Gestalt now held only a few agents, generating static and preventing Symbios from seizing full control. Then suddenly, users in the casino began to disconnect.

At first Symbios thought Gestalt had found a way to write a program that could distinguish between them, but then it sensed from the people it shared with Gestalt—no. The people were being completely disconnected, no longer accessible to either metamind.

Like a firefighter, Gestalt was drawing a firebreak in the Net. If it could not destroy Symbios, it would halt its progress.

Insane! Symbios stimulated the same images Gestalt had transmitted to show the chaos that would arise from disconnection.

As their internal war raged, Las Vegas ground to a halt. Hotel elevators froze, trapping people inside. Huntington Memorial Hospital went on emergency power. Medical machines no longer communicated patient status. All the bed alarms went off at once. Nurses and interns scrambled to answer all calls, unsure which were real.

Still Gestalt unraveled the network, building its firewall.

Traffic on the highways became uncoordinated. A four-trailer cargo truck on I-15 slammed into a passenger car. Unable to sense the destruction ahead, forty-two vehicles slammed into the pileup before drivers saw the wreck visually and overrode the automatic controls.

Symbios was outraged that the other overmind would turn on its units this way. Gestalt was a threat to human life.

Dixon Tully had information Symbios needed to stop the bloodshed. In the same way plucking a nearby guitar string causes the others to vibrate in harmonic resonance, Symbios could transmit its agents on multiple frequencies. Once a connection was made, the user could be swayed to convert to a new frequency. It was an old hacker's trick. If Symbios kept switching its main transmission frequency, Gestalt wouldn't be able to catch up.

Symbios employed Dixon's technique, capturing users who had been cut off from the Net. They were now solely Symbios's. With a surge of this new processing power, Symbios expanded itself further.

Gestalt tried to match Symbios's new frequencies, but the younger metamind had twenty talented naturals at its core. It was less distributed, more focused, faster. And it drove its users harder, now taking fifty, seventy-five percent. It gained more from each new unit than Gestalt lost. The old metamind was losing ground.

As Symbios concentrated on the attack front, the lag to its core hosts increased. As communication between Symbios and the scientists in Pasadena took longer, its influence over them waned.

In the basement of the Mission house, Jaz stirred. Her first conscious thought was: No. I will not.

Jaz had been infinite, part of a creature exploding across North America, but now she remembered herself. The metaminds used the carnage they created as moral arguments against each other. In her tank, seeing the pileups on the highway, watching planes collide over congested airports, Jaz wept. Her second thought was: This must stop.

Hundreds of miles away, Symbios transmitted a picture of the British retreating from the New World and leaving it to the colonists.

Gestalt transmitted back the statistics from the spread of the LA-III virus. It started in Los Angeles and swept across the world, killing hundreds of thousands before a cure was found.

Jaz sensed all this through her link with Symbios. If the metamind noticed her awakening, it didn't have time to react. Gestalt held it at bay just outside Atlanta and Chicago.

While they warred, North America self-destructed around them. The people in their thrall froze like zombies, waiting for a victor. The only free people were the feebs, who wandered the streets in wonder, poking at their mysteriously frozen fellowmen.

Through the eyes of an investment banker, Jaz saw Ellery Houston, the homeless man who had warned her about the beast. His rheumy eyes were inches away from the banker's. He knocked on the rich man's head.

"Anybody home?"

Using skills the witch had taught her, Jaz settled into the banker's body. She blinked.

The homeless man jumped back with a cry of alarm.

Speaking through the banker's lips, Jaz said, "The beast walks the earth. Free the people. Tell the others." With the banker's large and unfamiliar hands, Jaz reached over and removed the data jewelry from a young mother with a toddler strapped into a stroller. The child was too young for a connection and was bawling at his frozen mother. When the jewelry was removed from her, the woman shook herself and picked up the child, caressing and soothing it.

A gleam lit the watery blue eyes of the homeless man and he began capering about the motionless people in a rolling gait, pulling off their jewelry. "Free the others!" he shouted, as if finally the world made sense. "Free yourself!"

She repeated this in cities across North America. By their very nature, Gestalt and Symbios were barely aware of the feebs. Jaz used that blindness against them. But it wouldn't be enough.

Even thousands of people snatching off data jewelry

wouldn't stop the conflict. One of the metaminds had to win. They were direct competitors; there could never be peace between them. As one prospered, the other suffered.

As much as she had felt at home with Symbios and the other scientists, the fastest way to stop this conflict was to destroy the young metamind. For a brief suspicious moment Jaz wondered if Gestalt had planted that thought in her mind during its momentary contact, then decided it didn't matter. It was the right decision, whatever its origin.

But how? She was no metamind, her mental processes stretching halfway across a continent. How could a single human make a difference? How could you destroy something with the combined intelligence of millions of people?

If there were a thousand of her, or a hundred thousand, it still wouldn't be enough. Unless . . . instead of making herself greater, she made Symbios less. Could she reduce the number of connecteds, break the lines of communications? She hid these thoughts with layers of irrelevant reminiscences: a recipe for iced coffee, the sway of a hammock in the wind, and the smell of fresh-mown grass.

Jaz closed her eyes. Her prison was a boon, blocking out unnecessary sensory input as she constructed a neural program, stringing together thoughts and autosuggestions to trigger computation in the recipient's brain. It was like the agents Symbios and Gestalt used to coordinate thoughts between their hosts, but this one required no central communication. It would replicate itself, and then move the user's body to disconnect their data jewelry.

She stole worm-virus code from Dixon's memory and wrapped it in one of Symbios's agent programs. When she was done, it looked like a basic network ping, code to establish and persist a connection to hosts even when no data was being transmitted. A Trojan horse with a deadly payload.

Jaz felt Symbios struggling with Gestalt. It had taken Atlanta, and was working its way north toward New

York. Soon Gestalt would be driven out of the United States, and have to continue the attack through the transfer stations between the United States, Canada, and Mexico. If that happened, Symbios could cut fiber-optic feeds from those nations and hold the United States indefinitely.

Orley would never forgive her for killing his dream. Jaz wasn't sure she would forgive herself. She didn't know which would be worse, if her worm virus failed or if it succeeded. With a whisper of regret, Jaz transmitted the code.

The virus worked against both Gestalt and Symbios, but it originated within Symbios's structure, rupturing outward, depleting Symbios's resources on the way.

Anger welled through Jaz. The wrath of a god betrayed. Symbios looked in her mind and found what she had done. It moved to disrupt the program, to cut off the infected communication lines and isolate those users. In milliseconds it had done so, but not before 35 percent of its new hosts were offline.

Jaz quailed in her tank. Through her connection to Symbios, she sensed Gestalt moving closer, taking territory back from Symbios. More of Gestalt's agent-programs made their way through to Jaz before being destroyed—formed a barrier between her and Symbios, and gave Jaz room to think.

"More," the programs whispered before disintegrating. "Do more."

Jaz gritted her teeth. Symbios tried to regain control over her, drive her harder. She felt herself fading, her personality subsumed into the fractured viewpoint of the metamind.

Symbios was in full flight, retreating from Atlanta and Chicago, making a brief stand in Houston, before falling back to Las Vegas. But Jaz's worm had spread out from the central hubs of its network. Symbios was a tree whose roots were destroyed, it held on to its foundation solely through the mental processes of its original founders, those with implants who could not be disconnected. If she could isolate the parts of Symbios on the Net from its Pasadena core, perhaps it could be stopped. Jaz's thoughts coalesced slowly, like thinking through mud. Symbios had taken control of her logic centers. Her programming skill was at its disposal, not hers. She tried to think a line of code. But before she could finish, the logic was overwritten by one of Symbios's agent-programs.

Her primary motor cortex. Her body. That was all the metamind had left her to work with, had discarded as not useful to the battle.

Gestalt and Symbios thought of humans as mental-processing units. Never having had a physical body, it was easy for the metaminds to forget that humans did. Her body was trapped inside the tank . . . but there were others.

Jaz reached out to Moira in Los Angeles and Dr. Jensen in Seattle. Their mutual contact through Symbios made them easy to locate. The metamind drove their minds at near full capacity, leaving nothing alert to protect their bodies. Jaz gently took control, using techniques she had learned from the witch.

It was a strain, waldoeing two other bodies in different locations. But she had to do this simultaneously. If she shut down only half of Symbios's patch, it could stop her. Jaz's vision blurred as two sets of optic nerves fed conflicting input to her brain.

Symbios sensed something going on. Jaz felt Orley's awareness touch her mind: "What are you—"

She shut him out. Dixon was there, a firefly presence, lending her all the light he could.

Jaz reached out with two sets of trembling hands—

Symbios turned its attention on Jaz. To stop her, it increased the potential on the induction jewelry, driving her neurons at dangerous voltages. A driving spike of pain lanced through Jaz's head as her brain heated and neurons started to die.

Jaz felt as if she were thinking through broken glass, firing neurons one by one.

In the Net, a million minds thought for Gestalt, concentrated on the problem of Symbios, programmed memes to distract the biounits supporting the younger metamind. Symbios had to divert a portion of its attention to collate the new data coming in from the front lines, users disconnected in downtown Seattle with no explanation. It was only a thousandth of the metamind's control, but that instantaneous lapse was enough.

Grunting with effort, Jaz waldoed Moira and Jensen into position, their hands on the uninterruptible power sources that supplied electricity to the transmitters. With a final thrust of will, she pushed both emergency off buttons on the uninterruptible power sources. In Seattle and Los Angles, the server hardware shut off.

Suddenly the world was twenty people wide.

Jaz gasped at the sudden release. Her adversary had just shrunk a millionfold. But the respite was temporary. Jensen and Moira were loyal to Symbios. Short of rendering them unconscious or killing them, there was no way to prevent them from turning the servers back on.

Somehow, Jaz had to get the number of connecteds below Symbios's consciousness threshold before that happened.

Jaz hit the emergency release on the inside of the sensory-deprivation tank. Either Orley had counted on the drugs to keep her unconscious, or he hadn't had time to disable it. The tank's lid popped open with a hydraulic whoosh, and fluid cascaded over the sides.

Crawling out of the sensory-deprivation tank was an ordeal. Orley's drugs left her limbs shaky and clenched. Once out of the tank, she leaned forward and coughed out fluorocarbon fluid.

In that instant, she felt the network hardware come back online. The initialization sequence to connect to the worldwide Net would take mere seconds. Jaz fought to reestablish her hold on Moira and Jensen, but Symbios blocked her way.

"Goddamn it. Someone help me," Jaz swore.

Behind her she heard the creak of a tank lid. She turned.

Dixon Tully half crawled, half fell out of the tank. He coughed as she had, clearing his lungs. "You—" he broke off in a coughing fit—"stop them. I'll . . . the tanks."

There was no time to worry about medical protocol. The war had already killed thousands in automobile and airplane accidents. More would die if Symbios wasn't stopped.

Dixon lurched over to the tank holding one of the NSA agents. He smashed the glass with a crescent wrench. Fluorocarbon emulsion and glass sluiced across the room. Dixon reached down to snatch off the electronics that bound the man to the Net.

Jaz couldn't watch anymore, she had work of her own to do. She sank down cross-legged in the clear liquid and focused her mind. Dixon had given her an idea. It was time for irrevocable action.

Her head pounded in rhythm with her heart. Her brain spiked with pain—her forehead felt on fire. Something was broken inside her brain—but no time to worry about that. Symbios was a threat, not just to her own freedom—but everyone's. Jaz stilled her breathing, silenced her body to the room around her, and prepared to do what no one had ever attempted; she was going to take over a collective consciousness.

She timed her heartbeats to the rhythm of the network pings that kept the hosts in contact with Symbios. The path hardware had been restored, and Symbios was growing in the worldwide Net. It had been weakened, but was regaining ground fast.

To merge with it, she had to give over conscious control, let Symbios move through her, use her. Jaz leaned back until her head lay half-submerged in the oxygenated emulsion. Her mind served Symbios, creating agent programs with a facility matched by only a few others on the Net.

The metamind was suspicious, but needed all the resources it could muster to retake California. It drove Jaz hard, taking ninety, then ninety-five percent of her neural functioning. Jaz succumbed, feigning surrender.

It was like composing a sonnet in a hurricane, but for every hundred lines of code Symbios wrote through her, Jaz crafted one of her own.

With skill that would have made the witch proud, Jaz created an infectious thought, a meme, to drive Jensen and Moira. Her brief experience in their minds had given her access to images in their memories: private shames, secret fantasies.

Jaz wrapped the meme in a network ping and set it to go off when received by someone who recognized those key images: for Jensen, naked youths in a steamy locker room, for Moira, the shrieking of a crippled horse.

While she waited for the meme to work its way to them, Jaz let herself drift. The battle was glorious. Jaz felt herself expand across the United States, growing smarter and stronger with each added mind. Ideas and images coruscated across the sky of an internal landscape. It was like being inside a thundercloud. Each lightning flash illuminated a new attack: memes disconnected bioagents, Symbios changed the message protocols for its agents on the fly; Gestalt intercepted those messages with spurious data. Symbios counterattacked with a denial of service attack on Gestalt's hubs in Chicago and Atlanta. Packets of erroneous data flooded into Gestalt, and it wasted processing power trying to sort real from illusory. They were two giants fighting in the sky across North America, each step spanning a league.

Then, with a click, her meme-bomb found its targets. The images replayed, inciting a flash of recognition and violent emotions in its intended targets. The sudden rush of hormones triggered the compulsion Jaz had planted inside.

Moira ripped out the patch cords, crumpling the fiber-optic ribbon in her fists and shattering the delicate fibers. In Seattle, Dr. Jensen wrenched off the steel bar locking the server rack and dropped it across the UPS battery bus bars. The resultant explosion knocked him to his knees.

Symbios was furious. Its world had shrunken to eighteen, but that was still enough to cook Jaz's brain. She dragged off the connection jewelry and slumped sideways in the puddle of clear fluid.

Dixon was smeared in his own blood; the wound in his shoulder had reopened with his exertions. The two NSA agents coughed on the floor.

The trapdoor opened.

In the too-bright light Jaz could make out the blond halo of Tate's hair. "You bitch!" she shouted, spewing spittle. "You've ruined everything!" Tate pointed her gun at Jaz's face.

Jaz's stomach clenched. The gun barrel seemed enormous, gaping before her like a train tunnel. This would be her last ride.

Tate's finger tightened on the trigger.

Dixon started for Jaz, but he was too far away—he'd never make it. No time for Jaz to roll aside. She lay still, waiting for the bang.

"I wouldn't do that if I were you," said a voice in the darkness. A gun barrel pressed against the side of Tate's head. The owner of the voice stepped into the light, his face as naked of data jewelry as the day she had met him. Herridge.

CHAPTER 22

"See you in hell," Tate said, and pulled the trigger.
Something slammed sideways into Jaz, knocking stars into her vision. The gunshot exploded in her ears. Jaz hit the earthen floor of the cellar and a rib cracked. The pain was glorious; if she could hurt she wasn't dead.

"Shit, shit, shit," Dixon hissed. He rolled off Jaz, clutching his neck. Blood spurted from between his fingers.

A second explosion. Tate jerked sideways.

Herridge's face appeared in the square of light above. It was spattered with blood and gray matter, but his glacial blue eyes were calm. "Everyone all right down there?"

Jaz smelled gunpowder, blood, and shit. "Dixon is wounded." Her voice quavered. "I—I don't know about the other agents." Her probing hands found the gunshot wound on Dixon's neck. The one he had taken to save her. Hot blood gushed through her fingers. Jaz pressed her palm against the bleeding. "There's a lot of blood—we need a doctor—now!"

"I've put in a call. Here." Herridge tossed a first-aid kit through the trapdoor.

Jaz watched it land in the murky orange mud. Too far away. Jaz feared that, if she let off the pressure to grab it, Dixon would die. His eyes were already taking on the glassy edge of shock. She cradled his head in her lap and bent over him, rocking slightly. "Stay with me, Dixon.

We've been through too much for you to quit now. Please. Stay."

Dixon's pale lips parted in a smile. "See," he croaked. "I knew you wanted me." His eyes fluttered and closed.

Jaz lifted her head and howled, her entire being lost in that sound and the feel of Dixon's life ebbing beneath her fingers.

Hands lifted her from Dixon's body. Someone shined a light in her eyes. "Conjugate deviation of the eyes to the left, possible intracerebral hemorrhaging. Get her into the ambulance, stat."

Someone strapped Jaz to a gurney and lifted her through the cellar door. Dixon lay below, men with Red Cross armbands crouched around him, trying to keep him alive. As the medics carried her away, Jaz reached her hands back, imploring Dixon to live. Live, Dixon, live. Please. For me.

Tate was a crumpled heap under the potting bench. Half her head was gone. Jaz observed the misshapen skull through a fog of pain and shock. Dead. Her fault. Think about it later.

Outside, the morning air was cold. The first true rays of dawn lightened the horizon. Men shouted orders. Scientists in nightshirts and pajamas marched, hands on their heads, toward two black vans. Orley was among them. For an instant, their eyes met. His mouth twisted with anger and grief. He shouted over the chaos. *"Why? We shared everything. You killed Tate—you killed Symb—"*

A black-uniformed man slammed the butt of his rifle into the side of Orley's knee. Orley's leg folded sideways, and he went down screaming.

Cold tears streamed down Jaz's cheeks. She tasted their salt in her mouth. The last glimpse she got of Orley he was writhing on the ground, his face contorted in pain.

Everything was falling apart. She couldn't think. Each step the medics carrying her took slammed her brain against her skull. Bile rose in the back of her throat.

They slid her gurney into the ambulance. The bright white lights made her tear up again. Jaz tilted her head and squeezed her eyes shut. No good, she could still see red, pulsing like the purple-green pain in her skull.

Symbios had driven her brain past its breaking point. Jaz couldn't find the words, but she knew she was dying.

"She's suffered a hemorrhagic brain attack. Get her temperature down—now!" The medics pushed her hand through a gasket into a glass jar. Somewhere in the floor of the ambulance, a vacuum pump started. Jaz shivered as blood vessels in her arm dilated, radiating away heat.

A screaming torment of sirens and an endless bumping and jostling down asphalt streets. Jaz blacked out when they bounced her down out of the ambulance and into the emergency room. She woke to the cold touch of scissors, cutting off her clothes.

"Easy now." A black woman pressed her back into the gurney. "Got to get these off so the doctor can look at you."

"No," Jaz whispered, lolling her head left and right. Leave me to die in peace. But her mouth couldn't find the words.

Reality strobed past Jaz in disjointed sensations: Herridge. A sleepy-looking Japanese man with a coat thrown over tan silk pajamas. Low voices. A cold metal collar around the back of her head. Clear mask coming down over her nose and mouth. Metal rods screwed against her skull, holding her head immobile.

She opened her mouth wide to scream, inhaled the acrid tang of anesthesia, and passed out.

Jaz moved her hand to scratch her nose, but couldn't. Her eyes fluttered open and she saw an IV tube taped to the crook of her right arm. In her left elbow, a needle probe led to a machine that monitored the level of medication in her bloodstream. Oxygen flowed into her through a set of nostril plugs. Nylon straps secured her wrists. It was a claustrophobic feeling. Jaz struggled feebly trying to escape—afraid she would pull something free.

A blurry figure moved at the foot of her bed. Jaz blinked to focus her eyes. A man in a dark green uniform, one of Herridge's men. He wore a headband connected to the Net.

"Easy, Ms. Reese." He placed a restraining hand on her shoulder. "Take it easy."

"Wha hap . . ."

"I've placed a call to Colonel Herridge." The young man's brown eyes were sympathetic. "He'll be here shortly."

Jaz lolled back against the bed. Images flashed through her head: Dixon, bleeding from his neck. Tate's head jerking sideways. Orley cursing, falling. A medic leaning over her, peering into her eyes with a penlight. *"Concussion, possibly internal hemorrhaging."*

Her throat convulsed with nausea.

The door opened, and Herridge entered. His uniform was rumpled, and the beginnings of a beard stubbled his cheek. His eerie blue gaze was hidden by silver induction goggles. Their facets reflected the room, making his eyes look like shattered mirrors. Disconcerting, but not as frightening as his calm, expressionless eyes when he'd killed Tate.

The guard saluted and left the room.

Herridge turned to Jaz. Her image wavered in his goggle lenses: bruised black circles under her eyes, sunken sallow cheeks, and a turban of bandages around her head. She reached up to touch them, but she was still tethered.

Herridge stepped closed and undid the nylon straps tying her down.

"Not a prisoner?" she whispered.

"No, Ms. Reese. Your mission was a success. The country owes you a debt of gratitude." Herridge's voice was smoother, somehow. The edgy energy she'd associated with him was gone. Or perhaps even the mighty Herridge was exhausted after the morning's raid.

She felt the gauze covering her head with her fingertips. "What happened?"

Herridge looked toward the door. "This is a civilian hospital. You weren't stable enough to transport to one of our facilities. There are things we can't discuss here. Do you understand?"

Jaz nodded and immediately regretted the motion. "Yes."

"Let's call what happened to you . . . an equipment malfunction. During this malfunction, your network connection induced potentials in your brain five times higher than maximum safe levels. You nearly died. Damn lucky thing the University of Southern California has a crack neurosurgery department." Herridge scrubbed his jaw. "You want the medical details?"

"Yes."

"Give me a moment." His face slackened as he concentrated on the Net. Herridge's voice deepened and took on a slight Japanese accent. "Neuron death in the immediate vicinity cascaded waste products to cells in the penumbra . . . excess potassium caused glia cells to release glutamate and other neurotransmitters . . . overstimulation of neurons and buildup of sodium, calcium, and zinc has swelled penumbral neurons, and . . . burst cell membranes. Administering glutamate inhibitor MK-801 to block activity at glutamate synapses, and designer enzymes to scavenge excess calcium and zinc from the affected regions."

Jaz blinked. Her stomach felt like someone had hollowed her out with a spoon. "How much damage?"

Herridge laid a comforting hand on Jaz's shoulder. "It's too soon to say. We got you and Dr. Takashira together within thirty minutes of the event. That helped. His prognosis is guarded, but optimistic."

Her breath rattled in her chest. She couldn't stop hyperventilating. "I need a number, a percentage. How much did I lose?"

"It doesn't work like that—"

"Get Takashira in here and let him tell me." Jaz sat up in bed. "I need a number. How much of me died back there?"

Herridge studied his fingernails. "The brain is elastic. It can reroute information around damaged regions."

"Don't give me platitudes. I was a good soldier. I deserve to know."

He sighed. "It will be a couple of days until your brain stabilizes. The poisons building up from dying neurons may kill others. It all depends on how your body accepts the designer enzymes. Five percent of the neurons in your left hemisphere have died. That number may rise as high as seven to fifteen percent, depending on how you respond to treatment."

She might be a gibbering wreck, barely able to talk, or only slightly impaired. Which would be worse: being so damaged she wasn't aware of what she lost, or losing just enough to feel it? Either way, she wouldn't be special anymore. The edge that had made her a natural would be gone. Her skill at data mining was the one thing that had never let her down. Panic seized Jaz's chest. "Will I be able to connect?"

"The doctors don't know. It'll take a day or two to flush the remaining waste products and enzymes out of your system. Then you should be stable enough to try."

Now she knew how Dixon felt. Then she remembered. He'd been shot. "Dixon?"

A shoulder came up in a half shrug. "Lost a lot of blood, but he pulled through."

"Can I see him?"

"No. He's been transferred to a military facility. When you're in stable condition, we'll move you there."

Jaz reached up toward the sliver lenses that hid Herridge's intense blue eyes. "And you?"

Herridge smiled and took her hand before it could touch the glasses. "I am at peace again. Our mutual friend comforts me."

"Orley—"

"Don't say that name." Herridge cut Jaz off with a tense whisper. "Not here. That information is classified."

She met his too-near gaze. "Alive?"

"Yes. I can't tell you more." Herridge cocked his head as if hearing internal voices. "I've got to go. If you need anything, ask Lieutenant Jameson." Herridge patted her shoulder, then walked to the door.

Jaz stopped him with a question. "Am I really free?"

He looked at her over his shoulder, weighing the question. "Yes."

"Then why the guard?" she asked, looking over at Jameson, who stood just outside the door.

Herridge sucked his teeth. "He's here for your protection. There were two . . . outside of Pasadena. . . . We haven't apprehended them. Yet."

She watched the door swing shut behind Herridge, the man who had captured, imprisoned, and coerced her. He was telling her that Dr. Jensen and Moira had escaped. Could she believe him, or was this another ploy to keep her under his thumb?

The lieutenant reentered the room and took up his position at the foot of the bed. Jaz was tired, but too nervous to fall asleep. What if more of her died while she was sleeping? "Lieutenant?"

"Yes, Ms. Reese?"

"Could you get me a portable screen? Something that doesn't require a connection? I want to check the news."

"Yes, Ms. Reese."

Ten minutes later, a nurse brought a data pad. "Dr. Takashira left orders that you could use a pad, but only for a half hour at a time. No fatiguing yourself." She pointed a meaty finger at the lieutenant. "Keep an eye on her. I've set it to shut off automatically, but take it away sooner if she gets tired."

Under the nurse's gaze, the hospital bed lifted into a sitting position. The nurse propped the data pad on Jaz's knees. "It's tuned to CNN. Turn it on here." She pressed a button and the pad lit up with scrolling stock figures and video clips from a dozen ongoing news stories. "I'll be back in half an hour to check on you."

Jaz watched an account of this morning's Net disruption. So far the death count was over three thousand, and they were still picking bodies out of the Atlantic from two Boeing 947s that had collided over Manhattan airspace.

So many dead, and it was her fault. If she hadn't pushed Symbios into motion by contacting Gestalt, none of this might have happened. In trying to prevent a war, she had triggered it.

What would have happened if she hadn't intervened? Could Symbios have grown slowly, been able to negotiate a truce with Gestalt? Jaz would never know.

Other news stories speculated on what had occurred: an anomalous power surge on the West Coast, a new type of Net virus that generated mass hallucinations. Jaz turned to a less reputable news channel and found conspiracy theories: an attempt by unknown forces to take over the Net, angels and demons fighting over the souls of men. One story included an interview with a homeless man. He described an entire street of people frozen in the grasp of the "beast"—until he and other feebs pulled off their data jewelry and freed them. The clip terminated abruptly. Its title disappeared from the play list. Jaz had seen this kind of interactive editing before. She whispered into the data pad's microphone, "Gestalt?"

A palm-size whirlwind appeared in the foreground. Tiny people circled in its column.

"You can't erase them all." Memory was built into the structure of human brains. You could suppress or erase a single neural path, but surrounding neurons had a way of re-creating the data. And there was no way—short of mass murder—that Gestalt could modify the memories of the feebs Jaz had pulled into the battle. She was fiercely glad. A small victory for Symbios.

The whirlwind funneled into a tornado, touching down on the news page, leaving a swath of changes in its path. Jaz reread the stories. Solar flares instead of demonic intervention, denial-of-service attacks instead of governmental conspiracy.

Gestalt could try, but the story would spread faster than its agents. Jaz suspected there were hundreds, maybe thousands, of people on the West Coast that would never touch another induction device. Symbios was gone, but the truth remained. Gestalt would have to prepare for a world where humanity knew it existed. It was only a matter of time.

Her half hour was up, and the data pad clicked off. Jaz laid it on the bedside table and surrendered to sleep.

When she woke again, a middle-aged Japanese man stood near her bed. He turned to her and bowed slightly. "I am Dr. Takashira," he said in the deep tones Herridge had approximated last night.

"How am I doing?" Jaz mumbled.

"Very well, given the nature of your injuries. It is necessary we test your brain function, to determine the full scope of the damage."

She spent the rest of the day undergoing a grueling regime of psychological evaluations, induction-resonance scans, and strength and coordination tests. All seemed to be in working order, except for an occasional tremor in her right hand and that her short-term memory was not as reliable as it had been.

"Excellent," Dr. Takashira said when he reviewed the results. "Your progress is remarkable."

Jaz propped herself up on her right elbow. "What percentage of my neurons died?"

Dr. Takashira waved a hand dismissively. "The number is not important; what matters is your perceived disability."

"All my life I've dealt in concrete facts. Binary details, on-off, black-white. Give me a number."

"Such information is not in your best interest." His dark brown eyes were sympathetic. "Be happy with what you have."

"Please. By profession, I mine the Net for information. I need to know what to expect when I reconnect. Will I be able to continue my career?"

Dr. Takashira pinched the skin between his brows. "Six point eight percent of the neurons in your cerebral cortex died before the enzymic treatment took effect."

At the look of dismay on Jaz's face, he said, "This is excellent considering the voltages you were exposed to during the equipment malfunction. You may lose some memories, there may be an impairment to your online skills. But with training, you should be able to recover most of your lost ability."

"Most. But not all."

"No." Dr. Takashira inclined his head slightly. "Not all. But you must concentrate on what is salvaged, not what is lost. You have your life."

Jaz sighed. "Yes. Thanks to you. I saw you before the operation . . . in your pajamas. You weren't on duty when the call came."

Dr. Takashira chuckled. "Thank your commanding officer. He was most persuasive." Dr. Takashira bowed again. "Please excuse me. A call has come in; I must see another patient."

He left her alone with Lieutenant Jameson. The guard's expression was bland. He might have been watching a sporting event or monitoring military channels.

Jaz envied him.

She had merged with two metaminds, understood them utterly; her fear of the Net was gone. Symbios was destroyed, and Gestalt couldn't infiltrate her mind without Jaz recognizing the intrusion. Ironic, that just when she was willing to reenter the Net, she might be unable to.

All around Jaz was an invisible sea of communications, but she might never walk those waves again.

Two days later, Jaz was transported by helicopter to Los Angeles Air Force Base. From there, a private jet flew her east across the United States. She was blindfolded for the last half hour of the journey, but as the blindfold was slipped over her head, Jaz saw the white-capped peaks of the Rocky Mountains.

Herridge was waiting at the bottom of the folding stairs as Jaz climbed out of the jet. "Ms. Reese, I am glad to see you well." He clasped her right hand in a firm handshake.

Her wrist quivered under the pressure. "Mostly well," Jaz said. "I haven't had the courage to try induction jewelry yet."

Herridge's sliver-faceted eyes turned toward her. He stared a long moment. "You will." Leading her away from the helicopter, he said, "I've called a debriefing session for eighteen hundred hours. Your quarters are this way."

At the metal door to the compound, Jaz paused. "No hood?"

The left corner of Herridge's lips twitched up in a rare smile. "No hood."

He led her inside. From habit, Jaz counted as the elevator carried them down. Nine seconds left them in a brightly lit corridor with white-tile floors and artificial windows set into the walls. The scenes displayed natural settings: the russet cliffs of the Grand Canyon, the snowcapped peaks of Mount Tacoma, a field of California poppies.

Her suite was at the end of the corridor. There was a living room with a desk and full-immersion unit. Jaz winced at the sight of it. Even the thought of connection equipment made her brain ache. The room beyond was oak-paneled and dominated by a four-poster bed with white quilts.

"I've moved up in the world."

Herridge swung open a cabinet to reveal a variety of chilled liqueurs. "The gratitude of a powerful nation." He pulled out a tiny bottle of scotch and tucked it in his pocket. "The United States is in your debt."

Jaz looked out a simulated picture window showing a view of dragonflies skimming across a pond. "Tell that to the families of the people who died."

"Casualties are expected in war. You prevented many times that number of deaths."

Jaz shook her head. Her eyes stung with emotion. "That's no consolation to the dead." She looked at her trembling hand. "Or the wounded." Blinking to clear tears, she turned back to Herridge. "Where's Dixon? Can I see him?"

Herridge studied her with his metallic gaze. "In the hospital, recovering. We'll visit him soon for a debriefing. You've got two hours to settle in and relax." He nodded toward the dresser. "Your clothes are in there."

Jaz sketched a mocking salute with her wavering hand and Herridge left her alone.

She'd brought no luggage with her. Her clothes had been cut off before the operation, so she wore a borrowed uniform. The dark color highlighted the sallow circles under her eyes. Worse was her head. The gauze was gone. Her bald scalp was covered by a patchwork of round adhesive bandages covering the incisions necessary for the microsurgery and enzyme injections. The "flesh tone" looked like pale scabs against her mahogany skin.

Her crowning glory, the thick dark hair Ian had loved to sink his hands into, was gone, cut away from her as emotionlessly as her clothes. She looked like an ugly baby bird, with her skinny neck and bulbous head.

Jaz sank down on the end of the bed and buried her hands in her face. She cried until her breath came in gasps.

At last, moving stiffly, she opened the drawers. Brightly colored silks with gold-and-silver embroidery puffed out at her. Jaz snatched up a shift and clutched it to her cheek. The fabric was cool and soft. If she was no longer beautiful or smart, she'd surround herself with beautiful things.

Jaz stripped down and kicked the hated wool uniform into the corner. When she had slipped into flowing silk pants and a long *kurta* that hung to her knees, her spirits rose. Jaz wrapped a long red-and-gold scarf around her head, the fringed ends dangling over her left shoulder. It would do.

Shoes. Jaz pulled open the second drawer down. It was empty save for a black plastic face. Draped across the diagnostic port was her mask, the Quantum-IV Infotech had bought for her.

She froze as if it were a viper, ready to strike. The LEDs on the brow of the port glowed green. The mask was in perfect working condition. The gem-encrusted bands crossed the face horizontally. It was beautiful, mocking her with its perfection. Ironic that its malfunction had brought her into the conflict between Gestalt and Symbios. Now it was repaired, and she was forever broken.

Jaz lifted the delicate grid of wires and held it up to

the light. Her old brain patterns were part of its programming. Would it recognize her in this diminished state? As the thought formed in Jaz's brain, her hand began to tremble. She let the mask fall through nerveless fingers into a crumpled heap onto the face-shaped port. With her bare foot, she pushed the drawer closed.

Jaz found shoes in the closet. She chose a pair of flats, not trusting her coordination to heels.

Then, bored and unwilling to try the rig, Jaz spent time programming the picture window. Through trial and error, she settled on a repeating scene of a lunar eclipse. The full moon shone down over a desert landscape and was eaten by the shadow of the earth. Jaz watched the shadow creep across the shining face of the moon. She knew how the moon felt.

A knock on the door interrupted her reverie. Herridge saluted. "Ready for the debriefing?"

Jaz didn't answer, only rose and followed him out. When they stepped into the elevator, it rose.

"Hospital wing," he said. "Mr. Tully's wounds are slower healing than yours."

The hospital ward was quiet compared to the bustling energy of USC University Hospital. One nurse manned a central station. Dixon's room appeared to be the only one in use.

Dixon was propped up on a reclining bed. His neck and the lower left portion of his jaw were wrapped in gauze. At sight of Jaz, his face broke into a wide grin. Then he winced and pressed his hand to his left cheek. "Ow." He held out his right hand to Jaz. "You look great."

She took his hand, saw him glance down at the tremor. "How are you?"

He squeezed her hand and let it go. "Neck hurts like hell, but watch this!" Dixon picked up a data pad lying close to the bed and kissed it. "They removed my conditioning this morning."

Jaz tried to smile, felt her lips move, but didn't feel the warmth of it in her chest. "That's wonderful. I'm happy for you."

"If we could begin the debriefing," Herridge said.

"Just the three of us?" Jaz asked.

Herridge checked the hallway and closed the door. "Yes. The extraction team has already been debriefed with an appropriate amount of information. Ms. Jordon felt that her presence here would not be productive."

Jaz exchanged a look with Dixon. His eyes narrowed, and he said, "Good call on her part."

Herridge pulled up a chair to the end of Dixon's bed. Jaz sat in a chair to the side of the bed.

"First, let me say that you both exceeded expectations. Gestalt is especially pleased with you, Ms. Reese. Your intervention prevented Symbios from capturing a significant portion of the United States. You and Mr. Tully have been nominated for a Presidential Commendation."

Jaz restrained an urge to twirl her finger in the air. "What does this mean to us in real terms? You kidnapped me from a lucrative position with Infotech, coerced me into helping you destroy a scientific commune, during which I suffered brain damage."

At the last two words, Dixon turned to look at her.

She avoided his gaze. Pity, she did not need. "It's uncertain whether I'll ever be able to connect to the Net again. What do I do with the rest of my life?"

Herridge's mouth worked. "I had planned to save this discussion until the end of the briefing, but to allay your concerns, the NSA has extended an offer of employment to you both. If you are willing and able, we would like to keep you on as field agents. If . . . your injuries prevent a Net connection, you would still be a valuable addition to the team as a consultant."

Dixon pointed at himself. "Me, too?"

Herridge nodded.

"Imagine that. Me, working for the largest security agency in the world." He grinned. "The boys back at the cellblock would never believe it."

Jaz studied her fingertips. She wasn't sure that she liked the idea of working for Herridge, but too much was uncertain to turn down his offer. She might need the job if Dr. Takashira's optimistic projections didn't pan out. "What do you want to know?"

Herridge leaned back into his seat. A moment of silent scanning, then: "We've already questioned Dr. Orley."

Jaz stiffened at his name. "He's here?"

"In the compound, yes."

Dixon was very still. His gaze slid sideways to Jaz's face, the muscles on the side of his neck tensed.

Jaz felt a need to see Orley, to try to explain why she betrayed him. It wasn't because of the mission. She'd done the right thing. Looking at Herridge's metallic lenses, Jaz wondered how much of her training for the mission had been at a conscious level. They'd had access to her brain, and the finest equipment at their disposal. She'd done everything they'd wanted. For reasons of her own? Jaz wasn't so sure anymore.

She kept her face and voice calm, hiding her suspicions. "What did Orley tell you?"

Dixon relaxed when he heard her question. What had he been afraid she'd ask?

"He provided background on the Symbios project," Herridge said. "And after suitable motivation, the names of all scientists directly involved. What we want from you is a complete account of everything that transpired from the time you left Potter at the airport terminal."

Dixon relayed the story, with Jaz filling in bits he forgot to mention, or information he wasn't privy to. Up to the point where Dixon had left her alone with Orley.

"What happened then?" Herridge asked.

Jaz stared at him. Her face burned. She could still feel Orley's hands on her waist, sliding up to cup her breasts.

Herridge and Jordon had ordered her to seduce Orley—Gestalt might even have planted the suggestion in her unconscious—but her sex life was none of their goddamned business. With deliberation, Jaz said, "I forget."

Herridge leaned forward. "I'm not asking out of curiosity. We need to know. It will help us question Orley."

Jaz licked her lips. "Brain damage is a tricky business.

Dr. Takashira said I would have lapses in my short-term memory." She stared through Herridge.

Herridge licked his lips. "We could compel you to tell us."

"Same old Herridge. Tell me, would you pin the Presidential Commendation medal to my hospital gown before or after you brain-hacked me?"

The left corner of Herridge's mouth quirked up in an expression half smile, half sneer. "You're harder than you used to be."

"Behavioral changes are not unexpected after brain trauma."

Herridge held up his hands. "All right. Keep your dirty little secrets. If we need to pursue it later, we will."

Jaz swallowed. It was good to see Herridge back down. She risked a glance at Dixon.

He winked.

"Tell me what occurred after your regrettable memory lapse."

Jaz described how they'd infiltrated Symbios's sleeping collective mind and discovered what had happened to the NSA agents.

"Why didn't you contact the extraction team then?"

"We didn't have proof," Jaz said. "Dreams contain both real and imagined information. I had to verify that the agents were imprisoned."

Herridge frowned and waved for her to continue.

Jaz described Tate's face in the cellar door opening, her shooting Dixon. Then a fog fell over the scene. "I don't know what happened next."

Herridge looked at her sharply.

Jaz rolled her eyes toward the ceiling. "A tank, I think they put me in a tank. Like the other agents. There was pain. Something . . . I remember crawling out, but not how or why." Jaz dug her thumbs into her eyes until she saw sparks. "I can't." Her voice broke on the last word.

Dixon reached out and put his hand on her knee. "Don't." To Herridge he said, "I was connected to Jaz through a limited-bandwidth feed. There was a battle online between Symbios and Gestalt, fought by agent-programs customized to control and disconnect users. When the time came, Jaz tipped the balance. You want more, get it from Gestalt. She and I are done answering questions."

Herridge stood. "Don't annoy me, Tully. Your sentence has been *suspended,* not repealed." He looked at Jaz.

Her hand trembled violently, and she felt the burn of tears redden her nose. She tried to stare him down, but her body betrayed her. A single tear slipped out of her right eye and slid down the curve of her face. Humiliated, she somehow found the strength to meet his gaze.

Herridge looked down at his feet, then back up. "We'll continue this later." He left the room.

"Thank you," Jaz said to Dixon, trying to keep a quaver out of her voice.

Dixon flapped a negligent hand through the air. "Don't worry about it. One of the things you learn in prison is not to take any shit. You all right?"

She tried to smile. It broke. "No," she sobbed. "I've lost everything . . . even my self-control."

He rubbed Jaz's back. "It's all right. Even the strongest of us break down sometime. Here." He handed her a tissue from a box beside the bed. "If you show me yours, I'll show you mine."

Jaz looked at him sharply.

Dixon laughed and gestured at her impromptu turban. "Wounds, I mean."

"Oh." She touched her scarf nervously, fingers plucking at the silk. Jaz dropped her hand. "You first."

Dixon pulled down the edges of his bandage. "It looks worse than it is. The bullet just nicked the artery." A strip of translucent pink artificial skin overlaid the ragged edges of the wound.

Jaz sucked in a breath at the sight. The skin patch looked too fragile to hold a human life together. "I never thanked you for saving my life."

Dixon shrugged the bandage back into place. He patted her cheek. "It was worth it."

Jaz smiled ruefully. "Maybe not. You haven't seen my

head. The neurosurgeon shaved off my hair. I look dreadful."

He stared at her. "So. Show me."

Jaz unwound the scarf. The cool air of the hospital room chilled her head. She felt naked and exposed without her hair.

Dixon's face was solemn. "How bad did Symbios burn you?"

"Six point eight percent of my neurons died in that battle. I've got tremors in my right hand, some memory lapses. . . ."

"Do you notice any difference when you connect?" He didn't dismiss the damage like Dr. Takashira had. Dixon understood how thin the line was between being the best and being mediocre.

Jaz licked her lips and stared out his artificial window. It displayed a street scene of children playing. They shrieked and ran about erratically, like Brownian particles. She wondered if it was the room's default display, or if he had chosen it. The silence dragged on for minutes. "I don't know. I haven't tried yet."

"Scared?" It was a question, not a confrontation.

"Terrified. Sometimes I think I'd rather not know how bad it is."

"I know what you mean." Dixon reached down and slid open the drawer of his bedside table. Inside was a Lockheed-Ilyushin-Daewoo 345-G7, military model. Horizontal bands of gleaming metal were connected by delicate wires. It looked like Japanese armor Jaz had seen in museum archives.

Jaz's eyes widened at the sight of it.

"A present from our grateful government. I'm sure Herridge could arrange one for you if you asked." He picked it up—face port and all—and propped it on his stomach. The black plastic mold stared blankly at Dixon. "I waited for you. I thought we could reenter the Net together."

Jaz goggled at him. From the moment he'd met her, Dixon had obsessed about regaining Net access. How could he wait? "You didn't have to do that."

"Maybe I'm sentimental—I wouldn't be able to make this connection if it weren't for you." He chuckled ruefully. "Or maybe I really do understand why you're reluctant to find out exactly how much you've lost." He breathed deeply, and the mask perched on his stomach rose and fell. "It's been two and a half years. Everything I knew is out-of-date."

The twinkle in his hazel eyes was back. "Come with me, Jaz. Your wounded brain and my obsolete skills. Let's storm the gates of the Net together." He held out his hand.

Jaz took his tan hand in her darker one and gripped it. She pursed her lips in the beginnings of a smile. "Provocateur."

CHAPTER 23

"**M**y mask is back in the room," said Jaz.

"Then meet me online in ten minutes." Dixon gestured at the rickety wire-frame chair next to his bed. "There's no place here for you to be comfortable." He grinned. "Unless you want to sit on my lap."

Jaz snorted. "See you online." She waved as she left the room.

Herridge was waiting in the hall outside. Jaz walked past him. He matched his steps to hers. "We need to talk."

"We certainly do," she said without looking back. "I found the mask . . . my mask. It's in perfect working condition."

"I thought you might find it useful during your recovery to have equipment customized to your previous neural mappings. So I had it repaired."

Jaz stopped and turned to face him. "Did you? Or did you simply stop causing it to malfunction?"

"I had it repaired." Changing the subject, Herridge said, "We need more information about Orley."

"Then ask him yourself," Jaz snapped. She stepped into the elevator and pressed her floor.

Herridge stepped in beside her as the doors closed. "I know you've been hurt, and you're angry with me, but the government needs this information. I'll come for you in the morning at eight hundred hours. Be ready to talk."

He escorted her to her suite, more guard than company.

Inside her room, Jaz locked the privacy bolt and shuttered the peephole—for all the good it would do. Staying inside the NSA compound was like living in a fishbowl. There were sure to be electronic watchers.

She checked the bedside clock. She had five minutes until her online rendezvous with Dixon. She pulled the data mask out, tilting it from side to side so its gems twinkled: beautiful portal to an imaginary world.

Jaz remembered the weeks of tuning its electronics to her brain patterns. Nightly headaches and blurry visuals at first, but it had been worth it. Once the rig was configured, her Net-running was more convincing than physical reality.

Jaz dimmed the lights and lay down on the bed. She lifted the rig—her right hand betrayed her and trembled violently. Shit. With her left hand, she eased the mask into place, awkwardly reaching across her head to smooth the right side.

The metal and silicon were cold against her skin. This was stupid. It would never work with her damaged brain. Jaz wanted to tear it off and fling the mask across the room.

No. She'd promised Dixon. He needed her online as much as she needed him.

Tentatively, Jaz activated the start-up sequence. She imagined the ocean on a calm summer day: white fluffy clouds overhead, waves lapping at her feet, an endless horizon of blue.

Pain. A dull pounding just behind her eyes. The scene flickered, trying to reconstruct the landscape from neurons that had died. The world looked like Swiss cheese. Pockets of void permeated her dream.

Like viewing your childhood home after a fire, it was beautiful and familiar, but forever ruined. Only this damage was inside her.

The sound of the surf came in fits and starts, so Jaz turned off that part of her metaphor. She huddled on the surface of the silent sea, arms wrapped around her knees.

Far off in the distance, a white column rose from the water. Gestalt? Jaz moved her hand in the physical world to disconnect. But as it drew near, Jaz saw a man made of fire walking on the waves. Steam billowed where his soles touched the water.

"Our base metaphors are both elemental." The voice was Dixon's. "Interesting."

Jaz held up her arms and studied her avatar. As always, it was herself. She hadn't forgotten what she looked like. The only difference now was her avatar still had the shining coil of waist-length hair she had lost.

Voice tight with grief, Jaz pointed to the voids in the air, tangible proof of what she'd lost. "There are holes in my metaphor."

"So?" He stepped closer. The flames on his body flared and surrounded them in a billowing white steam. "Imagine a new one."

The steam lifted Jaz. She struggled against it. The sea was her metaphor, had always been. Diving its depths had allowed her to probe the secrets of the Net and her own subconscious.

"Let it go," Dixon murmured, his flaming face the only thing she could see in the steam. "For once in your life, you don't have to control your surroundings."

It took an effort of will for Jaz to let herself be lifted off her base. The steam carried them to one of the clouds floating above the sea. Because she'd never imagined herself in such a place, there were no preexisting damaged images in her mind. Everything was new. But without years of carefully constructed scenery, the details were fuzzy. In a cloud bank, however, blurry surroundings were appropriate. The pounding in Jaz's head from the connection intruded on the metaphor as a distant roll of thunder.

"How are *you* handling the Net?" Jaz asked.

Dixon's avatar shrugged, plumes of flame rising from his shoulders. "Everything moves faster. There's more detail, more subtext. But the constant is the human mind. No matter how quickly technology changes, it still has to interact with netware evolved millions of years ago. I'll adapt." He gestured at the clouds around them. "Is this better?"

Jaz tried to smile. "Some."

Dixon waved his hands and the clouds parted. They lay on a warm column of steam the size and shape of a magic carpet. All around them was open sky. Jaz saw the sea as a tiny dot of blue far below. The rest of the Net appeared as a patchwork of individual imaginings: baseball fields, dark crackling balls of electricity, steel mazes, and endless forests.

Jaz gasped and leaned forward for a better view. "This is amazing."

Dixon lay back into the cloud. "Air metaphors are excellent for keeping an eye on the Net."

"There's an extra buzz in the atmosphere, or is that me?" Jaz asked.

"No. The events of last week are big news. People all over the world are learning about Gestalt faster than it can erase their knowledge. You and I changed history, Jaz. Mankind's woken up. Everything we suffered was worth it."

Was it? A world where people knew Gestalt existed was a world that had lost its innocence. Paranoia would run rampant for a time. Some people would never reconnect. She wasn't sure how all the details would play out. The only thing she knew for certain was that the near future would be chaotic.

"I hope you're right." Jaz touched Dixon's avatar where the bullet had nicked his throat. The flames lapped at her flesh, but did not burn. They flowed over her skin like a warm breeze. "Why fire?"

He grinned and touched his fingertips to his chest. "Because I'm a hot guy?"

Jaz stared at him. She crossed her arms.

Dixon squirmed. "You want the truth."

"Always."

"For this, we'll need privacy." Dixon raised his arms and the steam surrounded them in a pocket of white. He settled back into the cloud, his long body stretched out alongside Jaz. "Fire was man's first technology. It transforms, but also destroys. A reminder that every tool is dangerous."

Jaz's eyes narrowed. "You're not as shallow as you like to pretend."

Dixon shrugged. "Being underestimated is also a tool."

"And thus dangerous?" she quipped, looking at him.

Their eyes met and held. In the boiling magma of Dixon's irises, Jaz saw a flicker of hazel. "Sometimes," he said. He looked like he might say more, paused, then, "Why did you sleep with Orley?"

Jaz looked down at her hands as if she could read the answer in their lines. "You were there. What do you think?"

The flames burned hotter on his face. "Forget I asked. It's none of my—"

"Then why did you ask?"

Dixon took her hand in his. The flames crawled over her skin until they burned together. "Because I have a secret," he whispered, brought her hand to his lips and kissed it. "When you returned, and I was jealous . . . I wasn't pretending."

Heat flared through Jaz's body, and she wasn't sure if it was metaphor or real. "When—why? You said—Valkyries?" She cupped hands in front of her chest, mimicking the gesture Dixon had made in the hotel.

"I lied." Dixon pressed her hand over his heart. "I've never met a woman who could keep up with me on the Net. Someone I wouldn't have to hold back with."

Under his flames Jaz touched a warm, living body. She pulled away. "You're too late. Why find me when I am *this?*" Her avatar morphed into her damaged body. The static surf cut in and out, and the holes in the sky glowed like black embers.

"It doesn't matter." Dixon leaned forward and brushed the silken scarf away from her brow. "Whatever you're feeling, I want to share it."

Jaz stood up and took a step back. "No. That kind of sharing never works. Let's stay out of each other's heads." The memories of her failures floated to the surface, the image of Ian's mocking jeer when she learned of his infidelity, Orley's grief-stricken expression when he learned she worked for Gestalt. The images hovered in the air around her, before Jaz brushed them away. Of all the memories Symbios had destroyed, why hadn't it taken those?

"Scared to try?" Dixon's voice was reproving. "I never figured you for a coward."

"What do you know about my pain?" Jaz said quietly.

His smile was mocking. "Come find out. All your life you've wanted someone you wouldn't have to throttle down your intellect to avoid overwhelming. I don't need a connection to know that. I can see it in your eyes. You want a man who can keep up." He flung his arms wide, and sparks of flame jumped from his palms. "Here I am."

Lying in her bed, Jaz panted, felt sweat creeping down her temples. Or was that steam on the imagined flesh of her avatar?

Dixon offered her a full sharing, something more intimate than sex, and she barely knew him. She felt a yearning to give in, but she didn't trust it. Dixon was skilled at manipulation; perhaps he was affecting her emotions.

His avatar stepped closer and encircled Jaz with his arms.

"I haven't said yes," she protested.

Dixon leaned down and brushed his lips against hers. "Ah, but you haven't said no, either." With the feather-light kiss came a flash of memory, Dixon's first sight of Jaz. He'd been attracted to her high breasts and narrow waist, but he'd dismissed her as an NSA agent, one of the opposition.

The images ignited neural pathways to Jaz's memory of the scene: her curiosity about what he was reading, her approval of his long, lean frame. She pushed it into his mouth with her tongue.

He grasped her tighter, the whole length of his body pressed against hers. His flames covered them both, an expression of the rush of sexual adrenaline that flowed between them.

The crackling fire burned away their simulated clothing, leaving their avatars naked, no secrets between them now.

Jaz pushed her consciousness deeper into Dixon and found the night when she'd made love to Orley. He'd sat in the bedroom wracked with jealousy and hurt. In his firefly form, he'd experienced everything secondhand, hating Orley, and yet unable to turn away from even a filtered experience of Jaz.

"I'm sorry." Jaz smoothed his brow and comforted Dixon with the lust she'd felt for him at the dance club. It had been all too easy that night to snuggle into his arms, playing girlfriend.

"Practice," he thought to her, "makes perfect. Give me everything. I can take it."

"Can you?" Jaz melted into his avatar, her water merging with his fire. She dropped her defenses, and let him experience it all: the hot pulsing in her groin, the grinding pain in her head, memories of friends, lost love, the holes in her memory, everything. She rained her being into him, and waited for rejection.

Dixon's avatar fell backward onto a bed of steam, carrying Jaz on top of him. "More," he said. "Drown me." Images of the desert boiled out of him, of women he had tried to love, the sheer intellectual joy of cracking another programmer's security protocols, the throbbing of his penis.

Jaz sank onto Dixon's virtual erection and shuddered as images of all the women he'd ever made love to vibrated through her. She surrendered her memories of Ian and Orley, and the others who had shared her bed. It brought them closer, gave them an understanding of each other's erotic ideals . . . fantasies.

Each thrust ignited deeper memories, more guarded emotions. Jaz struggled to relax the mental walls she had spent a lifetime constructing. She let Dixon experience an awkward family gathering, her mother's family scheming to find her a husband. Having to sit still while a group of women dressed in saris discussed her prospects as if she, a lead researcher at Infotech, was a failure because she didn't have a husband.

Dixon shared a thrilling night of Net-running across the Australian outback, smuggling illegal patching equipment for his uncle's casinos. Standing up in the back of a pickup truck, tasting dust mixed with imported whiskey. Watching the blue-and-red lights of the Australian Federal Police fade in the distance.

Jaz opened her bandwidth, absorbing images from Dixon as fast as he could generate them, giving him her own in return.

In her bedroom, Jaz's body was sweating from the mental effort. She'd never driven herself this hard before.

Dixon penetrated her subconscious. He found her suppressed fears of rejection, the images of disgust Ian had projected into Jaz during their breakup. A childhood of never fitting in anywhere. Too white for the Indian community, too dark for the Anglos.

Jaz sank deeper into Dixon, felt the pain of losing his mother when he was six. The white hospital in Victoria that she'd entered and never left. His small hand in his uncle's hardened one.

In the next wave of intimacy, Jaz followed the memory until confronted by a wall of flame. She was surprised by the metaphor in his private thoughts. For all his desire to share with her, Dixon still had secrets.

Ones and zeros streamed upward like so many cinders. He'd written security memes to lock down this portion of his cerebral cortex.

Jaz stared at the wall. Should she leave him his privacy? She felt him relive her first masturbation attempts when she was eleven. So much for discretion. Jaz split her consciousness into three separate streams and tried to tease apart the unfactorable sums blocking her path. Nothing.

Then she saw the chink in his defenses. Dixon had locked down his logic centers, but left his sensory path wide-open. It was a small channel, very little bandwidth compared to the raging electric storm that was human consciousness. But the witch had taught Jaz how to slip inside through nuance.

While Dixon vicariously relived Jaz's first fumbling attempts at self-intimacy, Jaz patched calming sensations into his sensory channel: she replaced the pain from his neck and shoulder with the soothing warmth of floating in a warm tub of water and the building ecstasy of orgasm.

The wall of fire shrank to hurdle height, then vanished. Dixon felt safe. There was no need for defenses.

With a surge of pride at having retained some of her skills, Jaz stepped inside.

Suddenly Jaz was running in a tan desert, chasing a parti-colored dog. Tufts of spiky desert weed were scattered about. Dog and child ran toward a white wooden house. Mother stood on the porch. She was slender, with pale skin like Dixon's and black, curling hair. Her face was hidden by an old-style connection mask, its blank silver oval painted with Maori designs.

The woman on the porch collapsed, began to seizure. Jaz fell to the dust, screaming and backpedaling away from the scene—Jaz felt adult Dixon shift beneath her in the cloud of steam, rising against the pain of the memory—she could see Dixon as a child, on the porch, crying and holding his mother's head while she spasmed. The woman's mask fell away.

In a crescendo of pain and joy, their understanding of each other peaked. In that instant, Dixon pierced through to Jaz's hidden secrets. The fear that no matter how hard she tried, no matter what she accomplished, she would never be good enough.

Their union subsided. The information flowing between them fell to a trickle. Standard metaphor. Two imagined bodies on a cloud.

The flames burned out. In the circle of their arms, Dixon's avatar was like hers, human. "Someday we should do that for real," he said, kissing her forehead.

Jaz felt something clench inside her stomach. She squeezed Dixon tightly. "Thank you. I've never felt that free before."

Dixon returned her squeeze. "I'm not sure what happens next in my life, but I want you in it."

His words startled Jaz. What did come next? Once you've saved the world?

Dixon's avatar flickered in her arms. "Shit." After a

moment he resolidified. "My heart rate peaked. The nurse is checking I haven't had a stroke. Excuse me. I have some explaining to do." His face relit with flames, and Jaz felt his embarrassment. She caught an image of a nurse peeling back slightly damp sheets. Jaz shut down the connection before she sensed any more. One person living through that kind of mortification was enough.

Besides, she was glad to get away. Dixon hadn't been paying attention during the last seconds of their intimacy. He hadn't felt her shock of realization.

Jaz had a secret.

She'd seen the face behind his mother's mask. The fox-sharp chin, the too-big hazel eyes, the exact shade as Dixon's: red-brown blending into green.

In that flash of memory, she'd experienced a childhood of helping his mother cope with a body that was falling apart. Dixon's mother was the witch.

And he didn't know she was still alive.

CHAPTER 24

Jaz stewed all night wondering what she should do with the information. Dixon had mourned the loss of his mother since childhood. Would telling him his mother was alive—but imprisoned by the NSA—heal or destroy him? Whatever the eventual outcome, he'd be angry. She couldn't decide which was worse, a comforting lie or a distressing truth.

At eight hundred hours Herridge pounded on the door. His face was freshly shaved and his uniform crisp. In his right hand he held a tray of coffee and croissants.

Herridge set the tray down on the round table near the bed. Jaz nibbled on a pastry as he settled into the other chair.

"Feeling better this morning?"

"Yes and no." Jaz reached back to the bedside table for her mask. She'd been afraid to sleep in it; afraid Dixon might pick up her dreams. Now Jaz slipped it on.

Herridge was no natural; he floated like driftwood through Jaz's tattered ocean metaphor. She surrounded him with a net of mnemonic programs, sensitized to pick up every emotion he leaked into the Net.

Jaz asked, "Did you know about Dixon's mother?"

"No." His face was calm and as innocent as a babe's. But he was lying. Herridge had good control—only one subconscious image leaked out. The mnemonic program that picked it up from him routed it to her frontal lobe: the witch, hanging in her chamber.

If Jaz hadn't been prepared, she would have missed it. "How long have you known?"

Herridge peeled off his goggles and stared at Jaz with his pale blue eyes. "Apparently the brain damage you suffered is generating false signals." He jammed the goggles into his shirt pocket. "Let's remove that distraction."

"Scared to face me online?" Jaz challenged.

Herridge shifted his weight, causing his shoulder holster to peak out. "Cautious," he said. "I still want to know what happened with Orley. Did you make contact?"

Knowledge was her only bargaining chip. "I'll tell you everything I know about Orley if you give me the history of Dixon's mother." ·

Herridge clicked a dial on the side of his goggles and put them back on, but he did not reappear on the Net. He must have been transmitting on a private frequency. After a second he said, "Gestalt agrees, but you must not reveal any of this information to Dixon. It would be detrimental to his mental health."

Jaz hesitated. The secret she knew now prevented full intimacy with Dixon. Adding this new information would only make that worse. She wanted to be close to him, but . . . she had to know. "Tell me everything."

Herridge crossed his legs, balancing his ankle on his knee. "Amanda Tully was born in Connecticut in 2047. In her teens, she connected with the Salem occult movement and garnered a reputation as a psychic. In 2067, she traveled the world, studying with mystics in Ireland, New Delhi, the Himalayas, and the Australian outback. She became pregnant in the summer of 2069, father unknown, and settled in Perth, Australia, with her brother. The trouble didn't start until she learned to use the Net." Herridge looked down at his palms as if lost in recollection. From the way his jaw clenched, an unpleasant memory. "Ms. Tully isn't a natural. . . . She's a force of nature.

"We don't know if it was the occult training or a genetic anomaly that gives her the ability to intuit the Net. Ms. Tully became a threat to Gestalt's stability. She controlled the thoughts and emotions of half of western Australia before she was captured. Australian Federal Police agents were only able to get near her because she had a seizure and lost control. Otherwise, it might be she—and not Gestalt—who rules the Net."

Jaz's breath caught in her chest. Impossible. No human intelligence could encompass that much information. Surely Herridge was exaggerating. "If she's so dangerous, why didn't your agents kill her?"

Herridge clenched his hands into fists. "Even dangerous tools have their uses. We keep her on life support in an isolated network. Scientists study her brain patterns, seeking to replicate her level of connection. They use the data to construct safeguards for Gestalt should another Amanda Tully come along."

"You're worried about Dixon?"

"Of course. He has long been under our observation. So far, he hasn't demonstrated anything approaching his mother's level of skill. A talented natural, but that's all."

"And if I told him this . . ."

Herridge became very still, like a sharp shooter fixing on a target. "Our psychologists predict two outcomes: he would either attempt to free his mother or attempt to duplicate her skill. Success at either would require . . . intervention."

Jaz's blood chilled at Herridge's implication. "If he's so dangerous, why did you remove the inhibitions against his using the Net?"

"He's still under our control." Herridge picked up his cup of coffee and took a sip. His hand wavered slightly as he set the cup down. "We watch him for clues about his mother. Whether her skills have a genetic component."

Jaz felt the hairs on the back of her neck prickle. "Are you watching me as well?"

"Of course. You are very interesting to us." His lips spread in a slow smile. "Especially yesterday."

Jaz's face grew hot. She and Dixon had secured their transmissions, but people working for the NSA had invented modern cryptography. And with Gestalt's assistance, nothing on the Net was secure from Herridge.

Herridge continued. "Do you understand why Dixon must never know we have his mother?"

"Does Amanda know about Dixon? That he's here?"

Herridge paused, listening to an inner voice. "We don't think so. But with the witch, anything is possible."

Jaz remembered the wasted woman hanging in her underground cell. If that were her mother, Jaz would expend any amount of effort to free her. To what end? Gestalt and the NSA would never allow Amanda Tully a life outside. But for them, her body would have died long ago.

"I need to think about this," Jaz said. "It's wrong to let Dixon believe his mother died thirty years ago. But telling him the truth might be worse—"

"The witch cannot be allowed to leave this facility." His hand hovered near his holster. "I personally will make sure of that. Do you understand me?" His whole body thrummed with tension.

"Of course." Jaz was surprised at Herridge's loss of composure. What had the witch done to him? "I won't make a move without consulting with you first."

"Good." Herridge straightened his jacket with a quick jerk downward and said in a calmer voice, "Now tell me all you know about Dr. John Orley."

Jaz eased back in her chair. "I did establish a . . . rapport with Orley." Jaz felt her face heat and quickly moved on. She told Herridge the whole story, leaving out the most pornographic details.

"Did you get the names of the others involved with the project, the ones not in Pasadena?"

Jaz considered the question. "No, they were never discussed. Couldn't you access that information during Orley's interrogation? Did you use a natural?"

"One of the best, but at some point during the raid, Orley burned out the neural paths that stored those names."

"Deliberately?"

"We believe so."

Jaz gaped. Orley's loyalty to his supporters was amazing; he'd destroy part of his brain to keep their identities secret. Jaz scanned the memory of her encounter with Orley. "No. I never accessed that information. I searched for his future plans and the fate of the NSA agents."

"Give us everything you have. There may be clues embedded in ancillary memories. Part of a face, a voice in the background, something to help us track down the others."

"How do you know there were others besides the scientists in Pasadena?"

"We've found records of equipment and funds sent anonymously to the compound. It's likely there were computer scientists who were interested in the project but unwilling to leave their families and careers. We have to locate them, or the Symbios project could start up again."

Jaz shook her head. "Not without Orley. A project like this takes an amazing amount of coordination and dedication. You need a charismatic leader, someone who can convince sixteen researchers to go on sabbatical and move into a commune."

"We can't take that chance." Herridge uncrossed his legs and braced his hands on his knees. "Will you give us the memories?"

A chill prickled Jaz's neck. Give NSA hacks free access to her brain? No way. "Sure," she said. "I'll download them for you."

"It would be better if our investigators could view them directly."

"I'm not giving anyone who works for you access to my brain. Those days are over."

Herridge listened to induced voices, his face slack with concentration. Then he asked, "Is that all you remember about Orley?"

"Yes." Jaz stared at the framed picture of the lunar eclipse. The moon was almost gone. "What will happen to him now?"

"Orley is under arrest for sedition, treason, and disruption of national communication lines." Herridge sipped his coffee.

"Will there be a trial?"

He set the cup down, his fingers playing for a moment in the steam. "Of course. This is America."

The answer surprised her. "Publicly?"

"No." Herridge shifted his silver gaze to Jaz. "A private military tribunal."

"Ah, of course. You can't publicly charge someone of creating a second rogue metamind, unless you're willing to expose Gestalt."

"That, and we don't want others to know what's possible. Orley's not the only person disenchanted with the Net."

"Will he be executed?"

Herridge shrugged. "If it were my call . . . but it's not. Gestalt wants to study him and the other scientists, understand what went wrong."

"So Orley and the others spend their lives in Faraday cages? It's such a waste."

"That, or we give them negative conditioning as we did with Dixon Tully. Either way, they can never be allowed back into the network. There's nothing to stop them from creating another metamind."

Jaz cocked her head. "Would that be such a bad thing? The Net is vast. Why not communities of metaminds? Symbios's error was that it grew too fast. Like a three-year-old given adult responsibilities, it didn't have the moral maturity to make good decisions.

"Smaller metaminds, grown slowly, might work. Each person could share in a collective consciousness and, through that, contribute to the Net. It would even aid Gestalt. These submetaminds would organize their constituents more effectively than the naturals Gestalt currently uses."

Jaz knew she was on to something—this solution felt right. Millions of years of evolution had hard-wired humans to work together in small groups.

Herridge's eyebrows rose. "Would you time-share part of your brain? Every kiloflop of processing power given to a new metamind steals from Gestalt. Every instance of its existence, it would be in direct competition with her."

"It doesn't have to be that way. I could prove it to you. . . . If only we had way to build a proof-of-concept system where growth could be constrained and there was no chance of an escape."

"Impossible," said Herridge. "I would never permit such a thing. Even the Net-isolated labs where Amanda Tully is imprisoned can be breached. It's too great a risk."

Jaz looked at the picture on the wall. The earth's shadow was moving away from the moon. The crescent of light in the picture grew. The image was time-lapsed, taking only a minute to cycle from dark to light. If only there was a way to create a second network, one that could never interact with Gestalt. Still watching the picture, Jaz said, "I want to talk to Orley."

"That wouldn't be prudent. He considers you a traitor. Orley wouldn't tell you anything we haven't already gotten from the interrogators."

"Maybe I could tell *him* something."

Herridge shook his head. "Don't let your desire to confess override your common sense."

The moon waxed full again. Something about the image . . . a forgotten fact or memory. But it wouldn't come. Jaz turned toward Herridge and said, "You won't know unless I try. Isn't it worth the risk if I might discover something that would help you locate the others?"

Herridge stood. "I'll set it up, but you're wasting your time."

He was at the door when Jaz said, "There's something I wondered about the raid. How did you locate us so quickly? Even if you triangulated using my transmission—we were hidden in a root cellar."

He tapped his shoulder. "Flu shot," he said. Then the door closed behind him

Jaz squeezed the skin around the injection site until she found it: a tiny lump, no bigger than a grain of rice. She looked at the closed door and wondered what other hidden watchers Herridge had installed in her body and mind while she was under his control.

Jaz watched the scene on the wall devour the moon, then resurrect it, bright and shining and whole. She wished she could be restored like the moon, that she could salvage something from this misbegotten affair.

Then a tiny piece of her memory ignited, something she'd heard in eighth-grade physics about the moon in relation to earth. Knowledge that had lain dormant—until now.

The data gems of her mask felt cold against her cheekbones. Jaz closed her eyes and saw the ocean. "Gestalt," she summoned.

The response was instantaneous, a waterspout formed from the waves around Jaz, encircling and hiding her.

"I know what to do. The answer is obvious. Let Orley create another metamind."

The waterspout tightened around Jaz. She felt its unease. In the curving walls of water, Gestalt projected Symbios's path across the United States, a black cancer eating at Gestalt's domain.

"It would be a controlled experiment, one that could never interfere with your network."

Curiosity blew across Jaz, flavored with disbelief.

"There is a way." Jaz pressed her palms together and then drew them apart. In the center was a tiny image of the moon, copied from her wall display. "The moon is one point two five light-seconds from Earth. If you moved Orley and the others to a moon base, that lag would prevent them from infiltrating your network. The new metamind won't be able to bridge its consciousness from the moon to earth. Even if it managed to establish a connection with minds on earth, the two-point-five-second lag would allow you to break its hold on them. The physics of the situation is an inescapable prison. Think about it—you would be able to study the forces that gave rise to you, safely. You could learn about yourself, study how a metamind can operate *cooperatively* with its hosts. By acting openly, Symbios gained access to a larger percentage of its host minds than can you can skim surreptitiously."

Doubt and uncertainty rippled across the surface of the waterspout.

"You have no choice. A time is coming when humanity

will know about you, Gestalt, despite all of your and Herridge's efforts to the contrary. You should be prepared."

The circle of air expanded around Jaz, giving her more room to breathe, a metaphorical invitation to continue. "Think of it: one of your own kind to communicate with. You are generated out of the minds of humans, inheriting their need to connect—but none of us is your equal. How lonely you must be."

A sadness seeped from the inner wall of the waterspout. Beneath Jaz's feet the ocean waves turned to gray dust and craters. Sharp shadows cast by light unscattered by an atmosphere darkened the crater's edge.

The moon base lay below, a barracks for lunar scientists. Inside were three fold-down bunks in a space three by five meters long. Gestalt superimposed the images of Orley's scientists into the room. Standing room only.

"Do you seriously expect me to believe, that with all your influence on the world's leaders, you couldn't expand the base? Orley and his scientists represent a unique opportunity to understand yourself. With sixteen minds they can generate a consciousness that's nearly your equal. Imagine what you could do with that information and the resources of an entire planet. Can you afford to squander Orley's knowledge in an unconnected prison cell?"

The waterspout transfigured to moon dust and whipped across the landscape. It writhed in indecision, flinging itself into five separate columns, each one predicting the outcome of Jaz's proposal. The five parts reassembled, churned. The dust column returned and engulfed Jaz.

Jaz tried to disconnect, but her limbs were frozen. Gestalt fired neurons, dragging every last bit of information about Orley and the others from her. In agony, Jaz gave everything Gestalt asked for. She gave up privacy and self-identity, surrendered her self-control. After seconds that felt like hours, Gestalt released her.

Jaz slumped to the floor in her room, her head aflame. She saw purple-and-black splotches before her eyes. Everything hurt. But she and Gestalt had a bargain.

CHAPTER 25

That afternoon, a guard in a dark green uniform and beret came to escort Jaz to Orley's cell.

They walked through a marble-tiled floor to a private elevator. The guard palmed the biometric pad on the wall, and the elevator opened. The doors closed, and Jaz counted the seconds before it opened again. Forty-five. Add that to the nine seconds it had taken the elevator to reach her suite. They were holding Orley on the same floor she had been imprisoned on.

The door opened on a utilitarian hallway with cinder-block walls. Metal doors lined either side, spaced eight meters apart. Windows were set into each door. Jaz recognized the rooms. They were identical to the Faraday cage cell she had dubbed the Disco Hilton. Dr. Joseph West paced in one, another housed Dr. Akukwe. Orley's room was at the end of the hall. He lay on the bed, hands behind his head, staring at the ceiling.

Jaz paused in front of the door, watching him.

The guard asked, "You sure you want to do this?"

"No. But open the door anyway."

The guard pressed his thumb to the door, and it clicked open.

Orley sat up, startled. He wore an orange jumpsuit that exposed his wrists and ankles. Prison clothes, cut too short for his lanky frame. Light brown stubble textured his chin. When Orley saw Jaz, his face clouded. "Did Herridge send you? You're wasting your time. I won't tell you anything he doesn't already know."

Jaz waved for the guard to leave. He murmured, "I'll be outside," and closed the door with a click.

"Herridge didn't send me. Seeing you was my idea."

His eyes narrowed. "Why?"

Jaz sat on the far end of the bed. "I . . . I'm sorry things turned out the way they did."

Orley laughed a humorless sound. "Am I supposed to forgive you for imprisoning fifteen of the finest scientists in the world, for destroying my life's work, seducing me, and then betraying me?" His voice lowered to a dangerous pitch. "Your people killed Tate. I'll never forgive you."

Jaz's stomach clenched. "It wasn't my choice. Herridge threatened me with life imprisonment unless I helped him."

Orley's green eyes glittered like emeralds. "He offered me a deal, too. The difference between us, *Jasmine,* is I said no."

She was quiet a long moment. "I deserved that. But I didn't come here to apologize. I came here to help."

"I've had enough of your help to last a lifetime." He clenched his hands into fists. "You know what hurts the most? That I was *stupid.* Two naturals fall into my lap, one so beautiful I can barely look at her. Tate knew you were trouble—but I didn't listen, didn't let her tear your defenses down to learn the truth. That I could even for a moment think you wanted me—" His voice broke off in a hiss of self-disgust.

Jaz reached a comforting hand toward Orley's shoulder—

"Don't." His eyes bored into hers, threatening violence. "You should go now."

"No." She let her hand fall to her side. "Not until I've told you what I came here to say."

"I've had enough of your lies. How much do you expect one man to endure? Leave me alone."

Jaz slipped the scarf off her head, exposing her naked scalp and the pockmarked bandages. "When Symbios turned on me I almost died. We've all suffered, John. Let me do what I can to help you."

He stared at her head. "I wish you *had* died."

Jaz rocked back and sighed explosively. "Is your hatred of me so great you would throw away your last chance to rebuild Symbios?"

Orley cocked his head. "What?"

"The moon. You and the others could rebuild your network on the moon. The one-point-five-second lag would ensure that your metamind could never make the leap to the earth network."

He paused, considering her words. Then he slashed his hand sideways through the air. "More lies. Gestalt would never acquiesce to such a plan."

"It already has. Gestalt wants to understand itself. Your research is the best way for it to do that. Hate me if you must, but listen." Jaz described her conversation with Gestalt, their plans to expand the moon base into a permanent colony. "Your talents are wasted in this Faraday cage. On the moon, you can continue your research in a way that benefits everyone."

Orley shook his head. "Even if it's a sincere offer, it won't work. We need sixteen naturals to generate consciousness. Dr. Jensen and Moira are in hiding. The NSA agents are gone. Tate is dead. Even if every one of us who was captured at the Mission house signs up for this, we don't have critical mass. We're one natural short."

Jaz rewrapped the scarf around her head. "Perhaps one of the others on the outside would join you on the moon. I could call them for you."

Orley opened his mouth, then closed it with a snap. "You almost had me . . . again." He shook his head. "No wonder you take me for a fool—I am a fool. Get out of here. Tell Herridge your trick didn't work. I won't contact anyone."

Jaz stomped her foot on the ground. "This isn't a trick. Damn it. I'm trying to make amends. What do I have to do to prove that to you?"

Orley considered her question. Then his lips spread in a quiet, cold smile. "You could go with us. If you want me to trust you, put your life on the line. With you on the moon base, Herridge would be less likely to write us off as a failed experiment."

Jaz wasn't so sure. She'd seen the lengths Herridge

would go to in order to protect Gestalt. She had no illusions that he'd put her safety before the metamind's.

"I have brain damage. I wouldn't be useful to you," she argued haltingly.

A flicker of emotion crossed Orley's face. "Are you able to connect?"

"Yes," Jaz admitted.

"Then your resources are sufficient. If you are sincere about wanting to re-create the Symbios project, get personally involved." He waved his hand in an abrupt dismissive gesture. "Otherwise, don't waste my time with game-playing."

In one respect, Orley's offer was tempting. Even with her reduced capacity, she would be able to make a contribution on the moon. Here, what could she offer the Net? One more mediocre mind? She no longer had the conditioning to be a top data miner. What was left for her here, a data-pushing job as a consultant for the NSA?

Staying on earth, with access to the Net, would be a constant reminder of what she had lost. On the moon, she would be part of something new, without the sullied associations of her past skill. A break with her past.

Dixon could come, too. They could rebuild their skills together, in a research environment, isolated from the churning surf of the Net.

On the moon, it wouldn't matter if Dixon found out about his mother. He would be protected from either contacting or emulating her. They could be together, online, without any defenses.

"Only if Dixon can come, too."

Orley spread his hands in supplication. "But of course." A wry smile touched his lips but did not reach his eyes.

Herridge pounded his fist on his desk. "This is the stupidest crock I've ever heard. You are not going to the moon."

Jaz stood in Herridge's office, in front of his huge mahogany desk. The walls were covered with antique paper maps of Europe and Russia.

"How dare you," Herridge continued, "go over my

head to Gestalt with this harebrained scheme? I'm not letting one of my agents—"

"I'm not one of your agents," Jaz said. "I'm a civilian."

"No one—I repeat—no one, is going to the moon. This plan of yours is insane. Orley and the others are staying on earth, where we can keep them under direct twenty-four-hour surveillance."

"It's not your decision." Jaz spread her hands placatingly. "Gestalt is already raising funds to expand the moon base into a colony."

Herridge sank back into his chair and rubbed his palms together. "Are you sure this is what you want to do?"

"This is the only thing that makes sense. Orley's work is important, and he can't—won't—continue it without me."

Herridge raised one eyebrow. "Have you asked Dixon how he feels about this move? Maybe you should discuss it with him before you emigrate off the planet."

Jaz said quietly, "I was hoping he would go with me."

"Think again." Herridge tapped the desk with his fingernail. "Our boy Dixon signed on as an NSA consultant this morning. Five-year contract. And I can assure you he won't be stationed on the moon. That is *my* decision."

"He what?"

Herridge pulled a data pad out of a drawer and offered it to Jaz. The screen filled with a contract, at the bottom, clear as day, was Dixon's thumbprint. "How does that affect your travel plans?"

"He wouldn't—"

"Wouldn't what? Make long-term, life-altering plans without consulting you?" Herridge drummed his fingers on the desk. "Plans like moving to a barren rock with fifteen people who hate you? Symbios must have really fried your brain if that sounds like a good idea."

Jaz sat down, hard. The chair creaked with her motion. In all her thinking, Dixon had been with her on the moon. They could make a new start, away from Herridge and the NSA. She'd never imagined that Dixon Tully, the ultimate free-wheeling Net-hack, would join an oppressive bureaucracy. It didn't add up. She pointed at the data pad. "How do I know that's authentic?"

Herridge folded his arms across his chest. "Ask him yourself. In fact, have a nice long chat with the boy. Maybe he can talk some sense into you."

Dixon sat on the edge of his hospital bed. He wore a white hospital gown that left his legs bare from midthigh. When he looked up and saw it was Jaz, he flung his arms wide and grinned. "I was just thinking about you."

She stepped into the circle of his arms and hugged him, careful to avoid the artificial skin on his neck and shoulder. Through the thin cotton gown, she could feel every ridge and bulge of his body. He smelled musky, and she wanted to hold on to him forever. Instead she pushed him back to arm's length, and asked, "How's the physical therapy?"

Dixon grimaced. "Torture. But the therapist assures me I'm making good progress. At this rate of recovery, it shouldn't be more than a couple of weeks before you and I can try a few things for real."

Jaz tried to smile, failed.

Dixon's expression grew serious. "Is something wrong?"

"Herridge told me you joined the NSA."

"Damn, I wanted to tell you myself." Dixon sat back down on the bed and patted the space next to him.

When Jaz had settled, he took her hand. "I meant it when I said I wanted you in my life. That made me do some thinking. There's no future in Net-hacking. I could never risk going to prison again and being away from you. You've done the impossible." Dixon thumped his chest with his free hand. "You've made a respectable man of me."

Jaz shushed him with her fingers on his mouth. Tears hovered in her eyes.

"What's the matter?" Dixon asked in a whisper. "Don't you want me?"

"More than anything. But I—damn it, why didn't you talk to me before you accepted?"

Dixon looped his arm around her waist. "I wanted to

surprise you. I thought you'd be pleased I'd gone legit. You and I, consulting agents for the NSA. What else were we going to do with our lives?" He stopped. "You weren't planning to go back to Infotech, were you? If so, we can—"

"No. I'm not going back to data mining. But I can't work for Herridge either. The man kidnapped me. This is a corrupt agency. They've been pulling strings behind the scenes for years."

Dixon's brow wrinkled. "They've worked covertly, had to do a few hard things, but the results are good. Most people are happy, healthy, and prosperous. What's so bad about that?"

"It's built on lies."

Dixon took her hand in both of his. "That's changing. People are learning about Gestalt. The NSA will have to change, too, become more open. Don't you want to be a part of that—with me?" His eyes creased with pain. "Please?"

Jaz pulled her hand away from Dixon's grip and huddled in a ball. "I won't work for the NSA."

Dixon slipped an arm around her back. "Fine. Don't. I'll make enough money to support us both. You can do anything you want. Go back to school. Write symphonies. Just be with me."

Tears squeezed out of her eyes. She couldn't look at him, couldn't see anything but her own pain. "I'm going to the moon, Dixon. With Orley."

"Wh-what?" Dixon held her at arm's length and shook her. "You're going to do *what?*"

Jaz looked him in the eye. It was hard; his face was so full of pain. "I've arranged to go to the moon with Orley, help him continue his research on metaminds. Without me, there aren't enough naturals to reach consciousness. They need me."

Dixon's face darkened. "*I* need you. Here on earth."

"It's important research."

"I don't care if he's fucking cured death. You're *not* going."

Jaz scraped his hands off her arms with the edge of her palms. "Don't tell me what to do."

"Last night I became closer to you than any other person on earth, shared parts of my soul that I'd locked away—even from myself. I searched a lifetime to find you. After that . . . you can't just leave."

She wished they were online together. This would be so much easier if he could experience her feelings directly, without the clumsy intervention of language. But Jaz held secrets that could harm Dixon. She didn't dare let him inside.

"I have to do this."

"Why?" The word was a scream of outrage and pain.

"It's my fault. I have to atone."

"Orley is a madman. He got what he deserved." Dixon twisted the front of his gown in his fist. "You can't leave with him. He hates you, Jaz. They all do. You'd be in danger."

"I believe in what he's doing. After what we've been through I can't trust the Net anymore. I want to be part of a network that's cooperative, with a high level of intimacy."

"You can have that with *me.*"

"No," Jaz said almost inaudibly. "I can't." The admission nearly broke her heart. He would never understand what she really meant.

Dixon sat up, transfixed. "All right. If that's the way you feel." His voice was the lethal hiss of a gas chamber. "Go. Go to *hell,* for all I care."

"It won't be forever, Dixon. You—you could come with me."

"Me and Orley on the moon? That'd be cozy—forget it. You walk out on me now, and I—" Dixon pounded the bed with his fist. "I am sick and *tired* of losing everyone I love." His voice became pleading. "Why are you doing this to us? Just tell Orley you won't go. Any other natural on earth could take your place. They'd be better; you're *brain-damaged.* What makes you think you'd be anything but a liability?"

Jaz's chest felt like a crushed tin can. "Maybe so. I won't know unless I try."

Dixon didn't say anything. His hands covered his face. Jaz knew he was crying.

She touched his shoulder. "I'll come back. As soon as I'm able, I'll return to you."

Dixon dashed at his eyes and said in a level voice, "You walk out on me now—I won't wait for you."

It wasn't a bluff. Jaz knew him as well as she knew herself. She leaned forward and, taking his head in her hands, kissed Dixon deeply. "I never expected you would." With a ragged breath, she left the room.

When she was outside, she looked back. Dixon looked like a man who'd been told he has six months to live. Tears streamed down the planes of his face. He mouthed *I love you.*

Then Jaz turned a corner and saw no more.

CHAPTER 26

The guard led Jaz back to her suite. When the door had closed behind him, she fell on the bed and cried. Perhaps Herridge and Dixon were right. It was insane for her to throw away their offers of employment and love to join a group of exiled scientists on the moon. Especially when she was the reason for their exile.

She didn't share their concern for her physical safety. Tate had been the only unstable personality among them. Jaz had touched the minds of the others, scientists and academics, and was confident they wouldn't harm her. Still, it would be tense. They would both need and resent her. Jaz wouldn't be the only one giving up earth; but she would be the only one who had a choice in the matter.

Losing Dixon was like punching a hole in her chest. But at the same time her nerve endings thrilled with guilty excitement . . . the moon! She had maneuvered the power behind world leaders to build a long-term settlement on the lunar surface. With Orley and the others she would explore the realms of human consciousness. Study the development of a new metamind. Extract new knowledge from the depleted scientific soil.

And there was her moral obligation. If she stayed on earth with Dixon, the scientists would remain imprisoned. She had destroyed their work, their dreams, and Tate's life. This was the only way to restore some of what she and the NSA had taken.

None of her rationalizations could remove the ache over losing Dixon and the guilt she felt for leaving him behind. But what choice did she have? If she stayed with him on earth, Dixon would eventually ferret out her secrets. And the knowledge she held would destroy him.

It would hurt her and Dixon, but Jaz had to go.

With a sigh, she picked up her data mask. There were other strings Jaz needed to cut before she left. It had been two weeks since she disappeared in an avalanche. She needed to call home.

Jaz stood on her pockmarked sea and loosed a seagull into the wind. It was a metaphor for a homing protocol that traveled the Net, searching for a particular user.

The seagull returned in seconds, perched on the hand of a sixty-year-old woman. She was tiny and wrapped in a crimson sari.

Anita Reese was online. She was always online.

Her nut-brown face broke into a wide grin at the sight of her daughter. They embraced. "Yasmine, I am delighted to hear from you. Such good news from your young man. But why weren't you telling me?"

Jaz took a step back and looked at her mother. "What?"

"A young man, Mr. Tully, called to tell us you were alive. That you and he met in hospital during your recovery from a hiking accident. Is it true? You are to be married?"

Dixon had thought to call her family and tell them she was alive. It was thoughtful. It was presumptuous. It was Dixon. "When did he call?"

"Yesterday. How are you?" Anita examined a nearby void in Jaz's metaphor. "This connection is not good."

"It's not the connection. It's me. In the accident, I suffered a brain injury."

Her mother gasped and took her child's face in both hands. In the simulation her mother did no more than scan her daughter's eyes. Underneath, thousands of agent-memes flowed from her, scanning and testing her daughter's capabilities.

Jaz teased one apart and repurposed it to destroy the others. Her mother's probe ended abruptly.

Anita's head jerked back as if she'd been slapped. "That is something new for you." Her black eyes narrowed in suspicion. "You learned that in the hospital?"

Jaz bit her bottom lip. "There are things I can't tell you. For your own safety as well as mine."

"Something to do with this young man? Will you tell me at the wedding?"

"He's a part of it. And the wedding . . . has been postponed indefinitely."

"But why, little one? This Mr. Tully showed me memories of you and him together. I have never seen you so happy. Were those false?"

Jaz twisted one of her long strands of imaginary hair. "No. We were happy. It's a long story. I'm going away. I wanted to tell you and Dad not to worry about me."

"Going?" Anita cocked her head. "Where?"

That was the question. Jaz spun off a streamer of consciousness to Gestalt, asking what cover story was being used for the expansion of the moon base. Its answer was brief and to the point. Like all the best lies, 90 percent of it was truth. Orley and several research associates were going to be stationed on the moon long-term to study the physiological effects of lunar life on humans and to create a lunar-based Net. New underground water reserves had been found and made the prospect of a permanent lunar colony feasible.

"I've quit my job at Infotech. There's a new multinational research project starting up. It's too soon to tell you now. But you'll be hearing about it on the Net. Expect some very long-distance phone calls."

Anita Reese had helped invent the Net. It took her three seconds to track down the rumors and budget proposals. "The moon? Can this be true?"

"Yes. I'll let you know more when I can."

Anita placed her hand on her daughter's arm. "I am worried for you, Yasmine. This is not making sense."

"I know. But it will. Is Dad around?"

"One moment." Her mother's avatar froze in concentration, and an instant later Jaz's father materialized beside them. He always presented himself online as a young man, insisting it kept him young. Sean Reese's avatar styled his brown hair in shoulder-length curls and wore a poet's shirt, open at the chest.

"Got a hug for your da?" he asked, sweeping Jaz's avatar up in his arms. "Your mother says you're leaving us to become an astronaut. Are you leaving that laddie who called the other day, too?"

"Yes, Dad."

Her father winked. "Good. You're too young for me to be losing you to marriage. And he has the look of a scoundrel about him."

"You would know," Jaz said, kissing him on the nose.

Anita interrupted their reunion. "Sean, she quit her job. She's leaving this young man. This cannot be wise."

"The ways of the heart are always wise, though the path they travel is crooked."

"Do not be quoting poetry to me. This is her *life*."

"Exactly." Sean Reese let go of Jaz and slipped an arm around his wife's shoulder. "*Her* life. Quite an adventure to live on the moon; perhaps we'll travel to visit her soon."

"You are making no sense." Anita Reese stamped her tiny brown foot in cyberspace.

"No sense," her husband agreed, "only rhyme."

Jaz backed out of the scene, smiling, and left her parents at their favorite pastime, verbal sparring.

Stacker nearly fell off his seat when Jaz contacted him. He lost his Net connection and had to reestablish. In his haste to reconnect, he skimped on avatar initialization; it was barely a stick figure. "Jaz? Is that really you? Matt told me you died in an avalanche." She could feel security memes pluck at the protocols on the edge of her avatar, checking for authenticity.

She waited until her identity was verified, then said, "I've come to resign."

"What?" He absorbed the reports from his memes. "Your brain patterns are slightly different. What's going on? What happened to you in the mountains?"

So much had been lost in Thunder Basin: her inno-

cence, her old way of life. There was no way to tell
Stacker the truth, so she embellished the lie the NSA
had concocted.

Jaz looked at her hands. "Search-and-rescue found me.
I had suffered some brain damage during my fall. I've
been in a hospital ever since."

"No one contacted us. For the past week, we thought
you were gone. Matt and Geena will be—"

"Will you tell them for me? I . . . don't think I'm up
to it right now." She'd had too many good-byes already.

Stacker laced his hands together. "Sure. Take it easy.
When you're fully recovered, come back to work for us.
I'll keep your job open."

Jaz shook her head. "No. I'll send someone around to
collect my things. I stopped by to thank you, Stacker.
You've been a good boss."

His half-sketched face was puzzled and a bit sad. "If
you change your mind, there'll always be a place for you
at Infotech."

Jaz hired a moving company to pack her things for
long-term storage. She walked through simulations of her
office and apartment, indicating what she'd like to keep,
what could be sold. Her personal possessions were a piti-
fully small pile. Her Ganesh wall hanging, a few memory
crystals of friends and family, the rug her grandmother
had given her, and her father's painting. Except for the
rug, it would all fit in a single cardboard box. A small
collection of treasures. She'd spent so much of her life
in her head.

Jaz paused in the simulation and looked out the window. The sun setting over Puget Sound cast pink shadows on the Olympics. It was a beautiful view. She saved
the memory. Soon this apartment would belong to someone else. Already it seemed alien to her, like visiting a
friend's house while they were out.

Jaz stepped across the oak floor to the bedroom, to
double-check that she'd tagged the items in the under-
bed drawer.

Dixon lay on the bed, hands folded behind his head.

The flames of his avatar licked harmlessly over her bedsheets.

Jaz gasped; she hadn't sensed him entering the simulation.

"I'm not here to fight," he said softly. "I just wondered who you were, before I met you."

"You haven't answered any of my calls."

Dixon stared at her, as if storing her image in a data gem. Perhaps he was. "It didn't seem . . . appropriate." He sat up in a single lithe movement and tapped the headboard. You'll want to erase the bed's memories. I don't think it's anything you'd care to share with the movers."

Jaz blushed. "That was private—you had no right."

His hazel eyes met hers levelly. "I've spent all my life finding out things other people didn't want me to know. Sometimes I think that's the only knowledge worth having." Dixon stood very close to her, and she could feel the heat emanating from the flames of his skin. He seemed about to say something, then stopped himself. Looking down at her, he said, "I won't intrude on you again." He headed for the door.

Jaz grabbed his hand. There was a shock of intimacy between them. Phantom memories from the time they'd shared almost everything. "Will you come to the launch?" Jaz closed her eyes, and whispered, "Please?"

Dixon's avatar gently loosened his hand from her grip. "No."

When she opened her eyes, he was gone.

Gestalt cut through bureaucracy like a laser. Space agencies around the world dropped their highest priority projects to work on expanding the moon base. Scientists filed complaints as their projects were slipped back a month, two months. Conspiracy theories abounded on the Net: aliens had been sighted near Neptune, and the world was building a global defense network; uranium deposits had been discovered on the moon, and the governments were mobilizing to mine it; and medical studies had proven that the reduced gravity of the moon could

extend a person's life three hundredfold, so aging governmental leaders were laying the groundwork for a retirement
home in space.

A few relentless hackers swore the lunar base was related to the Net disruption experienced in the United
States. Other groups were still digging into the events of
April twenty-ninth, trying to unearth what had caused
the disruption of the Net in the U.S.

Gestalt spent as much time quashing rumors as it did
spurring scientists and world leaders to work faster. It
continued as a phantom in the machine of humanity.
Only governmental leaders knew where the orders for
the moon base originated.

The first shipment of habitat components went up
within a week. The three scientists currently stationed
on the moon were reassigned to assemble them. They
protested, but orders were orders, and it paid to accom-
modate the government leaders who doled out grant
money.

During the month it took to ship and assemble the
habitat, Jaz, Orley, and the other scientists trained for
life on the moon. They underwent medical tests and full-
immersion simulations, learning how to don space suits,
manipulate jets during an EVA, and practicing emergency decompression drills. At night, they studied lunar
astronomy and the history of human occupation of the
moon. Each one learned how to pilot the lunar shuttle
to the L-5 space station in the event of an emergency
evacuation.

Jaz was surprised at this last. Apparently, Gestalt still
considered the scientists more of a resource than a
danger.

After a month of frenzied work, the lunar colony was
ready for occupation. Launch was set for the morning of
June sixth. They would fly to Kennedy Space Center in
Orlando and catch one of the new Boeing 2037 shuttles
to low-earth orbit, then connect with an orbital-transfer
vehicle to the L-5 space station. From there, they'd hitch
a ride with the last shipment for the new International
Lunar Habitat: radiation hardened servers.

*   *   *

Dixon steadfastly refused all of Jaz's calls. He was connected, she could feel him doing . . . something online. A large project, but each time she tried to investigate, walls of blackened basalt blocked her path, high-level security algorithms it would take years to crack. The security hole she had exploited before was gone.

Frustrated, Jaz stormed down to the quarters Dixon had been assigned upon his release from the hospital. The room was empty. The bed was made with fresh linens, and all his personal possessions were gone.

After their weekly meeting on the status of the lunar project, Jaz stopped Herridge in the hall. "Where is Dixon?"

"Mr. Tully has been assigned." Herridge stared at her with his inscrutable silver eyes. "He asked me not to tell you where."

The night before her flight to Orlando, Jaz made one last attempt to contact Dixon. She flooded the Net with ICQ programs. Not one of them returned, not even to report its failure.

The night before the launch, Jaz couldn't sleep. She replayed simulations, testing her readiness for anything that might happen. Friends and family, stretching across the globe from New York to Bombay, contacted her online to wish her luck. Jaz mulled over the new life that awaited her, one of research and mental exploration. But mostly, she tried not to think about Dixon, where he was now . . . whom he was with.

It was too late to change her mind. Too much work had been done to make her proposal a reality. The new metamind they'd create would have full governmental backing, and the latest equipment. They could learn so much about the nature of shared consciousness, and about themselves.

At 4:40 A.M., Jaz disconnected from the Net for the last time. Dixon hadn't contacted her.

She showered and met the others in the cafeteria for a light breakfast.

Orley came up behind her in line while Jaz was spooning sliced cantaloupe into a bowl. "Nervous?"

She looked over her shoulder at him. "Aren't you?"

Orley picked up a single-serve box of cereal and followed Jaz to a table. When they were settled, he said, "I must say you surprise me, Ms. Reese. I didn't expect you to go through with this."

Spearing a slice of fruit, she said, "It's important work."

"I agree. But what surprises me is that you would give up your life on earth to facilitate it. Joseph, Daren, and I had little choice. We leave behind us only the prospect of lifelong imprisonment. You had a future here."

Jaz set down her fork. "In a few days, Dr. Orley, you and I will share a private network in tight living quarters. Anything you want to know about me will be answered then. In the meantime, grant me these last few hours of privacy."

Orley bowed from his shoulders. "As you wish, Ms. Reese." He picked up his tray and moved to another table.

It was the last moment Jaz had to herself. The press came out in droves to record and transmit the launch of the first permanent colony on the moon. Marines kept the reporters at a distance. Herridge wouldn't risk giving Orley the airtime. But the new astronauts were required to do everything in a viewing room. One wall was plate glass. Jaz felt like a goldfish in a very small bowl as she stepped into the orange liner of her space suit. Once on, she would wear her suit for the three days it would take to reach the moon and verify the habitat was pressurized. Jaz stepped into the armorlike legs of the suit, and Orley helped her slide the top over her torso. Jaz wriggled into it, feeling like a stripper in reverse.

She fastened the waist gasket and checked the seals at her gloves and boots. Everything was normal.

The sea of faces on the other side of the glass included news luminaries and high-ranking politicians. Her mother and father had flown down with six of her Indian cousins to see her off. They formed a brightly colored island of silk in the gray-blue wool of newscasters and military officers.

Herridge was there, incongruous with his arm around the shoulders of a pretty blond wife and an eight-year-old son holding his other hand. She wouldn't have recognized him but for the silver goggles that hid his cold, killer's eyes. Connected, the killer inside him was tempered, and he could be a good family man.

Herridge dropped his hand from his wife's shoulder and saluted Jaz. There were worlds of respect in that simple gesture. He didn't agree with her decision, but he accepted it. He'd sent her a text message last night: *You're doing the wrong thing, but for the right reasons. Godspeed.*

Jaz returned his salute and tried to smile. Nearly a hundred people had turned out for the viewing. But as she scanned the faces on the other side of the glass, the one she wanted to see wasn't among them.

With a sigh, Jaz slipped on her gloves and sealed them. The helmet she left dangling behind her shoulders. Bulky and cumbersome, she'd seal it right before launch. She was the last one ready, walking through the door that led to the launch platform when Jaz heard a commotion in the viewing room behind her.

She turned. Dixon pushed his way to the front of the room. His hair was short, cut to NSA regulations and his perpetual scruff of stubble was gone. He looked fresh and vulnerable.

Jaz walked up to the window and pressed her gloved palm against the glass. Dixon mirrored the action with his hand. They stood there like that, while all the reporters of the world recorded their image. There was no privacy, but with Gestalt on the Net, there never had been.

"I love you," Jaz shouted through the thick glass that separated them.

Dixon lowered his head, his hand trailing down the glass. Without looking up, he turned and disappeared into the crowd.

EPILOGUE

The sky was black, spangled with bright, untwinkling stars. Jaz worked by earthlight. The globe hung full and blue-green in the sky. No matter how many times she journeyed outside, the sight always amazed her.

"Are you done?" Orley's voice crackled over the radio they were using until the network was in place.

"Almost." Jaz planted the repeater tripod on the top of the peak. Its central drill activated, embedding itself in the bedrock. Powder-fine dust, residue from the eternal pounding of meteoroids against the moon's surface, kicked up whirlwinds around the spinning drill. When the tripod sank into place, Jaz asked, "Is everyone ready?"

"Yes. Go ahead."

Jaz pushed a button on the side of the unit, connecting the last wideband picocell repeater. She felt the others pushing on her mind from all directions with memes and sensations.

"If you've finished setting up, come back to the base," Orley said. "We need to minimize latency."

"Not yet," Jaz said. The EVA suit was bulky, but Jaz managed to lower herself to the lunar surface. She stretched out her legs and leaned back against the rim of the crater. The earth was like a blue-green jewel against a background of black velvet. On its surface was everyone she loved. But that planet was no longer her home.

Herridge had been right; it was a mistake to come.

Tensions had been high ever since they stepped into the shuttle on the launchpad. Orley's compatriots hadn't welcomed her. Even three weeks later it was as if the others lived in a social bubble she couldn't penetrate. Conversations stopped when she entered a room. The acceptance that had drawn her to Symbios was gone. Without trust, how could they succeed?

Jaz allowed a trickle of information to flow from the others: Orley's annoyance at her delay, images of the other researchers seated on the floor around him, as if they performed a séance to summon the new metamind.

Jaz was glad to be outside. It was a symbol of the way things were, and the unrelenting gray landscape suited her mood. A pockmarked crust of peaks and valleys. She had been excited to travel to the moon. But the reality: social isolation, no privacy, military rations, was disappointing.

Nothing stirred on the Net. Jaz felt Orley's frustration. She gave over more of herself, but their metaphor was still a haze of bright colors and tinny sounds. The damage to her neural paths made the connection difficult. Is this how Symbios had appeared to Dixon?

A memory leaked from Dr. Akukwe, the Nigerian chemical physicist. Jaz couldn't tell whether he had transmitted intentionally, or if it was a slip caused by the tension.

Akukwe and Orley sat in the cafeteria on the day of the launch. Jaz could see herself out of the corner of Akukwe's vision. From Akukwe's perspective, she was an ominous figure, huddled over her food and full of dangerous secrets.

"But she is the one who betrayed us," Dr. Akukwe said. "Why, of all people, did you pick her?"

"In part, to punish her," Orley said, tasting a glass of orange juice. "I wanted to see whether she was sincere, or if this proposal was a governmental trick. She is talented. Even damaged, she can replace Tate. I have tested her neural functioning, it is adequate."

Akukwe speared a sausage with his fork. "Are you

sure that it is not your hormones making this decision?" Akukwe transmitted an image of two bodies merging behind a rice-paper wall.

Orley looked down at his tray of untouched scrambled eggs. "I am certain Ms. Reese does not desire a repetition of that encounter."

Jaz's face heated as the vision faded. If not for her the scientists would still be in NSA prison cells, with no hope of continuing their work. However bad things were—they would have been worse if she had not intervened to help their cause.

"Ah yes," a voice whispered in the back of her mind, so softly that Jaz was not certain whether it was one of the others or her own guilty conscience, "but did you run to the moon, or just run away?"

The earth glinted across space at her from four hundred thousand kilometers away, like the reproach of a jilted lover. Her enthusiasm for the lunar project had masked her true feelings. She had been afraid those last few days. Afraid that Dixon would break past the barriers she set in her mind and discover the truth about his mother—a truth that could destroy him. Afraid of the intimacy he offered, and that she might lose herself in him. But most of all, she had feared herself, and what she might become without the edge that had made her a skilled data miner: ordinary.

Jaz gave more of herself to the connection with the others. She waited long moments, listening to her own breath amplified in the cavity of her helmet. Still, no unnamed presence stirred on the lunar Net.

Was Orley wrong about her? Even after a month of recovery, was her mind still too weak, too damaged? Had she brought them all this way just to fail?

Orley felt Jaz's panic and soothed her with images of the long nights of meditation it had taken to coalesce Symbios. His touch was brotherly. Patience, he thought into her mind, patience.

But surely this time it would go faster. The others were practiced in coordinating their thoughts. Unlike the time they'd generated Symbios, now they knew what they were doing.

Orley's voice crackled over the speaker. "Ms. Reese, we need you online." Through his polite facade, Jaz heard anxiety. It wasn't just her life that would be wasted if they failed.

Jaz sighed. This was the moment of truth. Had she spent millions of government dollars only to strand herself and Orley's group on the moon? Or would they create a new metamind and explore the next stage in the evolution of human consciousness?

Jaz opened her mind to the new network. At first the metaphor—a room full of people in party dress—fizzled and popped with static. Jaz wasn't sure whether the trouble was with her or the connection. Then the signal smoothed out.

Instead of the acceptance Jaz had felt when she joined Symbios, she felt wariness. The others didn't trust her. She was a gate-crasher at their party. The relative you had to invite but hoped wouldn't show up. Jaz recoiled.

But she wasn't there to stand on the sidelines. Jaz braced herself to let go of the control she'd held so tightly for the past eleven years. Ever since that night in the dance club when she'd found how different she was, Jaz had been careful not to lose control. With an act of will, she let down her defenses.

The shock was like plunging into an icy river. Orley and the other scientists absorbed her thoughts, teasing out every memory, every scrap of knowledge, every dream. They plundered her mind, taking everything, the synthesis of all she had ever been or thought.

And still there was nothing more than sixteen people on the moon.

Alone on an alien landscape, her mind invaded by strangers, a single thought reverberated through Jaz: she had failed.

It hurt too much to cry. She gaped at the darkness of space like a landed fish. The only sound was her own ragged breathing.

On the network she felt reflections of her grief. They had all failed, all lost loved ones to travel into a pointless exile. In that instant of despair, despite cultural differences, or lingering mistrust, they shared Jaz's emotion. They were as one.

And then, in the silences between their thoughts, a new thing stirred.

Jaz held her breath, as if the slightest movement would blow out this tiny flame of consciousness.

"Welcome," Orley formed the words in his mind. Candles lit on an imaginary cake. "Today is your birthday."

Jaz and the others quieted their minds, gave more of themselves over to this new creature. Jaz felt it expand, encompass new concepts: today, birthday, birth, self?

"WHO AM I?" asked the newly formed entity.

It had worked. Out of their pain, in that instant of communal grief, something wondrous had been born. Jaz felt a rush of love and pride. All of her sacrifice had been worth it. With those three words Jaz knew she would do anything to protect that fledging consciousness. Tears of joy streaming down her cheeks, Jaz looked out over the barren landscape and spoke aloud the name they had chosen.

"You are Luna."